PRICELESS

"The very talented Ms. Stewart . . . provide[s] readers with outstanding stories and characters that are exciting, distinctive, and highly entertaining. Four and a half stars."
—*Romantic Times*

"The best of romance and suspense. Flowing dialogue, wonderfully well-rounded and realistic characters, and beautifully descriptive passages fill the pages of *Priceless*. . . . Not to be missed."
—RomCom.com

"Stewart's storylines flow like melted chocolate."
—America Online Writers Club Romance Group

"In the style of Nora Roberts, Stewart weaves a powerful romance with suspense for a very compelling read."
—*Under the Covers Reviews*

"An exceptionally gifted storyteller with a unique ability . . . and a rare talent that places her in the company of today's bestselling romantic suspense authors."
—CompuServe Reviews

WONDERFUL YOU

"Compares favorably with the best of Barbara Delinsky and Belva Plain."
—Amazon.com

Books by Mariah Stewart

Moments in Time
A Different Light
Carolina Mist
Devlin's Light
Wonderful You
Moon Dance
Priceless
Brown-Eyed Girl
Voices Carry

Published by POCKET BOOKS

MARIAH STEWART

Carolina Mist

POCKET BOOKS
New York   London   Toronto   Sydney

This book is a work of fiction. Names, characters, places and incidents are products of the author's imagination or are used fictitiously. Any resemblance to actual events or locales or persons, living or dead, is entirely coincidental.

 POCKET BOOKS, a division of Simon & Schuster, Inc.
1230 Avenue of the Americas, New York, NY 10020

ISBN-13: 978-0-671-52787-7
ISBN-10: 0-671-52787-8

First Pocket Books printing August 1996

10 9 8 7 6 5 4

POCKET and colophon are registered trademarks of
Simon & Schuster, Inc.

Cover design by Jae Song; Photo © Tad Sham/Picturesque

Manufactured in the United States of America

For information regarding special discounts for bulk purchases,
please contact Simon & Schuster Special Sales at 1-800-456-6798
or business@simonandschuster.com.

To Helen—who always hits the right notes—
for years of love and friendship, and for
encouraging me every step of the way. You're
a shining star.

Acknowledgments to . . .

Loretta Barrett, friend and agent, for letting me dream and for never being more than a phone call away, and to Gary Morris for his ever-cheerful assistance.

Linda Marrow, with love and thanks for being in my corner.

Kate Collins, for her insight, moral support and total dedication to making every book its absolute best.

Miranda Jarrett—the other half of the M & M Traveling Show—for her friendship and her uniquely *dented* sense of humor. (Welcome home!)

Suzanne Coleburn and her merry band of romance readers—Mary Jane, Maryanne, Michelle, Sharon, Debbie, Pat, Gail, and, of course, everyone's favorite beaux, Ken—for their love and loyalty.

Pat and Willie Farrell of Washington, D.C., who, once upon a summer, shared unforgettable sunrises on a tranquil stretch of North Carolina beach with a fellow traveler.

And to the *real* Meri Puppins, who surely is chasing butterflies and dancing for Pet Tabs in that big Puppy Palace in the sky.

Carolina
Mist

◆ *Prologue* ◆

Even the brutal cold of a distinctly belligerent mid-February had not kept them away. The antique dealers and the curiosity seekers eagerly sought to rummage through the bits and pieces of the lives of the locally celebrated deceased who had until so recently lived amidst the splendor of the palatial town house.

They came with their checkbooks and their credit cards and their cash, to carry away the Oriental rugs—the Kirman with the medallioned portraits of one hundred and one kings of Persia, and the Qum silk carpet, red and blue intertwined on a field of ivory—and the fine furnishings. It was rumored that the pair of Biedermeier mahogany tables that had stood on either side of the bed in the master chamber were expected to possibly set a new record, and the Hepplewhite secretary from the front hall would bring its value and half as much again before the gavel would pound the podium to mark the end of the sale.

And then there were the collections: the art, impressionists and modernists alike; the imported pottery, rare Oriental pieces like the pottery model of a house with a hinged door from the Han dynasty and an early Sancai warrior from the Tang dynasty.

For those having less exotic tastes and more modest bank accounts, there would be the household appliances and the record collections (classical and jazz only) and the books (not surprisingly, some first editions).

Then, of course, there would be silver and imported china and porcelain—a Sevres dinner service, circa 1823, a pair of Meissen candelabra, and, naturally, the Ming and Imari vases, the Satsuma and Cantonese bowls, the Royal Worcester and the Derby and the Minton—all carefully lined up

1

shoulder to shoulder on display tables around which selected employees of the auctioneer stood guard to ensure that the pieces were not handled.

Only those seeking a glimpse of the jewelry that had once adorned the lady of the house were to be disappointed. Because of their reported value, the rings and necklaces and bracelets with which Harold McKenna had so lavishly gifted his beloved Charlotte had already been sent to Sotheby's, where they were expected to fetch a fortune. Not enough of a fortune, of course, to satisfy *all* the debts left behind when the small plane owned by the extravagant couple had crashed in the Canadian Rockies some months earlier, but enough, it was said, to satisfy the IRS, which had acted swiftly to ensure that the contents of the brownstone would remain undisturbed behind padlocked doors until such time as their worth could be assessed and the government's pound of flesh exacted.

The slender young woman slid into the back of the room unnoticed by the others, who, having viewed the contents of the house the day before, were again checking their catalogs for the items upon which they would bid once the auction began. The young woman leaned back against the wall and fixed her eyes straight ahead. The rustle of anticipation that stirred through the crowd as the auctioneer mounted the podium swept through her on a wave of nausea.

She shook her head to decline the seat offered by one of the auctioneer's helpers. She had wanted to be in a position from which she could quickly and easily leave once her business was concluded. Jenkins, the lawyer, had promised that through an arrangement with the auction house, those items she sought would be among the first lots offered. She would not have to witness the frenzy as the fragments of her life were picked apart and swallowed up by the scavengers, who gathered like hungry jackals, biding their time until their desire to consume could be sated.

The auctioneer, a tall, balding man in a green cardigan sweater and dark-rimmed glasses, cleared his throat and checked the microphone before he reminded the hopeful seated before him of the rules. Bid by holding up your numbered card. Many pieces have reserves, that is, a minimum acceptable bid. To save time, certain items will be sold in lots. The crowd shifted restlessly. They knew all this. They wanted to get on with it. The woman leaning against the wall thought of the spectators of ancient Rome, anxious to have the games begin, and was sickened by the sport.

Lot one: photographic equipment. Sold to a young man in a brown suede jacket.

Lot two: table linens. Sold to a woman with a sleek hairstyle in the middle of the fourth row.

Lot three: photographs.

The young woman raised her hand, holding up her bright yellow numbered card for the auctioneer to see clearly. Her bid was acknowledged, and she relaxed. Then, to her shock, another bid was made. A man in a brown overcoat two rows in front of her had raised his card to enter his bid. The auctioneer looked to her, giving her an opportunity to respond. She nodded her head, yes, to which the other bidder again nodded. *Why*, she thought numbly, *would anyone else want these few boxes of old photographs?*

Her hands began to sweat as the bid continued to mount. Soon it became apparent that the price had gone beyond her reach. She stood in shock as the man in the overcoat accepted the boxes from the hands of the auction assistant, then turned to flash a look of good-natured triumph in her direction. The horror reflected in her eyes drew him to the back of the room. At his approach, she fled wordlessly through the open doorway into the foyer, now painfully stripped of its once celebrated works of art.

"Miss . . . hold up there." He grabbed her by the arm and pulled her to one side of the front door. "Look, I don't know why these old photos mean so much to you, but obviously you want them more than I do. I only wanted the album . . . all that fancy silver work on the cover must be worth a fortune. Never saw anything like it, have you?"

Yes, she could have told him. *There is one other.*

"Was it the photos you were after?" His voice had softened. He had clearly been touched by the pain so apparent in her eyes.

"Yes," she whispered.

"Look, for ten dollars, you can have all of the pictures."

She nodded, took a single bill from her wallet, and handed it over with shaking fingers. She watched patiently as he carefully removed the old photographs from the pages of the album, then accepted the boxes reverently as if they held her firstborn child.

"Thank you," she said simply, then turned to walk through the door, the hot tears burning her skin as they slid down her cheeks.

Never again, she silently vowed, tightly clutching the boxes that held her baby pictures, her parents' wedding pictures, to her chest. *I will never go through this again . . .*

✦ 1 ✦

1995

At nine thirty-five on the morning of her twenty-seventh birthday, on the very day she'd planned to present a killer report on the Adkins account—thereby ensuring yet another quick hop up the corporate ladder—Abigail McKenna received a most unwelcome surprise.

". . . and, of course, we'll make outplacement available to you." Nancy Joachim's thin lips appeared to move almost continually as she precisely recited her prosaic dissertation on all that White-Edwards would do to make Abby's entry into the world of the unemployed a smooth one.

As the director of human resources for a company that had, over the past six months, taken a financial beating, Nancy was well versed in sympathetic pauses and encouraging smiles. She'd had a lot of practice, particularly in the past three months, as one department after another had been forced to cut its staff. Nancy knew the drill by heart. The termination of Abby McKenna had been as swift as a knee jerk, and just about as impassive.

Abby had barely moved or changed expression since she'd taken her seat fifteen minutes earlier. In fact, the second she realized what was happening, her mind had clamped shut as firmly as a stubborn clam, making any response improbable.

There was no way this could be happening to her. It simply wasn't possible.

"I strongly suggest you take advantage of the outplacement, Abby." Dylan Forester leaned across the narrow space that separated their chairs and touched Abby lightly on the arm. As vice president in charge of her department, Dylan had shared in breaking the bad news. "They'll give you a nice office to go to every day while you polish your résumé and a secretary to type it for you."

Abby turned an ashen, uncomprehending face in his direction but did not speak, her heart pounding disconcertingly—loud enough, she was certain, to be heard in the lobby, some twelve floors below.

Nancy nudged some papers across the desktop, and Dylan handed her a pen. Abby uncharacteristically signed her name without question. She could not think, could not read, could not react. All her inner circuits had shut down with the shock of finding herself exactly where she swore she'd never be.

Numb feet carried her equally numb body to the elevator, where routine forced her fingers to the button for the eleventh floor. She'd gotten all the way back to her office and was about to close the door when she realized Dylan had followed her.

"Listen, Abby, I know this comes as a big shock. I didn't even know myself until last night." Dylan leaned toward her, a tall, thin body topped by a long, narrow face. "Believe me when I tell you, this was the very last thing I wanted . . ."

Of course, Dylan would have fought to keep her. It had been Abby who had produced the stellar reports that had helped Dylan's own star to rise and shine so rapidly. *Of course,* he would be reluctant to let her go. She had made the department—and Dylan—look oh so good for oh so long.

"Who else?" She managed to loosen her vocal cords.

"Wilson, Trina, Nick . . ."

"Barsky?" she asked.

"Well, no." He cleared his throat. "The decision was made to keep him on."

If you're going to keep at least one live body, it might as well be Barsky, she thought. He was the only person Abby'd ever met who was flattered—flattered!—when his ideas were stolen and passed off as someone else's, most often Dylan's.

"Listen, Dylan, I need some time to myself." She gestured impatiently for him to leave.

"Oh, sure. Hey, I understand." He backed toward the door as she advanced. "And listen, I'd be more than happy to provide you with glowing references. You can count on me. And Abby . . ."

She closed the door in his face and leaned back on it, taking in a few deep, highly controlled breaths before walking slowly to her desk. She dropped into her chair, permitting her shoulders to slump, not knowing what to do first. Pushing the whirlpool of panic to the back of her mind, she opened the bottom drawer of her desk and pulled out a box of business cards. Wooden fingers pried the lid off and pulled out one of the pale gray cards.

L. Abigail McKenna, Assistant Vice President.

Not anymore.

Without ceremony, she emptied the box into the waste-basket and watched as the avalanche of cards tumbled in slow motion toward the bottom. Biting her lip to force back bitter tears, she swung her chair around and looked out the window.

Abby had declined a larger office following her last promotion simply because she had loved this view. The Parkway spread out before her, a wide boulevard patterned, it was said, after the Champs Élysees. So many of Philadelphia's landmarks lay just beyond the window—the Franklin Institute, the Academy of Natural History, the Art Museum. A few blocks down, a fountain danced in Logan Circle. Frequently, on summer days such as this, she had bought lunch from one of the vendors and walked the few blocks to sit on a bench near the fountain, finding the delicate trickle of the water soothing after an intense morning. More often than not, during the school year, the Parkway would be lined with yellow buses from every adjacent state which would fill the air with exhaust fumes as each waited its turn to deposit its passengers in front of whichever landmark was first on their particular agenda. Each successive crop of class-trippers would spill onto the sidewalk, where they would crowd noisily into untidy lines while the teachers and chaperons attempted to count the ever-moving heads of their charges. The summer visitors to the city arrived with fewer fumes and less fanfare than the schoolchildren, and on many a day such as this one, Abby had enjoyed a few peaceful moments to herself in the shadow of some of the city's most popular tourist attractions.

She stood at the window, her face pressed against the glass. Steam rose from the sidewalks as the July sun turned morning dew into haze. One hand rested on the glass, as if to reach beyond and touch the trees lining the Parkway. The other hand had been drawn into a tightly clenched fist, her fingernails digging unconsciously into her palm.

Damn! How could this happen to me? I have worked so hard, planned every move so carefully . . . even chose White-Edwards from a wide field of contenders because of their stability. How could this have happened? A perplexed Abby slapped the open palm of her hand onto the flat window glass.

It's my own fault. She began to pace the length of the room. *I should have seen it coming a year ago, as soon as they started talking merger . . . should have started looking then. It's always easier to find a job when you have one.*

She pulled a tissue from the box on her credenza and wiped her face, careful not to disturb her makeup. Appearance was everything, she reminded herself.

Let it never be said that Abigail McKenna couldn't take it like a man.

It took a surprisingly short time to empty her desk of her personal belongings. One by one, the few bits of herself she had brought with her five years earlier dropped into her briefcase—a small crystal clock, a brass picture frame holding a photograph of her parents, a Cross pen-and-pencil set, her personal appointment book, a small phone book of navy blue leather with her initials in gold. Abby was all business. There had been little evidence in the room to give a hint of her personality or her preferences. The desk drawers held no cards from birthdays past, no personal correspondence, no magazines or books. The prints on the wall had been selected by the decorator hired when the company moved in, and Abby had not replaced them, as others had done.

Placing her leather briefcase on the desktop, she snapped the brass closures with trembling fingers. She glanced around the room, as if unconvinced that she'd packed all her belongings. It occurred to her that the office looked almost exactly the same as it had on the day she moved in. The desktop was cleared of all except the leather blotter, a Rolodex, the same In and Out bins she had inherited from her predecessor. Only the thickly bound sheaf of paper on the left side of the desk—the proposal on the Adkins account she'd completed the evening before—bore proof that she had been there. She studied it for a moment, that fat ream she'd worked herself into a near frenzy to perfect, and was tempted to stuff it into her briefcase, enjoying the mental image of Dylan's scrambling to come up with something between now and two this afternoon, when he would need to present it to the board. Ever the professional, Abby dropped the report into her Out basket, squared her shoulders, and inched her chin up a notch or two before opening the door.

Not allowing herself a backward glance, she strode down the hall to the elevator, forcing a perfunctory smile when she passed a familiar face. Grateful to find the elevator empty, she hit the button for the lobby. A woman got on at nine, Gail Something-or-other, Abby recalled, from the accounting department.

"Gonna be hot again today." Gail hit the button for four.

"It would appear so," Abby replied stiffly.

"I sure do hate these Philadelphia summers." Gail shook her head as the doors slid open and she stepped out.

Three men—all vaguely familiar and all wearing light-weight summer suits—got on at three and nodded in unison to Abby, who smiled wanly and dropped her eyes to the toes of her tan leather shoes, hoping to avoid even a cursory conversation.

She walked across the lobby and through the front doors, then out onto the sidewalk, where she paused for a moment before turning to cross the street, leaving White-Edwards—and her brilliant future—behind.

◆ 2 ◆

Two weeks, max, she assured herself as she fumbled with the key to her second-floor apartment. *Probably less. With my résumé, I should be able to walk into a great job by the end of the week.*

She dropped her purse and briefcase on the nearest chair and removed her dark green unlined silk jacket, walking into the neat bedroom to place it immediately on its hanger. She went into the kitchen and poured herself a glass of iced raspberry herbal tea with hands that suddenly felt weak. After taking a few long sips, she leaned back against the counter, her left foot tapping out the passing seconds in agitation before she began unconsciously to pace back and forth in a narrow path between the stove and the sink.

Eventually, she paced herself into the living room and slumped on the sofa, holding a throw pillow against her middle to force back the panic that had filled her and turned her legs to water. She heard herself sobbing as the fear and anger and confusion spilled out and splashed about her in heated waves. Knowing she could not stop it, now that it had begun, she gave in and cried mindlessly until her throat burned raw and her eyes were all but swollen closed. When the torrent had stopped, she sat motionless in a state of suspension, mentally protesting the improbable twist of fate that had taken all that she had prized most in her life.

Abby's job—her career—had been all she had, all she had wanted or needed. It had been her passport to independence, to security, to a future where she would never have to worry that what she had worked for could ever be taken from her.

Working hard in college to shine as a bright light to corporate recruiters had gotten her through four tough years at the University of Pennsylvania. The entry-level job at

White-Edwards, a small investment consulting firm, had been the best of the many offers she received. All the information she had gathered from her research indicated that the company was an up-and-comer, a company that rewarded hard work with promotions and good salary increases. Abby had been happy there, happy to work long hours for the satisfaction of knowing that her efforts were, in fact, noticed and applauded. Her goals had been so carefully defined. What, she wondered numbly, had gone wrong?

Abby poured a cold drink and told herself she should eat something. She had four spoonfuls of yogurt before admitting she had no appetite. A shower would feel good, though, she thought, maybe wash away some of the despair along with the stickiness of the city she'd brought inside with her. She ran the water and stripped off her clothes, pausing to inspect herself in the mirror above the narrow sink.

To say that she was small was an understatement. Having never grown past five feet, two inches, Abby always held herself as straight as possible, hoping to maximize what little height she had. She had read once that dressing monochromatically would make one look taller and thinner. Thin had never been an issue. Tall had, and so her business suits had always been of one solid line of color.

A mass of light auburn curls tumbled around a tiny face. The palest smattering of freckles danced like the footprints of fairies across the bridge of her nose. Vanity had led her to cover them with makeup. How many top executives have freckles? she had thought with disgust. Her naturally arched brows rose above her pale amber eyes like parentheses. She might have just stepped out of the Irish mist. Someone had said that to her once, she recalled as she stepped into the steaming water. Who . . . ?

Oh, Alex. Alex Kane. He had said that, that last summer. Must be ten years now, she mused. *At least ten.*

Her hair had been more red when she was younger, and that's what he had called her when they were children: Red. And she had retaliated by calling him Candy. Candy Kane.

She stepped from the shower and wrapped a towel around

her head before reaching for her terry-cloth robe. The hot water had helped to clear her head. She had allowed herself enough time to mourn for what could have been at White-Edwards. She would focus on what had to be done, update her résumé, pull out the Sunday paper, and make a list of headhunters. She was down but not out. There was no more time for self-pity. White-Edwards could keep its outplacement service. Abigail McKenna wouldn't need it, thank you very much. She'd have a new job in no time. She was certain of it.

With the return of the first fragments of her former confidence, her innate sense of determination urged her on. Abby snapped off the bathroom light and headed for the PC in the corner of the living room.

It had not taken long for Abby to recognize that there was a major difference between job hunting in the nineties and job hunting in the eighties. Good jobs with great futures had been plentiful when she left college. Today's market was overflowing with candidates just like her—top skills, great experience, superb references—and all of them competing with her for the same few positions. Middle management, the land of opportunity of the eighties, was a wasteland in the nineties.

Oh, she had heard about it, read about it. But all those articles pertained to someone else. Some *other* companies had phased out certain positions. Some *other* fields had dried up. It had never been germane to her. Until the headhunter she interviewed with on her first day out showed her a stack of résumés the size of a phone book.

"All just like you, Ms. McKenna. All highly qualified, highly desirable prospects. I have exactly three positions at your level—none of them in investment counseling, I might add—and seventy-three résumés." The employment counselor sat back in her chair and sighed. "Look, I'd love to be able to help you. I'd kill to be able to place every one of these people." She nodded toward the résumés she had plunked down on her desk. "But the positions simply aren't there. There are entry-level jobs—not many, but a few—

paying a fraction of what you're making now. Are you interested in any of them?"

Abby leaned forward and scanned the short list of positions, noted the salaries, and shook her head. She'd not even make her rent.

"No," she whispered.

"Look, I'll keep your résumé on file. If anything comes up, I'll be sure to call . . ."

Abby walked back to her apartment in a fog of disbelief and disappointment. She'd call another employment agency in the morning. Surely there'd be something.

But there was not, not the next day, or the next week, or the one after that.

She started buying out-of-town newspapers, calling employment services in Baltimore, Trenton, Lancaster, D.C., even Pittsburgh. Nothing was promising enough to spend the money for travel.

By the end of September, she was beginning to panic. Faced with a stack of bills, her rent due, and no prospects, she pulled out her savings account, her checking account, the list of her meager investments. She had received eight weeks of severance pay, which she had just about depleted, and there would be unemployment, she knew, but that wouldn't even cover the rent on her apartment. At this rate, she could last three months, four maybe, if she stopped eating, used no electricity, and had her phone removed. She had thought there would be plenty of time to save for her future. Unfortunately, the future had arrived much sooner than she'd anticipated, and she was totally unprepared for it.

Abby sighed and looked around at her apartment. Why had she moved into such an expensive building? It had been so perfect, she had thought at the time, close to her office, known for its security, and, besides, it had lots of space, high ceilings, and lots of windows. It had been an indulgence, and she had known it even as she signed the lease. Well, the lease would be up at the end of next month, and she wouldn't be renewing. She was too depressed at that moment to think about where she'd be moving *to*.

Slumped in the middle of the living-room floor, she stared glumly at the piles of bills on one side, her bank statements on the other. On the table beside her were two notices of attempts to deliver a certified letter. Had one of her debts gone into collection? She wasn't sure and had no desire to find out. Maybe next week she could deal with it, but not now. She'd just have to keep ducking the mailman.

Her stomach reminded her that it was almost noon, and she had yet to eat. On bare feet, she padded into the kitchen. No milk. No eggs. She checked her wallet and, after finding a few bills, pulled on her old running shoes and headed for the corner grocery.

The excursion was brief, Abby grabbing the two items she'd come for and making only the most perfunctory conversation with the old man behind the counter who greeted her so cheerfully. *One of the few things that can make you feel even worse when you feel this bad,* she grumbled to herself as she headed back up the street, *is to be confronted by a truly perky person.*

She was fumbling in her pocket for her key when she bumped into him on the top step. Smiling—"Gotcha!"— the mailman handed her the letter and a pen, pointing to the line on the little green card where she was to sign.

Could this day get much worse?

Tossing the unopened letter onto the small kitchen table, she boiled water to make egg salad and poured a glass of milk. A short row of neglected African violets, their velvet leaves dangling over the sides of their pots as if gasping, lined the end of the table nearest the window and seemed to beg for her attention.

"I don't know why I bother," she sighed, "since not one of you has ever shown me so much as one blossom."

She poured a half-glass of water into the dry dirt, oblivious to the fact that she'd created a near tidal wave inside the small plastic pots. The excess poured over the tops of the saucers and slid across the table. She grabbed a paper towel and chased the stream, but not before the letter had been saturated. She spread the envelope out flat on the counter

14

and blotted at the runny ink. For the first time, she noticed the return address:

Horace D. Tillman, Esquire
1263 Harper Avenue
Primrose, N.C.

It was the name of the town, not that of the sender, that caught her eye. Primrose, North Carolina, was the home of her Great-aunt Leila.

"Oh, no." The very softest protest slipped from her lips.

Had the envelope borne a thick border of black, it would have been no more apparent what news lay wrapped within the soggy folds of paper. She shook the remaining drops of water from the envelope and went into the living room. Deeply saddened, Abby sank into a chair.

With trembling hands, she carefully opened it. Aunt Leila would be, what, ninety or so? *And it's been so long since I visited,* Abby thought, guiltily recalling how many times over the past several years she had opted to forgo vacation time to complete a project at work.

I always meant to go back. Abby shook her head, already comprehending that it was too late. *I always intended to take a few weeks off and spend the time with her. Why didn't I go last summer? Or the summer before?*

> Dear Ms. McKenna:
>
> It is my sad duty to notify you of the passing of your great-aunt, Leila Abigail Dunham Cassidy, on September 1 of this year. Please accept my deepest condolences on your loss.
>
> I have enclosed a copy of the late Mrs. Cassidy's will, which, as you can see, is self-explanatory. For the sake of brevity, I will summarize by advising that your great-aunt has elected to make you the sole beneficiary of her estate . . .

The sole beneficiary of her estate.

Abby's heart began to thump wildly. Tears of sorrow mixed with tears of gratitude as she read and read yet again the one-page letter, trying to absorb the news and its implications.

Aunt Leila was gone.

And she had left everything to Abby.

The memory of her great-aunt and the days they'd spent together suddenly filled her mind. A sister of Abby's maternal grandmother, Aunt Leila had opened her home to Abby every summer from the time she'd been five until she was in high school. Abby's parents would drop her off in June, then sweep off to some romantic place together, coming back for their only child in August. Aunt Leila had shared more than just her home with the lonely girl. She had given Abby roots and a sense of family history, as well as a glimpse into another world, a world where ladies dressed in white linen gathered on broad porches in summer and perched on white wicker chairs for Sunday tea.

Abby leaned deeper into the cushion, lost in those memories. Summers in Primrose had been everything to her as a child. Aunt Leila's house had been like a treasure-filled castle to Abby, every piece of furniture a glimpse into her family's past, every portrait on the wall an ancestor whose story she had heard over and over until they had seemed more real to Abby than her friends back in Chicago.

Every summer had been a magical venture into a time of forgotten gentility and graciousness. Aunt Leila was a true Victorian lady all her life, a woman who treated all with the same courteousness and amity, a woman who never passed a day without observing afternoon tea, a woman who spoke softly and thoughtfully, a woman of intelligence and charm and wit. Coming to Primrose from Chicago every year had been like entering a time warp, going from the bustle of modern life into a gentler era simply by passing through the front door of the big, rambling house on Cove Road.

Abby's visits had been joyful and filled with wonder, as childhood summers should be. There were dirt roads to travel and dunes to explore, adventures of pirate legends to reenact, and, on rainy days, the lure of the attic with all its treasures packed in trunks or the old carriage house, where the smell of the horses still faintly lingered. There was

Sunday tea on the wide front porch, with other ladies of
Aunt Leila's circle.

And always—always—there had been Alex Kane.

The grandson of Leila's dearest friend, Alex, too, had
been sent east from California every summer to stay in the
big house that faced Leila's from directly across the street.
His sister, Krista, two years older than Alex, three years
older than Abby, would lounge in the hammock in the
backyard of their grandmother's house reading teeny-
bopper magazines and drinking diet soda, all the while
sniffing disdainfully at the childish pursuits of Abby and
Alex, who were inseparable from the last week of June until
the second week of August, every year for twelve years.

No. Abby corrected herself. *Eleven years. That last summer, Alex had not come.*

He had had to take a job that summer, his grandmother
had told her, a construction job that would help pay his
college tuition the following September, money being tight
now that his parents were divorcing. Abby knew instinctively that summers would never be the same again and that
a chapter of her life had closed forever.

Abby idly fanned herself with the letter, wondering what
had become of Alex and Krista and—what was his grandmother's name? Oh, of course. Belle. Annabelle Lee
Matthews. She had been a tiny, spry elf of a woman, whose
very eyes spoke of mischief. How peculiar that she and Aunt
Leila, who was the epitome of quiet grace, should have been
the very closest of friends.

No more peculiar, she mused, than for Aunt Leila to have
chosen as her beloved the adventuresome Thomas Cassidy,
a man who had scoured the continents seeking lost treasures
long before Steven Spielberg had dreamed up Indiana
Jones.

Abby reached to a nearby table and retrieved a box
of tissues as she shed fat, hot tears—tears for her lost
summers, tears for Aunt Leila, tears for the long-ago days
of her childhood, and yet still more tears for her long-lost
love.

When she'd wept herself dry, she pulled the will from the

envelope and read through the pages of legalese until she found her name.

To my grand-niece and namesake, Leila Abigail McKenna, I bequeath all of my personal and real property, to include the estate of my late husband, Thomas Andrew Cassidy . . .

All of my personal and real property.

That would mean the house and its contents. Abby tapped the nails of two fingers on the arm of the chair, contemplating the unexpected news. The house—the castle of her childhood—was now hers. Why, the furniture alone must be worth a . . .

A fortune.

"Oh, thank you, Aunt Leila," she half shouted, half sobbed. "Thankyouthankyouthankyou . . . you've saved my life!"

Horace D. Tillman had been the perfect Southern gentleman when Abby called to acknowledge receipt of the letter. Suitably sympathetic and kindly recalling Aunt Leila before getting down to the business at hand, he had assured her that she was, indeed, Leila's sole beneficiary. He apologized for the delay in notifying her, but there had been some difficulty in determining her whereabouts. He had finally traced her through her Montana relatives.

She would, of course, she assured Mr. Tillman, come to Primrose as soon as humanly possible. Early November would be just fine. Abby was all but dancing when she hung up the phone. Considering her circumstances, she would walk to Primrose if necessary.

Abby scanned the living room, taking stock of her surroundings with a critical eye. The furniture she bought two years ago had been expensive. How much would it be worth now? she wondered, an idea forming rapidly.

Suppose I sell it—give my landlord his thirty-day notice. My lease is up at the end of October anyway. I could go to North Carolina, sell the house, and, from there, I could go anywhere.

Abby brusquely pushed aside the sharp pang that accompanied the thought of selling the house. She would deal with the emotional aspects of *that* when the time came. Right now, she had to accept the bequest as the gift Aunt Leila had meant it to be. Surely, Aunt Leila would have known that a corporate type like Abby would not have moved to a sleepy little town like Primrose. Surely, she would have known that the estate would be sold . . .

I'll think about that later.

Abruptly, Abby rose and began to pace.

I would need a car. How can I buy a car? From the sale of my furniture. I can buy a used car—something small and inexpensive.

She grabbed the newspaper lying, still folded from that morning, on the table. She scanned the ads. There were lots of small, inexpensive cars to be had.

She walked to her desk, pulled the small red phone book from the top drawer, and looked up the number of her landlord to tell him the check he'd receive on Thursday would be her last.

She folded the will and tried to return it to its envelope, but something inside seemed to bar its way. Sticking her hand inside, her fingers found yet another envelope, a small square of thin yellow paper on which her name had been scripted in precise and flowing letters. Aunt Leila's own hand. She carefully removed the small wax seal and read the message that had been left only for her.

> *My dearest Abigail,*
> *I am hopeful that at some time between my writing this note and your reading it, we might have one last Sunday afternoon to spend over tea. Though your childhood may seem a lifetime away to you, it was, for me, but yesterday that the little girl with the big round eyes and the wayward curls descended upon Primrose to share the days of summer. Ah, child, you've no idea how I looked forward to June, and your arrival at my door . . .*

*the anticipation of having this house filled with your
youthful laughter once again. The glow of those
remembered joys would carry me, year after year,
through the chill of winter.*

*Knowing how you loved this house, it is fitting
that it should pass from my hands into yours. I
know I can rest in the peaceful assurance that you
will care for it—and for any dear and gentle spirit
you may encounter here—as best you can, as I have
done.*

*I remain, as always, your loving
Aunt Leila*

Abby's eyes stung as she understood for the first time how
much her visits to Cove Road had meant to Aunt Leila.
They had not shared tea on a Sunday afternoon since the
year Abby graduated from college. For five years, the old
woman had waited for her to return, and in each of those
five years, Abby had disappointed her.

"I'm sorry, Aunt Leila, I'm so very sorry," she whispered.
"I don't think I realized how much you loved me."

✦3✦

"How much do you want for everything?" the young
woman repeated.

Abby hesitated. It had cost twenty-five hundred dollars,
this stylish piece of nubby white upholstery. And the round
glass tables had cost half that. Extravagances she had, once
upon a time, been able to afford. The prints on the wall—
some of them originals purchased from students at the
Philadelphia College of Art—had been indulgences. Should
she include them as well?

"Four thousand dollars," Abby looked at the woman who

would sublet her apartment and tried not to blink. You had to start someplace.

"Does that include the artwork?"

"Yes." Abby wouldn't have included it if the woman hadn't asked.

"And the bedroom furniture as well?"

"Yes."

"I don't know." The woman strolled around the apartment as if taking inventory. "Four thousand dollars . . ."

"Nothing is more than two years old," Abby pointed out, "and, as you can see, everything is in pristine condition."

"Okay. I'll bring you a check the morning I move in," the woman said as she headed toward the door.

"Which will be . . . ?" Abby was pleased. She had expected to negotiate.

"The fifteenth of November."

"Not good." Abby shook her head. "I have to be out on the first."

"Can I drop off a check that morning, then? On my way to my office?"

Abby winced. The woman spoke with the same air of confidence she herself, until recently, had once had.

"I'm afraid I'll have to ask for cash." Abby realized she would have closed out her bank accounts by the first of November.

"Fine." The woman took one last look around at the apartment and its furnishings.

As soon as the door closed between them, Abby danced a silent arabesque across the living room before grabbing the morning paper and dialing the phone number she had earlier circled in red.

"Hello . . . I'm calling about the ad you had in this morning's *Inquirer?* For the Subaru station wagon? How many miles does it have?" She sat on the floor and made notes on the back of an envelope. "And how much were you asking? Yes, I am interested. Where is the car? Oh. No, I'm sorry, I have no way to get there . . . you would? Great. Yes. This afternoon would be fine."

She doodled on the envelope for a few minutes, contemplating the steps she had taken. With the contents of her apartment sold, she would be free to take a job anywhere, once she had tended to her affairs in Primrose. With the money from her furniture, she could buy a small car to take her where she had to go. A station wagon would permit her to take her clothes and the few personal belongings she would keep. After she sold Aunt Leila's house and its contents, she'd have more than enough money to take her time finding the right position, and then some. She stood and stretched, buoyed by her prospects. Feeling more content than she had in a long time, she decided to follow an impulse and venture out for a rare afternoon walk.

Abby stopped to purchase an ice cream cone from a sidewalk vendor before idly wandering with no particular destination in mind. It had been days since she had left her apartment, and she savored the fresh air, filled with the crisp promise of deepening autumn. The leaves that peppered the sidewalks leading through Rittenhouse Square rustled in the light October breeze and crunched beneath her feet. She sat on a bench in the sun to lick at the strawberry streams that slid down the sides of the cone.

She had never, she suddenly realized, really known this city she had called home for the past nine years. In four years of college and five years of working and living on her own, she had never made the time to explore its haunts or its historical treasures, had never found its heart. Abby's sole focus had been her career. Period. She had never developed friendships, had never made a social life to speak of. There was no one even to say good-bye to, no one to care that she was leaving. She had had few women friends in college, fewer still at the office. Those she had known at White-Edwards always seemed to view her as an oddity. She was the one who always worked late and took unfinished items home to work on even later. She would work on weekends, rarely sparing time for a night out except for those few occasions when one man or another had managed to get close enough to ask her out. No one had interested her enough for her to see more than a few times. Certainly, none of them had lit so much as a spark in her.

Memories of her sixteenth summer tugged playfully to be recalled. As if she had forgotten the summer she and Alex Kane had discovered each other as more than childhood playmates. They had spent hours biking along the back roads, winding slowly through the fields and woodlands, taking their time, talking about school, their dreams, their futures. Alex would be a lawyer, a criminal defense lawyer, a true Perry Mason. Abby would be an artist, painting the Carolina countryside and finding fame and fortune in the pricey galleries in New York City. And always they would return to Primrose—and each other. They had taken long walks along the river, holding hands and learning how to kiss. They had acknowledged their everlasting love for each other that summer and had experimented with more than kissing before the second week in August arrived and, with it, Abby's parents.

Abby dragged the toe of one shoe through the hard dust in front of the park bench. *That was the last truly happy time of my life,* she thought.

She tried to recall which of them had been the first to stop writing, but she could not be certain. She had auditioned for and won the lead in the junior play that fall, and Alex, as starting quarterback for his high school football team, had had a busy season. Before too long, it was June, and she had anxiously counted the days until they would meet in Primrose. It had never occurred to her that a time would come when he would not be there for her in summer.

How bizarre, she thought with a wry smile. *Alex set the standard by which I've judged kissing since I was sixteen, and he's never been bested.*

Not that I've had much time for such things, she reminded herself as she stood and started across the square. *I imagine that romance can take one's focus from one's goal. Working hard, getting ahead, is the only way to attain security. If my father had worked more and played less, things would have been different.*

But, ever the gambler, Harold McKenna had played fast and loose with the market for eighteen months. Confident that his latest little deal would turn a huge and speedy profit, he had invested every dime he had, as well as far too many he'd borrowed, and had lost everything. On the heels of Harold's sudden financial decline—the news of which Harold had not yet shared with his wife and daughter— death had cheated him of the opportunity to try to recoup his former wealth. And so, in the blink of an eye, Abby had gone from being the beloved daughter of a wealthy investor to being a penniless orphan.

She had sometimes wondered how her father, who so doted on her, who provided her with every luxury, would have felt had he known what his gamble had cost her. Each time, she had all but felt his pain.

Harold may have made some foolish decisions where his finances were concerned, but he never, never would have knowingly placed Abby in such a predicament. He simply had not expected to die.

She poked along solemnly, all too well aware that her own hard work, single-minded as it had been, had not insulated her from financial disaster.

That's different, she argued with herself. *I didn't fritter away what I had. Okay, I could have saved more, but if you want to move in executive circles, you need to dress like an executive. And besides, I didn't expect to lose my job.*

And my father hadn't expected to die.

Still pondering the quirks of fate, she failed to notice the woman who stood in front of her building until she had all but walked over her.

"Oh . . . I'm sorry," Abby mumbled, walking around the woman and heading for the steps.

"Excuse me." The woman held out her arm. "Do you live here?"

"Yes," Abby replied.

"I'm looking for . . ." She fumbled with a piece of paper. "Abby McKenna."

"I'm Abby McKenna." Abby eyed her suspiciously.

"I'm Debbie. You called earlier about my car."

"Oh, yes. I'm so sorry." Abby apologized for her tardiness. She had lost all track of time.

"Well, that's it, across the street." Debbie pointed somewhere down the block.

"Which one . . . the red one?"

"Yes." The woman nodded, and they dodged cars as they crossed the street to take a look.

Cherry red, five years old, gray cloth interior. It looked fine.

Debbie handed her the keys. "Take it for a ride."

"You do drive stick, don't you?" Debbie asked as Abby started the engine.

"Stick?"

"Manual transmission . . . the kind with a . . ."

Abby hit the gas pedal, sending the car into a sort of forward lurch. The engine promptly died.

". . . clutch."

"Oh. Right. Of course. Stick shift," Abby said dumbly. "Sorry. I used to know how to do this . . ."

She restarted the engine and tried again, this time making it to the corner before the car stalled again.

"Sorry. I, ah, haven't driven in a few years."

"You do have a license?" Debbie asked nervously.

"Yes. I kept renewing it, thinking someday I'd have a car again. I just haven't needed one, living in the city. I walk to work." Abby was more nervous than she'd expected. "At least, I used to walk to work . . . damn, I keep forgetting about the clutch . . ."

Abby pulled into a parking spot in front of her building after an excruciatingly long five-minute drive around the block.

"I'll take it," she said.

"Are you sure?" Debbie's eyebrows rose halfway up her forehead.

"Yes. It's just what I need." Abby returned the keys with a grin.

"Aren't you going to ask about the mechanics?"

"Well, it seems to be in good shape. I mean, anyone could tell it's been cared for," Abby said quickly. *And the price is right. All this sucker has to do is get me to North Carolina. One way. I can sell it down there and fly to wherever I decide to go from there.*

It would take most of the remains of her savings, but she'd make that up when Jane, the new tenant, paid her for her furniture. She and Debbie came to an agreement quickly. The car would be brought back to her on Friday, when they would transfer the title. Abby skipped up the steps.

Her course now set, Abby spent the evening going through her closet to pack up clothes that no longer fit. She'd lost weight since last winter, she realized, holding up a blue pin-striped suit she'd purchased in January. She caught her reflection in the mirror. Her face was gaunt and her color more pale than usual. *Too much stress,* she told herself.

Abby finished cleaning out her closet, carefully hanging in quilted garment bags those few suits and dresses and good slacks and blouses that still fit. Her few casual outfits—sweat clothes and two pairs of jeans—would travel south in her suitcase. She had boxes for other items, and she fervently hoped all—her Calphalon cookware, her collections of old perfume bottles and cookbooks, and two small boxes of well-played Motown tapes—would fit in the back of the small car along with her PC, her 20-inch television, VCR, and small CD player. She bagged her discards for the homeless shelter six blocks away. Highly pleased with her efforts, she stood back and surveyed the stack of boxes.

"Thank you, Aunt Leila, for loving me." She spoke aloud with all the reverence some might reserve for prayer. "Thank you for remembering me in so generous a fashion. Thank you for giving me options. Thank you for forgiving me for having stayed away so long."

◆ 4 ◆

The first of November could not have been more gray. The sun struggled to break through sullen clouds—themselves gunmetal gray in a bleak sky—barely dispelling the fog which wrapped around the city in an insistent tangle of wispy arms. Abby finished loading boxes into the car, having dropped the backseat to double her cargo space, carefully fitting her clothes and the boxes between the electronics before tucking the envelope filled with cash from the sale of her furniture into the glove compartment. She leaned over the front seat to root through a box, looking for some tapes of old favorites to keep her company as she drove.

After popping the Four Tops into the tape player on the dash, Abby started the engine and, without a backward glance, pulled into the morning traffic and headed for the interstate. Once she was on I-95, the city's skyline rose, shaded in mist, on her right. To her left, the Delaware River flowed choppy and muddy green. She drove past the exits to Veterans Stadium and the Spectrum, neither of which she had ever visited. Just beyond, the flat-roofed warehouses of the food distribution center opened their wide doors to the truckers who would transport produce all across the metropolitan area. A few of those trucks were already competing for her lane of traffic. She pulled to her right as the first of the tractor-trailers sped past on the approach to the huge double-decked bridge that spanned the Schuylkill River. Planes almost close enough to touch seemed to float past on their way to the airport just to her left.

Beyond the city limits now, Abby accelerated and moved into the passing lane to go around a small red pickup with Delaware plates. The City of Brotherly Love, along with all her dreams of corporate bliss, was lost in her rearview mirror, shrouded in the haze of a misty early-autumn morning.

She stopped in Delaware for breakfast and, later, had a leisurely lunch in Virginia. She'd expected to be in Primrose by dinner but zigged into North Carolina where she should have zagged, somewhere in the vicinity of the Great Dismal Swamp, and wasted an hour trying to get back onto the right road. A friendly restaurant across the street from the county courthouse in Elizabeth City served up wonderful crab cakes, a fresh salad, and a warming cup of coffee. Fortified, she set off on the last leg of her journey.

It was shortly after nine when she exited the highway, following, with a certain caution, the signs to the darkened road that led to Primrose. Though in her youth she'd known every bump on every road for ten miles in any direction, years had passed, and she was no longer definite. Overhead lighting was virtually nonexistent on this approach to the small town, and memory told her that there were at least two sharp curves somewhere ahead. The acres of dense woodland on either side of the narrow road seemed to close in on her, and she momentarily wished she had waited until the following day to make this last leg of her trip.

The first curve was upon her before she had time to brake for it, sending the Subaru into the opposing lane, which, fortunately, was unoccupied. She returned to her side of the road and slowed to a crawl, recalling that the next curve would be almost ninety degrees to the right. She all but crept into it, then sped up, knowing it would be a straightaway into the center of town from that point on.

Driving into a small town after it has closed for the night gives you the oddest feeling, she thought as she passed through Primrose proper. The sidewalks were long deserted, the stores long darkened, their proprietors having gone to their homes hours earlier. The old-fashioned street lights which hung from poles every thirty feet or so on either side cast an eerie glow on the shop fronts.

"Rolled back the sidewalks at dusk" was coined to describe *Primrose,* Abby mused as she passed the silent storefronts. Slowing slightly, she peered through the darkness at Mr. Foster's General Store, which appeared just as she remembered it. On past the Primrose Café, where the townfolk traditionally gathered for their early-morning coffee, and the hardware store, where one could purchase everything from string and thumbtacks to lawn mowers. And that was Primrose proper.

Or was, when I was a girl. Looks like maybe a few more shops than what I recall.

The new gas station at the corner of Harper and Cove Road took her by surprise, and she almost missed the turn. Ever more slowly, she crept down Cove Road, past the house where Aunt Leila's friend, Mrs. Lawrence, once lived, past the old Matthews place, where Aunt Leila's best friend, Belle, had lived.

Guess she's gone now, too, judging by the tricycles there by the front porch.

Abby pulled to the side of the road and parked in front of a structure that, in the darkened hush, appeared less than hospitable. She turned off the motor and the headlights, took a deep breath, and opened the car door. Standing in the middle of the road, Abby focused on the magnificent building that loomed before her.

Aunt Leila's house, built by Thomas Cassidy's grandparents in the 1830s and subjected to expansion and renovation by successive generations, rose imposingly from behind overgrown rhododendron which obscured the entire front porch and vast portions of the second floor as well. Only the wide front steps, which seemed to stick out from the porch like the tongue of a sassy child, emerged from the darkened facade. The entire house huddled in a dreary silence, the windows of the top two floors shuttered tightly against the world without. It was—had always been—an imposing sight. Now, wrapped in the opalescent glow of mist from the river that flowed behind and beyond, the house was downright spooky.

Abby approached the long path that led to the porch with a certain amount of circumspection. As quietly as the night had settled around her, she followed the path to its end, then tentatively planted one foot on the first step, which sagged with a faint *whoosh,* no louder than an exhale, beneath her weight. The handrail was wobbly when she reached out for it, and the floorboards creaked as if in pain as she tiptoed toward the front door, where she stood almost expectantly before reaching for the knob.

"Oh, good grief," she exclaimed, realizing she had no key with which to open the door. Exasperated with herself for having overlooked this one little item, she paced back to the top of the steps, then sat down.

"Damn. I can't believe this," she growled. "I can't believe I drove all this way to reach a house I cannot get into."

The last motel she'd passed was about sixteen miles back. She figured she had roughly enough gas to make it to Mr. Foster's General Store.

She rose with great annoyance, shaking her head in disbelief at her stupidity. As she turned her head to the left, she saw the outline of the planter on which Aunt Leila had kept her African violets in the warm months. Small clay pots lined its white wrought-iron shelves. Abby paused, a memory begging for attention. When she was a child, Aunt Leila had often left a key for her under the third pot on the third shelf. She lifted the pot and ran her fingers across the spot where it had stood. Grinning broadly, she held up the key.

Thank you, Aunt Leila.

Abby fitted the key into the lock, hoping Aunt Leila had not had cause to change it. As the key and the knob turned simultaneously, the door opened with the greatest reluctance. She gave it a tentative push, and it swung an arc into the big, dark entrance hall. Taking a deep breath, she entered—slowly and on tiptoe—into the hushed halls of her childhood.

Through the inky darkness, Abby could see the stairwell rising some twenty feet back from the doorway, along the right wall. The interior of the house was as familiar to her as her name. Even in the dark, she knew that to her immediate left was the music room, which opened into Thomas's library. A wide hallway led past the stairwell and on to the dining room, beyond which was a butler's pantry and the kitchen. To her right was a formal parlor, which opened to a sitting room, from which one entered a small conservatory, which Aunt Leila had called her morning room.

Standing in the middle of the entrance hall, Abby peered into the two front rooms without taking a step toward either. The furniture was covered with sheets, giving a ghostly form to every chair and settee. There was an eeriness about the house that she had not anticipated. Over all, the scent of lavender—Aunt Leila's signature fragrance —seemed to preside.

What had Aunt Leila's letter said about dear and gentle spirits?

Goosebumps sped up her arms, across her shoulders, and straight down her back into her legs and didn't stop until they reached her toes.

Don't be an idiot. There's no such thing as . . .

The floorboards overhead creaked menacingly.

Old houses have noises. It's just the pipes, she told herself.

She forced the air out of her lungs slowly, then set her purse down on a nearby chair while she turned on the overhead light. One last bulb of the large, ornate crystal chandelier flickered uncertainly, the sudden dim light causing shadows to lengthen across the spacious hall. She took four steps forward when she heard it again.

Abby froze.

This time, the creaking was accompanied by a light shuffling sound. Inching toward the wall parallel to the stairwell, Abby tried to disappear into it, straining her ears to try to identify the sound.

A soft footfall on the top step was followed by another equally as faint. Someone was making a slow, deliberate descent. It was not Abby's imagination, nor was it a ghost. Someone very real—a burglar? a vagrant?—was making his way downstairs. Abby flattened herself against the wall, her fingers fanning out on either side as if searching for something to hold on to. Without a sound, she slid sideways toward the back hallway. She hoped, the intruder, whoever he was, didn't know the lay of the house as well as she did.

Unless, of course, he's been camped here since Aunt Leila died.

Maybe he somehow found out the house was vacant and decided to move in.

Maybe he used it as his base of operations, lying low during the day and sneaking out to commit murder and mayhem in the dark of night.

The shadow cast by the figure paused momentarily, long enough for Abby to move toward the dining room. She took two quick steps and hit the table that stood, obscured in darkness, against the wall. Something crashed to the floor.

"If you're looking for money, you've come to the wrong place. I don't have any," a woman's voice—forced firmness barely concealing fright—announced from somewhere halfway up the stairs.

Abby slowly stepped out of the shadows and peered up the steps. An old woman, wrapped in a bright yellow chenille robe, her hand tightly clasping the handrail, stared down at her.

"Go on, do whatever it is you're going to do," the old woman bravely demanded, her voice holding a hint of the soft eastern Carolina accent Abby had heard so often in her childhood. "Just don't hurt me. Rob me, take what you want. But don't hurt me."

"Who are you?" Relief washed over Abby like a warm ocean wave.

"Now, what the devil of a difference would *that* make?" The woman's shoulders were tiny under the robe, frail, like the rest of her. Only her voice—the voice of one accustomed to being obeyed—appeared strong. "The silver's in the dining room. That's about all there is that you could carry away. Help yourself. Then get out of here so I can go back to sleep."

Abby approached the bottom of the steps.

"You don't look much like a burglar." The old woman eyed her suspiciously.

"I'm not a burglar," Abby told her.

"If you're not here to rob me, then what the Sam Hill *are* you doing, breaking in here in the middle of the night and scaring an old lady half out of her mind?" snapped the woman. "Unless you're one of them serial killers you hear about on the news these days . . ."

"I'm Abby McKenna," Abby told her gently. "I own this house."

"Abby McKenna," the woman repeated. "Abigail McKenna? Leila's grand-niece?"

"Yes." Abby nodded. Clearly, this was no vagrant. "Who are you?"

"Belle. Belle Matthews." The woman came down the remaining steps to study Abby's face. "Well, mercy me. You're Abigail, all right. Well, then, 'bout time you got here."

The two women eyed each other for a long moment. In spite of the old woman's bravado, Belle was flushed, her hands trembling as her white-knuckled grip on the baluster eased.

Taking great pains to present as dignified and controlled a front as possible under the circumstances, Belle asked, "Want some tea?" Without waiting for an answer, she pulled herself up to her full height of almost five feet and swept past Abby toward the kitchen.

In the poorly lit kitchen, Belle placed a pot of water on the stove and opened a cabinet to bring down two cups and matching saucers.

They sat at a small table overlooking the darkened backyard. Abby stirred her tea and wondered how she could go about asking Belle why she was living in Leila's house.

"Guess you're wondering what I'm doing in Leila's house." Belle looked at her from over the top of her cup.

"Well . . . yes." Abby's eyebrows rose in mild surprise that Belle's words so closely echoed Abby's own thoughts.

"If you'd made the time to visit once in a while, you'd have known that Leila invited me to move in with her about two years ago. Right before I sold my house." She nodded her head, presumably to indicate the house across the street. "Not that I wanted to. Sell it, that is. Couldn't pay the taxes. Sell it or watch it be sold for back taxes, that was my choice. Leila kindly offered me shelter. I kindly loaned Leila money to have the roof replaced, once I had cash from the sale."

"And she paid you back?"

"Nope. I figured it would come out of Leila's estate, once you got around to coming down here."

Abby's face took on the appearance of plaster of paris as she tried not to choke on the thought.

Belle finished her tea and rinsed the cup out in the sink. "I'm glad you finally got here, Abigail McKenna. I was wondering how I'd keep that dinosaur of an oil tank filled this winter. Leila and I used to pool our social security checks, you know, just to eat and pay our utilities. Never would have been able to keep the furnace running by myself. Guess now that you're here, I can quit worrying about *that*. Leila promised me I'd always have a home here. Nice to know it'll be a warm one. See you in the morning. Oh." She turned around to face Abby, who sat silent and wide-eyed as she tried to digest the news of her indebtedness. "Which room you figure on using?"

"I . . . I hadn't thought about it. My old one, I guess."

"Linens in the closet where they've always been." Belle tottered off down the hall, her voice trailing behind her. "Take a quilt from the chest at the foot of the bed. It'll be chilly by morning."

Abby sat motionless at the table, Aunt Leila's letter to her suddenly very clear.

"*. . . care for . . . any dear and gentle spirit you may encounter here—as best you can, as I have done . . .*"

Leila had passed not only her home but her best friend as well into Abby's hands.

✦ 5 ✦

Lost in a dreamless sleep after her marathon drive of the previous day, Abby had no sense of time or place when she finally awakened. The windows permitted no clue of dark or dawn beyond their heavy drapes and tightly clasped shutters. She reached for her watch on the table next to the bed. Seven A.M.

Grabbing her robe from the bedpost, she tied it loosely at her waist and opened the door. The house lay as silent as it had the night before when she had first crossed the threshold. She wondered if Belle was an early riser.

Wandering down the stairs, she checked for coffee. *Even instant coffee will do,* she thought, suddenly craving the gourmet beans she used to splurge on back in her more affluent days. The cupboards held nothing but a box containing a half-dozen tea bags.

She pushed aside the narrow blue-and-white-striped curtain that hung across the glass in the back door. Looking around, she found a wall hook upon which a key dangled on a thin piece of string. She fitted the key into the lock and turned it, the hinges protesting with a low-pitched shriek as she pulled it open. Abby took a few steps out into the morning air and peered at the old thermometer on the outside wall. Fifty-eight degrees. The sun was trying its best to will away a veil of clouds and make its appearance. Abby sat on the top step and stretched the long robe to wrap around her bare ankles.

That the grounds had fallen into a sad state of neglect pulled painfully at Abby's heart. Aunt Leila had been celebrated for her gardens. The local garden club had for many years included Leila's property on its annual summer tour. More often than not, the event would culminate in a garden party, for which a young Abby would be pressed into service. From her perch on the back porch, she could almost see herself, dressed in a starched white summer dress that had once been worn by Aunt Leila herself, offering delicate tea sandwhiches to the ladies who clustered around Aunt Leila's lilies or her arbors of roses. Here, Leila had hosted family weddings and grand parties. Abby's own parents had exchanged their vows right there, under that very arbor, when the white roses that once wound overhead had been at their very peak.

What a shame. She lamented the sight.

Vines and shrubs neglected for years had overtaken all. The cobbled paths that had once led from one pampered bed to another were obscured now, as were the beds themselves. Vestiges of Leila's herb garden remained around the ornate birdbath which had once stood proudly in the center of the garden. The birdbath was cracked now, one section hanging off its base at an awkward angle.

What a shame.

"Broke Leila's heart to let it go," Belle said softly from the doorway, "but, of course, these last few years, neither of us could tend to it. And there's been no money to hire out the work. 'Course, now that you're here, you can tidy things up a bit."

"I wouldn't know where to start." Abby turned to look over her shoulder at the slight figure behind the screen.

"You start with the obvious, Abigail," Belle sighed with exaggerated patience. "First, you pull out what doesn't belong there, then you tend to those things which do."

"I doubt I'd know the difference," Abby muttered.

"Read Leila's journals. Wrote down everything she did out here for almost seventy years. Sketched every plant she put in and dated every one of the sketches," Belle told her with a mild drawl. "You can read, can't you? Tea's ready, if you'd like some." Belle disappeared into the kitchen, and the whistle of the kettle ceased abruptly.

Abby tapped one foot quietly on the step, measuring out her patience.

"Gentle spirit," my ass.

"How about if I make breakfast for us?" Abby suggested

36

as she followed Belle into the house. "We could maybe eat in the morning room and get reacquainted."

And maybe I can find out where your family is, and what their plans are for you now that . . . well, now that Leila's gone, and soon the house will be passing into other hands, so to speak.

"That would be nice." Belle nodded agreeably. "I'll set the little table in there."

"What would you like for breakfast?" Abby asked.

"I'd like soft-boiled eggs, sausage, and biscuits with blackberry jam," Belle told her as she passed into the pantry for some dishes.

"Sounds easy enough." Abby smiled and opened the refrigerator door. The relatively new appliance was virtually empty, except for half a stick of butter in a pink Depression glass dish, a jar of grape jelly with only the faintest remnants of purple streaks up one side, and five slices of bread in their plastic wrapping.

"Belle," she called into the next room, "there are no eggs."

"And no sausage and no biscuits." Belle appeared momentarily in the doorway. "You asked me what I wanted. That's what I want. But we'll both have tea and toast, because that's all we have."

Abby put two pieces of toast in the ancient toaster, removed the butter from the refrigerator, and took it into the room Aunt Leila had called her morning room. She stood in the doorway and watched as Belle placed the teapot and cups on the small round table that stood between two straight-backed white wicker chairs. How many times had she watched Aunt Leila do these exact tasks in preparation for their morning meal?

The sun was beginning to beam through the back windows, casting aside some of the gloom that seemed to encase the entire house. As the light spread across the worn carpet, the shabbiness of the room became more apparent. In Abby's memory, the chintz on the settee was always fresh and new, the window ledges lined with lushly flowering plants, the lace curtains sparkling white. Now, all seemed faded and dusty, the paint on the window ledges peeling and the curtains almost gray. A few of the windows sat at slightly odd angles, the panes no longer solidly affixed to their frames.

As if reading her mind, Belle told her, "We just couldn't keep up with it, Abby. It was all too much. Before Leila died, we did manage to keep most of the downstairs open, but since she . . . it's all I can do to keep the dishes washed and the floors clean and the bed linens changed."

"You've had no help at all?" Abby whispered.

"Naomi, across the street—she and her husband bought my house—has been my salvation. She does my laundry, picks up some groceries for me when my social security check comes every month, brings me soup and homemade bread once a week or so." Belle's voice wavered slightly, and she gazed out the window to avert her eyes. It was a hard admission from a woman who had once presided over a handsome home of her own, who had been admired and sought after for her lofty social position as much as for her wit and charm.

"Belle, where's your family?" Abby set the plate of butter on the table.

"Abigail, the toaster . . ." Belle pointed toward the kitchen, from which the aroma of charcoal drifted.

"Good grief." Abby flew back into the kitchen and unplugged the toaster. She dumped the charred remains of bread into the sink.

"Well, there goes breakfast," Belle announced with a wry smile.

"I'll make two more." Abby shook out the last of the burnt crumbs.

"Not if you want lunch," Belle told her matter-of-factly.

"Belle, you can't live on tea and toast."

"Abigail, you can live on much less than that."

"This is ridiculous." Abby shook her head. "I'm going upstairs to change, and then I'm going down to the store for some groceries."

"What a lovely idea." Belle nodded slowly. "Abigail, while you are there, could you possibly see if Mr. Foster has

38

any blackberry jam? Not the regular store-bought kind, the kind Annie Thurman makes and jars, if it isn't too much? Young Foster will know."

No wonder the woman's so frail, Abby thought angrily as she pulled a sweatshirt and jeans from her suitcase and slid into them. *Living on the barest of necessities for who knows how long. Where in hell is her family?*

"What might you like for dinner?" Abby paused in the doorway.

"Dinner?" Belle spoke the word as if considering a foreign concept.

"Is there anything in particular you'd like?"

"Why, whatever you think, Abigail." Belle cleared her throat. "Though a roast chicken might be nice. I haven't had roast chicken since Leila passed on. She did all the cooking, you know."

"Fine. Chicken it is."

Abby grabbed her jacket and purse from the chair in the front hallway, where she'd deposited them the previous night. She checked her wallet and found she was low on cash. Opening the glove compartment, she withdrew some bills from the envelope and relocked the compartment. It was as safe there, she surmised, as it would be anyplace else.

She stopped at the new gas station on the corner. A tall, thin man in his early thirties dressed in jeans and a green and white flannel shirt came out to greet her.

" 'Morning." He smiled, wiping his hands on a light blue towel tucked into his waist. "What can I getcha?"

"Fill the tank, please." She smiled at his open friendliness.

"Check your oil?" He pronounced it "earl," and she smiled again, unconsciously this time.

"You still do that down here?" she asked.

He nodded and went about his business.

"You kin to Belle Matthews?" He watched Abby pull two five-dollar bills and three ones from her purse.

"No," she replied, puzzled.

"Thought maybe you might be, since you were parked there"—he nodded up Cove Road—"early this morning."

"Actually, my great-aunt owned that house." Abby grinned, reminding herself that in a town the size of Primrose, there were no secrets.

"You the one she left it to? The niece from up north or someplace?"

"Well, yes." She nodded.

"Welcome to Primrose, then." He pocketed the money. "Guess you'll be working on the place now. You planning on fixing it up and living there?"

"I haven't decided yet what I'm going to do."

No need for anyone else to know before she could break the news to Belle that the house would be going on the market as soon as possible.

"You might want to talk to Pete Phelps down at the hardware store. His son's a good carpenter—you'll be needing one for that front porch. Seems to me I heard that the building inspector was out there a few weeks ago looking around."

"Looking around at what?"

"That one chimney on the side is leanin' a little farther to the right than it should be. And the porch around that big turret looks like it's about to detach. Guess they'll"—he nodded toward town—"be glad to see you. They didn't know what to do, what with Miz Matthews livin' there and not ownin' the place. You might want to stop at the town hall and let someone know you're here."

"Thanks for the tip," she muttered sourly as she rolled up the window and drove toward the center of town.

Great. Not in Primrose twenty-four hours, and the building inspector's after me. Guess I better take a closer look at the house when I get back.

Abby parked along the sidewalk in front of the Primrose Café, where some of the locals lingered over their coffee to discuss the latest news. As she walked across the street to Foster's General Store, she was not unaware that curious eyes from the window of the café followed her as she opened the door to the one food market in Primrose. She smiled to herself, knowing that as quickly as she closed the door behind her, the folks across the street would be speculating on everything from her identity to her shoe size.

Housed in one storefront that was part of a row of shops in a two-story white clapboard building, Foster's was clean and bright, if limited in its selections. Rows of canned and packaged goods lined three aisles down the center of the store. A butcher's counter ran across the back, and along the left side, crates of fruits and vegetables sat in wooden bins. She wandered up and down the aisles, trying to decide what to buy.

"Need a basket, young lady?" a voice called to her from behind the butcher's counter.

"I guess I could use one, thanks." She moved toward the back of the store, trying not to dislodge the items she'd stacked in her arms.

The short, balding man in the white apron—"Young Foster," she guessed, though he had to be in his fifties— held out a red plastic basket, and she tried to drop the cans of soup one by one inside, but they rolled down her front avalanche-style. He lunged to hold on to the metal handles.

"Oops . . ."

"That's okay, miss, I've got it." He held the basket out to her. "Anything I can help you with?"

"Where would I find sugar?"

"Aisle two. Right there with the baked goods."

She put a five-pound bag into the basket, then paused in front of the flour. Maybe she could bake something . . . good, the package had a recipe for biscuits on the back. She grabbed a box of chocolate cake mix and a container of prepared frosting. She'd bake a little treat for Belle.

Eggs, butter, yogurt, milk from the dairy case filled a second basket. Orange juice from the small frozen-food section, carrots, potatoes, green beans, apples, bananas, and grapes from produce. She was on her third red basket when she arrived back at the meat counter.

Having proved herself a serious shopper, she had the full attention of the man in the white apron, who held out two whole chickens for her inspection.

"That one looks fine." She nodded, indicating the one in his left hand.

"That be all?" he asked.

"Ummm . . . blackberry jam." She recalled Belle's request. "Do you have some that's made locally?"

Young Foster held up a jar with a hand-printed label.

"Yes, that's it . . . and some breakfast sausage. Oh, and tea."

Belle's supply of tea was low. Abby had noticed that she used the one bag several times over. The last cup had been barely yellow in color.

"And coffee." She poked down the nearest aisle and found a can of already ground beans and returned with it to the counter.

"So," the grocer said as he tallied up her purchases. "You buy the old Landers place?"

"What? Oh, no." She shook her head as she scanned the front page of the local paper in the wire rack on the side of the counter.

"One of them new apartments out by the highway, then?" He never took his eyes off his work.

"No, actually, I inherited a property in town," she said vaguely.

"Oh, then you must be Miz Cassidy's grand-niece." He smiled in recognition.

"Why, yes, I am." She nodded her head.

"Fine lady, Miz Cassidy was. Best teacher I ever had."

"You were one of her students?" Abby fished in her purse for her wallet.

"Miz . . ."

"McKenna. Abby McKenna," she told him.

"Miz McKenna, everyone who grew up in Primrose and went to school here had Miz Cassidy for fifth grade. Why, she taught here for better'n forty years. Whole town came out when she retired. And again when she was buried. She was one of a kind." He shook his head fondly. "Wonderful woman, she was. A real lady, I might add. Not many left like her, that's for sure. She was like someone from another time."

Abby nodded slowly. She could not have described Leila better herself, she thought, as she loaded the bags into the car with Young Foster's help. Leila, with her elegant, soft clothes and her courtly grace, her strict observance of afternoon tea, her penchant for white gloves and hats in all seasons. Someone from another time, indeed.

After driving slowly into the narrow lane that ran next to Leila's house, Abby came to a stop and peered out the passenger-side window. The gas station attendant had been absolutely correct, she noted with a sinking heart. The porch was pulling away from the turret. What else was ready to take a tumble? She would make a thorough inspection this afternoon. Right now, she was going to prepare a proper lunch for Belle.

The old woman was like a child on Christmas morning, peeking into bags and exclaiming her delight upon finding something of particular preference.

"Seedless grapes . . . and bananas! I haven't had them in . . . well, who could recall?" She withdrew the favored items from the bag. "And you bought chicken, and, oh my . . . pork chops! And sugar. I've sorely missed sugar in my tea, the truth be told."

Good Lord, Abby thought, her face turning slightly red at the woman's unbounded joy. *This poor lady must be on the brink of abject poverty, if she can't afford a bag of sugar once or twice a year. Her family should be ashamed, letting her live like this. Alone in this big old house, no money, little food.*

She recalled Belle's comment about having been afraid she'd not have heat this winter. *If I hadn't come when I did, she might have frozen to death.*

Abby slammed the refrigerator door. *Wait till I get my hands on them. Krista and Alex and Josie, their mother. I have a few very choice words for all of them.*

The ringing telephone startled her. She followed the sound into the front hall, where Belle had picked it up.

"Why, yes, I am quite well. Thank you for inquiring," she was saying. "Yes, indeed, she is. Would you like to speak with her?"

Belle held the receiver out to Abby. "It's Mr. Tillman, Leila's attorney."

Word does travel. Abby grinned as she took the phone.

"Mr. Tillman, I was going to give you a call this afternoon. . . . Yes, I had a good trip. . . . Yes, it is good to be back in Primrose after all these years. . . . Well, I think we need to talk about that. . . . Yes, that would be fine. Ten tomorrow. I'll see you then."

Abby went back to the kitchen, thinking about what she might tell the lawyer. He'd asked if she was planning on keeping the house and making her home here. The answer was a definite no, but first she had to figure out what to do about Belle.

The woman has a family, she reminded herself. *She is their responsibility, not mine.*

Except that Aunt Leila had made Belle a promise and had bequeathed that promise to Abby along with the house.

✦ 6 ✦

Belle all but hung over Abby's shoulder as she prepared a lunch of chicken noodle soup and tuna salad. The woman ate slowly, savoring each bite, her eyes dancing with the sheer happiness of having a simple meal that was something other than tea and toast. For dessert, Abby presented her with a bowl of fruit and a few slices of cheese. Belle was in heaven.

"It must have been difficult to sell your house," Abby said over tea when the meal had finished. "I know it was terrible for me when my home—my parents' house, that is—was sold."

"Well, yes." Belle dabbed daintily at her mouth with a napkin. "I'd had better days. At least Granger wasn't alive to see it. Would have killed him, I think. He always set such store by that house, you know. Proud as a peacock, he was, the day he carried me over the threshold as a bride. Always romantic, my Granger was." Belle's eyes glazed, remembering.

"Couldn't Josie and her husband have helped?" Abby thought perhaps to turn the conversation to the absent family.

"Josie and Jack divorced about ten years ago," Belle told her. "Then Josie died—heart failure, they said—about two years later. If her heart failed, it was because that scoundrel of a husband of hers had taken off with his secretary. Little older than my granddaughter, she was." Belle shook her head sharply, her voice filled with bitterness.

"I had no idea." Abby felt stunned. "But surely her children could have helped you."

"Krista has about as much sense now as she had when she was nine. Probably less. Married some fool who can barely support her and the children. Four of them, she had, one right after another."

"And Alex?" It had been years since Abby had spoken his name aloud.

"Alexander is a lawyer." Her chin jutted out slightly. "The only one left in this family who'll ever live up to the Matthews name."

"Where is he living now?"

"Boston." Belle put down her cup and faced off with Abby. "But I've no mind to go running to that boy with my problems, missy. Alexander has had things tough enough, what with that fool father of his running off just when he was about to enter college, and his mother dying. He worked his way through school, law school, too. I imagine he's still paying back his loans. All those years, I thought I'd be able to do that for him." Her voice softened, almost as if she spoke only to herself. "I thought I'd be able to help him through school. All that boy ever asked of life was to study law and go fishing. No." Belle shook her head vehemently. "I'd not ask him for help. Not that I ever dreamed I'd be dependent on anyone."

"But you and Leila helped each other. That's not the same as being dependent."

"True enough. But now Leila's gone." She met Abby's eyes but did not add the obvious, *and I am dependent on you.*

Abby sensed Belle was waiting for some assurance from her, some words that would put her at ease, that would promise this home was still hers, now and always. It was a promise Abby could not, in good conscience, make, and so she said nothing.

Belle watched through narrow eyes that held questions they both wished to avoid as Abby cleared the table and carried Aunt Leila's equivalent of everyday dishes—some lovely old porcelain—into the kitchen.

"If Aunt Leila had fallen on hard times, why is there a new refrigerator? And a new stove?" Abby asked as she filled the sink.

"When things wore out, she replaced them."

"Where did the money come from?"

"She sold some things, when she had to," Belle told her.

"What did she sell?"

"Your great-grandmother's pearls went for the appliances, I don't recall what else, over the years. Some garnets, I think. And a diamond watch."

Abby searched her memory, trying to recall what jewelry there had been. Nothing specific came to mind except the garnets, a pin and a ring, which Aunt Leila had prized. It must have broken her heart to sell them.

"What do you do, Abigail?" Belle asked.

"What do you mean? What do I do for a living?"

"Yes."

"Well, right now, I'm unemployed. I used to work for a financial consulting firm."

"Doing what?"

"Advising people how to invest their money."

"People still have money to invest?" Belle asked wryly.

"Some do." Abby smiled.

"You left your job to come here?"

"Actually, it was the other way around." Abby let the water out of the sink, then searched for a towel to dry the dishes that stood in the drainer. "My job—and some others—were . . . eliminated."

Belle pondered for a moment, her eyes darting to Abby's face. "You don't expect to find a job like that here, do you? 'Cause there aren't any, I'd venture. Nobody I know around here has anything to invest."

"I don't know what I'm going to do." True, but vague.

"I see," Belle said softly.

"I think I'll take a look at that front porch, where it's sagging away from the house." Abby shoved her hands in her pockets, not wanting the conversation to drift further into her own plans. Not yet. She had far too many questions of her own, and far too few answers. She did not want to alarm Belle. There'd be time enough in the days to follow to face reality.

"You do that." Belle's eyes followed Abby as she went out the back door. "I think I'll take a nap. I feel very tired, all of a sudden."

The man at the gas station had not exaggerated. The chimney listed at an odd angle. It appeared that mortar was washing out from the bricks on one side. Abby wondered how it could be repaired, and at what price. She stepped back away from the house to study it.

When she was a child, she had believed this house to be enchanted. A wide turret rose three stories on the left, and the porches were trimmed with fancy woodwork. Gingerbread, Aunt Leila had called it. From the street, it did look like an oversized gingerbread house. Now, the paint peeled from the clapboard siding and several shutters hung loosely. The only thing that looked good was the roof, which Belle said Leila had replaced. With Belle's money.

Money, Abby reminded herself, that she would be obligated to repay.

She sat on the front porch and pondered the situation. She had an enormous house that was falling apart from every angle, an old woman to support, and debts she hadn't even known about. To pay Belle back, Abby would have to sell the house. If she sold the house, Belle would have nowhere to go. Even the money from the roof wouldn't take the old woman far, assuming she would agree to go. But go where? Abby could think of no option that would not inflict certain pain on Belle, whom Aunt Leila had trusted Abby to care for.

Damn Alex Kane, anyway. He screwed up my life when I was sixteen, and he's doing it again. Belle doesn't want to impose on him, doesn't want to disrupt his life. What about my life? I've worked every bit as hard as Alex has, and I've had my share of hardships, too.

She ambled around the back of the house and pushed open the old garden gate, which protested loudly having been forced from its long-inactive state. The pachysandra had spread to the drive, all the way back to the old carriage house which stood alongside the fence and overlooked the river. An ancient pine tree she'd climbed as a girl stood watch over the grounds. From where she stood, she could see the initials carved halfway up the trunk. *A.K. & A.M.* Alex had carved them that last summer, where Abby could see them from her bedroom window at the back of the house.

Without thinking, she had walked toward the pine, and now she ran her fingers over the rough bark. She had stood right here, in this spot, when he had kissed her good-bye the night before she left for Chicago. It had been an agonizing good-bye, Abby crying and unable to speak. Alex had done all the talking, between deep kisses they were still learning how to negotiate, in spite of all their practice that summer.

"It'll be okay, Ab, I promise," he had whispered. "I'll write every day, you will, too, okay? And I'll call you when I can. And before you know it, summer will be here again, and we'll both be back. It won't be so bad. Look, Ab, a shooting star . . . right there . . . quick, make a wish."

What had she wished for that night so long ago? That she and Alex would live happily ever after, here in Primrose. She hadn't asked him what he had wished for. He'd held her close and whispered his undying, never-ending love for her.

"I'll never love anyone but you, Abby," he'd said. "I just never could."

And the next summer, he'd stayed away. Job or no job, she'd childishly insisted, he should have come. She had never forgiven him, but neither had she ever forgotten him.

✦ 7 ✦

The bells in the tower that rose sixty feet above the town hall were just chiming ten o'clock as Abby opened the door to the law offices of Tillman, Dodd, and Readinger. Mr. Tillman was waiting for her, the perky young receptionist drawled as she summoned the attorney's secretary. The latter, a buxom blonde whose heavily perfumed self and swaying hips seemed out of place in the dignified suite of offices, beckoned Abby down a hushed hallway that dead-ended at a large oak door which stood open.

The sole occupant of the room sprang forth in a flurry of goodwill to greet them.

"Well, then, Abigail McKenna, no doubt." Horace D. Tillman, Esquire, friendly as a spaniel, extended a pudgy hand. "Come right in here and sit yourself down. Cerise"— he turned to his secretary—"please bring a pot of coffee and two cups in for Miz McKenna and me."

"Yes, Uncle Horace." The young woman cast a curiously intent glance in Abby's direction, returning Abby's smile with one that lacked warmth and revealed nothing behind cool gray eyes.

"The wife's niece." The attorney shrugged an explanation as he turned his attention to Abby. "You had a good trip, I trust?"

"Just fine, thank you." Abby took the chair to the right of the desk as the lawyer had indicated.

"How's it feel to be back in Primrose after all these

years?" Leila's lawyer—short, round, balding, and sixty-five if he was a day—smiled as he seated himself behind the desk, rustling through a stack of papers with his left hand. His glasses perched on the end of his nose as if pausing before taking flight, like an oversized moth.

"Odd." Abby nodded slowly. "Without Aunt Leila. But I've always loved being here. I only wish the circumstances were other than what they are."

"Perfectly understandable, my dear." Tillman's glasses seemed to slide a notch farther down his nose. "Leila Cassidy was as fine a woman as ever lived in Primrose. It's been my honor and privilege to have served as her attorney for the past twenty-five years, as my father served her for more years than I can tally up."

"Then you knew her well." Abby smiled.

"Oh, indeed I did. And Thomas, too, of course. He went to school with my father, so many years back. Bit of a legend around these parts, Tom Cassidy was."

"I'm sorry I never met him. He must have been quite a character, from what Belle tells me."

"Belle Matthews would certainly know. Her late husband, Granger, and Tom were kids together. Lifelong friends." He leaned back in his chair to allow his secretary to place a tray in front of him. He poured a cup of steaming black coffee into a porcelain cup and passed it to Abby, along with the creamer and sugar bowl. "Tom took off to find adventure the day after high school graduation. Granger went off to college up north someplace. Came back to run his daddy's bank—that's long gone, of course—and marry his childhood sweetheart."

"Belle must have been a child bride, if Granger went to school with Thomas," Abby murmured, stirring cream into her coffee. "Belle and Leila were pretty close in age, and Thomas was much older than Leila."

"Belle was Granger's second wife. His first wife, Annie, took off on him after about two years or so."

"Oh." Abby's eyebrows rose halfway to her hairline. "I had no idea."

"Well, it's a long-forgotten story." He sipped at his coffee.

"But yes, Annie took off with their child. Story was that she left with some traveling salesman or some such." He frowned, trying to recall the details. "Hadn't thought about it in years. It was a big scandal, of course, small town like Primrose. 'Course, there were those who weren't surprised, Annie Fields coming from the sort of no-account background she did, and Granger being a Matthews, son of the founding fathers, that sort of thing. My daddy handled Granger's divorce."

"Then Granger married Belle," Abby noted.

"Some year or so after." Horace shook his head, his glasses swaying slightly with the motion. "Belle was, as you say, quite younger than Granger, though, of course, they'd always known each other. Belle was friends with Granger's sister, Josephine—she died young, Josephine did, not long out of school. Drowned out in the Sound. Guess that was when Belle first came to Granger's attention as something more than his little sister's friend. Wasn't too long after that, it seems to me, that Belle and Granger were married, and order was restored to Primrose." His eyes flashed a twinkle of mischief, as if relating some long-hidden family secret. "Belle being the daughter of one of our finer families, you know, her marrying Granger set the social order right again. All the old biddies breathed a sigh of relief, and life went on as it was meant to. All that business with Annie was promptly forgotten. Not too much longer after that, Tom Cassidy brought his bride home from someplace out west."

"Montana," Abby told him.

"Exactly." He nodded more vigorously, his index finger catching the nosepiece of his spectacles to push them back at the precise second they were about to dive toward his lap. "Belle and Leila were inseparable, even in those days. Belle was the first to extend the hand of friendship to Tom's new wife, made sure she met the right people, that sort of thing. Made it easier for Leila to fit in."

"I doubt Aunt Leila would have difficulty fitting in anyplace."

"Well, now, keep in mind that more than one lady in this town had her heart set on being the one to corral Tom

Cassidy, Miz McKenna. Not everyone in Primrose was happy when he showed up with a bride." He refilled her cup. "But Belle smoothed the way for Leila, gave a big party for the newlyweds, invited all the right people, that sort of thing. Those days, Belle held a pretty lofty position in Primrose, you know, bein' the wife of the local banker and all. If Belle Matthews included Leila Cassidy in her close circle, you can be sure the other ladies followed suit."

"I see." Abby pondered this bit of information.

"Yes, their friendship goes back more years than either you or I have seen on this earth."

"What happened to the baby?" she asked.

"What baby?"

"Granger's child, the one his first wife took with her when she left him."

"Best I know, he just disappeared along with his mother." Tillman shrugged his shoulders. "Of course, Granger hired a private detective to track them down, aiming to bring the baby back, but he never did find a trace of them. My daddy said it was a terrible blow to Granger, losing that boy."

"I imagine it was." Abby could almost hear the buzz *that* must have set off in Primrose.

The lawyer tapped all ten fingers unconsciously on the desktop.

"He burned the house down." Tillman spoke the words softly, almost as if recalling a long-forgotten secret.

"What?" Abby leaned forward, certain she had not heard correctly.

"Granger. Burned down the house he'd lived in with Annie. Not more than a week before he married Belle. At least, everyone suspected it was Granger who did it. Far as I know, no one ever asked him. He and Belle moved in with Granger's mother—his father had already passed on, by then. Started their married life in that big house on Cove Road, right across from the old Cassidy place—your place now."

"What a fascinating story."

"And speaking of the Cassidy house, I guess we might as

52

well get down to business here," he told her, pushing aside local lore along with his coffee cup.

Tillman opened a fat brown file and removed a thick packet of legal-sized papers.

"This here's Miz Cassidy's will." He handed it to her as if it were some fragile figurine. "Take a few minutes to look through it. Let me know if you have any questions."

Again, Abby skimmed through the legalese, searching for her name. She reread the bequest—*all my worldly goods to my grand-niece, Leila Abigail McKenna*—and looked up at the lawyer to catch him studying her.

"Mr. Tillman, there's a reference here to a safe deposit box."

"I have the key." He held an envelope out to her.

"And several bank accounts." She held her breath, hoping against hope there'd be money in *one* of them.

"The bank statements are right here." He pushed the papers face-up across the desktop.

Trying not to appear overly eager, Abby glanced through the statements slowly.

"As you can see," he told her, "there was very little cash, once the debts against the estate—the funeral expenses and taxes on the property—were paid out."

The sum remaining would barely put oil in the furnace. She bit her lip, hoping to hide her disappointment, then asked, "Has your fee been paid?"

"Yes." He nodded. "The executor's fee was deducted and paid by the bank. If you would sign here"—he pointed to a form—"and again here, here, and here, I can have a check for the remaining funds issued to you."

She took the pen he offered her and signed line after line.

"Well, then, that's it." He smiled. "You are now officially the owner of Number Thirty-five Cove Road. How does it feel to be a property owner?"

"Overwhelming." She tried to return his smile, but it seemed to her that her mouth had instinctively twisted into a kind of grimace.

"What are your plans for the place, might I ask?" Tillman

glanced at his watch, then rose from his chair to indicate their business had concluded.

"Well, I'm not certain." She gathered her purse and the envelope containing her copies of the various papers she had signed. "I was thinking . . . that is, I was wondering . . ."

"Something I might help you with?" he inquired with studied courtesy.

"Well, I'm not certain that I will be staying in Primrose indefinitely."

"Ah, I see." He leaned back thoughtfully against the desk, his arms folding over his chest. "Would you be thinking of, at some point, putting the house up for sale?"

"Possibly." She nodded. "Very possibly."

"Then you would need the services of someone who could perhaps appraise the house, determine its value."

"Yes."

Tillman scribbled on a notepad, then handed her the paper on which he'd written a name and phone number.

"Artie Snow's the man you want to see," he told Abby as he escorted her through the doorway and down the hall, where the thick floral fragrance lingered. "Knows every piece of property in Primrose. Lived here all his life. If he can't put a proper number on that house, no one can."

"Thank you. Maybe I'll give him a call."

He nodded a greeting at the woman sitting in one of the visitors' chairs in the lobby, telling her, "I'll be with you in a moment, Carolanne. Now, Miz McKenna, you have any questions, you need any advice, you give me a call, hear?" He took her hand and gave it a perfunctory pump.

"I'll do that." Abby smiled as she passed through the door he held open for her.

"By the way"—he remained in the doorway—"where will Miz Matthews be going? When you sell the house?"

"Well . . ." Abby struggled for a response.

Perfectly reading her sheepish expression, Tillman nodded knowingly. "I see. Shame, isn't it? Belle's the last of her kind, sure enough she is. And after all these years in Primrose . . . well, it'll be a sad day when Belle Matthews

54

leaves town. Guess it can't be helped. Now, you need any assistance tracking down her people, you give me a ring." He said this last sadly, as if offering to volunteer to perform an odious albeit necessary duty.

Like cleaning latrines, Abby told herself as she walked down the sidewalk and across the street toward the bank, the safe deposit box key clutched in her right hand.

⋆ 8 ⋆

"Let's just see what we have hidden in here," Abby murmured as she fitted the key into the small lock on the front of the large metal box, hoping against hope that it would not be as empty as the bank accounts had been.

The vault of the Primrose National Bank was as quiet as a tomb and just about as well lit. She pushed the lid back as far as it would go and turned toward the only light in the room, a small wall fixture with one bulb. Biting her bottom lip in anticipation, she reached her hand inside and pulled out a thick envelope of papers. Shuffling through them, she found the deed to the house on Cove Road, a copy of Thomas's will, and some letters written on thin paper, yellow now with age. She tucked them into her purse to read later.

Smooth cases of flat black leather, shaped like envelopes with small buttons on their flaps, lined the bottom of the box.

"Oh, please be something good," she begged hopefully.

With trembling hands, she opened the top case. A necklace of amethysts the size of small birds' eggs slid onto the table.

"Sweet Jesus, Mary, and Edna!" The expletive long ago borrowed from a former McKenna housekeeper exploded from her lips.

She held it up before her, admiring the stones, their plum

55

hue lit by the light. *Gorgeous.* She sighed. *And worth a pretty penny, no doubt.*

Holding the envelope sideways, she carefully emptied its contents onto her lap. Earrings, a bracelet, a magnificent ring, all of the same fine purple stones, sent sparks of light through the poorly lit cell.

Hallelujah.

She gently placed the amethysts on the table, and, her heart pounding, she opened the second case and coaxed out its contents. A necklace of gold, incredible in its color and design, fell into her hands. It was totally crafted into leaves, graduated in size from front to back, the longest falling almost two inches in length from the heavy gold chain that held it. The sight of it absolutely took her breath away. She had never seen anything so regal.

After lining the necklace up with the amethysts, she opened the third envelope, her hands visibly shaking now. Sapphires, brilliant blue, tumbled into her hands. Two rings, a pair of earrings, and a choker of the clear blue stones.

The last of the leather cases held emeralds—a perfectly matched set of earrings, oval-shaped stones surrounded by diamonds, a necklace, and a ring in the same lush shade of deep summer green.

The jewelry was spread out across the table in sets. She sat and stared dumbly at the rainbow of precious stones.

I may not be a gemologist, but I know the real thing when I see it. And this—she mouthed the words silently as she fingered the gold necklace—*is definitely the real thing.*

Abby wished she had a mirror there, so that she could try on each piece, just once, before she sold them. And, of course, she would sell everything, first chance she got. She had no idea of the total worth of the jewels that lay before her, but she was reasonably certain there'd be enough to pay back Belle and have a fair amount of repairs done on the house. No, there was no question about keeping the jewelry.

She fingered each piece gingerly, studying the fine workmanship, the beauty of the stones, wondering if they had been gifts from Thomas to his bride or perhaps family pieces brought east by Leila. The sapphires looked familiar, and Abby wondered where she might have seen them before. She slipped a ring on her finger and held out her hand to admire the blue fire that lay deep within the large center gem. Had one of her own Dunham ancestors worn this very piece?

I can't afford to be sentimental, she scolded herself, sensing that it wouldn't take much to talk herself into keeping a piece or two. Which, clearly, she could not do.

But still . . . she had lost so much of her past, maybe just *one* ring. Just one little sapphire ring . . .

"Thank you, Aunt Leila," she said aloud as she returned all the jewelry—with the exception of that *one* not-so-little ring—to the soft cases and stacked them back in the metal box, which she locked before leaving the room.

Next stop, the hardware store, Abby decided as she skipped jauntily down the bank's wide steps. She drew her jacket closed against the sudden breeze and stopped on the sidewalk to orient herself. Phelps's Hardware was to her left a few doors down from the bank. She would treat herself to a coffee maker.

Buoyed by the knowledge that the contents of the safe deposit box would more than replenish her cash, she added a toaster to the pile of light bulbs she had stacked on the counter as she introduced herself to the tall man in the plaid flannel shirt who stood behind it.

"Pete Phelps," he told her cordially.

"Oh, then you're the father of the carpenter." She recalled her conversation with the gas station attendant.

"That's right." He nodded.

"Mr. Phelps . . ."

"Pete." He smiled.

"Pete, do you think your son could come out to my house—the Cassidy home—and maybe give me an idea of what needs to be fixed and how much it might cost?"

"Sure thing. I expect him back in about an hour, Miz McKenna."

"Abby." She returned the friendly gesture.

"I can see if he can maybe stop out late this afternoon, if that's a good time for you, Abby."

"I have all the time in the world, Pete," she said as she loaded her arms with her purchases.

This is great, she cheerfully mused as she strolled back to her car. *I can get an estimate and pay for some—maybe even all—of the work. I can pay off Leila's debt to Belle . . .*

Not really, she knew, her heart sinking as she started the engine of the small car. *How can Belle ever be repaid for all she did for Aunt Leila?* Abby wondered, recalling Tillman's tale of how it had been Belle who had welcomed Leila into a strange town and offered her friendship to the newcomer.

How difficult it must have been for Aunt Leila, coming east with her new husband, a man who was years older than she, to a new town and a new lifestyle, so different from the ranch and the small town in the valleys of Montana. Leila had been close to her family, and yet she had left them all behind for Thomas's sake. And Belle had been the one to reach out to her, to help her find her place in Primrose.

And I want to pay her back by pitching her out on her elderly little butt. Abby grimaced. *Not pitch her out, not really, but, God, am I supposed to stay in Primrose for the rest of my natural life? Belle could outlive me and her family . . .*

Not that I wish her ill, Abby hastened to add. *I just wish there was someone else to take her in, so that I can get on with my life.*

Not a very gracious way to treat Leila's best friend. And Leila did promise Belle she could stay in that house.

Forever. She sighed as she pulled into the driveway. *I will be in Primrose forever.*

But that's just what you prayed for, years ago, her little inner voice piped up mischievously.

That was then, and this is now, she growled back. *That was when I was young and didn't know any better.*

And when you were in love with Alex Kane. The little voice pricked at her.

I was sixteen years old, she grumbled. *What does a sixteen-year-old know about love?*

Seems that was as close as you ever really got, the voice jeered.

"Enough," she snarled aloud through clenched teeth, silencing the little whisperings inside her head as she got out of the car and slammed the door vigorously.

Forcing a cheerful tone, she called to Belle from the kitchen.

"What in heaven's name are you doing, Abigail?" Belle watched in alarm as Abby pitched the old toaster out the back door and into the open trash can at the bottom of the steps.

"Reducing our risk of death by fire," Abby told Belle, handing her the box containing the new appliance.

"Oh my, isn't that handsome?" Belle admired the new toaster.

Abby drew the new coffee maker from the bag. "And something to make my morning coffee in."

"Coffee is for heathens," Belle sniffed. "Ladies drink tea."

Abby laughed as she plugged in the coffee pot and ran water through the top. She fitted the basket with a white paper filter, measured and poured in some ground coffee beans, and turned on the switch. Belle watched in amazement as the coffee began to drip down into the pot.

"Why, I never," she declared, hands on her hips. "What will they think of next?"

"Belle, meet Mr. Coffee." She grinned. "Would you like to try some?"

"Certainly not." Belle filled the kettle for her tea. "But I'd surely like to try out that new toaster. Perhaps we can have an early lunch, and you can tell me about your meeting with Mr. Tillman."

Belle was delighted with her lightly toasted bread. She spread cream cheese and cherry preserves on first one, then a second piece, proclaiming the results "Perfect!"

Abby was pleased to have given Belle a treat that was so highly regarded.

"I have another surprise," she told Belle when they had finished eating.

"You don't," Belle protested, her eyes dancing with anticipation. "Truly, Abigail, this has been a day of surprises."

"Well, as the expression goes, you ain't seen nothing yet. I'll be right back."

True to her word, Abby was back in a flash, lugging her portable television, which she set on the floor beside the table that held Leila's old black-and-white set.

"Oh, my goodness," exclaimed Belle. "Would you just look at the size of that screen!"

Abby smiled as she removed the old television and replaced it with her own. When she plugged it in, Belle gasped.

"Lord sakes, Abigail. The picture's in color!"

"Belle, what show do you usually watch now?" Abby asked, grinning from ear to ear.

"Why, I watch 'The Price Is Right.'"

"And what channel is that on?"

Belle got up from her seat to search for the channel, but Abby waved her back to the chair.

"Here, Belle." Abby passed a black plastic wand-type thing to her. "This is called a remote control. You press the number of the channel you want to watch, then press this button, and voilà! Instant channel change."

"Oh, good night!" The old woman chuckled with glee. "You mean I don't even have to get up to change channels? I can do that from this chair?"

"Absolutely," Abby assured her.

"Show me again."

Abby did, and Belle giggled like a young girl as she skipped up and down the dial.

"Oh my, Abigail." She laughed. "What will they think of next? Wouldn't Leila have loved this? Channel-surfing, you say? Oh, yes, Leila would have enjoyed the remote control."

"Well, I'm glad you're enjoying it so much." Abby rose and stretched. "I think I'll bring in the rest of my things from the car. I'll be back in a few minutes, Belle. Oh, by the way, if you want to increase the volume, you just do this." Abby demonstrated the features of the remote control to an astounded Belle.

"Belle, when Aunt Leila sold the jewelry to buy the new refrigerator and the stove, who did she take her things to?" Abby, arms laden with suitcases, poked her head in as Belle prepared to watch her afternoon game show.

"Why, I believe the man's name was Robinson." Belle eyed Abby curiously as she settled in for some serious TV time. "You planning on selling something?"

"Well, I stopped in the bank and looked through Aunt Leila's safe deposit box after I left Tillman's office." Abby's eyes sparkled.

"Ah, so you found them." Belle nodded slowly as she propped a pillow up behind her back.

"Belle, you wouldn't believe . . ."

"Of course I would," Belle snapped. "I know exactly what's in that box."

Abby set the plates back down on the table and stared at Belle.

"There were sapphires, amethysts, and a heavy gold necklace," Belle told Abby without looking at her, "and emeralds big enough to choke a horse."

"Well, yes." Abby folded her arms across her chest.

"And you just can't wait to sell them, can you?" Belle prodded her peevishly.

"Belle, it isn't that I *want* to sell them. I just don't see where I have a choice. I need a great deal of money to repair this house." Abby fingered the outline of the sapphire ring in her jeans pocket, forcing herself to remain calm. "And I don't have any. That jewelry would bring in a substantial amount of cash. I can't understand why Aunt Leila held on to it all when she could have sold some of it to have the roof fixed, instead of borrowing money from you."

"Oh, you can't, huh?" Belle's chin jutted out indignantly.

"Belle, I look around, and I see windows nearly falling out." Abby could barely restrain herself from shouting.

"Wallpaper dancing its way backward down the walls, a front porch that's ready to drop into the front lawn, and a chimney that won't make it through the next big storm."

"Forgive her, Leila," Belle muttered. "She has eyes but cannot see."

"What the devil is that supposed to mean?" Abby yelled in exasperation as the doorbell rang from the front of the house. "Now, who the hell is that?"

Abby stomped to the front door and struggled to open it. A young man in his early twenties stood before her.

"Yes?" she bellowed.

"I . . . I'm Paul Phelps, ma'am," the young man stuttered, taking a few steps backward. "My daddy—that'd be Pete Phelps, down to the hardware—said you wanted me to look at some work you might be wanting done."

His voice trailed off, leery of the wild-eyed woman with the wild curly hair who stood blocking the doorway like some petite and ornery sentinel.

"I didn't expect you until later this afternoon." The words bounced from her mouth before she realized how rude she must sound to the poor young fellow who'd had the misfortune to ring the doorbell at precisely the wrong moment.

"I . . . I can come back," he told her as he took a few steps toward the porch and away from her.

"No, no." She regained both her senses and her composure at the same time. Damn, Belle had riled her.

"I apologize"—she smiled sweetly—"for snapping at you. You startled me, that's all. Now, Paul." She stepped out onto the porch and took his arm. "Suppose I show you around the outside first, then we can go inside and look. I need to know what has to be done and how much it would cost. Can you prepare an estimate for me that's broken down like that?"

"Sure could." He bobbed his head up and down. His light brown ponytail flopped against his back, and his gold earring glittered. Primrose, meet MTV.

Almost two hours later, a broadly grinning Paul headed

back to town in his pickup truck, anxious to begin writing up the estimate for the old house on Cove Road. Abby had stood on the sidewalk with her hands on her hips, trying to comprehend the extent of the work. Paul's "eyeball number" was somewhere between forty-five and fifty thousand dollars.

No wonder he was smiling when he left, she grumbled to herself. *He's planning on whistling all the way to the bank.*

Abby tapped one foot in agitation, then turned toward the house. Might as well put a call into Leila's jewelry man, she decided. She would make an appointment with him to appraise—and, she hoped, purchase—the treasure she had left in the bank vault.

She started toward the morning room, where Belle was still glued to the television, but decided she'd try looking through Leila's desk to see if she could find the phone number herself. She'd just as soon not get into another discussion with Belle over the fate of Leila's jewelry.

I don't know why it would matter so much to Belle, anyway, she thought to herself as she entered Thomas's study.

Abby had assumed Leila's desk would be there, where Thomas's own desk stood, a massive roll-top affair. Never having known the man, Abby felt every bit the intruder. Standing in the center of the room, she surveyed Thomas's private domain. Wide shelves with glass doors completely wrapped around the walls of the room. A well-used, overstuffed chair and matching ottoman stood at an angle to the fireplace. Other than the desk and a small table upon which rose a tall brass lamp, there was no other furniture in the room.

Next to a photograph of Leila in a wide frame of thick polished wood, Thomas's notebook lay open on the desktop, a pen resting in the valley made by the spine of the book. Leila obviously had taken care not to disturb her husband's personal things in all the years since he had died. Abby had no intention of doing so now. She all but backed out of the room.

Abby discovered the small oak lady's writing desk in the sitting room next to the front parlor. The writing surface squealed slightly as she let the top fall forward to reveal a dozen small compartments and a flat surface upon which sat a stack of pale yellow writing paper. The top three sheets had been written on. Abby took them to the window to better see the words.

Dear Susannah—that would be Sunny Hollister, Abby's first cousin—*Thank you ever so much for the lovely birthday greetings.* Abby flinched, trying to recall if she, herself, had sent a card the previous February. *I did greatly enjoy your note, and deeply appreciate being remembered. I so rarely hear from anyone in the family, and so am very happy when someone thinks to bring me up to date. I am delighted to hear that your business is doing so well, dear. I do hope you will be able to stop in Primrose on your way to Atlanta later this fall. I would like to pass on to you a few family mementos which I feel should go to you. In remembrance of our shared February birthday, I would like you to have several amethyst pieces which I have cherished and a gold necklace made in the shape of leaves. (Quite an interesting piece, by the way. Thomas had brought it back on one of his forays into treasure hunting, though I seem to forget the origin of it.) And also the portrait of my mother, your great-grandmother, Serena Dunham, whom you so resemble. I'd never realized how much you look like her, dear, until you sent the photograph from your wedding. Of course, I remember you best as a child . . .*

Abby's heart was in her knees. The amethysts and the gold necklace—probably the single most valuable piece in the vault—were intended for her cousin, Sunny.

Unconsciously, she began to pace the length of the room, the letter clutched in one hand. It was dated just two days before Leila died. Sunny obviously did not know of Leila's intentions. Who would know if Abby didn't tell anyone that Leila had planned to give the jewelry to Sunny?

I would know, she told herself as she plunked down on the chair closest to the window. *And Leila would know.*

Her eyes scanned the room, coming to rest on the portrait

that hung over the fireplace. Serena, the great-grandmother she and Sunny shared, seemed to arch a dark eyebrow in her direction. Did Sunny look like her? Abby wouldn't know. They hadn't seen each other since they were fifteen.

"And you'd know, too." She addressed her great-grandmother from across the room. Serena's wry smile was as good as a nodded acknowledgment.

Abby stared up at the portrait. If Sunny looked anything like Serena, she'd be magnificent. Thick dark hair piled high above an unforgettably lovely face. The high cheekbones Serena had inherited from her mother, Elizabeth, a full-blooded Cherokee. The deep blue eyes—a gift, no doubt, from Serena's father, Stephen Cameron—close in hue to the blue satin dress. Closer still to the stones in the necklace that wound around her graceful neck. The same necklace Abby had held in her hands earlier that day in the bank vault. From her ears dangled ovals of sapphires surrounded by diamonds. The ring that graced Serena's left hand lay, at this minute, in the bottom of Abby's jeans pocket. Leila had chosen not to sell them because they had belonged to her mother.

Belle's invocation to Leila rang in Abby's ears. *She has eyes but cannot see.*

Okay, Aunt Leila. Serena's sapphires will stay in the vault. And Sunny will have her inheritance, just as you intended.

Sighing deeply, she went back to Leila's desk and rummaged through the cubbyholes, hoping to find an address book. She had no idea where Sunny was living these days or what her married name might be. She located the small book and flipped through it till she came to the H's, where she found the listing for Susannah Hollister. Either Sunny had not changed her name when she married, or Aunt Leila had not bothered to change the entry in her book. Abby wondered if the Connecticut address was current. She would to write to Sunny and tell her of their aunt's bequest.

Several small pieces of paper escaped from the inside cover of the book. On one was written the name "Edwin Robinson" and a phone number. Abby tucked the paper in the pocket with the ring, thinking that perhaps she would call him in the morning. She wondered what the emeralds would bring.

"Okay, Belle," she said with resignation as she slumped onto the small sofa in the morning room. "I know about the sapphires. And I know that Leila wanted the gold necklace and the amethysts to go to my cousin, Susannah."

"Did she, now?" Belle asked without taking her eyes from the television. "I thought perhaps she was holding on to them because of their sentimental value."

"Which was?"

"Thomas gave the amethysts to Leila on their wedding day. Which was also Leila's birthday."

"Well, it was apparently Sunny's birthday, too," Abby noted. "And the gold necklace?"

"Thomas gave it to Leila when he proposed to her. He had brought it back with him from a trip he'd made to one of those Asian countries that ends in 'stan.' I can't remember which one. His next expedition was in search of some silver mines in Montana."

"Where he met Leila."

Belle nodded without taking her eyes from the television. "He came back to Primrose a changed man. He only stayed a few weeks before returning to Montana, where he married Leila. He gave her the gold necklace. It was a symbol, he said."

"A symbol of what?"

"That he loved her more than he loved the life he had led before he met her. He never went on another trip, just stayed here in Primrose and wrote books about his adventures."

"And she chose to live in a house that was falling down around her, rather than sell it?"

"There are some things that are worth more than money, Abigail," Belle said pointedly.

"Well, it just seems to me that . . ."

"Oh, for pity's sake." The old woman fairly exploded. "Hasn't there ever been anything that meant something to you, not because of its monetary value but because you loved the person who gave it to you? Hasn't there ever been anything you simply couldn't bear to part with, because of the memories?"

Abby straightened her spine and glared across the room at Belle. "I think it's time to start dinner," she said flatly as she turned heel toward the kitchen.

The bells from the center of town were chiming three A.M. Abby punched her pillow for about the twentieth time and tried to find a comfortable spot on the ancient mattress. Maybe she was chilled, she thought.

Maybe if I pull up the quilt . . .

Abby searched in the darkness at the end of the bed but could not find it. She turned on the lamp on the bedside table, threw back the covers, and got out of bed. The quilt had slipped to the floor. She retrieved it and spread it over the blanket.

Sitting on the edge of the bed, her feet dangling almost to the floor, she looked around the room. It had been reserved just for her as a child and had known all her childhood dreams.

My childhood dreams, she mused.

Almost without thinking, she rose and opened one of the suitcases she had carried in that afternoon. There, in one of the satin compartments, was a small wooden box wherein rested her most cherished possessions. Her mother's plain gold wedding ring, the one her father had placed upon his bride's finger, the one that years later had been replaced by another that had been much more expensive. Pearl earrings given to her on her twelfth birthday by her mother. A thin gold chain with a tiny gold heart, a gift from her father when she turned sixteen.

At the bottom of the box lay a small ring, two lengths of thick silver rope that wound endlessly around each other. Turning it around and around in her hand, she glanced out the window toward the pine where Alex had carved their initials the night he placed the silver band on her finger.

"Hasn't there ever been anything you simply couldn't

bear to part with, because of the memories?" Belle had asked her, and she had not answered.

Abby dropped the ring back into the box, snapped the lid closed, and turned off the light.

✦ 9 ✦

Abby sat on the front porch steps in the late-November sun, unconsciously fanning herself with the sheets of notepaper on which the Phelps lad had composed his estimate for the repairs on her house: $53,475, a nice, round, tidy number. *It might as well be fifty-three million,* she thought, questioning for the first time the wisdom of having so promptly sent off a letter to her cousin Sunny to let her know what was awaiting her in Primrose. She leaned back against the wobbly railing, rethinking her decision to keep Serena's sapphires in the vault.

She made a mental note to call Mr. Robinson. At least no one seemed to have a claim, emotional or otherwise, on the emeralds. She doubted they'd bring enough, but whatever she'd get for them, it should make a dent in the repair bill.

Abby raised her head at the sound of a passing car that had slowed, then stopped as the driver leaned out the window to exchange a few words with a young woman who had been about to cross the street. The woman was tall and well built, with dark wavy hair pulled into an untamed bun at the nape of her neck. Short wisps of curly hair wound around her face, which, even from Abby's perch on the porch steps, appeared open and friendly. She was dressed in a white sweatshirt and jeans, and she fumbled with the pins in her hair as she leaned forward toward the driver and patted him on the arm before he pulled away from the curb to continue down the road.

The young woman smiled broadly and waved as she

crossed the road and made eye contact with Abby. "Mankind is one," proclaimed her sweatshirt.

"Hi," she called pleasantly as she walked slowly, deliberately, and with a very pronounced limp toward Abby's front porch. "I'm Naomi Hunter. I live across the street."

"Oh, of course. The new owner of Belle's place." Abby forced herself from her gloomy mental retreat and tried to return the cordiality. "I'm Abby McKenna."

"Yes, I know," the woman told her. "I remember you."

"Remember me?" Abby frowned, trying to place the name, the face.

"Sure." Naomi seated herself on the bottom step and stretched her left leg out in front of her. "Gosh, I remember as a kid, watching you and Miz Matthews's grandson go trekking off on your bikes. I always thought there was something so . . . I don't know, *exotic,* about you. Big-city girl with big-city clothes." Naomi laughed without a trace of self-consciousness.

"I didn't think any of the kids from Primrose even knew I was alive." Abby laughed.

"Are you *kidding?* You and Miz Matthews's grandson were an *event.* It was like summer didn't *begin* until you arrived," Naomi drawled softly, smiling at the recollection. "I always envied you your freedom, and the way you always seemed to be off on some adventure, you know? Sometimes I even got up early, just to watch you from my bedroom window. You'd be riding your bikes off into the early-morning mist, that wild red hair streaming behind you. I used to pray that one day, you'd see me in the window and wave me down to go with you."

"Why didn't you just come out and introduce yourself and come with us?" Abby asked, flattered and curious at the same time.

"I just never would have had the nerve." Naomi shook her head, a few strands of hair sliding loose as she did so.

"Why not? Did I act snobby or something?"

"No, not really. You just never seemed to notice anyone. You and . . . what was his name?"

"Alex."

"Right. You and Alex just always seemed to be in your own world, somehow. Like you didn't see nothin' or no one else." Naomi slipped cozily into a little Southern vernacular. "Like you were in a bubble that just sort of floated around Primrose for two months or so, then disappeared." Her eyes looked skyward. "Just sort of floated away until the next year."

Abby sat in silence. *It was exactly like that,* she could have said. *We were in our own world. It never occurred to either of us to seek out the company of anyone else.*

"Besides," Naomi continued, "I lived up on the other side of town, not down here where the old money lived. But I remember what it was like when I was growing up, when all the houses down here were so fancy, and all those genteel old ladies were still alive. Sundays, I'd ride my bike down here, like I was headed out to the cove. I'd ride real slow past this place." She nodded her head back toward the house behind them. "When your aunt would have her fancy teas, in the warm weather, they'd all sit out here on the porch, all the fancy old ladies of Primrose, all gathered around that big wicker table, sitting on the edge of those high-backed wicker chairs. Are they still in there?" she asked, referring to the chairs and the table. Abby, fascinated by the accuracy of the young woman's recollection, nodded that they were. "If you ever want to sell that set, you let me know, okay? Anyway, there they'd be, and it looked so elegant, you know? The old ladies in their white summer dresses and their big hats . . . it was right out of a picture book. Have you ever seen *Victoria* magazine?" Without waiting for an answer, Naomi plowed ahead, almost as if Abby was not there. "It was just like what you see in that magazine sometimes. Except the women in the magazine are always young and beautiful, and the women on Miz Cassidy's porch were old. Not hard to imagine them being young and beautiful once, though. And the women on the porch were real, not models posing for a picture. They really lived like that, didn't they?"

"For as long as I can remember, Aunt Leila did." Abby nodded. "And she was beautiful when she was young. Tall and straight and regal."

"Even as an older lady, she still had that elegance, you know?" Naomi twisted her body and looked thoughtfully toward the side of the porch, where the fabled teas had taken place. "I cannot tell you how many times I fell off my bike for staring over here instead of watching where I was going. Broke two fingers on my left hand once." She held up her hand as if to show off her old injury. "And in the summers, you'd be there, too. You and Alex, all dressed up in white, a white straw hat on your head."

"And white gloves." Abby smiled fondly at the memory. "Aunt Leila insisted that I wear white gloves."

"I'd be so jealous." Naomi laughed again. "Wanting to know what it felt like to sit there, so grown-up like, being part of that . . . tableau." She spoke the word tentatively, as if testing it for its sound. "Wondering what you all were talking about. Wondering what secrets you learned from those old ladies. When I heard Miz Matthews's house was being sold for taxes, I had to have it. I bugged the bejesus out of Colin—that's my husband—until he said yes. Got it cheap enough, but God knows we'll put more into it than what we paid for it by the time we're done with the repairs."

Abby grimaced, knowing full well just how much went into restoring these old homes.

"I don't know." Naomi glanced across the street toward her own house. "But I guess I thought living in one of these grand houses would make me feel grand somehow, too."

"Has it?"

"Sometimes. I guess I thought living here would some-how make me more like them—the old ladies, I mean. Like maybe somehow some of their secrets were still in the house and that maybe when I got older, there'd be teas on the front porches again, only maybe this time I'd be part of it." She sighed and blushed faintly. "You must think I'm really daft."

"Not at all." Abby shook her head. "I miss those days sometimes, too. I didn't appreciate it then, but it was a gentler time. Mostly what I remember was being hot and uncomfortable and bored to death by the chatter. 'Yes, thank you, Mrs. Chandler. I did quite well in school this past year.' And 'Thank you, Mrs. Evans, I am happy to be here.' 'Yes, it is quite humid today.' 'Yes, Aunt Leila's garden is particularly lovely this summer.' "

"Don't tell me that was all?" Naomi slapped her blue-denimed knee. "Here, all these years, I thought they were imparting their secrets of the genteel life."

"In a way, I guess they were. If knowing how to serve a proper tea, bake a perfect sponge cake, and make authentic Devonshire cream counts for anything." Abby pondered the lessons learned and their value in the grand scheme of her life.

"Can you do all those things?" Naomi grinned.

"Actually, I can." Abby laughed. "Aunt Leila was a superb cook. And so am I, if the truth were to be told. Maybe I picked that up from her, without even realizing it. I remember watching her in the kitchen when I was little. She could make the most fabulous meals from the most simple ingredients. And she was a very thrifty cook. She used everything. I never really thought about it before," she said thoughtfully, thinking back to her college days, when she could stretch a lone chicken into two weeks' worth of meals, "but I guess I was more influenced by her than I realized."

"Well, maybe someday we'll have tea together," Naomi said wistfully, "you and me and Miz Matthews."

"That's a wonderful idea." Abby stretched her legs down until they reached the top of the third step. "I'll see if I can find Leila's old cookbooks and see if I can bake a scone as well as she did."

"Then you can show me, and I can reciprocate on our porch." Naomi gazed across the street. "If it wouldn't upset Miz Matthews too much, coming back to her old place."

"That must have been terribly difficult for her, to have left that house." Abby leaned forward thoughtfully, resting her elbows on her bent knees.

"It was a very sad day." Naomi nodded. "I had such

mixed feelings, being the one to move in while she was having to move out. On the one hand, I wanted the house—and we had the cash from the insurance company settlement; I was hit by a drunk driver a few years back, that's why my leg is messed up—but on the other hand, I felt like Snidely Whiplash, foreclosing on the widow."

"Well, from what I understand, your buying the house at least gave her money to live on and saved her from the humiliation of seeing the house go to sheriff's sale, which would have been much worse for her. And someone would have bought the house. I'm sure she takes pleasure in knowing that the people who have it love it, just as she and her family did for so many years."

"That's what Colin said," Naomi told her. "And Miz Matthews's grandson, too, when he came to help her move out."

"Alex was here then?" Abby's head jerked up.

"Came down from Boston to help out with the move." Naomi turned to look up at her. "Carried her things over to here and stored some other things—furniture and such—in the carriage house out back there."

Abby's toes began to twitch in agitation. "So he knows she's been living here," Abby said half aloud.

"Oh, sure. He moved her in and stayed for a few days." Naomi studied Abby's face. "How long's it been since you've seen him?"

"Ten years or so." Abby shrugged as if it was of no importance to her.

"Well, he sure did grow up nice." Naomi grinned, her brown eyes twinkling.

"If he's so nice, why was his elderly grandmother living alone in a house that's falling down?" Abby snapped. "Where I come from, that's not considered nice."

"I meant he's one fine-looking man." Naomi watched for a reaction. "Tall and broad-shouldered. Really grew into his looks, if you know what I mean. You should have seen Janelle, down at the Primrose Café, when he'd go in for his coffee in the mornings. Why, she just about . . ."

"Was that the only time he was here? When Belle moved in?" Abby cut her off, not interested in Alex's local conquests.

"No, he's been back a few times. Not since Miz Cassidy passed on, though. I think back in the beginning of last summer, he was here for a few days. Think Miz Matthews said he fixed the plumbing in the front bathroom when he was here."

"That's the least he could have done," Abby grumbled.

"Funny, you know, I always thought that you and he would . . ." Naomi stopped in mid-sentence, her words cut off by Abby's frozen gaze. "Then again, maybe not." She shrugged.

Naomi stood and brushed a few dried leaves off the back of her jeans. "I guess I need to get back on over to the house. My son will be getting up soon, then it'll be time to run down to the school and pick up my daughter."

"How old are your children?" Abby made an effort to be neighborly.

"My little girl will be five in a few months—she goes to the preschool down at the church. My boy is almost three." Naomi smiled. "Just the right ages to make you want to pull your hair out half the time and smother them with kisses the other half. Now, listen, if you need anything—anything at all—don't be hesitating to knock on my door. I'll be baking bread tonight, so I'll bring over a loaf in the morning."

"That's very nice of you."

"I've been sending bread over to Miz Matthews—and Miz Cassidy, before her passing—since we moved here. And stew or soups, when I make a big batch. Seems the least I could do for them." Naomi brushed off her acts of kindness as easily as she had dispatched the leaves from the seat of her pants. "Which reminds me of why I was stopping over here this afternoon. I usually do Miz Matthews's laundry for her once a week. There's a washer and dryer in the basement"—she gestured toward the house—"but I was afraid for her or Miz Cassidy to use the steps."

"I'm glad you told me. I guess I would have been

wondering where to take our stuff . . . though it seems to me that Belle did mention that you had been helping out. I'll take a look when I go inside."

"The dryer's fine, but the washer stalls a bit between the first two cycles. I'd be happy to show how to get around that when you're ready."

"I appreciate that. Thank you, Naomi."

"Just give me a call." Naomi waved as she started toward the sidewalk. "I'm glad you're here. I'm glad we finally met after all these years."

"So am I," Abby said sincerely. "I'm sorry it took so long. I would have liked to have known you, back then. And I want to thank you for taking such care of Aunt Leila. And of Belle."

"Think nothing of it," Naomi said with another wave of her hand. "It was just my way of paying them back."

"For what?"

"For giving me dreams," Naomi called over her shoulder as she crossed the street.

✦ 10 ✦

It was almost midnight by the time Abby checked all the locks on the doors and began to turn off the downstairs lights. She'd been in the sitting room at Leila's desk all night studying the carpenter's estimate, then had gone room to room, checking off those things she could do herself. Scrape peeled paint, strip old wallpaper, repaint the walls and the wood trim—how difficult could those things be?

The list was the size of a small manuscript by the time she finished, exhausting her by its overwhelming proportions. She tapped her fingers on the desktop in agitation.

What had she done back at White-Edwards when she had a massive project assigned to her?

She'd broken it down into manageable sections, focusing

her energy on each section until the whole had been completed.

So I'll go one room at a time, she told herself resolutely. *I'll finish one room, then go on to the next. If I take it little by little, maybe it won't seem so bad.*

It'll take months. She sighed, tossing her pen onto the writing surface. *But then again, it doesn't look as if I'm going anywhere in the near future. And maybe by the spring, the job market will have opened up and I'll find something. The house will look better by then, and maybe I'll be able to find a buyer. I'll sell the emeralds and use the money to have the heavy work done, the things I can't do for myself.*

Cheered at having a game plan, at having found a use for her old management skills as well as for her overabundance of spare time, she snapped off the hall light and climbed the steps.

She paused at the top of the stairs, where a sudden whiff of lavender seemed to welcome her. With a sigh, she followed the hall to the right and carefully, almost reverently pushed open the door to Leila's suite of rooms.

Here, the scent of lavender was strongest, Leila having tucked sprigs in her dresser drawers, hung bunches from the drapery tie-backs, and filled porcelain bowls with potpourri, all of which combined to give a sweet yet spicy heaviness to the still air. Abby stood in the doorway for a long moment, trying to recall where the light switch was. She located the old wall switch, which clicked loudly as she flicked on.

Aunt Leila's old carved oak tester bed stood along the near wall. The spread of palest yellow silk, embroidered with silken threads of dark green and purple to create a striped pattern of chain stitches, ran the length of the bed and spilled onto the floor. Lacy shams stood across the front of the headboard, which was nine feet in height. A heart-shaped needlepoint pillow spelled out "Peace—Be Still" in dark burgundy letters through which wound some white flowers on shaded green vines.

The room remained exactly as it had been in Abby's

memory, with the porcelain clock and matching vases on the mantel and the heavy drapes of dark gold velvet blocking the light from the windows. There were paintings on one wall, a doorway leading to Leila's bath on another. Yet another doorway to the right led to Leila's sitting room, the second floor of the tower, and it was in this room that Abby had often sat with Leila on rainy nights or stormy mornings. Abby followed the worn carpet to the door and pushed it open.

The old Belter parlor set of the deepest crimson velvet and carved rosewood—Leila's pride and joy—still graced the alcove formed by the curve of the tower.

She could almost close her eyes and see Aunt Leila perched on the velvet upholstery of the chair, like a princess in her tower, her reading glasses set upon her long fine nose, her legs crossed at the ankle. In her hands, she would hold what she laughingly called her family Bible—the silver-covered book she had brought from her mountain home in which she had preserved the precious photos of the family she left behind when she ventured east to marry Thomas Cassidy.

Leila would point to her siblings and name them, pausing over each to tell some story or other, so that by the time Abby was six years old, she knew their names and faces and the anecdotes that over time became family legend. There were Leila's parents, the beautifully exotic Serena Dunham and her rancher husband, Will. And the only existing photo that Leila had ever seen of her maternal grandparents—Elizabeth, whose Cherokee name had been Song of the Wren, and Stephen Cameron, the Philadelphia blue-blood who had forsaken his birthright for the love of a woman who had, as a small child, walked the Trail of Tears.

Leila's brothers and sisters were, in Leila's books, ever youthful, ever strong. There was William, the oldest, who, like his father, had become a rancher. And Jonathan, who had gone back east to claim a place in his grandfather's family bank. Then the sisters, Sarah and Eliza, so much alike they were called the twins, though they were a little more than a year apart in age, who were followed by Avery, the family wanderer. Lastly, Leila herself. Somewhere in the recitation of Sarah's children had appeared Abby's own mother, Charlotte, who had defied family tradition by marrying late in life and producing but one child.

Abby sat on the very edge of the sofa, the fabric, roughened with the passing years, scratching at the backs of her legs. The sensation conjured up the memories of a hundred times when she had sat on that very spot and leaned closer to the old woman who held the photos under the dim lamps to cast the best amount of light on the faces she had loved so well and never stopped missing. Holding a small pillow to her chest, Abby could have sworn the smell of lavender had grown stronger for a moment. With a sigh, she replaced the pillow at the corner of the sofa and snapped off the small reading lamp that stood on the marble-topped table. Looking around Leila's room once more before turning off the overhead light, Abby made a mental note to come back in on the next rainy day and look for the albums.

Sleep was a long time coming, Abby's head spinning with the visions of the faces remembered from the old photographs. For a time, Grandmother Sarah's face intertwined with her mother's and then with Aunt Leila's. Great-grandfather Dunham and Great-uncle Avery's faces blended, one into the other, then, to her amusement, took on the features of Alex Kane. She could see herself and Alex, squirming uncomfortably, perched on the edges of their chairs, her fingers tugging at the starched collar of her organdy dress. What had happened to those clothes? she wondered.

Leila's own childhood frocks, carefully preserved through the years, freshly washed and starched, had been waiting for Abby every summer. Sometimes on rainy days, Abby would go into the attic and poke through the trunks and the freestanding wardrobes that lined one wall, looking at those things she could not yet wear, dresses waiting for her to grow into them, waiting for other summers when it would be their turn to be worn once again. Abby had made a game of sifting through stacks of old photographs to find pictures of Leila wearing whatever it was that Abby had worn that year.

On a whim, she got out of bed and went into the hall. The house crouched in sleepy darkness, and she felt along the wall for the light switch. She opened the attic door and turned on that light as well before tiptoeing up the ancient steps. The old attic was airless and closed, the lavender fragrance heavy even there. Abby pushed a window open slightly, wondering how long it had been since anyone had been up there.

Perhaps not as long as one might have suspected, she noted, glancing at the footsteps that remained in the dust around the windows. Maybe one of the roofers had been up there, she thought, then frowned as she followed the trail of steps from one trunk to the next. She opened first one trunk, then another, anger filling her as she realized that the contents were in total disarray. Leila had been meticulous about keeping everything neatly packed away. Her roofers must have ransacked them. What had they taken?

She emptied each trunk and carefully returned the contents. Old fans with handpainted peacocks or roses, soft elbow-length leather gloves, boxes of hat pins and hair combs, silk evening shawls—was anything missing? She pecked through her memory, searching for a hint of what might have been taken, but it had been too many years since she had last removed and replaced the old items. She recognized each and every one of the old treasures but could not recall what else the trunk once held. Judging by the amount of things remaining, if anything had been taken, it hadn't been much.

Abby closed up the trunks and walked through the dust on the creaking boards to the wardrobes, opening the door before her. In the attic's dim light, her hand ran along the row of dresses from a bygone era, dresses that spanned the decades of Aunt Leila's life.

What a shame no one dresses like this anymore, she thought, fingering the high-necked ivory silk dress that had been one of Leila's favorites. On a whim, she stripped off her nightshirt, carefully removed the dress from its hanger, and floated it over her head. On Leila, the dress had been calf-length, but on the much shorter Abby, the hem skimmed the floor. She gathered it up to keep it from the dusty floor and started downstairs to find a mirror. Seeing the stack of hat boxes, she stopped to open first one, then another, until she found Leila's favorite summer hat, a vision of ivory netting and palest pink cabbage roses. Abby pulled her hair up on top of her head and put the hat on.

She crept down the steps, giggling in anticipation of beholding herself in the old clothes. Playing dress-up in the middle of the night . . .

"Oh my!"

Belle had opened her door, and at the sight of Abby, she slumped back against the wall, her hand flying to her heart.

"Belle!" Abby rushed across the hall to catch the old woman before she landed in a breathless heap on the floor.

"Oh, Abigail, you gave me such a start," Belle exclaimed as Abby helped her into her room and seated her on the side of her bed. "I thought I was seeing a ghost. My goodness, child, you look just like Leila in that dress."

"Belle, I'm so sorry. I couldn't sleep, and I thought I'd go into the attic and see if the old clothes were still there. Here, let me get you a glass of water."

Abby rushed to the bathroom and back. She sat on the edge of the bed and guided the glass of water into Belle's trembling hands.

"I have it, dear, thank you." Belle's breathing was still labored. "Oh my." She shook her head as if to clear it. "Oh my."

"Belle, are you all right?" Abby leaned forward a bit, truly concerned.

"Yes, I'm quite fine, Abigail. I thought I heard the noises in the attic again—you know, sometimes at night you hear things, but you're not certain that you've really heard anything? Well, I thought I'd just peek in and see if you were awake. If you'd heard it, too."

"I'm so sorry, Belle. I was the noise in the attic. I probably should have waited till morning to satisfy my curiosity."

"That's all right, Abigail. How strange to see that dress again. It was one of Leila's very favorites for, oh my, for as long as I can remember. And that hat." Belle, relaxed now, began to chuckle. "Why, I remember when Luellen Bronson made that hat for Leila. That hat was her pride and joy. Wore it every Sunday afternoon for years."

"I remember." Abby lifted the hat from her head and shook her hair loose. "I thought she was so grand, presiding over the ladies of Primrose at tea like a duchess. Funny, Naomi and I were talking about that this afternoon, about the teas Aunt Leila used to have in the summer. I guess that's what got me thinking about the clothes in the attic."

"Naomi is a dear." Belle sighed and moved back on the mattress slightly, her tiny feet dangling over the side like a child's. "Hard as it was to give up my house, it would have been infinitely harder had it passed into the hands of someone who'd never love it. Naomi loves that house, as I did. It made it seem not quite so bad."

"She is a very nice woman," Abby agreed, "one I'd like to get to know better."

"Naomi is very kind." Belle yawned. "I am very fond of her, as Leila was. And, of course, we both doted on those two little ones of hers."

"We were talking about maybe having a tea some Sunday afternoon," Abby told Belle as she helped the old woman back against her pillow and pulled the blankets up around her.

"Oh, how I miss those days," the old woman murmured wistfully. "No matter what was really happening in our lives, for just a few hours, all was well. The day before my house was sold, Leila and I sat and had tea—never mentioned what the next day would bring."

"Ignoring reality isn't always a good idea." Abby paused in the doorway.

"Nor were we, dear. It just all went away for a while.

There is a certain solace in sharing a quiet cup of tea with an old friend. Observing the tradition, you see, life is, just for a while, pleasant and gentle once again. I do miss Leila most at tea time . . ." Her voice began to trail away. "Haven't had a decent scone since she died . . ."

Then tomorrow you will, Abby promised silently, closing Belle's door and tiptoeing quietly the length of the hall to her room. After removing the silk dress, she laid it carefully on the other twin bed, placing the hat next to it. Realizing she'd left her nightshirt in the attic, she debated whether or not to return for it. Deciding against the risk of waking Belle again, she took another shirt from the suitcase and slipped it over her head.

Tomorrow, she would put her clothes in the dresser drawers. She would go to the hardware store and buy the tools she would need to begin her work on the house. And she would find Aunt Leila's cookbooks and look up the recipe for scones. She began to drift into sleep, opening her eyes once, thinking she'd heard something overhead. Then she recalled the window she'd opened.

In the morning, she told herself as she faded into a deep slumber. *I'll go up and close it in the morning.*

✦ *11* ✦

"Abby?" a voice called up the steps.

"I'm in the back room, Naomi," Abby called back.

"Wow, you're ambitious." Naomi looked up at Abby, who was perched on the ladder she'd bought just that morning.

"Not so much ambitious as desperate." Abby grimaced, turning to sit on one of the top steps. "You wouldn't believe how much money I'll save by doing this myself."

"Yes, I would." Naomi laughed. "Here, I brought you some coffee and a slice of zucchini bread. Miz Matthews said you've been hard at work since early this morning, so I thought you could use a break."

"Thanks." Abby smiled, touched by the thoughtfulness of her new friend.

Friend. How long has it been since I had a friend? Abby mused. She enjoyed the prospect.

"Now, tell me what you're going to do in here." Naomi cleared a spot on the old four-poster bed, which Abby had moved to the center of the room, and sat on the edge, her coffee mug perched on her knee.

"Well, once I get the rest of the paper stripped, I think I'll just paint the woodwork and the walls." Abby looked around the room as she spoke, envisioning the changes she would make.

"You sure did get a lot done in a few short days," Naomi noted.

"Well, the paper is so old and the glue so dry, it practically jumps off the walls." Abby moved the old drapes she'd taken down from the windows and flung onto a chair and sat down, nibbling on the zucchini bread. "This is great bread, Naomi."

"We had a bumper crop of zucchini last year." She grinned. "The freezer's full of zucchini bread, zucchini muffins, stewed zucchini, zucchini quiche . . . you name it, we've got it. I took five loaves out of the freezer this morning to send down to the church for their Christmas bazaar tomorrow night, and you'd never know anything was missing."

"Are we that close to Christmas?" Abby frowned.

"A few weeks. Something wrong?" Naomi asked.

"I just haven't much enjoyed the holiday these past few years," Abby noted, recalling Christmases when she'd sat alone in her apartment. The city of Philadelphia had always dressed gaily for the season, though none of its spirit had ever seemed to permeate the little home Abby had made for herself, where no carols played and no tree had been decorated. She had stopped acknowledging the holiday the year her parents died and, alone since that time, had simply ignored it.

"Well, maybe this year we can change that." Naomi smiled. "Folks in Primrose pull out all the stops this time of year."

"Momma, Sam needs to use the bathroom," a child's voice called from the bottom of the steps.

"Oh, of course he does." Naomi sighed. "Abby, can we . . . ?"

"Second door to the right." Abby nodded.

"Bring him on up, Meredy," Naomi instructed her daughter. "I'll be right back, Abby," she said, then told the tiny girl who entered the room tentatively, "Don't you touch anything, Meredy, and don't get in Miz McKenna's way."

The biggest, roundest, darkest eyes Abby'd ever seen darted around the room before settling on Abby's face.

"What're you doing, Miz McKenna?" she asked without a trace of shyness.

"I'm taking off the old wallpaper." Abby smiled. "And you can call me Abby."

"My momma says it's impolite to call grown-ups by their first name," Meredy said as she watched Abby climb the ladder.

"Well, maybe your momma will make an exception," Abby told her, "since we're neighbors."

"I'll have to ask," the child replied seriously. "Are you going to have to clean up this mess all by yourself?"

"I certainly am." Abby nodded, wondering what to say next. She'd had no experience with small children and felt uncomfortable left in the company of one so small and unfamiliar. "What was your name?"

"Meredith Dare Hunter," the child told her matter-of-factly, "but everyone calls me Meredy. My middle name is Dare, 'cause that was my momma's name before she married my daddy. Momma's Lumbee."

"What?" a confused Abby asked.

"Momma's *Lumbee,*" Meredy repeated.

"What's Lumbee?"

"Lumbee Indian, of course," the child explained with politely disguised exasperation.

"Oh." Abby digested this information as she resumed scraping long, dry pieces of wallpaper which flopped in clumps to the floor. "I'm sorry, Meredy. I'm not familiar with the Lumbee Indians."

"That's 'cause you're from up north," Meredy reasoned forgivingly. "Lumbee's mostly in North Carolina."

"Meredy, I told you not to bother Miz McKenna," Naomi said, returning with the little boy in her arms.

"I'm not bothering her," Meredy informed her mother, "and she said I could call her Abby, since we're neighbors."

"Meredy was just starting to tell me about the Lumbee Indians," Abby told Naomi. "I wasn't familiar with the name."

"Most folks outside North Carolina aren't." Naomi shrugged. "We're a relatively small tribe, don't live on reservations, and are pretty well integrated into the mainstream. We never were involved in a war with the government and never entered any treaties with Uncle Sam, so we never got much attention. Except from folks studying the Lost Colony."

"The Lost Colony? You mean, as in Roanoke?" Abby asked as another chunk of paper flopped onto the floor.

"Right." Naomi nodded as she stood her son on the floor and tucked his shirt in. "Some folks think that that English settlement was not lost at all. Some think they met up with the Lumbee and moved inland, intermarried with members of the tribe."

"Really?" Abby stopped her work and peered down at Naomi. "I never heard that before."

"And you're not likely to." Naomi grinned. "At least, not from anyone who's not Lumbee. There's a great romance to the legend, you know, the first English settlement in America vanishing without a trace. Look at all the tourist dollars that would be lost each year at the reenactment. And history books would have to be rewritten."

"Do you believe it?" Abby asked.

"Well, let me just say that an awful lot of Lumbee have English surnames. Like Lowry, Oxendine, Dare."

"Like Virginia Dare? She was, what, the first English

child born on American soil?" Abby sought to recall her elementary school history lessons.

"That's right," Naomi told her. "Dare was my maiden name."

"Sounds pretty convincing to me." Abby nodded, sending a hunk of dried paper to join the others at the base of the ladder.

"Names can be borrowed." Naomi frowned. "I think it's more telling that early explorers reported meeting up with some fair-skinned, English-speaking Indians along the Lumber River, inland and south a bit from here. I'm full-blooded Lumbee, but I've got blue eyes and naturally curly hair—not your typical Native American characteristics. Good grief, would you look at the time. Meredy, get your jacket, baby. We have to get you to school," Naomi instructed her daughter, who was quietly piling the discarded wallpaper into a neat stack on the floor. "Afternoon session starts at twelve-thirty."

"Thanks for the snack," Abby told her. "I didn't realize how hungry I was. I guess I should go down and make some lunch for Belle."

"I made a sandwich for her before I came up," Naomi said. "I figured you'd probably lost track of time."

"I had, and I thank you." Abby paused in her work, silently blessing Naomi's thoughtfulness.

"Gotta run." Naomi herded both son and daughter toward the door.

"Miz Mc . . . Abby." Meredy stopped in the hallway. "Would you come to my Christmas play?"

"Meredy, I'm sure Abby has better things to do on Christmas Eve," Naomi began.

"Not at all." Abby smiled at the child, who waited expectantly for a reply. "I'd love to go. And I appreciate the invitation, Meredy."

"I'm going to be an angel," Meredy told her. "Momma's making my costume."

"A serious bit of miscasting on someone's part," Naomi muttered as she followed her daughter to the first floor.

Abby swung the ladder toward a virgin turf of wall and began to loosen the paper, amusing herself by recalling the last Christmas pageant she herself had been in. She was seven years old, and one of the live sheep brought in for the occasion had butted Tommy Picard off the stage. She paused, thinking she heard the sound of a ringing telephone from the entry hall below.

After climbing off the ladder, she hastened down the steps. By the time she reached the bottom step, Belle had picked it up in the kitchen.

"Why, Alexander, what a surprise," she heard Belle coo delightedly. "Why, yes, dear, I am quite well . . ."

Abby's heart turned over at the sound of his name.

"You are? How wonderful . . . why, I'd love that, dear . . ."

This is perfect, Abby thought as she regained the momentary lapse of her senses. *Belle will tell him that I'm here. He'll understand the situation, maybe take Belle to live with him. I know as soon as he knows, he'll . . .*

"Oh, well, no, dear. Leila can't come to the phone right now. She's . . . napping."

Abby stopped dead in her tracks just outside the kitchen door, certain she'd not heard correctly. She stepped quietly into the room and leaned against the door, her arms crossed over her chest.

"Certainly, dear. I'll tell her you were asking for her." Belle turned, sensing Abby's presence. Flushing slightly, she ignored the eavesdropper. "And have you heard from your sister?"

Abby waited out the conversation, and when Belle had hung up, she repeated wryly, "Leila is *napping?*"

"In a manner of speaking." Belle sniffed with indignation and pulled her sweater more closely around her shoulders. "Really, Abigail, I'd have thought you'd have better manners than to listen in on other people's conversations."

"Belle, why didn't you tell him the truth?" Abby asked pointedly.

"I don't want to worry him." Belle turned her back and

busied herself rinsing out her teacup. "That boy has enough on his mind. Just starting a new job, moving to a new city . . ."

"Where'd he move to?"

"Hampton, Virginia."

"That's only a few hours away," Abby thought aloud. "Will he be coming to visit?"

"Sooner or later," Belle replied, still not facing Abby, "I expect he will."

"Don't you think he'll think something is odd, if Leila is 'napping' the entire time he's here?"

"I will tell him, Abigail." Belle's voice dropped to a low whisper of resignation.

"I can't believe you haven't told him before this." Abby shook her head. "Why didn't you tell him when Leila died?"

"Because he'd never have permitted me to stay here alone, Abigail." Belle turned slowly, the pain of being forced to speak the obvious filling every line of her face. "And I have noplace else to go."

She brushed past Abby without meeting her eyes as she shuffled, shoulders slumped, from the room.

◆ 12 ◆

"Abigail, I simply cannot thank you enough for taking me down to the church tonight." Belle beamed as Abby helped her off with her worn winter coat. "I cannot recall when I enjoyed an evening more. Why, the last time I went to one of those little Christmas pageants, my Josie was in it. So many, many years ago . . ." She shook her head at the thought of how much time had passed.

"Well, I had a good time, too." Abby hung their coats in the front hall closet. "And wasn't Meredy absolutely adorable in her little white organdy dress and those little gold wings?"

"She was the cutest one on the stage." Belle nodded vehemently. "Just like I told her, she couldn't have been one bit cuter."

"What the choir lacked in heavenly voices, they certainly made up for in enthusiasm." Abby chuckled, the wide-eyed little faces from which emitted the most uncelestial notes still fresh in her mind.

"Oh my, yes. They were off-key, weren't they?" Belle tucked her black wool gloves into her purse. "You know, I couldn't help but think of one time when our Josie was right up there on that same stage. Singing 'Away in a Manger' to beat the band. If I live to be a hundred—and at the rate I'm going, that's a distinct possibility—I will still see that earnest little face peering out to the audience"—the memory flickered across her face, softening the lines for just a second—"looking for her daddy and me in the crowd. Josie never had much of a singing voice, but she sure was loud. Must have heard her clear out to the Outer Banks."

Abby followed Belle back to the morning room and turned on the lamp as the old woman lowered herself into her usual chair. Belle reached for the remote control, absentmindedly turning it over and over in her hands yet not activating the television, as if she had slipped off somewhere.

"Belle?" Abby gently touched her shoulder.

"Ever wonder where it all goes, Abigail?" Belle's eyes were as clear and as wide as a child's pondering the flight of a bird for the first time.

"Where what goes, Belle?" Abby seated herself on the edge of the hassock, near Belle's chair.

"All the little bits and pieces of your life. All the minutes of all the hours, all the days and all the years. Sometimes, in my mind, I can see so much of it so clearly. Just as clear as the pictures on that television." Belle spoke softly but distinctly, as if being drawn to some far-off place. "Granger's face when he asked me to be his bride, his eyes so intense, deep and warm as the good brown earth after a summer rain. Some nights, when I close my eyes, I can still see that face, clear as I see yours. And sometimes I can even hear his laughter . . ."

Belle raised a hand to her face, lightly brushing her lips with her finger tips. Her voice was low, like a voice in a confessional.

"I still miss him in my bed at night. All these years he's been gone, I still reach for him in the night. And sometimes, when it storms, I hear Josie calling me from the foot of the bed. Always scared of thunder, Josie was. She'd stand there till one of us woke up and patted the blankets, then she'd jump in between us and snuggle down and go out like a light . . ."

Abby listened, pondering the ability of the human mind to transcend time. Had she herself not heard voices from her own past, glimpsed within her own mind her own mother's face as she kissed Abby good-bye that last time they had been together?

Swallowing hard, a tight wedge of compassion blocking her throat and stinging her eyes, Abby studied the face of the woman who sat before her. This tiny woman who had loved so greatly over the course of her many years, who had been so dearly loved, was now alone with only memories of family and friends to sustain her, dependent upon a stranger for even the most basic necessities of her existence. And who knew how long Abby could be here for her?

"And then, of course, there's Leila," Belle said.

"You must miss her terribly."

"Well, yes, but, of course, she's never really left us," Belle told her in hushed tones.

"They say those we love are always with us." Abby reached out a hand to pat Belle's arm.

"Never more true than with Leila, dear." Belle sighed.

"So many times since I've been here, I've caught the scent of lavender," Abby confessed, "and sometimes it takes me off guard. I almost think that she's there. I find myself turning to look for her."

"You haven't seen her, have you?" Belle leaned forward, her brow folding into an instant crease.

"Of course not." Abby giggled at the thought.

Belle raised an eyebrow, as if to speak. Instead, she merely stared at Abby for a long moment or two.

"I think I'll go up to bed," Belle told her, and she placed the remote control on the table, and the moment passed as if it had not been. "I don't believe I much feel like watching television, after all."

"I'll be up in few minutes." Abby braced her hands against her thighs and pushed herself up from her low seat on the hassock.

"Good night, then, Abigail."

"Belle . . ." Abby called to her as she reached the doorway and turned slowly.

"Belle, would you like me to take you to the Christmas service in the morning?"

"Why, that would be a delight, Abigail." The faint hall light veiled Belle's face, but her pleasure was evident in her sincere response. "Thank you. I would very much like that. I would indeed."

"It's at nine o'clock, Naomi said."

"What lovely surprises this day has held," Belle said as she turned toward the hall. She stopped momentarily and looked over her shoulder. "Thank you, Abigail. And Merry Christmas."

"Merry Christmas, Belle."

Abby turned off the light and stood in the darkness, the only sound in the house being Belle's light footfall on the steps. After walking into the front room to turn off the lights, she stopped to straighten a candle on the mantel. The smell of the pine boughs she'd cut and draped around the brass candle holders evoked memories of other Christmases when trees had reached upward to graze the ceiling of the Chicago brownstone and the piles of gaily wrapped presents reached end to end across the living room. Her mother had insisted on a touch of the holiday in every room, and Abby smiled to herself as she recalled Charlotte's zeal as she decked every window with greens.

"Oh, Mother, what you must think of me," she sighed as she looked around the room.

The pine branches had been scattered on the mantel only for the sake of Meredy, who had so proudly presented Abby with a chain of red and green circles to hang on the tree. When she was told Abby and Belle would have no tree, Meredy's tiny face had clouded with confusion. Did Abby not want her carefully crafted garland?

It was then that Abby realized that she could not, this year, ignore the holiday as she had grown accustomed to doing. She invited Meredy to help cut branches from the old pine in the backyard and place them on the mantel, where they twined the colorful paper chain around them. Not quite as good as having a tree, Meredy had told her solemnly, but better than nothing at all.

Abby turned off the light and moved into the hallway, stopping to check that the latch on the front door was secure. She started toward the steps, then paused before going into the dining room.

She and Belle had taken all their meals every day in the morning room. What a treat it might be for Belle, who clearly missed the formality of years gone by, to have Christmas dinner in a more traditional setting. Abby turned on the overhead light and looked around the room, which obviously had not been used in ages.

The low, wide silver candle holders that stood at the center of the table were badly tarnished, as were the serving pieces displayed on the old mahogany sideboard. A built-in closet with double glass doors at one end of the room held row after row of fine crystal and stacks of porcelain plates, all coated with a layer of gritty dust. The dust was thicker on the furniture, and she whispered an apology to Aunt Leila as she gathered the darkened silver pieces in her arms and headed toward the kitchen.

Barely three hours later, all the silver as well as the dark wood furniture had been polished until it gleamed. The crystal, carefully washed and dried along with Aunt Leila's best china, glowed from behind the glass doors. Abby replaced the candle holders on the table and stood back to admire her work.

Something was not right.

She opened drawers in the sideboard and rummaged until she found a creamy colored damask cloth, wrapped in tissue paper into which had been tucked sprigs of lavender. Abby shook out the cloth, then draped it over the table and returned the candlesticks.

Still not right.

A holiday table called for a centerpiece, she told herself as she scanned the room for something suitable. A long, low silver bowl, freshly polished, all but waved to her from the small server near the side window. She carried it back into the kitchen and plunked it onto the counter, where she stacked it high with the bright red apples she had bought with the thought of baking a pie for Christmas dinner. She'd think of something else for tomorrow's dessert.

Almost perfect, Abby noted as she placed the bowl of shiny fruit in the center of the dining-room table, *but not quite.* She went back into the kitchen to see if she could scrounge up something else to add the finishing touch.

The moon, wide and full, lit the yard behind the house, sending a long, fat shadow of the pine tree to bisect the back porch.

"Of course," she said aloud, grabbing a jacket and the key from a hook just inside the back door. She unlocked the door and stepped into the first cool, dark hours of Christmas morning.

By the light of the moon, Abby gathered pine cones and stacked them on the back steps. As the pile began to grow larger, she went back into the house to fetch a basket. On her way out the door, she grabbed a pair of scissors, which she used to snip some branches of boxwood from the ancient hedge. She cut some long, still-green arms of ivy from the side of the porch, then piled it all into the basket.

The night was so still, the far reaches of the sky so boundless, that she stood for a moment looking upward, her face tilted toward the endless procession of stars so high above. The serenity of the night held her, motionless, for what seemed to be forever. In those few moments, without words, she said a prayer of thanksgiving for her many blessings. For the first time in ten years, there were people in her life she cared about, people who, in turn, genuinely cared about her. It was all she had, but it was more than she'd had in a decade, and she was grateful.

When the spell was broken by the sound of the wind shaking a loose shutter, she turned back to the house, filled with the first true sense of goodwill toward her fellow men she had known in a very long time.

⋄ *13* ⋄

"I simply cannot get over how old Sarah Williamson looks." Belle shook her head as she raised her teacup to her lips.

"How old is she?" Abby asked.

"Well, Sarah must be . . . let's see now, she was the youngest of the Baldwin girls. Eloise, the oldest, was two years behind me in school, that'd make Sarah maybe seventy-five or so."

Abby suppressed a giggle. Sarah was roughly fifteen years younger than Belle.

"No excuse for letting yourself go like that." Belle touched a hand to the back of her head, as if checking to make certain the pins holding her hair in the fat bun were secure. "But it was a lovely service. How wonderful to see so many familiar faces again, Abigail. People who were just children when Josie was a child, now parents, grandparents, some of them. And how lovely to have been remembered by so many. It was the nicest gift I've had in a very long time, Abigail, and I thank you."

"You are most welcome." Abby stood and stretched. "I'm only sorry I couldn't afford to buy you a present."

"There is nothing you could have bought for me that would have meant more. However, while we are on the subject of gifts . . ." Belle reached down next to her chair and retrieved a small white box which she extended to a startled Abby.

"Belle, you didn't have to . . ."

"Now, child, it's just a token. A little something I thought you might like." Belle folded her hands in her lap and waited expectantly while Abby opened the box.

"Oh, it's beautiful, Belle." Abby lifted the gold filigree butterfly from its cotton perch. "Belle, are you sure you want to give this to me? I mean, it's obviously not a costume piece."

"If it was a costume piece, I wouldn't have kept it all these years." Belle sniffed at the mere suggestion.

"Thank you, Belle, for giving it to me. I absolutely love it." Abby smiled inwardly at Belle's indignation as she pinned the butterfly to her green sweater, then picked up the plate holding the few remaining scones and began to clear the table.

"I only meant," Abby said as she started toward the kitchen, "that I would have expected that you'd want to keep a piece like this in your family."

"And that's exactly what I aim to do, my dear," Belle said softly as she heard Abby push open the kitchen door.

Abby leaned back against the kitchen counter, trying to decide how to spend the rest of the day. The dinner preparations were, for the most part, well in hand, and Belle's menu requests carried out to the letter, right down to the sweet potato soup Abby made from Leila's old hand-printed recipe. The only compromise had been on the green beans, which Abby had refused to cook for hours in pork, the way Belle liked them. They would be lightly steamed and crisp, all their vitamins intact.

The turkey Belle had craved was ready to go into the oven at the appointed time. The large bird was an extravagance for just the two of them, but Abby could stretch leftover turkey thirty different ways. The savory cornbread and sausage stuffing—also Leila's recipe—was resting in a bowl in the refrigerator.

Dinner wouldn't be until six. It was only eleven o'clock. She had hours to kill.

She tapped a foot impatiently. Belle would be watching television for the next few hours. The earlier holiday glow from the Christmas service had worn off. Now, it was just another day.

She poked her head into the morning room. "Belle, I think I'll go up and scrape paper in that back room for a few hours."

"On Christmas?" Belle appeared horrified.

"I hate to waste the day." Abby shrugged. "And I already have everything lined up for dinner."

"You'll get that flaky stuff all over you," Belle protested. "You'll be a mess."

"It washes off." Abby laughed and headed toward the steps. "I promise to be cleaned up by dinner."

"Oh, dear," Belle whispered to the empty room, through which the faintest scent of lavender began to flow. "I'm afraid that may not be quite soon enough."

In spite of Abby's best efforts, the paper stuck to the wall like a two-year-old clinging to his mother's leg. Reluctantly, she climbed down from the ladder and hunted around the room for her spray bottle. Once located under a sheet she'd draped over a chair, the bottle of water accompanied her to the top of the ladder, where she sprayed its contents onto the wall. She hated this technique of loosening the old glue, knowing that the wet paper, once its glue had been reactivated by the water, would stick to everything. The hair on her head, as well as the hair on her arms, her shirt, the drop cloths, all would soon be covered with the sticky confetti.

Abby turned up the radio, which was tuned to the country music station she recently discovered. At first, she'd listened only because it was the only station without static. Soon, however, she grew accustomed to the flavor of the songs and the voices that sung them and found herself turning it on every day as she worked. She developed a true fondness for

Patsy Cline, learning every word to every song, which Abby sang aloud at the top of her lungs.

Good-bye, Motown. Hello, Memphis.

She and Patsy were wailing "Walking After Midnight" when she sensed his presence without having heard his footfall on the worn oak steps. She turned on the ladder in disbelief just as he crossed the threshold.

"Little Abby McKenna." He grinned with true delight as he crossed the room in three strides and reached up to pluck her from her perch. "All grown up."

"Alex?" She blinked her doubting eyes.

Ohmigod, it's true. Listening to country music nonstop for two days does cause hallucinations.

The strong arms of her hallucination spun her around the room.

"Alex?" she repeated again, somewhat dumbly.

"Abby, you look wonderful. I can't tell you how happy I am to see you." The spinning stopped, but he did not release her. "You look just like you did the last time I saw you. You haven't changed a bit."

Her head was buzzing loudly, swirling as if some giant whirlpool within her threatened to pull her under. She pushed her hands against his chest to distance herself from him while she sought to compose herself and hush the roar between her ears. After so long, he was suddenly too close too soon.

"Abby, you always were just a wisp of a girl." He reached down to touch her hair. "Now you're a wisp of a woman."

Flakes of wallpaper fluttered around her like a dusty halo.

"Ah . . . I'm afraid I'm a bit of a mess." She flushed, knowing what she must look like. "You've caught me completely off guard. If I'd known you were coming . . ."

"Gran didn't tell you?"

"You mean Belle knew?" Abby's eyes widened. How could Belle have neglected to tell her?

"Alexander?" A woman's voice—not Belle's—called from the top of the steps.

"Oh." Alex looked momentarily over his shoulder. "In here, Melissa."

Melissa?

Abby's hands dropped to her sides as the young woman strode into the room, one eyebrow rising in frank curiosity as she viewed the scene before her.

"Melissa Pendleton, this is Abby McKenna." Alex turned Abby around with his right arm still around her. "Abby was my very best buddy for many years."

"How very nice for both of you." Melissa extended a patrician hand in Abby's direction as her eyes tried to size up both Abby and her importance—past and present—in Alex's life.

Abby smiled woodenly as she in turn sized up Melissa, whose red silk shirt and black crepe slacks were distinctly out of place in the wreck of the partially stripped room. Abby slid one sneakered foot self-consciously toward the other, painfully comparing her rumpled and dirty self to the carefully made-up, beautifully manicured, and perfectly coifed Melissa. Stubby-nailed fingers sought solace in the pocket of ripped jeans. There was no way to hide the hair, short of draping a drop cloth over her head.

"Abby's aunt owns this house," Alex explained, oblivious to the two women's mutual albeit silent assessment of each other. "She and my grandmother have been best friends forever."

"Really." Melissa was relaxing. She had scanned Abby's appearance and had clearly labeled her no competition.

Abby's cheeks burned, and her ire began to rise as she sensed Melissa's blatant dismissal.

"Where is Leila, anyway, Abby?" Alex asked.

"Oh, for pity's sake," Abby groaned. How long did Belle intend to carry on this silly charade?

"Abigail?" Belle called from the bottom of the steps. "Meredy and her little friends are here to sing carols for us. Please do come down for a moment."

Abby tossed her hands up in exasperation. What was the point in beating around the bush?

"Leila is dead," she announced flatly as she headed for the door, "and has been for months."

She left Alex standing in the middle of the room, his jaw hanging open halfway to his knees.

· 14 ·

"I think we had better talk about this." He leaned against the counter as Abby prepared to chop carrots. She could have bounced the entire bag off the top of Belle's head for inviting Alex—and therefore Melissa—to join them for Christmas dinner without telling Abby she had done so. "Just what is going on here? What happened to Leila?"

"Leila died in September. She left the house to me." Abby was clipped and to the point.

"So you've been here since September?"

"No. Only for the past month."

"The past month?" He leaned closer. "Who was taking care of Gran between the time Leila died and the time you got here?"

"Naomi looked in on her every day. And brought food over for her, and ran her errands, did her laundry . . ."

"Are you saying that my grandmother lived alone in this big house for two months by herself?" he asked incredulously. "Abby, how could you have let her stay here alone?"

"How could *I* have let her stay here?" She slapped the carrots loudly on the counter. "How could *I* have let her stay here? Where the hell were *you*? How could *you* have let her stay here?"

"Up until four weeks ago, I was in Boston. I didn't know." He was wide-eyed that she would assume that he would permit his elderly grandmother to live alone in this huge old house.

"Well, neither did I."

"How could you *not* know? It's your house."

"How could *you* not know? She's your grandmother." She spat the accusation back at him.

"Nobody told me Leila was dead." His brown eyes crackled with angry sparks, his voice rising defensively.

"Nobody told *me* Belle was living here." Abby went him one octave higher.

They stood almost toe to toe, in the same stance, hands on hips. Only their difference in height prevented them from being nose to nose.

"Abby, Miz Matthews asked me to tell you that she'd like you to serve tea soon." Melissa peered into the kitchen, making no effort to conceal her small pleasure at having found the two of them in obvious disagreement.

"Oh, did she now," Abby snapped.

"Yes, she did." Melissa clearly enjoyed the opportunity to pass along the orders. "Oh, and she said for you to make a *fresh* batch of scones. *Buttermilk* scones, she said specifically. My momma had a cook that made the best buttermilk scones in Georgia. Now, you *do* put raisins in yours, don't you, Abby?"

"Yes," Abby hissed.

"Well, I was just checking, no need to get huffy," she purred sweetly as she turned her baby blues on Alex, who was still glaring at the back of Abby's neck. "Alexander, I'd sure like that little walking tour of this quaint little town right about now." Melissa looped a hand through his arm possessively and tugged seductively at his shirt sleeve. "Unless, of course, Abby'd like some help with tea."

"I do not need help." Abby turned her back abruptly and made a pretense of searching in the cupboard for the bag of flour.

"How much time before tea?" Melissa asked sweetly.

"Forty-five minutes to an hour," Abby said flatly, refusing to turn around.

"That should be plenty of time. Come on, then, Alex. I want to walk down to that cute little town square we passed on the way in." She guided him toward the door.

"Abby." He spoke her name crisply, as if being forced to. "We will finish this conversation later."

"Count on it." She tossed the words over her shoulder like a well-aimed fastball.

"Come along now, *Alex*." Abby mimicked Melissa's drawl when she had heard the front door close. "I'm just dying for you to show me around this cute little ole town, *Alex*."

She measured flour, baking powder, and baking soda into the bowl, muttering in exaggerated imitation, "Now, Abby, Miz Matthews would like her tea soon. And *fresh* scones, Abby. *Buttermilk* scones, Abby, which couldn't *possibly* be near as good as my momma's cook's were. Now, you do *know* enough to put raisins in, don't you, Abigail?"

Unsalted butter was cut with her fingers and dumped into the flour mixture.

"What the hell do I look like, the downstairs maid?" Abby snarled.

Actually, she knew, that was exactly what she did look like. Her hair was a tangle, and her sweatshirt bore streaks of paint and strips of gummy paper. The knees were out of her jeans. She recognized the painful contrast to Melissa's impeccable clothes, her carefully groomed hair, each blond strand of which lined up perfectly with the one next to it. Abby hadn't had a good haircut in six months. Melissa's nails were perfectly manicured. Abby's were blunt little stubs worn down by weeks of scraping and painting and cleaning. Melissa's bearing and self-confident demeanor announced that she was a woman who knew her way around a boardroom. She had "Serious Suit" stamped all over her.

Abby sighed with misery.

I used to look like her, she wanted to shout.

I used to be her.

Tears stung her eyes as she furiously slapped the dough for the scones onto the baking sheet. *After all these years, why did he have to show up here today? And why did he have to bring Melissa, who, six months ago, could have been my clone? Of course, these days, I look more like "Hazel" meets "This Old House." He, of course, has to look like a Gap ad.* Abby had not failed to notice how great he looked in perfectly casual wool tweed slacks. A yummy soft sweater of misty brown that set off his eyes . . .

Get a grip, Abigail, she sternly chastised herself. *This is the same man who had the utter gall to yell at you because his grandmother was left alone here for months.*

Her temper continued its steady rise until it forced its way from between her clenched teeth in a semi-growl.

"You *betcha* we've got things to talk about, buddy boy." She slammed the oven door. "You bet your sweet ass we do."

Abby set up the tea table so that Belle could serve her guests when Alex and Melissa returned from their walk, allowing Abby time to check on the turkey before running upstairs to shower and change. Grumbling as she washed the sticky paper from her hair and arms, cursing aloud as she picked through her clothes, the early morning's sense of peace on earth, goodwill toward man had definitely made a hasty departure. Blinded with anger, she tripped over the sneakers that sat where she'd dropped them in the middle of the floor, then stumbled, stubbing a toe on the iron bedpost.

"Damn!" she yelled, hopping to the bed, where she sat on the mattress and rubbed her throbbing toe.

Taking a minute to calm down, she forced herself to take deep, slow breaths as she assessed the situation. She thought back to her days at White-Edwards.

What had been her strong suit as an up-and-coming executive?

The ability to define a problem, evaluate the possible solutions, and formulate an aggressive and rational game plan once the most expedient resolution had been identified. She pulled one leg up under her on the bed, leaned forward slightly, and focused on the present situation.

The problem is that I am virtually stuck in this house with no money and no job. I cannot sell this house or otherwise get on with my life as long as Belle is here. I need Alex's help if I want to be free to leave Primrose at any time in the near future. Alex has to take responsibility for his grandmother. Therefore, Alex must become my ally.

The solution was really quite simple, she reasoned. First, she would calmly and rationally make Alex aware of her dilemma. Surely, he would be sympathetic to her plight, once he knew. It followed that he would then recognize his own part in the eventual resolution of the situation. All she had to do was get his attention and keep it long enough to explain the facts of her life.

Of course, she would have to neutralize Melissa.

Abby flushed, recalling how Melissa had seemed to effortlessly and obviously stamp "No Competition" across Abby's forehead.

What had she done at White-Edwards when she had vied with one of her peers for a particular account? Had she rolled over and played dead? Adopted the role of shrinking violet?

Hell, no.

She'd looked to her strengths and always—but *always*— was better prepared than her opposition.

Abby rose and studied herself in the mirror. She pulled her hair back and caught it with a wide gold barrette, allowing wisps to fall in curls around her face. She applied makeup with the concentration of a soldier readying for battle. She slipped into a dusty-green silk shirt and matching short skirt, then hunted through her shoes, which had been confined to a suitcase since she arrived in Primrose. The taupe suede heels would be perfect. She hunted in another suitcase and found the green and gold leather belt she always wore with the outfit. As a finishing touch, she pinned Belle's gold butterfly slightly below the left shoulder and accented her ears with big gold button earrings before stepping back to assess herself.

Take that, Ms. Melissa.

Abby smiled confidently at her reflection and plotted her strategy.

A superb dinner—Alex has always loved to eat—served with charm, here in the bosom of his childhood.

And if that doesn't work—she grinned as she unfastened the top two buttons of her shirt—*there's always cleavage.*

◆ 15 ◆

Belle was a bundle of emotions at the dinner table, torn between the delight of once again presiding over a beautiful holiday feast, the joy of having her grandson and Abby reunited as she had so carefully plotted, and the distraction of Melissa's unexpected—and unwanted—presence.

That Melissa made no effort to hide the fact that she had her sights on Alex disturbed Belle to her core. The woman was brash and obvious, anyone could see that. Why wasn't she home with her own family, instead of here, intruding on Belle's holiday?

Alex and Abby were supposed to have fallen into each other's arms, found each other again. Then she, Belle, could live here, happily ever after, surrounded by the warmth of love that comes only when you are securely fixed in the bosom of your family. She intended for Abby to become family, just as she and Leila had long dreamed, and to be surrounded by a swarm of great-grandchildren before too long. Who was this Melissa person to threaten her dreams, her security, her future?

"Now, Marisa," Belle addressed her from the head of the table, "what do you think of our little town?"

"It's Melissa, Miz Matthews." Melissa smiled charmingly as she accepted the plate of salad from Abby's hands.

"Oh, of course." Belle shook her head slightly, as if to imply that she was a bit absentminded.

"And to answer your question, it's positively adorable. Just like what you'd read about in the travel magazines. You know, those articles about those little places tucked away off some side road. Those little, undiscovered villages that time seems to have forgotten." Melissa fairly gushed—the sweet Southern belle at her best. "It'd be just delightful here in the

104

summer, I'm sure, with the water so close and all the big tall trees. I do hope Alex'll bring me back next summer. If y'all'll have me, of course."

Belle ignored the ploy for a return invitation and smiled at her grandson. "Alexander, do pour a little of that lovely wine into my glass."

"Abby?" he offered without looking at her. "More wine?"

"Not just yet, thank you."

There was a terseness to their voices, some underlying tension that was barely discernible, but Belle had not missed it. *Oh, dear.* She sighed anxiously.

"Alexander, you hadn't told me that you'd be bringing a friend along with you today." Belle decided to get to the bottom of this woman's presence the easy way.

"Oh, I hope it's not an intrusion." Melissa feigned a concerned expression. Belle pretended not to have heard.

"Well, we're both sort of stuck in Hampton this week, working on a case, and since there are depositions scheduled for tomorrow, I thought it would be nicer for Melissa to spend Christmas here rather than alone in her hotel room."

Abby removed the salad plates, fighting the urge to allow the last bit of dressing to slide from Melissa's plate onto her black crepe lap.

"And tell me again what you are doing in Hampton, darlin'? I thought you said you were working in Boston. Or Baltimore . . . someplace that started with a B. Though Hampton's so much nicer. So much closer." Belle smiled gently. Melissa wasn't the only one who could play the Southern belle.

"The firm has opened a temporary office in Hampton to handle a rather sizable case that requires a lot of work. It was easier and less expensive to simply rent office space there temporarily and send a few attorneys in to handle the work than to have us traveling back and forth."

"And what is this big case?" Belle sipped at her wine.

"Maybe you heard about the Alden Boatyards fire?"

"Was that the one where so many people were trapped in

the warehouse and couldn't get out? So many were burned?" Abby asked as she placed the platter of perfectly golden turkey on the table.

"Yes." He nodded. "Our firm represents the manufacturer of the heater that was involved."

"Alexander, would you carve?" Belle motioned for Abby to pass the ivory-handled knife and fork to Alex.

Abby repositioned the platter in front of him, and he took the carving knife from her hand.

"It's been a long time since I did this," he mused. "I remember Gran and Leila giving me lessons one time on a roast chicken. I must have been all of ten. I couldn't hold the bird still and cut it at the same time."

"I remember that." Abby laughed. "It was Belle's birthday, and Leila had such a fine dinner party for her and her friends."

"And we had to get all dressed up, and you had to serve hors-d'oeuvres to all the little old ladies." He half-smiled at Abby for the first time since they had exchanged words in the kitchen.

"And as soon as they began eating, we snuck out and ran down to the cove . . ."

"And I pulled off that tie and pitched it off the dock." He chuckled, and the memory seemed slowly to erase the traces of the earlier tension from his face.

"And are you a lawyer also, Alissa?" Belle smoothed her napkin onto her lap and attempted to divert Melissa's attention from the giggling duo at the end of the table.

"It's *Melissa*," the woman corrected Belle, more firmly this time, "and yes, I am. My daddy started the firm in Atlanta with one of his brothers about thirty years ago. We now have offices in five cities throughout the South," she announced with a good deal of family pride. "Alex is one of the few Yankees Daddy ever hired. Daddy thinks he shows enormous promise." She smiled ever so sweetly as she added, "And so do I. He's just a *tiger*." She wrinkled her pert little nose and winked in Abby's direction. "In *court*, that is, of course."

Abby concentrated on cutting the thin slice of white

meat, which was beginning to take on the form of Melissa's little heart-shaped face. Abby gave it an extra stab, right about where that pouty little mouth would be.

"Carrots, anyone?" she asked.

"Why, yes, dear." Belle accepted the porcelain bowl. "Isn't this just the loveliest dinner? Abigail is simply the most wonderful cook."

"Everything is excellent, Abby." This from Alex, who was submerged behind a stack of carefully seasoned green beans. "Makes me think of all the Sunday dinners we had, right here in this room. No one cooked like Leila."

"Well, I was very fortunate to have had her as a mentor in the kitchen." Abby smiled at him from across the table. "And lucky to have found her old recipes in the pantry."

"My, you cook like a pro, bake scones from scratch, and make home repairs, too," Melissa drawled. "Why, you'll just make the *cutest* little housewife for one of these local boys."

Abby choked. "Excuse me," she said as she rose from her chair and headed for the kitchen.

"Are you all right, dear?" Belle asked with some concern.

"I'm fine. I just need to check a few things in the kitchen."

We'll start, she grumbled silently as she swung the kitchen door wide, *with my blood pressure. Then we'll move on to my temper.* She took a glass and filled it with water, counting the sips until she reached twenty. She simply could not afford to let Melissa's condescending attitude rattle her.

Alex was still happily eating away as Abby reseated herself at the table.

"Well, isn't this nice to be together on Christmas," Belle said. "Though, of course, it isn't quite the same without Leila."

"Gran, I think we need to talk about that. About Leila." Alex added a small pile of new potatoes—his third—to his plate.

"There's really very little to say, dear. She is dead, you know." Belle squirmed, not anxious to have the conversation turn to unpleasant reality just yet.

"I understand that, Gran. I'd like to know when and how." He put his fork down quietly.

"It was September the first, dear," Belle sighed. "Leila always made breakfast—she did all the cooking, of course—and on that morning, she just never came downstairs. I had her tea all ready and waiting for her, as I always did, but she simply did not come down."

Belle related her tale with the same mix of bewilderment and fear that she must have felt that day some months earlier.

"Well, when she hadn't made so much as a peep by eight-thirty, I went back up. And there she was, sleeping soundly. At least, I thought she was sleeping. And knowing how Leila hated to oversleep, I thought to wake her. But she was gone, you see?" Belle spread her hands out before her, as if awaiting an answer. When none came, she continued.

"I tried everything to rouse her, you understand. When she wouldn't wake up, I came down here and called Naomi. Well, she was over here in a shot, bless her heart. Took one look at Leila and said, 'Well, for heaven's sake, Miz Matthews. Miz Cassidy has passed on in her sleep!'" Belle's hand hovered over her heart as if to stop its fluttering. "Now, of course, it had never occurred to me that Leila would be dead. I mean, it was so unlike her to stay in bed so long, but *dead* . . ."

"I'm sure that was just the most ghastly shock." Melissa sought to be a part of the drama.

"Gran, why didn't you call me?" Alex asked gently.

"I wasn't really sure just where you were," she hedged.

"Come on, Gran. I was in Boston. You knew that."

"I must have forgotten." Belle dabbed her napkin to her lips. "I'm almost ninety years old, Alexander. One does tend to become forgetful about things."

Abby suppressed a giggle as she gathered up the dinner plates. Belle could probably tell you exactly what she wore on her very first day of school, right down to the color of her hair ribbons. Her attempts at playing the doddering old woman were laughable.

"Well, then, I will leave my business card with Abby, so that you won't have that excuse should another crisis arise," Alex was saying, and Abby looked over her shoulder in surprise as he did so. Good grief, was he buying into Belle's act? "But I still don't understand why Abby wasn't here with you all that time."

"Abby was in Philadelphia, Alexander, though I didn't know that at the time. Leila's lawyer tracked her down."

"What were you doing in Philadelphia?" He turned his attention to Abby.

"I was working for an investment firm," she told him.

"Doing what, exactly?" He leaned back in his chair.

"Investment counseling." She tried to appear blasé. "Vice president of new accounts."

Melissa's flat smile seemed to insinuate, *Of course you were, dear. And I'm Mother Teresa.* "Now, why would you leave a position like that to come all the way down to this quaint little town?" Melissa's eyes narrowed.

"The company was taken over in a merger," Abby reluctantly admitted.

"And you were let go." Melissa pointed out the obvious with a smile.

"Yes."

"But now you have this handsome old house, in this sweet little town, and Miz Matthews to keep you company," Melissa cooed, happy to take advantage of the opportunity to pour a little salt into the wound she had just forced open. "Who could ask for anything more? Why, I'll bet the social life around here just leaves you breathless."

"Why, actually, it does." Abby squared her jaw and glowered across the table. "Just last week, we were as busy as a couple of beavers. Let's see, now, on Friday night, we had the lighting of the tree down on the town green. Cocoa and cookies for everyone back at the Primrose Café, of course. Then, on Saturday, we had the church Christmas pageant, couldn't have missed that. Now, mind, all this follows on the heels of a month of revelry—the church bazaar, the ham supper at the firehouse—did I leave anything out? Oh, the Christmas house tour two Sundays ago. No one who's *anyone* in Primrose misses the house tour."

"It's all just as I remembered it," Alex said wistfully.

Abby and Melissa both turned to stare at him.

"That's what I loved best about Primrose. All those wonderful community events that made life so special here," he told them. "I sure have missed it. It sure is good to be back."

Belle took a sip of wine, hiding her pleasure behind the rim of the glass. Things were looking up.

Melissa rolled her eyes to the ceiling.

"Alex, could you give me a hand with clearing the table?" Abby asked sweetly.

"Of course." He stood up, lifting the turkey platter with one hand.

"Abby," he said when they'd gone into the kitchen, "I still don't understand why Gran was alone here so long."

"Alex, I didn't know Leila had died until I got the letter from Tillman in October," she told him. "Then it took me a while to get some things settled up there."

She couldn't bring herself to admit that she'd spent six weeks in a frenzy of job hunting.

"And that's when you found that Gran was living here?"

"That's right. Just as you found out when you showed up today," she said as they passed back into the dining room.

"I see." He nodded slowly, putting it all together, offering Abby a smile of apology for his earlier accusations of granny abandonment. "But, Gran, I don't understand why you didn't tell me about Leila. All those times I called . . ."

"I'm sure I must have mentioned it, dear."

"And I'm sure you did not. The last time I called, you told me she was napping."

"Now, did I say that?" Belle shook her head slowly, as if trying to recall. "I just get so forgetful sometimes."

Abby's head swiveled around as she reached for the empty vegetable bowls. Why was Belle persisting in this absurd imitation of one whose faculties came and went?

Belle's mind and memory were as sharp as a tack. She glanced over at Alex to see if he was falling for his grandmother's little act. The lines gathering on his brow assured her that he was.

"All the more reason why you should not be alone here," he told Belle with gentle concern.

"But I'm not alone, dear." Belle smiled. "Abigail is here now, and she takes excellent care of me. And you're close enough to come and help out whenever we need you."

"Absolutely whenever." He nodded.

Melissa's eyes narrowed, and her lips grew taut over her teeth as her face settled into an unpleasant mask.

"How many for coffee?" Abby asked brightly from the doorway.

"And what marvelous surprise do you have for dessert, Abigail?" Belle tapped her fingers in happy anticipation, hoping it would be something with chocolate.

"Dessert?" Abby stopped halfway through the dining-room door. She turned and looked at the apples piled in the centerpiece along with the pine cones, sprigs of boxwood, and trails of ivy. Those same apples had been destined for the apple pie. That very apple pie she had not made.

"Ah, dessert will be a real surprise, Belle. It's . . . I'll bring it out in a minute."

"Dessert," she whispered aloud to the empty kitchen. Even she couldn't throw something together in forty-five seconds.

Panicked, she dialed Naomi's number.

"Abby, is that you?" Naomi said. "Speak up, honey, I can't hear you."

"I can't speak up," Abby whispered into the phone. "I said, do you have any desserts left over?"

"Why, sure. We have some peach pie and some pecan pie and, let's see here, a few slices of coconut cake."

"No, no. I need a *whole* something. Something that hasn't been cut yet."

"Well, the only thing that's not been cut is the Yule log my sister brought over last night."

"Can I have it?" Abby cut her off.

"Sure, Abby, but . . ."

"Could you bring it right over? *Right now?*" Abby pleaded desperately.

"Yes, but Abby . . ."

"Thank you, thank you." Abby breathed a sigh of relief. "And Naomi, would you bring it to the back door?"

Abby was waiting for Naomi as she walked up the driveway, the Yule log perched on a silver tray.

"Abigail, what is going on here?" She laughed as she handed the tray to an obviously frazzled Abby. "You and Belle planning on a little sugar binge to top off the holiday?"

"Belle invited Alex to spend Christmas Day with us—without telling me, I might add—and the apples went into the centerpiece instead of a pie because I thought we needed a centerpiece. I mean, I did intend to bake the . . ."

"Alex is here? Now?" Naomi's eyes widened at the news. "But how lovely for Belle. And for *you.* How's it going, after all these years?"

"Not so good," Abby told her as they filed through the back door. "We sort of got off on the wrong foot, and he brought along . . ."

"Well, I just have to poke my head in and say Merry Christmas." Naomi grinned and disappeared through the door into the dining room.

Three minutes later, Naomi was back. "Abigail, who is that woman in there?"

"She's with Alex." Abby turned her back.

"I know she's with Alex." Naomi plunked herself down on the nearest kitchen chair. "Just who is she? In his life, I mean?"

"I know they work for the same law firm. Which her daddy and uncle own, by the way. Beyond that, I'm not sure. Naomi, you didn't tell them that you brought over that Yule log, did you?"

"What? Of course not. Are you trying to pass that off as your own?"

Abby nodded, her lips drawn into a tight smile.

"Why would you do that? Oh, for Pete's sake." Naomi's eyes lit with mischief. "Abigail McKenna, are you aiming to seduce that man with food?"

"I can't deny the thought crossed my mind." Abby sat down opposite her friend at the small table.

"I always knew it." Naomi grinned triumphantly. "I always knew you two would end up together. Is this just the most romantic thing?" She pounded her fist twice on the table to emphasize her glee.

"No, no, Naomi, see . . ." Abby attempted to explain.

"Oh, my stars, Abby, it's just like one of those romance novels. Childhood sweethearts, torn apart by time and circumstances, reunited at last." Naomi almost swooned.

"Naomi, listen. It's not like that."

"Now, tell me what happened. He showed up here today, and you just fell head over heels when you saw him again?"

"Naomi," Abby said sternly. "This is not love we're talking about here. It's a matter of convenience. I need Alex . . ."

"Say no more." Naomi held up one hand to stop her. "I understand completely. Passion often leads to love, Abby. It's nothing to be ashamed about."

"Naomi, I need him to help me figure out what to do about Belle." Abby grasped Naomi's arm, shaking it gently. "I can't afford to keep this house. I cannot spend the rest of my life in Primrose. I need to find a job. I have to support myself. I need Alex to take responsibility for Belle so I can get on with my life."

"That's all?" Naomi asked in mock horror.

"That's all." Abby nodded.

"You sure?"

"Positive."

"What a pity." Clearly disappointed, Naomi shook her head and stood up to let herself out. "What an absolute pity."

"Them's the facts." Abby shrugged.

"Enjoy your dessert," Naomi told her as she closed the screen door behind her. "But Ab?"

"What?"

"Didn't I tell you he'd grown up real nice?" She grinned, the touch of mischief returning to dance in her eyes.

Abby laughed out loud as she lifted the tray holding the Yule log and carried it into the dining room.

◆ 16 ◆

The rest of the evening seemed to go downhill after dessert, which Melissa had declined, saying, "Oh, I just never eat dessert, Abigail. I'd just end up looking like a house. Of course, you doin' all that *manual* labor, you probably just burn it right off."

Abby had glared, mentally stuffing the meringue mushrooms, which adorned the Yule log, firmly into Melissa's nostrils.

With one eye on the clock, knowing she was running out of time, Abby was fitfully stacking dishes on the counter when Alex appeared in the doorway.

"Can I give you a hand?" he asked.

"Sure." She opened a drawer and pulled out a linen towel. "You can dry as I get these washed up."

"Great."

She ran hot water over the plates, then stacked them on the counter while she filled the old porcelain sink, mentally searching for her opening line. She just couldn't say, *Look, Alex, I want to leave Primrose, so you are going to have to get your grandmother out of this house by the time I sell it.*

"Abby, I owe you an apology. If I'd thought before I opened my mouth, I'd have known that you'd never have deliberately left Gran here alone all that time." The apology came easily, without embarrassment or hesitation. The brown eyes that had earlier snapped in anger were once again soft and warm as molasses. "It was just such a shock,

114

finding out that Leila was dead. And imagine Gran forgetting to tell me."

"Alex, Belle did not forget." Abby handed him a wet plate. "She didn't want you to know."

"Didn't want me to know?" He laughed. "How long did she think she could get away with that?"

"Apparently, she got away with it for about three months," she reminded him.

"That's my fault. I should have made time to visit before this. I just got all caught up with this new job—you know how you get when you let your job absorb you?"

"Yes, unfortunately, I know all too well." She nodded. "It's been years since I visited with Aunt Leila. Far too many years. And I regret it more than I can tell you. I can still hardly believe that she left everything to me, after the way I neglected her."

"She loved you, Abby. And she knew how much you loved this house. I think she always intended for you to have it." He took another plate from the rack. "Besides, you always said someday you'd live in Primrose. How many people get to live their dreams?"

The dream, a tiny voice inside her threatened to confess aloud, *was to live in Primrose with you.*

"And you don't know how lucky you are," he continued. "I have such wonderful memories of this place. The happiest times of my life were spent in Primrose. You don't know how much I envy you, coming back here to stay."

"Well, Alex, that's something I need to talk to you about." She took a deep breath and prepared for the launch.

Melissa chose that moment to be helpful. "Abby, here's the dessert plates and the cups. I'll be back in a second with the saucers." She flashed an efficient smile at Alex as she blew in, then back out, only to return with the promised dishes in hand.

"Melissa, why don't you keep Belle company while Alex and I tend to the dishes?" Abby smiled a sweet smile of her own.

"Great idea." Alex nodded.

"Well, now, Alex, there's so many things to be washed up, and since Abby worked so hard on that lovely dinner, I think I should help out a little." Melissa, having clearly reevaluated the cleaned-up Abby, was reluctant to leave Alex alone in the company of such obvious competition for his attention.

"It's no problem," Abby assured her, "and it's a good opportunity for you to get to know Belle a little."

Melissa hesitated, pondering the advantages of getting to know the grandmother over keeping an eye on what Abby might be cooking up in the kitchen.

"Go on, Melissa," Alex said as he opened the kitchen door and held it for her.

"Well, just keep in mind that we have a long day ahead of us tomorrow," she said somewhat disagreeably.

"I know." He nodded. "This shouldn't take too long."

Abby waited for the kitchen door to close before opening her mouth to give the speech she was mentally preparing. She hesitated a few seconds too long.

"Listen, Abby, I didn't know what to get Gran for Christmas." He leaned back against the counter. "I was going to give her cash, but if you have a better idea . . ."

"Cash is good." Abby smiled wanly.

"Can you think of anything she might really need?"

"New glasses," Abby told him without a second thought. "She desperately needs new glasses. She can barely read and has a real problem seeing the television."

"That's a great idea." He grinned. "I knew you'd know just the right thing. Can you arrange that? Take her for her glasses, and I'll reimburse you?"

She hesitated, knowing this could be her opening. "I'm afraid my cash is pretty limited right now."

The realization that it embarrassed her to admit that to him slowed the momentum that had surged within her for the briefest of seconds.

"Oh. Of course, you shouldn't have to pay for them." He seemed to study her face. "I'm sorry, Abby. How 'bout if I leave you with . . ." He fished his wallet out of his back pocket and counted bills. "Three hundred dollars enough?"

"That should cover the exam and the frames and lenses." She nodded without looking at him. "But don't you think you should give it to Belle, so she knows it's from you?"

"Good idea." He put the wallet back into his pocket and, with the cash still in his hand, started toward the dining room.

"Alex, are you just going to hand that to her?"

"Well, yeah." He looked confused.

"No card?"

"I sent her a card," he told her, still perplexed. "Is something wrong?"

"I guess not." She turned back to the dishes in the sink. "Abby?"

"Well, don't you think it's a little insensitive to hand your grandmother a pile of cash and say, 'Here, go buy yourself some new glasses'?"

"What would you suggest?"

She turned around and leaned back against the sink to think, then took the towel from him and dried her hands.

"Wait right here," she told him.

She returned with a sheet of writing paper and an envelope, purloined from Leila's desk, and handed them to him with a pen.

"Write her a note. Tell her what the money is for. That way, she'll feel obligated to spend it on her glasses, instead of . . ." Her voice trailed off.

"Instead of what?" He looked up from the paper.

Instead of on food, she could have said. *Or on oil for the furnace.*

"Instead of on something else," she said, and resumed washing the dishes.

She could feel his eyes on the back of her head for a very long minute, but he did not speak.

Finally, he said, "Here, do you think this is okay?"

He leaned over her shoulder, holding the paper in front of her.

Gran, it read, *you can't do the crossword puzzles if you can't read the clues. This is for new*—he had drawn a pair of glasses. *Merry Christmas. Love, Alex.*

"I think it's perfect," she said softly.

He was close enough that she could feel his breath on her neck. It tickled her ear and sent a shiver someplace deep inside her. She stiffened herself against the unexpected nearness of him.

"I think I'll give this to her now. Excuse me for a moment."

Abby bit her lip. Time was slipping away.

"Alex," she said when she heard him breeze back into the kitchen, determined that the moment was now. She would get this agenda back on track and ignore the fact that she'd spent the last five minutes trying to regulate her heartbeat.

"Abby, that was a brilliant idea." He put his arms around her waist from behind, his hands resting lightly on her hips. "Gran was thrilled. You know, she had tears in her eyes when she was reading that little note? Thank you, Abby. It was just the right thing." He leaned around her shoulder and pressed his lips to her cheek, saying, "Thank you."

"Alex." She cleared her throat, hoping to clear her head, and thrust the dish towel in his hands.

"Right." He grinned. "Dry."

"Alex." She chose her words carefully. "I'm really glad that you came today . . ."

"So am I, Abby." He lifted a plate from the dish rack. "You know, I never stopped wondering where you were. If you were well. If you were happy. What kind of man you had fallen in love with . . ." His voice trailed off.

I never loved anyone but you, the voice inside her pronounced, loud and clear. Her head jerked up with surprise, fearing for a second that he had heard it. Her cheeks flushed with relief as she realized the words had not tumbled from her mouth.

"And I hoped he would be someone good enough for you. You were always so special, Abby," he told her softly. "The most special person in my life, for a very long time. I can't tell you how happy I am to see you again. Funny, isn't it, to be here together again?"

"Alex, that's what I want to talk to you about." She seized the moment.

"You mean about the arrangement you and Gran have? She told me all about it. I think it's wonderful that you've invited her to stay on with you. I realize that a lot of people wouldn't want to have an elderly person around all the time."

Abby barely heard a word from that point on. What on earth had Belle told him? And how could she set the record straight without calling his grandmother an out-and-out liar?

Melissa entered the room with agitation written all over her face. "Alex, do you realize it's going on nine o'clock," she whined, "and we have depositions tomorrow morning, and we still need hours to prepare. Could we *please* get moving?"

"Well, I really wanted to help Abby finish the cleanup." He reached for another plate, and Melissa took it from his hand, returning it to the rack.

"I'm sure Abby will understand," she said pointedly. "You do understand, don't you, Abby? This is a very important case."

"Of course," Abby said, her words clipped.

"Abby, are you sure?" Alex asked, holding the towel limply in one hand.

"Of course, she's sure." Melissa took the towel and tossed it onto the counter. "Abby is perfectly capable of finishing up."

"Abby?" he said.

"It's fine, Alex." She forced a smile. "Really."

"Well, then. That's settled. Come get your jacket and say good-bye to your grandmother." Melissa held the door open for him, and Abby's heart sank as he shrugged an apology and walked through it.

"Abigail." Belle poked her head in a few minutes later. "Alexander and what's-her-name are leaving now. Aren't you going to come out and say good-bye?"

"Sure, Belle," she said. "I'll be out in a minute."

She dried her hands slowly on the towel Alex had used to dry the plates, then folded it carefully and placed it on the counter, silently berating herself for having blown her big chance. She walked into the hallway, accepted Melissa's thanks, and put her face up for Alex to kiss as he left.

"Gran, thank you for inviting me to spend Christmas with you." His eyes sought Abby's over the head of the tiny woman who stood between them, and for the briefest moment, Abby was propelled back to a time when the boy he had once been had stood in this same spot, that last night so many summers ago, his brown eyes drinking her in as if to preserve her face forever in his mind.

She blinked, and it was Belle he was kissing good-bye, not the girl of long ago.

"You'll be all right, won't you, Gran?" he was asking.

"Of course, she'll be all right." Melissa poked him. "She has Abby to take care of her."

"Thanks, Abby. For everything," he said, then hesitated, as if he wanted to say something more. When Melissa opened the door and stepped through it to walk swiftly down the steps, there appeared to be little choice but for him to follow.

✦ *17* ✦

"My, aren't we the crabby one this morning?" Belle noted dryly after Abby had snapped her response to Belle's inquiry about whether the breakfast scones were yesterday's leftovers.

"Of course they're not," Abby had grumbled. "There were only two left, and I fed them to the ducks out on the Sound this morning."

"Melissa ate more than her fair share at tea yesterday." Belle chuckled. "Then she had the nerve to launch into her little 'Why, I just never eat dessert' routine. After three scones with butter and jam, it's a wonder she had any room for dinner. Though I noticed she put away a hefty enough portion of cornbread and sausage dressing."

"Hmmmph." The mere mention of Melissa's name destroyed Abby's appetite. She took her cup into the kitchen to see if Mr. Coffee had done his job.

She was crabby. Crabby and tired from a fitful night when sleep would not come and stay. She'd tossed and turned, alternating between anger with herself and anger directed toward Alex.

"How could he just walk out of here, assuming that I will just go on taking care of his grandmother so that he and Melissa can live happily ever after, skating along together from one big case to another?" she had hissed to the darkness.

"How could I have been stupid enough to let him leave without explaining the situation to him? Why didn't I sit him down and make him listen to the truth?"

Somewhere between anger and self-recrimination, she would feel his lips pressed against her cheek, his soft breath on her neck, the strength of his arms as he had lifted her from the ladder, and she'd turn over and punch the pillow, as if to beat away the memory.

All in all, it had not been a very good night.

She stewed all day and again through the following night, until she remembered that he had, in fact, left a business card with his office number near the phone in the hallway. First thing in the morning, she resolved, she would absolutely, positively call him.

Belle was happily enjoying a game show when Abby dialed the number.

"Alex Kane, please," she said when the receptionist announced the firm.

"One moment, please."

Abby tapped impatient fingers on the old black receiver as the phone rang, once, twice, three times.

"Alex Kane's office." A woman's voice answered on the fourth ring.

"Is Mr. Kane available?" Abby asked.

"Not at the moment." The voice was at once uncomfortably familiar. "May I ask who is calling?"

"Abigail McKenna."

"Oh, Abby. I thought that might be you. This is Melissa."

How did I know it would be? Abby leaned back against the wall.

"Alex will be in court all day," Melissa told her flatly. "Of course, I'll be seeing him at dinner, if you'd like me to pass on a message." She paused. "Is Miz Matthews all right?"

"She's fine. Just ask him to give me a call."

"Sure thing." Melissa tried to sound agreeable. "Thanks again, by the way, for taking us in for Christmas," she said, as if it was expected of her.

"Our pleasure." Abby made a face at the phone. She, too, could play the cordiality game.

"Well, I just can't tell you how relieved Alex is that he doesn't have to worry about his grandmother. What with you being there and all. With that off his shoulders, he can concentrate on his career."

"Is that what he said?" Abby twisted the phone cord into a noose, picturing Melissa's neck at the center of it.

"Not in so many words, but I know that's what he's thinking. You do develop a sort of sixth sense, don't you think, when you're so close to someone," Melissa cooed. "And Alex is a real up-and-comer, he can really go places in the firm. At least, if I have anything to say about it."

That Melissa would have plenty to say about it went unspoken.

"You will remember to tell him that I called?" Abby did her best to ignore Melissa's reminder of whose firm Alex was employed by.

"Oh, I sure will," Melissa promised. "And do give Miz Matthews my best."

Melissa's voice lingered with Abby all day like a bad hangover. It rang in Abby's ears as she patched plaster on the newly stripped walls in the back bedroom and sang discordantly in her subconscious as she painted the woodwork. It taunted Abby as she lay in bed that night, cursing Alex's name and his failure to return her call.

After all these years, he had come back into her life, only to let her down again.

"You know, Abigail," Belle said the next morning when

Abby returned from the paint store, a gallon of paint in one hand and a new roller in the other, "I've thought about it, and I don't believe she means a thing to him."

"Who are you talking about, Belle?" Abby asked, setting the can of paint on the counter while she removed her jacket.

"Alexander, of course. I don't think there's much between him and Melissa."

"I couldn't care less." Abby shrugged.

"Really?" Belle's eyes narrowed with blatant skepticism. "Well, it matters to me. I want better for him."

"Melissa is attractive and apparently successful." Abby gathered up her equipment and headed toward the front hall.

"Pooh." Belle sniffed. "She owes her looks to her hairdresser and the makeup she piles on that little face of hers. And she owes her success to the fact that her daddy is her boss. I found her rude, unappealing, and unsuitable."

"Your grandson apparently does not," Abby said over her shoulder as she climbed the steps, "and he is welcome to her. Frankly, I think they deserve each other."

The painting had gone quickly. By the time Naomi stopped in later that morning, Abby was washing out the roller and brush in the bathroom sink.

"Wow, what a difference," Naomi exclaimed. "Tell me what you're going to do with the rest of the room."

"As little as possible," Abby grumbled, and pushed past Naomi to return to the bedroom.

"Whoa there, Miz McKenna." Naomi grabbed Abby by the sleeve of her sweatshirt. "Look, I don't know what's gotten into you these past few days, but you're not going to take it out on me. And while we're on the subject, you should lay off Belle."

"I don't know what you're talking about," Abby said flatly, prying Naomi's finger from her shirt.

"Of course you do. You've been an absolute bitch since Christmas. Which I take to mean Alex was not receptive to whatever it was you wanted him to do." Naomi followed Abby into the room. "Well, that's not Belle's fault."

"That's not exactly true." Abby turned to face her. "Belle apparently told Alex that she and I had come to some sort of living arrangement."

"Have you?"

"No."

"Well, I suggest you call him up and get it straightened out."

"I did call him. He didn't call me back."

"Then call him again. Keep calling him until you get through to him. But stop jumping down everyone else's throat because you can't jump down his."

"You're right, of course." Abby removed the drop cloth from the bed and dumped it on the floor. "And I owe you an apology. I'm just getting a little concerned, Naomi. I do not know how we will get through this winter. I have very little cash left, maybe enough to keep the house heated and to pay the utility bills and to keep us fed for three or four more months. It scares me to think about what will happen after that. What if that chimney finally goes over, or the rest of the plumbing goes bad? It just may be time to give Aunt Leila's jewelry man a call."

"Who's that?"

"A man Aunt Leila sold some things to a few years ago when she needed cash. If she trusted him, I guess I can, too."

"What will you sell?"

"Leila's emeralds," Abby told her, then smiled wryly. "The rest of the real stuff goes to my cousin, Susannah. The emeralds are the only pieces of value that I can, in good conscience, sell."

"What a shame to have to part with a piece of your family history." Naomi shook her head.

"I'm starting to get used to it." Abby shrugged. "And besides, the emeralds won't keep the furnace going or pay the plumber when the pipes finally crumble."

"Yes, but they haven't crumbled yet," Naomi pointed out. "Why not hold on to them until you absolutely have to sell them?"

"That day may not be too far away." Abby grimaced.

"But it's not here yet. And besides, what if you sell them now and have the plumbing repaired, and then something else happens that's worse than leaking pipes? Then you have nothing to fall back on."

"Well, I guess there's always room for a disaster greater than leaking pipes." Abby tried to force a smile.

"Are you kidding? In a house like this?" Naomi's eyes widened. "Why, there's no end to what could go wrong in a house this old . . ." Naomi stopped herself, then said sheepishly, "I guess these are not exactly comforting thoughts."

"Not very encouraging." Abby laughed. "But all so true. And you're right. Keeping the emeralds is like having money in the bank—especially since there's so little of that left."

"And besides, sooner or later, you'll get through to Alex." Naomi patted her on the back. "I think he simply isn't aware of what the situation is. He'll come through for you, Abby, as soon as he knows the truth. Sooner or later, I just know he will."

"Better hope it's sooner"—Abby smiled wistfully—"or it could be a very long, cold winter."

✦ 18 ✦

"Oh, my stars, Naomi," Belle exclaimed. "What in the name of God's heaven is that?"

"It's a dog, Miz Matthews." Naomi scooped up the small, dark, furry bundle with one hand.

"A dog, you say?" Belle peered at the squirming critter suspiciously. "Not like any dog I ever saw. My stars, Naomi, are those *barrettes* I see in that dog's hair?"

"It's a Lhasa apso," Naomi announced, "and the barrettes are to keep the hair out of her eyes."

"Lasso whatso?" Belle inquired, eyebrows raised.

"Lhasa apso. They're from Tibet."

"Oh my. That little dog came all the way from Tibet?"

"Well, not this one, but her ancestors sure did." Naomi stroked the back of the tiny dog. "Cute, isn't she?"

"Hmmm." Belle inspected the animal as Naomi set it back on the floor. The dog turned her head to one side, inspecting Belle in precisely the same fashion. The long dark hair, parted exactly in the middle of her head, was indeed held back by tiny red barrettes, while the fur on her back, parted evenly all the way to her tail, swept the floor like a ball gown.

"Her name's Meri Puppins," Naomi offered.

"Meri Puppins, you say?"

At the sound of her name, the little dog began to wag her tail. She looked up at Belle winsomely.

"I declare, Naomi, that dog is smiling at me," Belle noted with no small pleasure.

"Why, Miz Matthews, I do believe she is."

Meri Puppins took small, tentative steps in Belle's direction, her tail wagging more slowly, as if unsure of her reception.

"Aren't you just the sweetest thing?" Belle cooed, and the wagging resumed in earnest.

"She is a good little dog, Miz Matthews. My sister brought her over for the kids on Christmas—you know that Sharon works over at the small animal shelter three days a week?—but Sam's allergic, and I have to return her. I thought maybe I could leave her here until I can get her back to the shelter. I had Sam to the doctor's this morning, and he said to get the dog out of the house as soon as I could, Sam's wheezing so badly. I was hoping to catch Abby before she left for the store this morning so I could ask her. 'Course, I hate to take the little thing back." Naomi knelt and petted Meri behind the ears. "No tellin' where she'll end up. Only had one owner, Sharon says."

"Oh?" Belle sat on one of the chairs in the hallway. The little dog came to her and stood on her hind legs, her front paws resting on Belle's knees. The two seemed to study each other quite seriously. "One owner, you say?"

"Sharon says a lady from out at Edenton who raised these

dogs had a heart attack two weeks ago. Her daughter, who lives out on the other side of the interstate, found homes for all the others—her mother had all show dogs—but no one wanted Meri Puppins. Something about her tail not being quite right. In any case, we can't keep her, either."

"Poor little girl," Belle whispered, and the tail wagging began again. "Is she housebroken, Naomi?"

"She most certainly is, Miz Matthews. She goes out first thing in the morning, a few times during the day—she will tell you when, incidentally—then after dinner, one more time before you lock up at night. Since we've had her, we've just opened the back door when she's told us to, let her out, and let her back in when she asks us to. She is a smart little dog, that's for sure. And judging from her appearance, I'd say she was quite pampered."

"Hmmmm." Belle stood up. "Perhaps Miss Puppins would like to watch a game show or two this morning."

Meri danced around happily at Belle's feet, as if she knew that if she played her cards right, she'd not have to worry about returning to the shelter, that night or any other night. She lifted her head and sashayed into the morning room, close on Belle's heels, without so much as a backward glance at the woman who'd brought her to Belle.

Naomi chuckled and let herself out the back door.

"Belle, Mr. Everett down at the pharmacy told me to tell you he was asking for you." Abby shook the remains of cold late-December rain from her hat as she came into the morning room. "I told him you were . . . Belle, what is that thing on your lap?"

"Abigail, meet Meri Puppins." Belle smiled happily. "Our new pet."

"Our what?"

"Actually, she's a dog. From Tibet. A Lahaso mopso. Or some such. Ask Naomi." Belle explained Meri's presence in the house, then lifted her chin and announced, "She is the loveliest dog, Abigail. I would like very much to keep her."

"Oh, Belle, I don't know. I've never had a dog. I've never even wanted a dog."

"She's not so doglike, Abigail. Truly. She's just like a

sweet, small person. She's been just the most delightful company." Belle looked Abby full in the face and repeated, "I would like very much to keep her, Abigail."

Abby and the little dog sized each other up. Meri Puppins turned on the charm.

"Belle, the dog looks like she's smiling." Abby peered more closely for a better look. "I never saw a dog smile before."

"Good. Meri likes you. Then it's settled." Belle patted the dog on the head, as if it had been Meri's decision to make and she was being complimented for having made the right one.

"I guess I should call Naomi and find out what it eats." Abby sighed. There was no point in denying Belle her newfound friend.

"Meri is a 'she,' not an 'it,' " Belle told her pointedly.

"I'll try to remember that."

"And Naomi left her bowl and dog food in the kitchen."

Abby placed her wet scarf on the radiator and smoothed it out. The dog jumped from Belle's lap and followed Abby into the hallway. Abby knelt down and held her hand out for the dog to sniff.

"It's not that I don't like you," Abby whispered. "You're actually very pretty—love the barrettes, by the way—and you seem like a nice enough dog. It's just that, well, you're just one more thing that it will hurt Belle to give up. Or leave behind when she goes . . . well, when she goes to wherever it is that she ends up going. So don't get too comfortable here, okay? And try not to get too attached. For both your sakes."

Meri promptly turned tail and fled to the morning room and the warmth and comfort of Belle's lap.

"Do you mind so much?" Naomi asked as she and Abby rounded the corner onto Cove Road. "I mean, she hasn't been any trouble, has she?"

"No," Abby admitted, "she's no trouble at all. And Belle is so delighted with her, I couldn't ask her to part with her even if *I* was the one with the allergy. I'm just afraid it will be hard for Belle if she has to give her up."

"Not a good enough reason to deprive her of all that puppy love now." Naomi slowed her pace, then leaned over and rubbed the side of her left knee.

"You okay?" Abby asked with concern. "Want to sit on the bench?" She motioned toward the bus stop across the street.

"It's okay." Naomi grimaced. "The cold is bothering it a little. We'll just walk a little slower, that's all."

"Let me know if you want to rest, and we'll stop. Or, if you want, I'll run home and get the car."

"No, I'll be fine. Really, Ab, it's okay. I'm used to it."

"I'm sorry," Abby told her. "That you've had to get used to it. I'm sorry it happened to you."

"Well, you know, for a time, I was sorry for me, too." Naomi leaned on Abby's shoulder as they walked along. "But, you know, Abby, everything I hold most dear in this life was a result—directly or indirectly—of that accident. Colin, and, because of Colin, my children. Shucks, even the money we bought the house with came from the insurance settlement."

"What did Colin have to do with it?"

"Didn't I tell you that story?" Naomi frowned, then laughed. "It's my worst news/best news story. I was in school in D.C.—coming back to the dorm from the library one afternoon. Crossing the street, daydreaming, sauntering along. Then *pow!*—out of nowhere—and I do mean *nowhere*—came the car. I literally never knew what hit me. I mean, I've read accounts of people being bitten by sharks, and they describe the same sensation—just *pow!* When I woke up in the hospital, I didn't know anything. I didn't know where, and I didn't know why. The first thing I saw when I opened my eyes was Colin's face. I didn't know it was *Colin,* of course, I just opened my eyes, and this handsome blond man was sitting there, watching me with these dreamy brown eyes." In spite of the pain, Naomi smiled at the memory.

"You mean you had amnesia, so you didn't recognize him?"

"No, I mean I didn't know him. Never seen him before in my life."

"What was he doing in your hospital room?"

"Waiting for me to wake up." Naomi's eyes began to dance. "Colin was the police officer who brought down the man who hit me. I mean, people who witnessed the accident told me later that Colin—he'd been in a patrol car two lanes over when I got hit—got out of his car and chased this guy on foot until he caught up with him three blocks down, stopped at a red light. Pulled him right out of the car, they told me, then slid in, pulled the keys out of the ignition, and left the car there while he walked this drunk back to the patrol car. He came every day to the hospital, Colin did. Every day for ten days, till I woke up. Said he wanted to be the first person I saw, and he was." Naomi increased her weight on Abby's shoulder. "Do you believe in miracles, Abby?"

"Well, I don't know that the age of miracles hasn't passed," Abby told her.

"Sometimes, in my dreams, I think I hear Colin prayin' for me. Prayin' for me to wake up." Naomi slowed to a stop. "And every time, I *do* wake up, and I take that man in my arms and love him like there's no tomorrow. Because I know he brought me back, Abby. Colin's prayers brought me back. That's miracle enough for me."

They walked slowly, in deep silence.

"Know what he said, Ab? Colin said he came to the hospital to see if I could give a report on the accident. And when he saw me lying in that white bed, he said all he could think of was Sleeping Beauty, waiting to be brought back with a kiss. Can you believe that? Me? Sleeping Beauty?" She laughed.

"That is absolutely the most beautiful love story I've ever heard."

"Every story of true love is beautiful." Naomi smiled.

"And he followed you back to Primrose?"

"Yes, ma'am, he did. Quit the police force in D.C. and

came down here and asked me to marry him. My daddy did put in a good word for him at the police station, but it probably wasn't necessary. I mean, by that time, everyone in Primrose had heard the story of what a hero Colin was, chasing after that car, nabbing the suspect, then waiting day after day for me to wake up. Chief Kennedy was real glad to have an officer like Colin on his force, to be sure." Naomi nodded. "I'd never have met Colin if it hadn't been for that drunk driver. I'd never have had Meredy or Sam."

They'd come to Naomi's driveway, and she bent to pick up the errant piece of newspaper that had blown onto her lawn.

"You are a most remarkable woman, Naomi," Abby said with sincere admiration.

"Well, now, it doesn't take a genius to figure out that what I've got is more important than what I lost." She smiled wryly. "Thanks for the use of your shoulder."

"Anytime, my friend," Abby told her as she crossed the street. "Anytime."

·19·

Meri Puppins was a very smart dog, indeed. Smart enough to wake Abby, rather than Belle, early in the morning when she wanted to go out.

"Oh, Meri, please, can't you wait?" Abby groaned. "It's not even six."

The little dog continued to dance around the side of Abby's bed with increasing impatience.

"Okay, okay. Damn, and it's cold, too. Cold and early," Abby whined and reached for her robe. "If you're as smart as Belle says you are, why don't you teach yourself to tell time? See, then you'll know not to wake me up until the big hand is on the twelve and the little hand is on the seven."

Abby slid her feet into her slippers and followed the dog

to the steps, turning on the light at the wall switch before descending. She yawned as she made her way to the kitchen. She had not slept well again. She had thought that a noise somewhere in the house awakened her, but she had not been able to tell where it came from. It had happened before, this vague noise-in-the-house sensation, and she did not like it. It was creepy. The house was too big, and there were too many places where someone could sneak in.

Maybe she should get a dog. They say that burglars avoid houses that have dogs.

Oh. Of course. She had a dog.

She was, in fact, following it to the back door right at this very minute. Not bothering to turn on the kitchen light, she felt for the back-door key on the wall and fitted it into the lock. As Abby pushed open the back door, Meri froze on the back step and barked with the zeal of a Doberman. In that second, Abby saw a dark form rise from the top step. She slammed the back door, frantically fumbling with the lock.

"Abby! Abby, it's me, Alex."

Alex?

"You scared the crap out of me," she grumbled as she unlatched the door. "What are you doing sitting on the back steps at six A.M.?"

"Drinking coffee and waiting for you to get up." He held up an empty cardboard cup from the local convenience store. "Can I come in? It's pretty damn cold out here."

Abby stepped aside to let him in as Meri sniffed at his pants leg suspiciously. Satisfied that he posed no threat, the little dog brushed past him and continued her path to the backyard.

"Abby, what was that little furry banshee thing?"

"That was Meri Puppins. And there'll be hell to pay if your grandmother hears you call her a thing."

"What's a . . . what did you call it?" He peered through the curtains at the back door.

"Meri Puppins. She's your grandmother's dog. A gift from Naomi. Belle adores her, so unless you want to incite Belle's wrath, you'll refer to Meri as 'she' rather than 'that thing' or 'it.'"

"I'll try to remember that." He grinned as he took his jacket off and slung it onto the back of a nearby chair.

"So." She leaned back against the cold enamel of the stove, as if finding a man on her back porch at the crack of dawn was an everyday event. In truth, she was struggling for something to say. After several weeks of calling him with no response, having him there in the dimly lit kitchen, with the morning sky not yet aglow with the new day, disconcerted her.

"So," he replied as he crossed his arms over his chest. "I guess I'm a little early."

"I'm sorry you had to wait outside," she offered.

"I didn't mind," he told her. "It was sort of pleasant, just me and the stars and the new day. I actually enjoyed it. At least I did until the cold set in."

"How long were you sitting out there?"

"Maybe forty minutes or so."

"Why so early?"

"I came right from the airport. I was in Dallas all week for depositions. When I called into the office yesterday, my secretary told me that you'd called. I thought I'd just as well come here on my way home, just in case something was wrong."

Meri Puppins announced her presence at the back door by lightly scratching on it. Abby turned the key, let Meri in, then relocked the door.

"Was there?" he asked.

"Was there what?"

"Something wrong?"

"Not exactly wrong," she told him, "but there are some things we need to talk about."

"No time like the present." He shrugged.

"Right." She nodded. "Let me just run upstairs and get dressed."

"Well, if you'll tell me where you hide the coffee, I'll put a pot on while you're changing."

She directed him to the cupboard and fled quietly up the steps. Rummaging for a pair of clean jeans and a sweater, she tried to shake the sleep from her brain.

This is it, she told herself. *This is my chance. Unless he left Melissa in the car, I have him all to myself. I can tell him everything. And we will find a solution. And I can start making plans to get on with my life. Yes!*

She pulled long woolly socks up to her knees, then danced into her soft, near-threadbare jeans. She was almost whistling as she drew the gray-and-white-flecked sweater over her head and tied her sneakers. A stop in the hall bath to dash water onto her face and tame her hair as best she could, and she was on her way down the steps. She was rehearsing what she'd say as she swung open the kitchen door.

"Look, Ab," he said softly from the back door, where he stood looking out the glass panels toward the Sound.

He moved slightly to his right to make room for her without turning.

She shared his silence as the sun poked its first light through the skeletal trees that rimmed the waking waters just beyond the carriage house.

"It never changes," she heard him say. "All these years later, it looks exactly the same. The water still turns the same shades of orange and gold, and Leila's carriage house still looks like it's on fire when that first light hits it. I can remember when I was a kid, waking up early and looking out the window to this house, and seeing it all, the house and the carriage house and the trees, all wrapped in the early-morning mist. Some days, it would be so thick, I couldn't see the house at all, as if it had floated down to the river and drifted on out into the Sound while we slept. I'd watch until the sun came up and burned away the fog, so that I could see that the house was still here, and that you were safe."

She looked up at him wordlessly, the sudden image of a young Alex, silhouetted in the front bedroom window of Belle's house, flashing before her eyes.

"I wondered what you were looking at," she mused. "Sometimes, I'd wake up early and look across the street and wonder what you . . . that is, wonder if anyone else in

Primrose was awake yet. Sometimes I thought I'd see someone at the window."

"That was me." He looked down and smiled. "Thinking about you. Seems I never thought about anything else, back then."

"They were good summers." She nodded as she turned from the rising sun and sought to busy herself by getting out cups and the sugar bowl and cream for their coffee.

"They were the best," he agreed, "the very best days of my life. There came a time when only the memory of Primrose kept me focused on what mattered and what didn't. That first summer, when I stayed home, sometimes when things hurt badly, sometimes I'd picture myself in Primrose, out on Leila's dock, or down by the inlet, just watching the water. I'd try to picture what you'd be doing each day, and I'd try to imagine myself there with you."

"Why didn't you write to me?" she asked.

"Sure. 'Dear Abby, I'm sorry I can't join you in Primrose this summer, but my dad has run off with his secretary, who is, oh, a year or so older than my sister, and Mom is, needless to say, a bit unnerved. Particularly since Dad closed out their bank accounts before he and little Courtney left last week for Mexico. Good-bye, Stanford, hello, state school (assuming I make enough money on my construction job to pay the tuition). Have a good summer. Have a good life. Your friend, Alex.' How would that have sounded?" he asked somewhat bitterly.

"It would have sounded like the truth," she said. "It would have sounded like something I could understand."

"I'm sorry, Abby," he whispered. "Everything just hurt too damned much that summer. Not the least of which was thinking about you being here and me not. I wanted to be riding bikes with you down Cove Road. I wanted to row out to the Sound to fish in the early morning. I wanted to climb the ladder to the loft in Leila's carriage house on rainy days and smell the hay and sit on the front porch at night and talk about who we'd be when we grew up. I wanted not to be in Seattle, watching my mother's life fall apart and knowing that nothing I did or said could give her back the slightest bit of what had been taken from her."

The sound of small dog feet tap dancing across hardwood drew their attention to the front hallway.

"Ha!" Belle exclaimed as she passed into the kitchen, her eyes lighting up as she spied their unexpected visitor. "I could tell by the way Meri P. was dancing around my bed that something was going on, but I didn't dare hope to find you here, Alexander. What a wonderful surprise!"

Belle reached both arms out to her grandson and all but disappeared within his embrace.

"Good morning, Gran." He kissed the top of her head, his large hands unconsciously smoothing back the errant strands of white hair that had slid from their pins at the nape of her neck.

"It is, in fact, a good morning." She beamed. "Now, what brings you here at the crack of dawn?"

"Well, I was on my way back from a trip and decided to come here first before going on to Hampton." He watched as the tiny woman filled the tea kettle with water and placed it on the stove. "I thought I'd stop in and see how you two were doing."

"We're doing just fine." Belle patted him on the arm. "What do you think of my new little friend?" Belle nodded toward the floor where Meri Puppins sat.

"Cute, Gran," he told her. "Who brushes out all that hair?"

"Why, I do, of course." Belle grinned. "You know all these articles about the elderly doing better when they have a pet? It's all true, Alexander, indeed it is. Why, I just feel happy all over when that little dog sashays into the room and I know she's looking for me. She knows who her best friend is, don't you, Meri?"

Alex and Abby exchanged grins as Belle leaned over to scratch Meri between the ears.

"Now, what's for breakfast, Abigail?" Belle asked as she poured her tea and headed toward the morning room. "Bring your coffee, and come keep me company, Alexander.

If we don't bother her too much, perhaps Abby will make blueberry pancakes."

"Now, this seems to be a familiar sight," Alex said from the doorway, where he paused to watch Abby as she aimed the nozzle of the water canister at the wall and attacked the old green paper.

He'd spent much of the morning chatting with Belle, then, exhausted from not having slept on his late-night flight from Dallas, he had fallen asleep on the sofa in the front parlor after lunch. Having awakened a few hours later in a silent house, he had gone searching for signs of life. Belle had fallen asleep in the morning room while watching a movie. Not finding Abby on the first floor, he'd gone up to the second, then followed the sound of her radio until he found her scraping yet another wall in yet another bedroom.

"Only way to get it done is to do it." She grinned.

"What can I do to help?" he asked.

"If you're expecting me to be polite and say, 'Oh, nothing,' you're going to be disappointed," she told him.

"No, no," he assured her. "I'd like to help."

"Great. You can take one of those large trash bags and fill it with the scrapings, then take it downstairs and out to the back where the trash cans are."

"Are you planning on doing this in every room in the house?" he asked as he filled the third plastic bag with sticky pieces of spent wallpaper.

"Yes, sir, I am." She smiled resolutely.

"Why?"

"Because"—she took a deep breath—"the better the house looks, the better the price I'll get for it."

"You'd sell this house?" Alex dropped the bag onto the floor, and it landed with a *whoosh,* sending paper dust like cold, gooey lava through the opening of the bag. "Abby, I can't believe you'd even consider such a thing."

He sat down on the edge of the bed, clearly stunned by her announcement.

"I really don't have a choice." She turned to face him. "I

can't afford to keep it, Alex. I have no income, and what little cash I had when I got here is just about gone."

"Abby, I can't imagine this house belonging to anyone else."

"I can't think about that." She turned back to the wall.

"Look, there has to be some way," he began.

"There isn't," she snapped. "And besides, I have to get on with my life. I have to get back to the business of finding a job. Of getting back on track. I cannot spend the rest of my life in this house with no one but . . ."

His head jerked up, and she stopped mid-sentence.

"With no one but an old woman?" he finished the sentence for her.

"Alex, I am very fond of Belle," she said more gently, "and I didn't mean to imply that I . . ."

"Abby, she's not your responsibility," he stated matter-of-factly. "You shouldn't be expected to make your plans around her."

There. It was said. And Abby had not been the one to say it aloud.

"Alex, this has been very difficult for me." She put down the scraper and perched at the top of the ladder. "I came here with the sole intention of selling this house and the furnishings and everything else. I had no idea that anyone—least of all Belle—was living here."

"Must have been quite a surprise," he noted wryly.

"Must have been." She smiled. "I arrived late at night, and I still do not know who scared who more, me or Belle."

"But you stayed."

"Right now, I have nowhere else to go." She added hastily, "That is, I haven't had time to look for a job, because I've been busy getting the house fixed up. I know I won't get much for it, not now, anyway, the sad shape it's in. So I figured I'd spend a few months and do the best I could with it, maybe increase its value. Besides, the Realtors all say that spring is the best time to sell." For some reason, she could not meet his eyes.

"Well," he said, "spring is just a month or so away."

"Yes."

"And this arrangement you had with Gran?"

"Alex, there was no arrangement. I don't know what she told you. Leila and Belle had an arrangement, that Belle could live here for as long as she wanted. I'll honor that arrangement for as long as I can, but I can't promise that it will be for as long as Belle might wish."

"I guess I showed up at just the right time," he said softly. "Just in time to take Gran off your hands."

"Well, I'm not ready to sell the house yet, Alex," she told him. "She can stay for as long as I'm here. I just don't know how long that will be. At least several months. It's taking me longer than I'd expected, going room to room up here, and I haven't even started on the first floor."

"Does Gran know about this?" he asked.

"No," Abby admitted. "I didn't know how to tell her. I know she'll be upset."

"Upset? The woman has lived all her life in this town, Abby. Everything that has ever mattered to her has happened right here in Primrose. We'll be lucky if it doesn't kill her."

"Oh, gee, thanks, Alex," she snapped. "Heap a little guilt on me, why don't you?"

"Aw, Abby, I'm not trying to . . . look, Gran's not your responsibility. She's mine. I'm grateful to you for not pitching her out in the street when you got here. And I'm grateful that you're willing to let her stay for a little while longer, especially since it appears she's tried to hoodwink both of us. But the fact remains that once the house is sold, she will have to leave and go someplace else."

"She could go with you," Abby ventured, wishing she had the nerve to add, *Wonder how sweet Melissa would like that?*

"Yes, she could." He nodded. "But it wouldn't be here. It wouldn't be Primrose. How on earth will we tell her—I mean, how will *I* tell her—that she has to leave Primrose?"

He stood and walked to the window and looked out at the river flowing cold and misty behind the peaked roof of the carriage house.

"Tell me what your timetable is," he said without turning around.

"Ideally, I'd like to have the house ready to be listed with the real estate company by April or May, but . . ."

"But?"

"Well, with everything that needs to be done, I'll be lucky if I have the house ready to sell by the end of the summer. The scope of the work overwhelms me at times."

"Show me."

Abby came down off the ladder and gave him the handyman's tour of the house, inside and outside.

"Wow." Alex shook his head in disbelief as he looked over the contractor's estimate. They had completed the rounds of necessary repairs and sat now in the kitchen, where Abby prepared scones for Belle's afternoon tea. "How much would you get for the house if you didn't do all this work?"

"Probably next to nothing," she admitted as she poured water into the coffee maker with one hand and turned on the oven with the other.

"I guess you really need to get all you can from it."

"Every blessed penny." She sighed. "If I don't get some positive response to my résumé soon, I may have to think about maybe starting a business of my own."

"Doing what?"

"I haven't decided."

"Where would you go?"

"Don't know."

"You just know you want out of Primrose," he noted quietly.

"There's nothing for me here, Alex," she told him more stiffly than she'd meant to.

"I see."

"Alex, there are no major companies within miles. There are no jobs, there is no future in Primrose for someone like . . ."

She turned to find Belle in the doorway.

"I must have slept longer than usual, dear," Belle said calmly. "Is it almost time for tea?"

"Yes, Belle." Abby could not meet her eyes. How much had she heard?

"Good." Belle watched with satisfaction as Abby dropped the scone dough onto the baking tray. "Is there any of Elvira's marmalade left, Abby? Oh, come on, Meri, would you like to go out back? Let me just get my sweater on. Come along, Meri."

Belle pulled on the heavy dark blue sweater that hung on a hook near the porch window. She opened the door and followed the little dog onto the back porch.

"Do you think she heard you?" Alex asked tensely.

"I think it's a question of how much she heard." Abby grimaced.

"Alexander," Belle called through the open door. "Come out here and look at these geese down toward the river."

He looked as if he was about to speak, but, apparently changing his mind, he rose to join Belle on the back porch.

Abby could hear his light banter with Belle, and she peered out the window. They stood facing the river, Alex's arm around the tiny shoulders of the old woman, as if protecting her from what was to come.

Oh my, Abby thought with a sigh. *Well, at least it's done. At least he knows the truth. Let's see what, if anything, he's willing to do about it.*

✦ 20 ✦

"This is a great dinner, Ab." Alex winked at her across the table as he helped himself to more chicken. "The sauce is wonderful. Have you ever tried making it with portobello mushrooms?"

"Not since I've come to Primrose." She laughed. "I fear that neither portobello nor shiitake have yet to grace the shelves of Foster's market."

"I'll bring you some next weekend," he promised. "Anything else you can't get here that you'd like?"

"Are you kidding?" She rolled her eyes. "Let me count the ways—fresh basil, pine nuts . . ."

"Ummm." He nodded. "Sounds like pesto."

"I am dying for it. Young Foster carries no fresh herbs."

Belle's eyes flickered from Abby to Alex and back again in disbelief.

"Alexander." She cleared her throat as she took pains to speak slowly, lest they think she was too excited. "Did you say you'd be back next weekend?"

"Why, yes, Gran, I did," he told her solemnly. "Since Abby has fed me so well these last two visits, I thought the least I could do was come back and treat her to some of my world-famous vegetarian chili."

"Why, that would be lovely, Alexander." Belle nodded cheerily, wondering what in the world *vegetarian chili* could possibly be.

Not that it mattered. What mattered was that he would be back again. Soon. And that he and Abby would spend time together and get to know each other as adults. It had been foolish for her to have expected them to fall in love immediately, she admitted to herself. But it would, with the right luck, all work out in time. There would be the rest of this weekend and all of the next.

Belle felt a feather of hope tickle at her insides.

She cautioned herself not to get too hopeful. She wasn't out of the woods yet, what with Abby so antsy to get the house fixed up so that she could sell it, and that stupid Melissa—brazen little hussy—chasing Alexander.

Belle looked across the table to the face of her beloved grandson, then to that of the young woman who had given life back to the old dreams she and Leila had shared.

I should tell Alexander that Melissa called while he and Abby were outside talking to Naomi and Colin, she thought. Her toes wiggled as a surge of something akin to mischief swept over her.

There was such lively banter between them as they cleared the dinner table together. Alexander's laughter, clear and strong and deep, floated down the hall from the kitchen. It was as she had hoped it would be—she and

Alexander and Abby, all happy together, here in Leila's house. Here in Primrose. He'd be staying the night. Staying the weekend.

Later, she mused. *I'll tell him about the call later.*

Anyway, Naomi had invited them over for birthday cake for Colin, and here was Abby with Belle's coat. A phone call would hold them all up.

Maybe later, she told herself as she slipped her thin arms into the sleeves of the coat Alex held for her. She watched with pleasure as he helped Abby into her jacket, then turned off the light on the sideboard, just like he belonged there.

Then again, she considered as she pulled on her gloves, *maybe not.*

"You know, this entry just doesn't look the same without that hall piece you used to have on this wall, Gran." Alex shook his head and looked around at the house that had, for so many years, belonged to his family. "You remember, the piece with the tall mirror and the marble top on the table?"

"I certainly do." Belle nodded, glad he was with her to hold on to, this first time she ventured into her home, which now belonged to someone else. She hadn't been quite sure how she would feel, and so she had avoided it.

"Oh, my, Miz Matthews, I remember that, too. It had brass swans up around the top of the mirror." Naomi took Belle's arm as Colin took their coats. "What a lovely piece that was. We keep looking for something like it but so far haven't found anything that even comes close."

Naomi led Belle slowly into the living room.

"Well." She seemed to hold her breath. "What do you think, Miz Matthews?"

Belle slowly studied the room, knowing that Naomi was seeking her approval of the newly papered walls and the furniture that was so very different from Belle's own.

"Why, this is a lovely shade of green, Naomi." Belle nodded. "Just lovely. And I just love the way you've filled the room with plants and light, dear."

"Oh, Miz Matthews, are you just saying that?" Naomi asked earnestly.

"No, dear. You've truly made this your own home." Belle swallowed a lump in her throat as she patted Naomi's hand. "Which is just as it should be. Now, show me what you've done in the dining room. Oh, Alexander, do come see."

"Do you think she is all right?" Colin whispered in Abby's ear, nodding toward Belle as the threesome disappeared into the next room.

"I think she'll be fine," Abby assured him.

"It really means so much to Naomi that Miz Matthews feel *all right* about us having her house," the husky blond man explained.

"Colin, there is no one Belle would feel *more* right about than you and Naomi. And it's your house now, not Belle's," Abby reminded him as she followed him into the kitchen.

"Well, Naomi was worried that Miz Matthews wouldn't like what we've done, or that she'd be upset about being here."

"She seems to be just fine. And maybe it's good that Alex's here with her, this first time she's come back."

Abby peered into the dining room, where Naomi was showing off some pottery pieces she had made. Alex stood with his back to the door, but the mirrored sideboard reflected his concern as he studied his grandmother's face. Abby, in turn, studied his.

He is still the only man who makes my heart beat faster and makes my hands shake. Abby shook her head in grudging admission of her closest secret. *All these years later, he's still the only one.*

But no one needs to know that. She bit her lip and turned her face away from his reflection. *He may spend an occasional weekend in Primrose, but he'll always be going back to his job and his real life and Melissa. And I cannot let myself forget that.*

"Abby." Meredy tugged at Abby's hand. "Want to see the present me and Sam made for Daddy's birthday?"

"I certainly do." Abby smiled, pushing aside the sharp twinge that shot through her when Alex looked into the mirror and caught her gaze.

If I didn't know better—she winced as she turned from

him and followed Meredy into the den—*I'd swear that man could read my mind.*

"See?" Sam pulled a papier-mâché badge from its wrappings. "It's 'cause my daddy's a policeman."

"Sammy!" Meredy snatched the present from her younger brother's hands. "Daddy's supposed to unwrap it, not you!"

Sam's wail of contrition brought his parents, followed by Alex and Belle, to investigate. Colin soothed Sam while Naomi placated Meredy by offering to hastily rewrap the gift in new paper. Alex guided Belle into a chair, then sat on a stool at her feet, her tiny hands held gently within his own. Abby could not hear what he was saying from across the room, but whatever it was, judging from the look of tenderness that crossed his grandmother's face, the words were precisely the ones she needed to hear. Belle beamed and nodded enthusiastically. Abby smiled to herself. For Belle, coming here tonight had been the equivalent of facing her own personal dragon. Judging by her face, Belle had won the fight.

The birthday cake, an elaborate affair that looked for all the world like a 1966 Corvette, Colin's dream car, was brought with celebratory fanfare into the dining room. The birthday song was sung, the candles blown out, and the cake cut and distributed to the small group. Abby poured a cup of coffee for herself at the sideboard and trailed Naomi into the den, where Colin sat unwrapping the present his wife and daughter had, only minutes earlier, rewrapped. The adults oohed and ahed over the gift so lovingly crafted by the two youngsters, who beamed their pleasure.

"See, Miz Matthews?" Meredy proudly showed Belle. "We painted it gold so it would look like Daddy's real badge."

"And it does indeed look just like your daddy's real badge," Belle clucked. "Why, I can barely tell them apart myself."

Abby sat down on the edge of the sofa just as Belle said, "And Colin, Alex and I have a gift for you, too."

"Now, Miz Matthews," Colin began a protest.

"You hear me out, now, Colin." Belle straightened her back and pulled her chin up almost imperceptibly. "I'm very pleased to be here. I must admit that I was nervous about coming. After all, I lived in this house for more years than anyone else in this room has lived on this earth. I raised my daughter here, buried my husband from that very room." She nodded in the direction of the front parlor. "But it's your home now, Colin. Yours and Naomi's."

"Miz Matthews, you're just gettin' yourself all upset, now." Naomi handed Belle a tissue with which she dabbed at wet eyes.

"It's all right to be upset, Naomi," Belle told her firmly. "It helps you to know you're still alive. Now, where was I? Oh, yes, well, Alexander and I got to talking just now, and we both agree that the old hall piece—the one you've been looking to replace, Naomi—should come back to this house, where it belongs. And first thing tomorrow morning, Alexander is going out to the carriage house to find it. He's certain he moved it over there when I moved in with Leila."

"Miz Matthews, you would be good enough to sell that piece to us?" Naomi's eyes widened. "Why, that's a family piece. Alex, are you certain that you won't want it someday?"

"Absolutely certain." He nodded. "It belongs here. It will never belong anywhere else, Naomi."

"It was Alexander's idea, Naomi." Belle patted the young woman on the back as Naomi bent to hug her with thanks. "But it's a gift, dear, to you and Colin, for all you've done for me over the past year."

"Miz Matthews, that's most generous," Colin told her, "most generous indeed. But we can't possibly accept such a gift. It's too valuable."

"Now, Colin, you don't want to insult my grandmother by refusing her present." Alex stood up and folded his arms across his chest. "Won't it be grand to see it there again in the front hall?"

He clapped Colin on the back, and they gravitated toward the front door, followed by Belle and Naomi. The foursome stood in silence, each imagining how grand it would be.

Abby stood just outside the doorway, watching as the two families almost seemed to momentarily merge, as the family home of one became in truth the family home of the other. The proffered heirloom would seal the bond and serve to link the two families. Abby, feeling suddenly the outsider, made a quiet retreat to the dining room.

The sense of isolation hung over her for the rest of the evening and followed her to bed. She found herself in her own kitchen at two A.M., her sleep disturbed by some old house noise or other. She poured a small glass of milk, snapped off the light, and went into the front parlor, where she cozied herself onto the loveseat and wrapped herself in Belle's fuzzy afghan.

Pulling her feet up under her, she shuddered in the cold darkness and shrank back into the cushions. The feeling of isolation she had felt earlier returned to invade her. For so long, she had been accustomed to her role as a loner and had grown comfortable with the solitary nature of her life. Over the past few months, the solitude had been breached, as first Belle, then Naomi, had moved into her life. And now there was Alex.

She sighed very deeply, acknowledging that things were much more complicated than they had been just six short months ago. Back in Philadelphia, there had been no friend who mattered. In fact, she had never really had a girlfriend with whom she shared secrets and clothes and dreams, but she recalled how in junior high and high school, she had wistfully envied those girls who had. It was nice to have Naomi for a friend. She was fun and clever and capable and caring and warm, everything a friend should be. And Belle, feisty though she could be at times, was almost like the grandmother Abby had hardly known.

Abby found herself thinking how much she would miss them both when she left Primrose. Before too long, she was sniffling. She fumbled in the box next to the table for a tissue and blew her nose. She wiped her eyes and drew the warm blanket more tightly around her shoulders, crossing it over her chest to create a kind of cocoon in which she could ponder the pros and cons of letting people into your life.

A creak on the floorboards in the front hallway told her that Alex, too, was unable to sleep. Abby sank her small self as deeply into the cushions as possible and pulled the blanket over her head, hoping to remain undetected. The footfalls paused briefly outside the music room, before passing through to the opposite side of the house. Perhaps Alex was looking for something to read in Thomas's study.

As long as it keeps him from poking in here, she thought. *I would not care to discuss why my eyes are red and my face is blotchy. So if I am really quiet and keep very still, he'll never know I'm here. And that's just fine with me.* She began to drift off to sleep. *Just perfectly fine . . .*

"Ah, so this is where you've been hiding," the voice from beyond the cocoon chuckled. "Very good, Meri Puppins."

With the tips of the fingers of one hand, Abby drew aside the flap of the afghan which was still semiwrapped around her face like a chador. Alex stood, hands on hips, in the center of the room, watching as Meri P. tried to jump onto the loveseat with Abby.

"You can hide from me," Alex told her solemnly, "and you can hide from Gran, Abigail, but you cannot hide from your dog."

"She's not my dog." Abby unsuccessfully smothered a yawn. "What time is it?"

"Almost seven-thirty." Alex sat down on the edge of the chair opposite her.

"Oh, my gosh," Abby gasped. "Meri has to go out."

"Relax. She's been out. I just came in to see if you'd like to have your coffee in here."

Abby sniffed the air. Sure enough, the scent of brewing coffee drifted from the kitchen.

"That would be a treat." She attempted a smile.

"I aim to please, ma'am. One sweetener—artificial, of course—and some cream, right?"

"Right." She nodded and sat up, dropping her shroud to try to straighten the tangle of auburn curls that spilled out of control around her face.

Like a phantom, Alex had moved almost effortlessly to

where she sat and, reaching out one hand, had taken a strand of hair between his fingers.

"Like silk," he mused as he caressed the tangles. "Strawberry silk. Remember when I used to call you Red?"

"Remember when I called you Candy?" She smiled in reply.

"So long ago." He seemed to loom closer. "Where did the years go, Abby? Where did we go?"

"We grew up. We went about the business of our own lives."

"Funny, isn't it?" he asked earnestly. "After so long a time, here we are again, just as if nothing has changed at all."

"But everything has changed, Alex," she reminded him. "Nothing has stayed the same. Appearances aside, Primrose is different, the people are different. We're different, you and I."

"Are we? I don't feel different when I'm here," he told her. "When I'm here, I feel like . . . like *myself* again. I don't know if I can explain it, but I like the way it feels." He nodded thoughtfully, then grinned. "And I like the way you look, all wrapped up there in that blanket. Snug as a bug."

He leaned toward her slightly, and for a very long moment, she thought he was going to kiss her. He was, she was certain, debating just that. And at precisely the second he decided that he would, at the exact second that Abby knew she wanted him to, Belle's voice drifted from the top of the stairs, calling to her grandson.

"One minute, Gran," he called back.

The same hand that moments earlier had entangled in Abby's locks cupped her face, his thumb gently tracing the outline of her chin. Their eyes locked, and Abby almost thought that if she closed her eyes, she would, in fact, be sixteen again, sitting on this same loveseat, about to receive her very first kiss from the very same boy. He smiled, and she knew that the same scene was playing out in his memory, too.

"Seems like a lifetime ago, doesn't it?" he asked.

"It was a lifetime ago," she told him.

Belle called to Alex again, banishing the moment and bringing them back to the present. Abby looked toward the front hallway to break the spell, knowing that one of them had to be the first to look away. Alex rose and left the room with obvious reluctance.

Abby watched as his long denimed legs carried him to the doorway.

That was close, she told herself. *Too close.*

"Gran is ready for breakfast," he announced as he stepped back into the room.

"Okay." Abby nodded and started up from the loveseat, wondering how to gracefully extract herself from the afghan without falling on her face or worse, exposing her worn flannel nightgown to his scrutiny.

"My turn this morning," he told her. Was he fighting a grin as he watched her wrap the blanket around her small body like a sarong? "What's your favorite breakfast?"

"Oh, eggs Benedict. Freshly squeezed orange juice. And, of course, perfect coffee." She tossed her order out lightly as she swept passed him, slinging the end of the blanket jauntily over one shoulder.

"As you wish, madam." He bowed low as she left the room. "Say, in twenty minutes?"

"Twenty minutes?" Her eyes widened. "You can do all that in twenty minutes?"

"No sweat." He folded his arms across his chest and leaned back against the door.

"You're on, bucko." She poked him in the ribs as she sauntered regally into the hallway.

She pitched the blanket in the direction of her bed, stripped off the flannel nightgown (what the well-dressed sex symbol of the nineties will wear, she noted ruefully), and turned the hot water on in the shower. She washed her hair with absentminded efficiency but left the shower without rinsing off the soap.

"He has you rattled," she accused the face in the bathroom mirror. "Twenty-four hours under the same roof, and you think you're a teenager again."

She returned to the shower and rinsed the soap from her

hair, then towel-dried it before pulling on jeans and a clean sweatshirt.

"You," she whispered aloud as she pointed sternly at her reflection when she returned to the bathroom to hang up the towel, "are *not* sixteen. You are playing with fire of the worst kind. He and Melissa are . . . whatever it is that they are. The last thing you need right now is *one more thing* to complicate your life."

She shivered, recalling the touch of his fingers on her face, the way his eyes burned into hers with that same soft fire that had lit her dreams for so many years. She raised her fingertips to her lips, and for a moment she could feel it, just as she remembered it, that same sweetness of kissing him. That same rush. That same longing.

Ah, but that was *forever* ago, she reminded herself. *That* Alex Kane and *that* Abby McKenna didn't exist anymore. *More's the pity.* She shook her head as she took the steps two at a time. She forced a smile onto her face as she pushed open the kitchen door.

He doesn't have to know, she told herself as she met his eyes from across the room and her heart resumed its errant banging against her chest.

He won't know, she promised herself as she accepted the coffee from his hands and allowed him to usher her to the morning room where her eggs Benedict—perfectly prepared—and freshly squeezed orange juice awaited her.

⋆ 21 ⋆

"Walk down to the river with me," Alex said as Abby started for the stairwell and the room that awaited her attention on the second floor.

"I really have . . ." She began a weak protest.

"I know, a lot to do," he teased. "Just half an hour, at the most, and then I promise to stay out of your hair."

Abby looked into the morning room, where Belle was happily situated in her viewing chair with a second cup of tea, the remote control, and Meri Puppins.

"We're going out back for a few minutes," Abby told her.

Belle wiggled the fingers of her right hand in a sort of semiwave to indicate she had heard.

"The African Queen," Belle said brightly, her eyes never leaving the television screen. The early Saturday morning classic film had become the highlight of her week.

"Really?" Abby paused in the doorway. "That's a favorite of mine."

"One of the all-time best." Belle nodded. "I still cannot believe I can sit here in this chair and bring Kate Hepburn right into the morning room with me. Leila would have loved it."

Abby smiled as she left the room. Belle said exactly the same thing every Saturday morning. Last week, it had been Myrna Loy; the week before, Ginger Rogers. Abby was pleased to have brought such wonders into Belle's life. And yes, most certainly, Aunt Leila would have loved it.

Joining Alex on the back porch, Abby inhaled deeply, her nostrils flaring to drink their fill of the heavy scent of pine washed down with early-morning dew and mist.

"It always smells so good here first thing in the morning." She sighed. "Some mornings, I just want to come outside and inhale, as if I can't get enough of it."

"Isn't it funny how there are some things you just never forget?" Alex asked as they walked into the yard. "The smell of pine always makes me think of Primrose. Every time I get a whiff of it, even from those little cardboard trees you hang in your car to freshen the air, it brings me right back to this spot."

Alex walked to where he had, years ago, carved their initials into the trunk of the pine and reached a long arm upward to trace the letters with his fingers.

"They're still there," he said, as if surprised. "Look, Ab."

"I saw." Abby walked past without breaking stride or pausing to wait for him to complete his inspection.

He caught up with her as she approached the old carriage house.

"I'll have to get Colin over this afternoon to help me get that piece of furniture out of there"—he motioned to the outbuilding as they passed it—"and over to his house."

"That was really nice of you to offer that old hall piece to Naomi and Colin."

"It belongs in that house," Alex told her. "Gran said that Grampa's father had that piece designed for that spot in that house." He gestured toward the street and the old Matthews house on the opposite side of Cove Road. "And besides, when you consider all that Colin and Naomi have done for Gran, I'm more than pleased to see it going back where it was meant to be."

The whine of the outboard on the back of a small boat broke the early-morning silence and drew their attention to the river, where a small craft fled toward the sound out beyond the wooded point a quarter-mile down the river on their right. The last of the boat's frothy white wake rode toward them on small, undulating waves as they stepped onto the old dock. Silently, they stood at one end, surveying what the years had done to a once-favorite spot.

"I'd say the decking needs a bit of shoring up." Alex frowned, bouncing slightly to demonstrate the deterioration of the old boards, which groaned slightly beneath his weight.

"Careful." Abby laughed as the decking under her feet swayed slightly. "Or we'll both end up in the river."

"Remember when I used to tie Grampa's old rowboat up here?" He pointed toward the end of the dock, almost as if expecting to see the small boat still tied to the bulkhead where he'd last seen it.

"You mean the *Pirate's Prize?*"

"Aye, and a proper prize for a swashbuckling pirate she was, lassie." His voice dropped several octaves and turned to gravel as he pretended to search his pockets. "Where's me eyepatch, lass? And have ye seen my sword?"

"The pirate summer." She laughed. "What were we that

year, nine and ten? I remember we spent most of the summer going up and down the river, looking for Black-beard's treasure."

"We filled an old tin biscuit box with marbles and pieces of quartz."

"Excuse me, but I distinctly recall that they were diamonds," she reminded him. "Pink diamonds. And priceless."

"All part of the pirate booty we buried up on the point. Plunder from raids on the high seas." He lowered himself onto the decking, stretching out the length of the dock like a big, lazy cat, until he lay flat on his back, one arm cushioning his neck, the other draped casually across his face to shield his eyes from the rising sun. "How many times do you suppose we buried that box and dug it up again?"

"Over the course of that summer? Maybe a hundred times." Abby plunked herself at the edge of the dock and leaned back against the pilings. "Do you remember taping the label onto the top of the box?"

"Valuables,' I wrote on it." Alex raised his head slightly to look at her, his left hand shading his eyes. "I wonder what happened to that box."

"I imagine it's right where we last buried it." She shrugged, tilting to dip one hand into the river below. She tapped her fingers lightly on the surface of cold water, as if tapping out a tune, her tiny, rhythmic splashes scattering drops in every direction. The sun had risen high enough above the trees to bathe them with the first rays of the day, and she pulled the sleeves of her old crewneck sweater up to her elbows to expose her winter-pale skin to the comforting warmth. Accustomed to the harsher Februarys common north of the Mason-Dixon line, Abby delighted in the delicious comfort of the toasty North Carolina morning. It felt good to relax on the dock in the sun, she thought. Every bit as good as it had felt when she was seven and twelve and sixteen and had spent the first hour or so of the morning lounging by the river.

"Do you remember where that was?" He lay back down

flat on the dock, one hand still draped across his face. "Where we last buried the box?"

"No." Abby stretched out her right leg, thinking that if she extended it as far as it would go, and if she moved it slightly to the left, the bottoms of their feet would be touching. *Sole to sole.* She smiled wryly to herself, her mind playing on the words. *Soul to soul.*

"Neither do I." He sighed and closed his eyes.

Abby leaned back, grateful for the opportunity to study his face without him knowing she was doing so. The light sandy brown hair of his youth had deepened to a honey brown and was just long enough to fall across his forehead, right above his dark brown eyes. The lankiness of his teens, which had once given him an unfinished look, had given way to a muscular hardness that had tormented her from the moment he had lifted her from the ladder on Christmas Day and swung her around as easily as he would have twirled an umbrella.

"He sure did grow up nice," Naomi had said.

Abby smiled at the memory. *Nice* didn't begin to describe the man who stretched out before her. Soft, loose jeans wrapped his legs in denim. The dark blue fleece of his sweatshirt stretched across his chest and pulled up above his waist to expose the flat expanse of his bare abdomen when he suddenly moved both arms behind his head to rest his neck. Abby felt a flipping sensation in her stomach.

I can't believe he can still make me feel this way. Her face flushed a sudden scarlet. *What on earth would he think if he knew that I still had a crush on him after all these years?*

He doesn't have to know, she told herself sternly. *Unless, of course, I make a complete ass out of myself.*

She pushed unruly hair behind her ears and tapped more rapidly on the water's surface. *Besides, he already has a "significant other." One who is in a position to do things for his career that I could never do.*

Abby pulled up one knee and rested her head on it, forcing her attention to the brown ducks that floated past, bobbing up and down in the water like feathered corks.

Darkened by the ancient, gnarled cedars that lined the banks, the river was the color of iced tea that had steeped just a little too long. The few remaining swirls of mist seemed to evaporate before her eyes with the grace of waltzing couples leaving the dance floor.

"This was the greatest place in the world, back then." Alex sat up suddenly, a touch of wistfulness in his voice. "The greatest place for a kid to spend summer vacation. We had the best times here, didn't we?"

"We surely did," she agreed softly.

"You know, I've been thinking," he began slowly, looking not at her but rather at a point somewhere across the river, where the trees stretched their thin shadows into the water.

She waited, sensing he was collecting his thoughts.

"I want to pay you for Gran's keep, so to speak. Room and board, you can call it."

"She doesn't eat much, Alex." Abby smiled.

"You have no income," he reminded her. "I know it has to be difficult for you, maintaining such a big house. And buying materials for all the work you've been doing—even just the paint—has to be expensive."

"Actually, things are very tight." She cleared her throat.

"Well, if I contribute on Gran's behalf, it could only help."

"It would help," she admitted. "Thank you."

"Thank *you*. You've been wonderful to take care of Gran these past few months. I'm incredibly fortunate to have you here with her. The very least I can do is kick into the kitty."

Abby swung her legs over the side of the dock, letting them dangle just inches from the water, pondering the reality of the situation. *I am falling in love with him all over again, and all he sees when he looks at me is a temporary solution to his oh-what-to-do-with-Granny dilemma.*

"The carriage house needs work," Alex observed. "The shutters on the second floor are half hanging off."

She turned to her left, where the carriage house loomed at the end of the dock. The glass panes of the windows were heavily glazed with the residue of the years, and paint peeled from every surface, giving the once handsome structure the look of a building that has long been abandoned.

"Thanks for pointing that out to me," Abby replied dryly. "I'll put it on the list of things to do."

Alex got up and walked the length of the dock, inspecting the back of the carriage house. He pushed gently on the door, which stood in the very center of the wall, and frowned when it swung open at his easy touch. Abby watched as he disappeared inside. With a sigh, she rose and followed him.

The sudden assault of dust twitched Abby's nose as she stepped into the dimly lit area that had once served as a tack room. Brittle pieces of leather, old bridles, and leads, hung upon the wall hooks so long ago by the Cassidy grooms, now lay like outgrown and discarded snakeskins on the brick floor. She sneezed lustily just as Alex appeared at the end of the little hallway, his hands on his hips and a look of concern on his face.

"Abby," he called to her. "Someone has been in here."

"How can you—*achoooo!!!*—tell?"

"The area around the base of the ladder leading up to the loft is disturbed." He motioned to her to come and inspect the evidence.

"Probably just some neighborhood kids." Abby shrugged. "Looking for a place to neck."

Wordlessly, two pairs of eyes strayed up the wooden ladder, step by step, to the loft, where they met over a shared memory before looking away, neither of them speaking the obvious: *Just like we used to do.*

"Or whatever it is kids do these days." She broke the spell by pretending to inspect an old glove she found on the floor.

The casual intimacy of the morning had tumbled too suddenly upon her, propelling disordered emotions to grate like sandpaper against her nerves. She sought as quickly as possible to sweep aside the muddle of her feelings to some small, secret place within her, someplace where she could store it all away until she could be alone to sort it out.

"They could set fire to the building, burn the damn place

down. The damage to your property aside, Gran has some valuable pieces of furniture stored in here."

"If they're that valuable, they shouldn't be in here."

"Maybe I'll see if Colin can help me move that hall piece over to their house now." Alex lifted the corner of a sheet and seemed to inspect the furniture beneath it.

"That's probably a good idea," she said, needing something to say, something to mindlessly fill the space between them, something that could push aside the growing awareness of him that had begun when she watched him stretch out along the dock.

He looked as if he was about to say something, then changed his mind.

"I think I'll do that right now," he said. "Talk to Colin, that is." He backed away from her and followed the light from the open back door. "You coming?" he asked her.

"Yes."

Once outside, Alex tried to wedge a stick into the lock to secure the door. "You really need to get this fixed," he told her.

"I'll send the handyman around first thing on Monday morning," Abby snapped. "As soon as he's finished the porch and the chimney and the plumbing and the electrical work."

"You really do have your hands full, you know," he noted.

"I can do a lot of it myself." Abby turned her back and started up the slight incline toward the back of the house.

"Ab, you can't possibly do everything that needs to be done." Two strides of his long legs, and he was beside her on the path.

"No fooling."

"I mean, if you expect to have this place ready even by late spring—which really isn't realistic, by the way, when you think about it—you need to have help." His pronouncement appeared almost to cheer him in some perverse way.

"Alex, you saw the estimate from the contractor. So,

unless you happen to have an extra fifty thou or so you haven't earmarked for anything else—or unless you know where I can find a handyman who'll work for food—I'd appreciate it if you'd refrain from reminding me of just how much more I have to do and just how unlikely it is that I'll be able to do it."

In her frustration, she had stood up, and her fisted hands had instinctively found their way to her hips. No one knew better than Abby how extensive the repairs on the house would be. She did not need Alexander Kane to point out to her just how much of it she could not do by herself.

"Remember how pretty this garden used to be?" Alex stopped just outside the gate. "How the roses fell over the fence . . ."

"Feel free to reminisce as long as you like." She kept walking even as he paused to look around at the remnants of the old rose arbor. "I have work to do."

Abby could feel his eyes on her back as she strode toward the house. How very annoying for him to rub it in. Of course, it was to his advantage that the repairs were so extensive. The longer it took her to get the house ready to sell, the longer it would be before he would have to make alternative arrangements for Belle. No wonder he was so cheerful.

Abby checked in on Belle and found her still headed downriver aboard the *African Queen*. She filled her spray bottle with water in the kitchen sink and headed up the steps to the small bedroom where earlier in the week she had launched an assault on peeling walls. She dragged the ladder to her starting point, turned on her radio, and attacked the old paper with an unexpected fury. Two Loretta Lynns, one Marty Robbins, and a Johnny Cash later, Patsy started singing "I Fall to Pieces."

"Patsy, you traitor," Abby muttered, leaning down to fumble with the dial, searching for a rock station, settling for the Stones' "Honky Tonk Woman."

Abby managed to finish scraping one entire wall before she realizing that Belle would be awaiting her overdue lunch. She wiped her scraper off on an old towel before hopping down the steps to the kitchen, where she searched for luncheon provisions. She stood in front of the open refrigerator, pondering the small array of leftovers. Would it be the beef stew for lunch and the chicken—perhaps in a pot pie—for dinner? Or would it be the chicken in salad for lunch, with the beef stew—dumplings added—for dinner? She would ask Belle if she had a preference.

Belle wanted *tuna* salad for lunch, and shouldn't Abby check with Alex to see if he'd be joining them for dinner? Abby went back outside, where Alex had just pulled his red Saab convertible into the driveway. She reached the car just as he lifted two brown paper bags from the backseat.

"Would you believe I had to drive all the way to Elizabeth City to find veal?" he asked. "And a store that carried more than two kinds of red wine?"

"Does this mean you're staying for dinner?"

"This means dinner's on me. I hope you like veal marsala."

"You cooking?"

"You betcha."

"Beats the heck out of the chicken pot pie I was going to make."

"I'm sorry. I should have asked first." He stopped midway up the back steps. "Abby, I owe you an apology."

"Apologize for forcing us to dine on veal rather than leftover something?" She shook her head. "Don't even think about it."

"How 'bout for overstating the obvious, then? Abby, what you have accomplished here on your own is truly impressive. But, without help, you'll be here forever. It isn't right that this house—and my grandmother—should hold you hostage when what you want is to move on. It's only fair that you have the opportunity to do that."

"So what are you saying?"

"I'm saying you've found your handyman. I'll do all those jobs that you can't do. I'll replace the plumbing, do all the heavy carpentry, replace the electrical outlets . . ."

Clearly taken off guard, Abby said nothing as she digested his words.

"Alex, it would take months, working every weekend, to do the things you're talking about."

"I understand that."

"You know how to do all that stuff? Plumbing and everything?"

"I worked for a general contractor every summer during college. I think the only thing I might have a problem with is the chimney, but everything else I can do."

"Alex, you've already offered to contribute financially."

"One has nothing to do with the other. The money is for Gran. The work is for you. I want to help." He squeezed her hand. "And besides, I've dreamed about living in Primrose for years. At last, I'll be able to do that. If only on the weekends."

"And only till the house is sold," she reminded him.

"Only till then. I know that selling the house is your goal. I understand that getting your career back on track is very important to you, believe me. But I also understand that to get the kind of price you need to get for the house, certain work has to be done. If we work together, over the next few months, we should be able to take care of business. Maybe by the end of the summer, you'll be on your way to wherever it is that you decide to go. What do you say, Abby?"

Every weekend. Working together. Just the two of them. Or would Melissa be part of the deal? She dared not ask.

"Abby?"

"I'm thinking," she told him.

"Is it that difficult to accept my help?"

"Of course not, it's just that . . ."

"Okay, you drive a hard bargain. I'll throw in half the cooking. Saturday breakfast and dinner. You do Friday dinner and Sunday breakfast."

Abby thought it over. "But that means you'll be spending more time cooking and less time working on Saturdays."

"Okay. We'll compromise. I'll do breakfasts, you'll do dinners, except for tonight. But that's my final offer."

"Is your veal marsala as good as your eggs Benedict?" She pretended to ponder the situation.

"Better." He winked as he began to unpack the grocery bags. Fresh mushrooms followed a package of angel hair pasta onto the counter.

"It sounds like an offer I can't refuse."

"You can't." He grinned, clearly pleased. He pulled a wine bottle from a long thin bag. "Corkscrew?" he asked, and she pointed to a drawer near the sink. "Why don't you grab the wineglasses, and we'll drink to our deal?"

Abby had just raised a goblet of thinnest crystal to touch the rim of the one in Alex's hand when the door swung open and Belle appeared. She studied the tableau for a long moment, trying to decipher the significance of the upraised glasses.

"I give up," she said crisply. "What are we celebrating?"

"Well, I guess you could say that we're sealing a bargain, Gran," Alex told her.

"What sort of bargain?" Belle asked.

"I've indentured myself, so to speak, to Abby," he said. "I've offered to help her with the work she's doing on the house. Do the heavy work for her."

"Really." Belle looked from Alex to Abby, then back again, as if attempting to get a read on the situation. "And when do you propose to do this?"

"On the weekends."

"Weekends," Belle repeated softly.

"Every weekend, till we're done." He nodded firmly.

"And when do you suppose that will be?" she asked.

"No way of telling until I get started," he said. "I won't know what needs to be done until I start doing it. That's a problem with an old house like this. You start taking things apart, you don't know what you'll find. To replace the plumbing, the wiring, the rotted wood outside—I don't know, it could take three months or six. Who knows, it could take as much as a year."

"My, a whole year?" Belle fought back a smile as she pondered the possibilities. A lot could happen in a year.

"So. Would you like to join in the toast?" Alex raised an empty glass in Belle's direction.

"What? Oh, yes. Please." Belle took the wineglass he offered her, careful not to spill the pale red liquid.

"To this wonderful old house and all its quirks," Alex offered. "May we get the best of it, and not the other way around."

"To the successful renovation of Thirty-five Cove Road," Abby added.

"To Leila," Belle piped up unexpectedly. "May she watch over your efforts and guide you both."

"To Aunt Leila." Abby took a sip of her wine.

Yes, indeed, most definitely, to Leila. With twinkling eyes, Belle observed the two of them together. *Wouldn't Leila be pleased?*

A whole year of weekends. Here in Primrose.

There was never any question that they belonged together. She and Leila had always known it.

How long, Belle wondered, her nose twitching as the first faint touch of lavender invaded the room, would it take for them to realize it?

✦ 22 ✦

"Where did you learn to cook like that?" Abby asked as they cleared the dishes away after a perfectly wonderful meal.

"When I was in law school, I worked for a friend who owned a restaurant. He had a wonderful chef who, fortunately for me, was very generous when it came to sharing recipes and technique. I soon found that I liked cooking more than I liked waiting on tables. I actually thought about chucking law and opening a restaurant of my own."

"Everything was delicious. You would have made a great chef, I'm certain of it." Abby sighed as she scraped the plates of the last remnants of veal marsala and angel hair pasta with mushrooms and green onions.

"Coming from someone who is as accomplished a cook as you are, I am flattered by the compliment."

"I learned how to cook out of necessity, to keep myself from starving while I was in school. I had so little money to live on, especially the year after my parents died and everything they had was tied up by the bank and the lawyers and my father's creditors . . ." She turned her back on him so that he would not see her pain. She was half a second too late.

"I'm so sorry for all you had to go through, Abby," he said quietly. "I'm so sorry that I was not there for you."

"From what Belle has told me, you were having some rough times of your own."

"Well, you're right. I guess it was right about that same time that my parents' divorce became final and Dad married Courtney." He snorted scornfully. "Can you imagine having a stepmother named *Courtney?*"

"It's a pretty name." Abby shrugged.

"Abby, Courtney was two years older than my sister and had a chest measurement higher than her IQ." Alex slapped the dish towel at the edge of the counter in agitation. "And you know what just kills me? It took my mother three years to accept what happened—to accept that her husband had in fact not only left her for a younger woman but did in fact marry the girl. She had even begun to believe she could make it through life alone, when she died. Just like that." He snapped his fingers. "Just that quickly, she was gone. And she never got the chance to prove to herself that she could support herself. That she could stand on her own."

"Did your father . . ." Abby began.

"I would prefer not to talk about him."

"Alex, I can understand why you'd be angry, but . . ."

"There are no buts, Abby," he said flatly.

"You may not understand what he did or why," she could not help but add, "but he's still your father, and at least your father is alive."

Alex's jaw set tightly, and his eyes narrowed. "He hurt my mother more than he needed to and turned his back on her for the sake of his new wife and his new son."

"You have a half-brother?"

"So they tell me."

"You've never seen him?"

"My sister sent some pictures."

"Does he look like you?"

"Not a bit."

"Don't you want to know . . ."

"I know everything I need to. Could we please drop it now?"

Abby rinsed the last of the dishes in silence, then drained the sink.

"Why don't you get the contractor's estimate," Alex suggested, his voice still flat and cool, "and we'll look over his list and see what kind of schedule we can come up with."

It took a while, but over the next few hours, Alex's natural warmth and enthusiasm began to return as they dissected the areas of work to be done and divided it into a neat schedule. Abby had retrieved a calendar from her purse, and she began to methodically date the entries on the schedule.

"Umm, better let me see the calendar for a minute." Alex frowned as he studied Abby's notations. With her pen, he circled several dates. "There are a few weekends when I know I'll be out of town. Let's see . . . *this* weekend, I'll be in Pittsburgh for depositions. And *this* weekend, I'll be in Atlanta from Thursday through Monday . . ."

"Atlanta?" Abby asked aloud.

"Melissa's sister is getting married," he noted offhandedly.

"I see." Abby bit her bottom lip. "Thursday through Monday? Sounds like one hell of a wedding."

"From what I've been hearing, it will be." He laughed. "Melissa's parents are pulling out all the stops for this. Nothing is too good for their little girls, you know."

All weekend, the name had not been mentioned. She'd

begun to hope against hope that somehow Melissa had just sort of disappeared. She should have known better. Beautiful, wealthy, A-type women like Melissa do not just fade away. Especially where a man like Alex is concerned.

"Where is Melissa this weekend?" Abby asked.

"What?" He looked up from the schedule. "Oh. An aunt in Georgia was having a wedding shower for Carlene, Melissa's sister. Why?"

"No reason." She shrugged. "Just wondering."

He looked at her quizzically, then said, "And you know, I'm not certain that we're not being overly optimistic here." He pointed to a weekend four weeks away. "I think if I get the wiring done in the three bathrooms on the second floor before the end of next month, I'll be doing really well. So we may want to reschedule . . ."

Okay, so she's still a part of his life. On the weekends, he'll be with me. Maybe not the way he's with her, but he'll be here. With me. And for a while, I can pretend . . .

Pretend what? That Alex and I are on the road to happily ever after?

Don't even start to look down that road, she told herself sternly, *'cause there's nothing but one big heartache waiting at the end of it.*

She sighed deeply, unaware that he had turned to stare at her at the sound.

"Hey, I know what you're thinking, Ab," he told her gently.

"You do?" She was horrified at the thought that at this minute he could read her mind.

"Sure, but don't let it get you down. It may all seem overwhelming now, but we will finish this someday. And you'll be able to get a good price for the house, you'll see. Who knows? Maybe I'll even buy it myself." He smiled and went back to his scheduling.

Oh, swell. Just one more happy possibility to look forward to. Alex and Melissa wallowing in domestic bliss in my house.

The image of a score of perfect children, all blond and sporting Melissa's tiny upturned nose, following Alex down the steps like so many ducklings to a waiting schoolbus, made Abby want to choke.

She rested her chin in her hand and studied his face from across the kitchen table. *He's too adorable,* she thought as he looked up at her and smiled absentmindedly before going back to the calendar that lay open before him. He was up to June already. She wondered if she would be able to bear spending two days a week, every week, under this roof with him, knowing that he had someone else in his life the other five days. She wondered how Melissa would feel about him spending the weekends in Primrose and brightened slightly.

She'll hate it, of course.

Somehow, just knowing that gave Abby a perverse sense of satisfaction.

"Abby, don't forget on Monday to call the lumberyard and order this material." Alex handed the list to her. "Tell them I'll pick it up next Saturday morning. Colin offered to let me borrow his pickup."

"Okay," Abby stuffed the paper into the pocket of her jeans without looking at it and watched from the bottom step as he tossed his overnight bag into the backseat of the Saab. What the upwardly mobile young attorney will drive. She folded her arms across her chest to ensure that they did not somehow find a way to wrap themselves around him and draw him to her. Then, just to make sure that her hands had something else to busy themselves with, she forced them to pull with deliberation at some errant strands of vine which, inspired by the unseasonable warmth of the past few days, had optimistically begun to twine around the porch railing.

"If I get the chance this week, I'll call around and see if I can find some of the tools I'll need for the plumbing," he said, almost cheerfully. "Don't look so glum, Abby. It'll be fun. It'll be just like old times, you'll see. Just like the old days."

Just like old times? she thought as she waved to him as he pulled out of the driveway and gave the horn a few short, jaunty beeps. *Just like the old days?*

In the old times, we had a lifetime of dreams, just waiting to come true. Now we have, at the most, a few months to spend together before we go our separate ways for good. Now we're all grown up, and someone else is sharing your life and starring in your dreams.

In the old days, I trembled at the thought of touching you, because we were just beginning to learn how precious, how good a loving touch could feel. Now I tremble at the very memory, because I want to touch you that way again, but I dare not. In the old days, we were learning to love, not quite yet lovers, but ever best friends. Now I do not know what we are.

How could it ever be just like old times again?

She gave a final hard tug on the last piece of vine, snapping it off at the root before going inside to make Belle's lunch.

The following weekend brought biting February winds and rain. Alex called on Friday night to say he'd wait till Saturday to drive down. On Saturday, an icy rain fell in fierce sheets against the windows, and when the phone rang at nine in the morning, she knew that he would not be coming. He could use the time to work on a new case he'd been assigned, he told her. Maybe the weather would be more cooperative the following week.

It was not. The winter, which had begun on so mild a note, had turned positively arrogant, locking Primrose in the grip of a raw wet spell that lasted three long weeks. Abby was down to her last dozen logs for the fireplace in the morning room, which she liked to keep toasty warm for Belle, when the warm temperatures returned with the arrival of March. The first warm weekend brought Alex.

Abby tried her best to act normal as she watched his car pull into the drive and park behind hers. As he bounded with all the exuberance of an overly large pup into the morning room to kiss his grandmother. As he chatted casually with Abby while dialing Colin's number to arrange for the use of the pickup truck. As he discussed with her his plans for the day and what he hoped to accomplish. As he opened the refrigerator and stashed the bottle of wine he'd brought to share at dinner. As he moved effortlessly back into her life as if he belonged there. As if he had never left.

A few times during the day, he would consult with her, but for the most part, they worked independently, she painting woodwork in one bedroom, he replacing the electrical wiring in the hall bathroom. They broke at noon to have lunch with Belle, then returned to their tasks. Abby cleaned up at four, showered, and had dinner on the table by six-thirty.

"I'd forgotten how tiring physical work can be." Alex yawned over the warm cherry cobbler Abby had served for dessert. "I guess I've been riding the desk too long."

Abby leaned back in her chair and watched him cover his yawning mouth with the back of his hand, his eyes blinking closed momentarily. She would give anything to be able to get out of her chair and go to him, to stand behind him and ease the knots from those broad shoulders, to drape her arms around his neck and nuzzle him, to . . .

"Sorry, Ab." Alex's mouth quirked into a lazy grin, interrupting her daydream just as she had mentally begun to turn his face to hers and lock lips with that all-too-inviting mouth. "I'm afraid I'm poor company tonight."

"It's okay," she managed to squeak. "I'm tired, too."

"Gran, what was the movie today?"

"Why, it was *His Girl Friday.*" She beamed. "Rosalind Russell and Cary Grant. Your grandfather and I saw that film in the theater on a trip to New York City in 1940. We had a wonderful two weeks. I remember we stayed at the Plaza, and my sister Barbara—God rest her—and her husband, Peter, who was her second husband . . ."

"Alex, why don't you go to bed?" Under the table, Abby's foot nudged a rapidly fading Alex. "It's silly for you to force yourself to sit here and make conversation when you are clearly falling asleep before our very eyes."

"You know it isn't the company, it's the hour."

"Whatever it is, your eyes are sailing at half-mast."

"Are you sure you wouldn't mind?"

"Of course not," Abby assured him.

"Well, then, in that case . . ." He rose from his chair, leaned over to kiss his grandmother, then smiled at Abby, telling her, "Don't forget that the waffles are on me in the morning."

"You're on, pal." Abby began to stack the dishes, thinking about the last weekend he had spent under her roof and the wonderful breakfast he had prepared for her and Belle. "I guess, as tired as you are, you won't need to be going in search of reading material tonight."

"What do you mean?" Alex looked back over his shoulder, puzzled.

"I just meant, like the last time you stayed here."

"I don't understand."

"Last time you were here, you came downstairs and went into Thomas's study. I assumed you were looking for something to read."

"No, I didn't."

"Alex, you did. It was around two in the morning. I was on the couch in the morning room, and I heard you."

"Abby, if you heard someone come down those steps at two in the morning, it was someone else. I slept like a log both nights, and I fully expect to sleep as well tonight. Gran, you're not taking late-night strolls around the house, are you?"

"Of course not." Belle brushed the suggestion aside with the wave of her hand. "Perhaps, Abigail, you were dreaming."

"I don't think so." She frowned. Hadn't she heard him on the steps? Hadn't she heard the study door open and seen the faintest bit of light?

"Well, if you catch me sleepwalking, just turn me around and point me back to my room." Alex yawned again and headed toward the stairs, leaving Belle to finish her cobbler and Abby to wonder just what she *had* heard that night as she huddled under the afghan in the parlor and pondered the fates that had brought Alex Kane back into her life.

✦23✦

Abby sat on the top step of the back porch and swished the last bit of coffee slowly around and around in the bottom of the cup while trying to decide if she wanted a second cup and, if she did, whether she should call Naomi to see if she had a few minutes to come over and join her on the steps on this fine afternoon to savor the first elusive scents of the promise of spring. Recalling that Naomi would be at the library with Sam for the Tuesday afternoon story hour, Abby sighed and with some reluctance splashed the remains of the coffee onto the grass. She stomped her sneakered feet against the step to dislodge bits of drying mud before going back into the house. She rinsed her cup and checked in on Belle, who was snoozing comfortably with her beloved pup on her lap.

Smiling at the cozy scene, Abby pushed the red power button on the remote control to turn off the television. If she worked steadily over the course of the afternoon, she told herself, she could finish painting the last of the windows in the right front bedroom. Then tomorrow, perhaps, she could paint the walls. Maybe a light pink, she reflected as she opened the front door to check the contents of the mailbox. The very palest strawberry-pink. With a touch of white lace at the windows and the quilt on the old maple bed, the room would be certain to charm prospective buyers.

She flipped through the mail—advertisements for a new pizza place out on the interstate, the electric bill—pondering Naomi's suggestion that she paint an old dressing table white, then trim the top and sides with tiny stenciled roses. Could she really spend so much time to personalize one room, when she could go on to the next?

The next stop on Abby's agenda would be the sitting room off Belle's bedroom. Perhaps a true and sunny yellow in there, she mused, then recalled that at some point over the past few years, the gutters had leaked, allowing water to seep in around the window. The sill would have to be replaced—Alex would have to do that—before the painting could be done.

Movement from the driveway caught her eye, and she turned just as a figure disappeared behind the huge rhododendron at the corner of the house. Abby crossed the porch and peered around the side of the house, but dense shrubs obscured her view. She hopped down the steps and crossed the lawn to follow the curve of the drive to the back of the house.

What, she wondered at the sight of the unexpected visitor who strolled casually toward her backyard, was Alex doing there in the middle of the week?

At her approach, he turned toward her.

Of course, it's not Alex, she realized. *This man is stockier and not so tall. And they look nothing alike. How could I possibly have thought . . .*

"Hi." The stranger smiled.

"Is there something I might help you with?" she asked somewhat warily.

"Is this your house?" He started toward her.

"Yes." *It's the walk,* she realized. *He walks like Alex.*

"Lucky you." He was still smiling pleasantly. "It's quite a place."

"It certainly is." Abby returned the smile slowly, still cautious. Primrose had few tourists. Could this be a prospective buyer?

"Funny how things look so different when you're a child," he mused, and stepped back, as if to gain better perspective.

"Oh, did you grow up in Primrose?" Abby relaxed slightly. A Primrose boy returning home.

"No," he told her. "And as far as I know, I was only here once, with my mother. And I was very small at the time."

He continued to walk the length of the house slowly, as if

172

taking in every inch of the building, a curious Abby watching his every step.

"I apologize," he said, as if it had just occurred to him that he was in fact intruding upon her property. "I am so sorry. I should have knocked on the door and asked if I might wander a bit. Forgive me, Miss? . . ."

"McKenna. Abby McKenna."

"Drew Cassidy." He smiled with the utmost charm and extended his right hand to clasp hers warmly.

"Cassidy? What a coincidence. The name of the family who built the house was Cassidy."

"No coincidence at all." Drew shook his head. "Thomas Cassidy was my grandfather."

"What did you say?" Abby was certain she had misunderstood.

"I said, Thomas Cassidy was my grandfather."

"How is that possible?"

"Because he was my father's father. Is there something wrong?"

She stammered. "Thomas Cassidy was married to my great-aunt. They had no children, so I don't understand . . ."

"Obviously, my grandmother and your great-aunt were not the same person," he confided with apparent amusement.

"Oh. Of course." She nodded slowly. "I'm sorry, it's just that I wasn't aware that Thomas had been married before he married Aunt Leila."

"He hadn't been, as far as I know," the young man told her. "From what I understand, he and my grandmother never married."

"What?" Abby exclaimed, thinking of the portrait of the serious-looking Thomas that stood on Aunt Leila's bedside table. "Why, whoever would have guessed?"

"My mother told me that my father had said that his mother was a stage actress, from Chicago," Drew told her as they walked toward the back of the house. "The story goes that my grandfather was head over heels in love with her, but she refused to give up the stage to marry him. They quarreled, and he left Chicago for some trip or other. Apparently, by the time he returned, she had left the city—pregnant with my father, though, of course, Thomas couldn't have known that—to go to stay with her sister in Dayton, Ohio. Apparently, sometime later, my grandmother relented and sought Thomas to let him know that he had a son, but by that time, he had married and settled down. I guess she had too much pride to come knocking on his door. Or so goes the story as related by my mother."

"And Thomas never knew he had a son . . ."

"No. He never did."

"How sad." Abby shook her head. "Then your father never knew his father."

"Apparently not. My father died when I was very young, so I never really knew him, either."

"And your mother?"

"I'm not certain. I haven't seen or heard from her in many years." Then, as if to provide some explanation, he added, "I'm afraid things fell apart for my mother after my dad died. I was in foster care for many years."

"I'm so sorry," Abby said. "Do you have sisters, brothers?"

"I was an only child."

"I know exactly how you feel." Abby sighed, feeling a sudden kinship with this stranger. "My parents died ten years ago. I was an only child, too."

"Then you know what it feels like to have absolutely no one." His eyes flickered, and he looked away, down toward the carriage house.

"I do." She nodded, then corrected herself, thinking of Belle and Naomi and the world of love that had begun to envelop her since she had come to Primrose. "At least, I did. I can't say that I feel quite so alone as I once did."

"I'm glad for you," he said with seeming sincerity.

"Would you like to see the house?" she offered.

"Would I ever! But, really, Miss McKenna . . ."

"Abby."

"That's very generous of you, Abby, but really, I would not want to impose."

"Are you kidding? We're practically related. Come on, Drew." She gestured for him to follow her toward the back porch. "We'll give you the downstairs tour and a cup of coffee. I'm afraid the upstairs is pretty well disrupted right now."

They stepped into the kitchen, and Drew looked around as if studying every corner and cranny.

"I wasn't back in this part of the house when I was here as a child," he told her. "Just in the front hallway."

"Looks pretty much like any kitchen built in the mid- to late eighteen hundreds," Abby noted. "Give me a second, I'll throw a pot of coffee on."

"Abby, don't go to any trouble."

"Don't be silly, it will only take a second." She filled the pot with water and poured it unceremoniously into the top of the coffee maker. "What brings you to Primrose? Obviously, you wanted to see the house, but, I mean, why now, after all these years?"

"I was passing through the Raleigh-Durham area on business."

"What business are you in?"

"I sell athletic equipment to colleges. I made a stop at Duke, looked at the map, and saw that Primrose was just a few hours away, and I thought, what the heck. I sure didn't expect to find family here . . . well, not family, I realize that, but . . ."

"I know exactly what you mean," Abby said to ease his discomfort. "Now, Drew Cassidy, how do you take your coffee?"

Before he could answer, a low growl followed by a shrill bark emitted from the end of the short hallway leading to the morning room.

"Oh, Meri, it's okay," Abby called over her shoulder.

The dog proceeded with the greatest of caution toward the stranger, grumbling all the while, even while she sniffed with deliberation at the fingers of the hand he held out to her. When Drew attempted to pet her, she snapped and fled with a yelp back down the hallway.

"Meri, you can be so rude sometimes," Abby called after the little dog. "Did she bite you?"

"No, no." He tried to smile. "I think she just wanted to assert her authority. Little dogs do that sometimes. I think maybe it makes them feel like big dogs."

"She normally doesn't do such things." Abby frowned. "I hope she's not going to turn snappish. We haven't had her but a few months. And she's very protective of Belle."

"Belle?"

"Belle Matthews," Abby explained as she refilled an empty sugar bowl and set it on the table. "She was Aunt Leila's best friend for years. She lives here with me."

"I see." He nodded.

"She's a lively old sprite, I must tell you." Abby searched in the refrigerator for the cream, which had managed to become lost behind a bowl of pudding. Belle had apparently sought and found a second dessert after lunch.

"I'm sure you appreciate the company." Drew watched as Abby poured a cup of coffee and offered it to him.

"I do," she agreed. "Well, if you'll come this way, we'll begin the two-dollar tour."

Abby led the way from the kitchen through the swinging door to the butler's pantry which opened to the dining room.

"This is lovely," Drew noted. "So many beautiful old things . . ."

"I doubt much has changed since the first Cassidys moved in," Abby said.

"That's quite a collection of silver," he noted, nodding in the direction of the sideboard. "Don't you think you might be pushing your luck, leaving it all out in the open, in full view of the window?"

"Normally, most of it is in the sideboard, rather than on top of it," she told him, "but I did some polishing a few nights back and just didn't get things put back."

"Well, you could be inviting a theft. Anyone looking through that window"—he nodded to their left—"would be blinded by all this." Drew gestured toward the row of gleaming bowls and pitchers and candle holders.

"I never thought about it." Abby shrugged. "The last burglary in Primrose proper was, let me see, I think Colin said it was about four years ago."

"Colin?"

"The chief of police." Abby pointed toward Cove Road. "He lives across the street."

"The police chief lives across the street?" he repeated.

"Yes. In Belle's old house."

"Well. That's . . . convenient."

"It is. He and his wife are close friends of ours. Mine and Belle's. They took very good care of Belle between the time Aunt Leila died and the time I arrived in Primrose."

"Well, that's all well and good. But I'd still put those away. You never know who might be poking around."

"Maybe you're right," she said.

She led him into the hallway, and he stood very still for a long moment before seeming to position himself inside the front door, as if he had just entered the house. She watched him, puzzled. A frown of confusion passed across his face.

"Is something wrong?" she asked.

"What? Oh, no. No. Of course not. Everything seems so different, that's all, from the way I remember it."

"Well, you were only . . . how old did you say you were when your mother brought you here?"

"Three or four, I guess. Still, I just seemed to recall . . ." He appeared to be struggling with something, looking to his left, toward the wall where the small marble-topped table stood. "But I'm sure you're right, of course. Things always seem so different when you're small. I'm sure that's it."

"This is the music room." She gestured for him to follow her to the left. "Aunt Leila's baby grand. Which she played for half an hour every morning. For Thomas. Even after he died."

"And through there?" Drew seemed anxious now to continue the tour.

"Thomas's study." Abby slid open the pocket doors.

Drew followed her into the room, his eyes darting around as if searching for something before coming to rest on the massive desk.

"Doesn't much fit the image of the adventurer, does it?" Drew noted. "Looks more like the room of a college professor. Or a lawyer."

"By the time he settled down and married Aunt Leila, Thomas had apparently lost his wanderlust. So the story goes." Abby smiled. "Though I've often wondered if that was completely true."

"What do you mean?" he asked.

"Well, I don't know that anyone but a consummate adventurer could have written these."

Abby opened one of the glass-doored cabinets and removed a stack of paperback books.

"The Treasure Seekers." Abby handed him the books and gestured for him to sit at the desk. "Are you familiar with the series?"

"Of course." He took them from her hands. "My grandfather wrote these books."

"He surely did." She smiled.

"Abby, could I have a few minutes to look at these?"

"Certainly. I'll get you a refill," she told him as she took his cup and headed off toward the back of the house.

What a perfectly odd turn of events, she thought. And what a tragically romantic story. As she poured coffee into his cup, she tried to imagine the mysterious woman who had mourned the loss of her beloved Thomas while bravely raising their love child alone.

"These are wonderful stories," Drew told her when she placed the mug on the desk blotter. "Is this the entire set?"

"There may be a few others. I'm not certain."

"Where were they?"

"Excuse me?"

"Where were they? In the room."

"On the third shelf, second cabinet. Why?"

"I just thought, if there were others, they'd be in the same place."

"Those were the only ones on the shelf."

"Where do you suppose he got his ideas?" Drew fanned through the stack, reading the titles aloud. *"The Silver Saddle. The Golden Griffin. The Tears of the Maiden."*

"Well, there is a school of thought that holds that each book was written around an element of truth. That is, that Thomas wove his real-life adventures into his stories. And that he even wrote about treasures he found but did not take."

"How could you find a treasure but not take it?"

"Well, a few years ago, someone claimed to have found a sunken ship off the coast of Georgia by following the clues in one of Thomas's books. The story was that Thomas had located the ship back in the thirties but did not have the resources to raise it. How true that is, only Thomas would know."

"If these books had been written about treasures Thomas had found, where do you suppose they would be? The treasures, I mean." He sifted back through the books and held one up. *"The Tears of the Maiden.* Look at the size of the pearls on the cover, Abby. They look like hens' eggs. Do you know what one pearl that big would be worth?"

"A small fortune, I'm sure." she laughed. "Unfortunately, if in fact he ever found them, he kept it strictly to himself. Or, at the very least, he didn't leave any clues for me to follow. Are you ready for the rest of the tour?"

"Have you looked for any?"

"Any what?"

"Clues."

"Of course not."

"Then how do you know there aren't any?"

"I guess if there was such a thing, Aunt Leila would have told me years ago. Are you ready to move on?"

Drew hesitated for a moment, then stacked the books neatly on the edge of the desk, picked up his cup, and followed her out of the room. As she slid the pocket doors back across the doorway, he asked, "You always keep the study closed up like that?"

"Keeping the room closed up keeps the dust down." She smiled as she crossed the foyer. "This was Aunt Leila's parlor, where she entertained her lady friends at tea."

"Is that her? Your great-aunt?" Drew gestured to the portrait over the mantel.

"No, that was her mother, my great-great-grandmother. Serena Dunham."

"Abigail, who on earth are you talking to?" Belle called out from the morning room.

"Oh, she's awake. Come meet Belle, Drew." Abby motioned for him to follow her. "Belle, you'll never believe this. Guess who this is."

Belle's eyes narrowed as they settled on Drew's face and lingered for a long minute.

"I am sure I do not know," she said pointedly.

"Belle." Abby walked all the way into the room. "This is Drew Cassidy."

"Cassidy, you say?" Belle arched an eyebrow.

"Yes. As in Thomas Cassidy." Abby's eyes twinkled, the scandalous story bubbling within her. "Belle, wait till you hear. Drew is Thomas's grandson."

"Oh, is he now?" Belle's eyes narrowed a notch further. "Is he indeed?"

"His grandmother was a stage actress who was from . . . where, Drew? Chicago, you said? Which is really a coincidence, when you think that Aunt Leila's mother was a stage actress in Chicago at one time. Sometime before the turn of the century, I believe. Which would have been long before your grandmother . . ."

"What year was your father born?" Belle's eyes were now the width of a strand of thread.

"I think it was maybe 1919 or so."

"Really," Belle said flatly.

Her blatant unfriendliness—her not-so-subtle skepticism—was making Drew uncomfortable and Abby annoyed.

"Belle and her husband, Granger, lived across the street for many years. They were very close to Aunt Leila and

Thomas." Abby sought to offer an explanation for Belle's animosity.

"Then you knew my grandfather very well."

"Oh, very well indeed," Belle told him steadily, then turned her attention from him as if he were no longer there. "Abigail, do you think I might have my tea now?"

"Of course, Belle. Drew, would you like to join us?"

"No, no thank you. I've already taken far too much of your time." He looked at his watch. "It was nice meeting you, Mrs. Matthews."

Belle appeared not to have heard.

"I'm going to walk Drew out," Abby told Belle, "and when I come back, I'll make your tea."

Belle dismissed them with a click of the remote control.

"I'm really sorry, Drew," Abby told him as they went through the front door. "I cannot imagine what got into Belle. She's usually much more gracious."

"Well, maybe she's having a grumpy day," he said pleasantly. "At her age, she's entitled."

"Well, I would have expected her to have at least been polite to the grandchild of an old friend."

They walked to his car, which was parked at the end of Cove Road.

"Well, you know, it may have come as a greater shock to her than it did to you, finding out that Thomas had a grandson," Drew told her. "After all, you never knew him, and he was her friend. And your aunt was her best friend, right?"

Abby nodded.

"Well, then, there you go." He held his hands out in front of him as if holding the explanation before her. "I'm sure she felt disloyal to your aunt's memory just by having me in the house."

"You think so?"

"I'm sure that's it."

"Well, I hope she gets over it," Abby told him, "because I'd like you to stop back. It must be like finding a missing piece of yourself, coming to this house, sitting at your grandfather's desk."

"Yes. That's it exactly. Thank you for understanding." He had brightened. "And for letting me see my grandfather's books." He shook his head slowly, as if awed by the experience.

"Look, there must be a complete set of Thomas's books around someplace. If you give me your address, I'd be happy to send them to you if I find them."

"Abby, that's very nice of you. But I'll be traveling the next few months with this new job. But, say, I will be back in Durham at some point over the next few weeks to check on an order. Would it be okay if I stopped back?"

"It would be fine," she assured him. "I'll see what I can find for you between now and then."

"Abby, this has been one of the happiest days . . ." He shook his head as if overcome by emotion.

"I understand. Believe me, I do," Abby assured him, and she stepped back onto the curb so that he could pull away. "You take care," she said as he pulled away.

"You, too," he called through the open window. "And thanks again."

Her smile faded into a grim line as she started back toward the house with a deliberate stride.

Belle had some explaining to do.

◆24◆

"Well, Miz Annabelle Lee Matthews of Primrose, North Carolina." Abby stood in the doorway to the morning room, hands planted firmly on her hips. "I'd surely like to know what that was all about."

"Whatever do you mean, Abigail?" Without glancing from the television screen and the afternoon soap of choice, Belle raised her chin, a movement of the slightest defiance against the interrogation she knew was about to commence.

"You know perfectly well what I mean."

Belle continued to stare at the screen, calmly scratching the back of Meri Puppin's head, but she did not offer a response.

"Belle, why were you so rude to Thomas's grandson?"

"That boy is not Thomas's grandson," Belle pronounced matter-of-factly.

"Belle, why would he come here and say that he is if he isn't?"

"Perhaps there's something of value to be gained by the charade."

"What? Belle, I am working my fanny off just to . . . to . . ." She paused, the words *to get this house in shape to sell it* catching in her throat. It was not time to have *that* discussion with Belle, and no amount of annoyance on her part was going to force a premature disclosure. ". . . to keep things going. There's no money at stake here." At least, Abby thought, not yet.

"Abigail, what he wants or what he is after is another matter entirely," Belle explained with exaggerated patience. "The point is, that boy is no kin to Thomas Cassidy." Belle crossed her thin arms over her chest and resumed her viewing of the daytime drama unfolding on the screen.

"I don't understand your attitude at all. If it's because you feel a certain loyalty to Aunt Leila's memory, I can appreciate the sentiment. But on the other hand, I think we owe it to Thomas to welcome Drew, who has come here seeking his . . . his roots. It's not his fault that his father was born on the wrong side of the sheets, Belle." Perhaps, Abby thought, logic and reason could overcome Belle's obvious emotional rejection of Drew. "Could you please try to put your own theories aside and be a little kinder next time?"

"Next time?"

"Yes. I invited him to come back."

"Why?"

"Because he has every right to be here, Belle. His father's family built this house. When you think about it, he has more of a right to this house than I . . ."

"Don't ever say such a thing!" Belle cut her off sharply.

"Leila preserved this house and everything in it for you, Abigail."

"Leila's family did not build this house, Belle."

"And neither did Drew's."

Abby sighed. "We're getting nowhere with this. Whether you like Drew or not, whether you accept that he's Thomas's grandson or not, he will be back, and I will welcome him. So let's see a little of that gracious Southern hospitality that I know you are capable of, okay?"

With her jaw set solidly, Belle's nose drifted a tad higher in the air. Damn, what a stubborn soul she was! Acknowledging that Belle was not going to agree to offer a personal welcome mat to Drew, Abby shrugged, throwing her hands up in resignation.

"Okay. Enough said. It's time for tea. Would you like strawberry or elderberry jam with your scones today?"

"Elderberry, please." Belle's pert little nose was still in the air, as if sniffing at something unpleasant.

Shaking her head in frustration, Abby headed for the kitchen, Belle's whispered insistence, "That boy is no kin to Thomas Cassidy," hanging in the air between them.

In preparation of her assault upon the room—third bedroom to the right of the stairs, next to Abby's own room but larger in size—Abby had removed the heavy drapes from the three tall arched windows that formed the deep bay overlooking the driveway side of the house. With the windows now bared to the late-afternoon sky, light flooded in, giving a whole new perspective to the room and its furnishings. Abby sat on the dressing-table stool and crossed her arms, one foot tapping unconsciously as she debated her color options for the decor. The two three-quarter-sized beds stood along one wall, an oval marble-topped washstand between them, its mirror caked with years of dust. A tall bonnet chest rose along the short wall near the door, a massive armoire along the wall near the closet. All of the furniture was of darkest mahogany, the bedspreads were white chenille yellowed with age, and the walls were papered with a sallow peach print on a grayed background. Overall, the room was inhospitable and depressing. Abby rubbed her wrists, anticipating yet another week of scraping. Her arms almost ached at the very thought of it.

"So, there you are." Naomi's head peeked around the door frame. "Wow, I hadn't seen this room before. What great light." Naomi drifted into the room and gravitated toward the windows.

"I took those down this morning." Abby nodded to the heap of dark green velvet piled on the floor next to one of the beds. "Just letting in some light makes a big difference in the way the room feels."

"It's wonderful." Naomi nodded. "And those beds with the high carved posts are beautiful."

"Aren't they? I was just trying to decide what to do in here. The peach and dark green really don't do much for the room."

"Ummm." Naomi's eyes darted around the large room. "I'd do this room in a really soft ivory—the walls and ceiling—with ivory lace curtains at the windows. White would be too stark with all this light, and too much color on the walls would detract from the dark natural woodwork and the dark furniture. But ivory would soften the afternoon sun. And then you could use quilts on the beds for color."

"Naomi, I've used quilts on the beds in every room so far."

"Well, you can't have too much of a good thing, especially since you're trying to create the kind of homey warmth that will attract a good buyer. In a house this size, you need all those little touches that make a house seem more welcoming and less formidable." Naomi leaned back against the deep sill of the center bay window. "And, besides, you're lucky to have so many of them. I'd kill to have antique quilts on every bed in my house."

"Well, there are two large trunks filled with them in the attic," Abby told her. "You are welcome to help yourself."

"You have to be out of your mind." Naomi laughed. "Old quilts like these are worth a lot of money. You should actually be thinking about selling them, not giving them away."

"Selling them seems so . . . final. Giving them to you is more like passing them on," Abby said thoughtfully. "Belle said that Aunt Leila doted on Meredy and Sam. I think she would have liked for them to have something of hers."

"Well, I'd think you'd want to keep some for your own children."

"Don't know that I'll ever have any." Abby shrugged. "And I can't see hoarding things for children who may never be born."

"Don't you want a husband, some young ones, some-day?" Naomi seemed to choose her words with care.

"Naomi, every woman doesn't have to marry and have a family to live a successful life." Abby seemed to bristle slightly. "The right career can be very fulfilling. Very rewarding."

"I've no doubt of that. I was asking about what you wanted."

"Why, I want what I have always wanted." Abby's answer was too quick, Naomi thought. Too clipped. "I want to be successful . . . though maybe in my own business this time."

"Owning a business does not preclude having a family, Abby. Millions of women do it. And many do it very successfully, I might add. Surely you know that."

"I don't know that I could do both. I tend to put too much energy into my job. I don't know what I'd have left to offer anyone else."

"The right man, the right job . . . ," Naomi began.

"There's not necessarily a 'right man' for everyone, Naomi. Some of us are just better off going it alone."

"You really believe that?"

"It's worked for me for the past ten years."

"Guess that carves it in stone."

Pointedly ignoring Naomi's last remark, Abby began to

remove the spread from the bed closest to her. Naomi crossed the room to help fold the wide chenille square.

"Well, then, what about Alex?" Naomi asked bluntly.

"What about him?"

"Abigail, are you going to stand there and try to tell me that you do not break into a sweat every time that man looks at you?"

"Is it that obvious?" Abby grimaced.

"Well, you do get the most becoming glow . . ."

"Ouch! Stop!" Abby cringed. "Do you think he's noticed?"

"I think he notices every little thing you do." Naomi grinned.

"Not likely." Abby sat down on the side of the bed. "I'm just his old best buddy, Naomi. His old best buddy who so conveniently is around to take care of his grandmother while he plays big-time lawyer and romances the boss's daughter."

"You sure about that?"

"I'm certain." Abby nodded firmly.

"Then where's she been?"

"What do you mean?"

"The last few weekends he's been here, he's been here alone. Where has Melissa been, if they're so cozy?"

"Her sister is getting married soon, so they've had a few bridal showers, that sort of thing."

"I'm not convinced." Naomi shook her head. "He didn't impress me as a man in love when I saw him at Christmas. He didn't have *that look* when he looked at her."

"Naomi, you are the most hopeless romantic I ever met. Maybe he's not head over heels in love with her, but maybe the thought of marrying the senior partner's daughter is enough to make his heart go pitty-pat. I can't see any man who wants to get ahead turning his back on the kind of doors someone like Melissa could open for him."

"Then what was he doing here this afternoon?"

"Alex wasn't here this afternoon."

"I thought I saw him walking up the drive."

"Oh, that wasn't Alex. That was Drew. I almost forgot." Abby drew her legs up under her and twisted slightly to face Naomi, who was perched on the other bed, one arm wrapped around the high post of the footboard. "Wait till I tell you. Thomas Cassidy's grandson was here!"

"What? I had no idea that he and Miz Cassidy had a child!"

"They didn't. Thomas and another woman—to whom he was not legally wed—had a son. Can you believe it?"

"What a very proper little scandal for Primrose." Naomi chuckled.

"More of a scandal than Belle can cope with, I'm afraid. She refuses to entertain the thought that there could have been such an indiscretion in Thomas's past. Belle was absolutely rude to poor Drew, who had come here with the intention of just looking at the house. He was as surprised to find family still living here as I was to have him show up. But he was charming and so grateful for the opportunity to actually tour the house . . ."

"You gave him a tour of the house?"

"Just the downstairs. The upstairs is, for the most part, off limits to visitors, since it's so torn apart. Why?"

"Do you think that was a good idea? Opening your house to a stranger?"

"He didn't *feel* like a stranger, Naomi. There was something that almost seemed . . . *familiar* about him. And, besides, he's almost like family. You would have done the same thing. I know you, and I know you would have felt the same way."

"Probably." She shrugged. "Why did he come here?"

"To see his grandfather's house."

"Why do you suppose he waited till now? Why not years ago? Why not when Leila was still alive?"

"Drew works for a sporting goods manufacturer. He's been assigned to this area." Abby toyed with the fringe on the bottom of the bedspread, unconsciously braiding several strands together. "Well, I, for one, thought it was an interesting twist. And being pretty much alone myself for so long, I was happy to be able to offer a little bit of family connection—however tenuous—to Drew. Next time, you'll meet him, and you'll see for yourself. I invited him to come back. I hope Belle will be a bit more gracious."

"It's so unlike Belle to be less than charming to a stranger."

"The best I can figure, she's just being protective of both Thomas and Leila. After all, back in their day, illegitimate children were the object of scandal. I'm certain she would do anything to protect the memories of her dearest friends from any such taint."

"Maybe so." Naomi glanced at her watch and rose to leave. "I need to get back across the street. I'm sure the young ones have Colin in a frenzy by now. Sam was really wound up—the storyteller at the library had selected *Where the Wild Things Are* as today's book. Every time Sam hears that story, he becomes a wild thing himself." Naomi chuckled. "Funny, though, you know, when I glanced over, I thought it was Alex standing there," Naomi said over her shoulder as she started down the steps.

"Drew looks nothing like Alex." Abby frowned. "Nothing at all. Though I admit I thought so at first. There's something similar in the way they walk, that's all."

Abby followed Naomi down the steps and unlocked the front door, agreeing to share a coffee break with her friend the next morning. Relocking the door, Abby tried to bring Drew's face into view in her mind's eye to mentally compare it with Alex's. True, they both had brown hair that parted naturally to the right. And they both had brown eyes. Lots of people have brown hair and brown eyes. Alex was taller, Drew was stockier. Alex was more muscular, Drew was older.

And, she mused, her senses suddenly ambushed by the memory of Alex's long, lean body stretched out along the dock, as charming as her surprise visitor had been, he had none of Alex's appeal, none of his casual sexiness.

Still, there had been *something* . . .

Abby paused at the bottom of the steps, trying to put her finger on it, wrestling with some errant fleeting image that had seemed to skip across her inner field of vision.

Perhaps, as she had noted earlier, it *was* just the walk and nothing more.

◆ 25 ◆

". . . so I guess the best thing for me to do is to drive down to the hardware store and see if they have a longer ladder." Alex leaned back in his chair after a hearty Saturday lunch, both arms resting along the arms of the kitchen chair. "Abby . . . Abby?" He leaned slightly to the left, as if to invade her field of vision.

"What?" Embarrassed at having been caught daydreaming, Abby blushed. *At least,* she thought gratefully, *he can't read my mind.*

"I said, the ladder is too short to reach the top of the windows on the second floor. I'm going to Phelps's to see if they have a longer one." He was clearly amused by her discomfiture.

"Oh. I'm sorry. I was . . . ah . . . just thinking," she stammered. *I was just thinking of how adorable you look with all those little curls of paint in your hair.* "About dinner."

"Do you need anything from downtown?" he asked as he began to clear the table of their lunch dishes.

"I don't know. That is, I don't know what to have for dinner." *That was a stupid thing to say,* she chided herself. *You've had the dinner menu planned all week.*

"Oh? Looked like beef Stroganoff, last time I looked in the refrigerator. Beef. Mushrooms. Sour cream." He winked as he went through the door into the kitchen.

Get a grip, she commanded. *You are acting like a lovesick adolescent. Find a way to get over it. Or at least function normally when he's around.*

"You're right." She laughed self-consciously. "I had planned on Stroganoff for tonight. I don't know what I was thinking of."

"Probably all that old dust you're stirring up has gone to your head. It's a beautiful afternoon, Ab. Let's walk downtown."

"If you walk, how will you get the ladder back here? Assuming that they have one. And wouldn't it be easier to call and ask what size ladders they have?"

"Yes, of course. Okay, I admit, I'm only looking for an excuse to take a walk with you. Come on, Ab. You've been cooped up all week, breathing in dust and dirt and who knows what else. Take thirty minutes and get some fresh air."

Just a short thirty-minute walk, she told herself. *I do need the fresh air.* As if to convince herself, she coughed a dry cough. *Alex's right. Too much dust and old plaster, too much dried old wallpaper glue.*

He slowed his pace to match hers as they followed the uneven sidewalk toward the end of Cove Road, toward the center of Primrose.

"Remember old Mrs. Lawrence, Ab?" he asked as they walked past the home of the woman, now surely deceased, who had been a regular guest at Aunt Leila's Sunday teas.

"I certainly do. She was tall and angular and smelled of cloves."

"And she had that dog that used to bark like a demon when we rode past on our bikes."

"A boxer, it was. I remember how she was so proud that she was the only person in Primrose to have a boxer."

"I always wondered what that dog would have done to us if he'd gotten loose."

"Probably the same thing he did to the Marshalls' cat." Abby made a face. "I heard from Aunt Leila that it wasn't pretty."

"I wonder what happened to that dog."

"Died. Just like Mrs. Lawrence and Mrs. Marshall and the Marshalls' cat. Most of the people we knew back then are gone. Except for Belle."

"Naomi's still around," he noted.

"I didn't know her back then. Did you?"

"Not that I remember. She said once that she used to see us around town."

"She told me that, too. I asked her why she didn't join us, and she said . . ."Abby hesitated, recalling Naomi's words.

". . . that we just looked like we belonged together, alone." Alex finished the sentence for her. "And she was right. I never needed anyone's company but yours, Ab."

They walked in silence past three or four houses, then crossed the street.

"Primrose is remarkably the same, don't you think? There are some new shops, but for the most part, the town has changed very little."

"You sound happy about that," she noted.

"I guess I am. Maybe it gives me a certain sense of security to have a constant in my life again."

"What about your job?" she asked. *What about Melissa?* is what she meant.

"I'm very good at what I do," he told her pointedly.

"I'm sure that you are. What I meant was, don't you get a certain amount of satisfaction—of security or self-esteem or whatever—from what you do?"

He seemed to mull over the question before offering an answer. "I get satisfaction when I win a case. If that kind of satisfaction means self-esteem, then I guess I get that, too."

"And security?"

"You don't get that from a job. You get that from . . ." He appeared to struggle. His facial expression hardened.

Abby looked up at him, anticipating the completion of his sentence.

"Who knows where that comes from?" he mumbled, kicking a stone from the sidewalk with a quick, fierce deliberation.

"When I was working for White-Edwards, I felt very secure," she confided. "I was very proud of myself. I had worked hard and deserved every perk, every raise, every bonus, every promotion. I felt as if I had made a very safe little world for myself."

Abby's shoulder brushed against his arm as they walked. She thrust her hands into her pockets to keep herself from looping an arm through his as they strolled along.

"One of the reasons losing my job had hurt so much was that I had really believed it was mine for as long as I wanted it to be mine. That it was something that could not be taken from me unless I wanted to give it up." She cleared her throat.

"Was that naïveté or arrogance? Everyone is expendable."

"Tell me about it." She frowned at the memory of her exit interview. "Well, it's a mistake I won't make again."

"Are you still looking for a new position?"

"Yes. I still have résumés floating throughout half the major cities in the country. And I have a few headhunters looking for me."

"What would you do if a really great offer came in before the house was ready to be sold?"

"Well, I guess I would take the job and hope that the local Realtors could find a buyer for the place in whatever condition it is in by then."

"Won't you miss it? The house, Primrose, Naomi . . ."

"Yes. Of course." She frowned at the obvious, though she herself had not, she realized, given much thought to this aspect of leaving town. "But there's no work for someone like me around here. There's no market for what I do in Primrose."

"Do something else," he suggested.

"Easy for you to say, Mr. Kane, Esquire. Attorneys can find work just about anywhere. With experience in *only* investment counseling, my résumé is a bit thin, sir."

He was about to say something else when they reached the doorway to the hardware store. He put aside whatever thought he'd been about to share and held the door for her. While Alex discussed the availability of a ladder of the required height and arranged for its delivery that afternoon, Abby poked around at the eclectic array of goods for sale. Kitchen gadgets from apple corers to microwave ovens. Shower curtains, bathmats, and toothbrush holders in the latest colors. African violets and flower seeds. Spatulas and barbecue grills, paring knives and Scotch tape.

"Don't you just love stores like this?" Alex grinned as he sorted through a bin of loose nails.

"I do. Almost as much as I love stationery stores," she told him as they walked back outside. "I could fill an afternoon looking at notebooks and writing papers and notepapers and cards and calendars and appointment books—not that I need one of *those* these days," she added ruefully.

"Well, the right position will come along, sooner or later." Alex took her by the arm and led her across the street.

"There's a lot to be said for sooner," she said, enjoying the feel of his hand on her arm. "Where are we going?"

"All of a sudden, I have a craving for a double chocolate ice cream cone." He grinned, steering her through the door of the Primrose Café. "And you'll have strawberry. Single dip. Chocolate sprinkles."

"I can't believe you remember that." Abby laughed.

"You have to be kidding. We did this every day for years." He nudged her, his hand lingering on the small of her back. The small act seemed to both soothe and agitate her.

Soon they were headed back to Cove Road, paper napkins wrapped around the bottoms of the cones to keep the ice cream from dripping onto their hands.

"Look, Ab, they've paved Patton's Road." He pointed to where the once-dirt road angled into Cove.

"I noticed."

"Remember when we used to ride our bikes out to the Point?"

"And just about anyplace else we wanted to go. Bikes

were definitely the prime mode of transportation back in those days. Especially since neither Aunt Leila nor Belle had a car. It was bike it or walk."

"Wonder where those old bikes are now?"

"After all these years, they're rusted and useless, wherever they may be."

"Ummm, I guess." He sighed.

"You're slowing down, Kane." She poked his side. "Not losing momentum, are you?"

"Nah. It just feels good to kind of amble along. It's a nice change of pace for me. Not rushing. Not pushing. Just enjoying the sunshine and the company."

"Well, there'll be plenty of sunshine atop that ladder— which, it appears, is being delivered as we speak." Abby pointed to the pickup that had passed them as they rounded the corner onto Cove Road. "And the company is not likely to change for the rest of the weekend."

"Suits me just fine," he told her. "There is noplace I'd rather be. And, Abby . . ."

"Abby, Abby!" Meredy was jumping up and down on the opposite side of the street.

"Hi, Sweet Pea," Abby called back.

"Someone's at your house, Abby."

"I know, baby. Mr. Phelps is bringing us a new ladder." Abby sighed, wondering what thought Alex'd had that Meredy's enthusiastic pronouncement had pushed aside.

"Are you going to paint?"

"I don't know." Abby frowned, wondering how many good work hours were left in the day. "I had planned to."

"Momma said she was going to get out into her garden today." Meredy was parallel to them across Cove Road, trying to keep up with Abby and Alex by taking two steps to each one of theirs while tugging with pudgy fingers at the dangling ribbons of an overlarge straw hat that threatened to slide from her head. "And she said I could help."

"I like your hat," Abby told her.

"Momma says I have to wear it when I go out into the sun, so's I don't *burn up.*" Meredy repeated her mother's words with the same emphasis as Naomi must have used, and both Abby and Alex smiled at the child's recitation. "Momma says . . ."

"Momma says you are going to talk everyone near to *death,* Meredith Dare Hunter." Naomi appeared at the end of her driveway, a pair of large pruning shears in one hand, a pair of heavy gloves in the other. She smiled and waved to Abby and Alex as they passed by, then shooed her daughter into the backyard, where she could keep an eye on her.

"Well, there's your new ladder." Abby pointed up the driveway before turning back to check the mailbox.

"Can I help you with something?" Alex called.

"I'm just getting the mail," she replied, before looking up and realizing he had spoken to someone beyond her.

Curious, she closed the mailbox and followed Alex around the side of the house.

"Drew!" she exclaimed. "I didn't expect you back so soon."

"I hope that doesn't mean it's *too* soon." He flashed a smile.

"Of course not." Abby smiled back at him.

A very solid pause hung in the air, heavy as a block of concrete, as the two men approached and looked each other over warily.

"Alex . . . *Alex.*" She tugged at his sleeve to get his attention. "This is Drew Cassidy."

"Cassidy," Alex repeated, and for a moment, Abby was uncertain if he was addressing Drew or merely repeating his name.

"Alex Kane," Abby told Drew, "is Belle's grandson."

"I see." Drew extended a hand with little enthusiasm. The two men shook and more or less grunted a greeting of sorts.

"Alex is helping me renovate the house," Abby explained. Then, to Alex, "Drew is Thomas's grandson."

"Thomas who?" Alex's forehead creased into a frown.

"Thomas Cassidy."

"I don't recall that he and Leila had children."

"Leila was not my grandmother." Drew addressed Alex directly.

"Drew's grandmother was a woman Thomas met before he met Leila."

"And did not marry," Drew added.

"I see."

"I hope I'm not intruding on anything." Drew turned to Abby. "I just thought I'd stop by and see if you'd had any luck in locating any more of Thomas's stories."

"Actually, I found three more. Come on into the study, and I'll show you." She motioned for him to follow her.

Alex remained in the driveway and watched, hands on his hips, as Abby and Drew approached the back of the house. As she reached the steps, Abby turned and asked, "Would you like to see Thomas's books?"

"I have work to do," Alex snapped.

"Suit yourself." She shrugged and led Drew into the kitchen, unaware that the man she'd left standing in the middle of her driveway was muttering curses and clenching his fists.

Dinner proved to be an unexpectedly somber event.

Once having invited Drew to look through the additional books she had found in Thomas's library, Abby could not very well have asked him to leave when it came time to sit down at the dinner table. Abby's guest could not have been less popular with the Matthews clan. Alex addressed Drew in short, clipped monosyllables, and Belle ignored his presence entirely. Immediately after dessert, Belle excused herself and retired to her room, claiming a headache. Alex, pleading exhaustion, followed at her heels, throwing one last barb—"I'm sure Drew will be more than happy to help you with the dishes"—over his shoulder as he left.

"Was it something I said?" a faintly amused Drew asked after Belle and Alex had made their exits.

"I doubt it." Abby looked to offer a plausible explanation. "I think Alex is just tired, and I think we both know how Belle feels. I do apologize for them both."

"No apology is necessary," he replied, the very essence of

understanding. "But I do have the distinct feeling that somehow my being here has put Kane's nose out of joint."

Abby stared blankly at him from across the table.

"Your relationship with Alex? . . ."

"Oh. We're old friends."

"That's it? Friends?" Drew raised a questioning eyebrow.

"That's it," Abby assured him. "He's helping me to fix up the house in exchange for me taking care of Belle. Our relationship is strictly platonic." *All too.*

"Then why do I have the feeling that I stepped on his toes just by showing up?"

"I have no idea," she told him, turning her head as she reached for the coffee pot, "but there are no toes to step on."

Abby heard the slight creak of the old bed in Alex's room as he flopped onto the mattress in the room over their heads.

Unfortunately, no toes at all.

✦ 26 ✦

"Well, Mr. Personality." Abby greeted Alex as she strolled into the kitchen for her morning coffee. "Did we sleep away last night's grumpies?"

He turned from the bowl of eggs he was beating for the French toast and glowered at her with brown eyes dark with malice.

"Ooh, I guess not." Abby's eyebrows rose slightly, and her mouth stretched into a grim line as she reached past him for her coffee mug.

"There is nothing I hate more than coming into a messy kitchen first thing in the morning," he said pointedly. "It puts me in a foul frame of mind if I have to wash dishes and clear counters before I can start making breakfast."

"Oh. I'm sorry, Alex." She tried to look contrite for having committed a major infraction of the cook's rules. "I meant to do the dishes last night. I really did, but, you see, Drew wanted to see if we could find some of the notes Thomas would have used to write the *Treasure Seekers* stories, and we just lost all track of time. See, we were going through . . ."

"*Treasure Seekers*. How apropos," Alex muttered dryly as he slid butter into a frying pan and turned the flame on low.

"Just what is that supposed to mean?"

"Gee, what a coincidence that Thomas Cassidy's hitherto unknown *grandson* shows up out of the blue so shortly after the *widow* Cassidy passes away and leaves all to her grandniece. Who happens to be single, beautiful, and bright. Not to mention gullible."

"You sound just like Belle."

"Well, maybe Gran's not quite as dotty as I thought."

"Alex, there is nothing dotty about your grandmother. She has as much of her faculties as you or I have."

"You're half right," he mumbled, slipping several pieces of bread, drippy with egg and milk, into the sizzling butter in the frying pan.

"What does that mean?" Abby challenged him.

"It means that at least *I* have enough sense to know a phony when I see one." Alex gestured at her with the long-handled spatula.

"What is wrong with you? I can understand Belle not wanting to accept Drew—I think she sees this as a stigma against her best friend's name. But you don't know Drew. You don't know what it means to him to find family. Alex, he's had *no one* for so many years. You didn't see his face when he was going through Thomas's papers. He was totally overwhelmed by the experience."

"Overwhelmed by the possibility of finding a fortune, is more likely."

"You are really infuriating, you know that? You have absolutely no reason to believe that Drew is not exactly who he says he is."

"And you have absolutely no reason to believe that he is."

"Why would he say he is if he isn't?"

"Abby, people do a lot of things when they think there is money at stake."

"What money? There is no money here, Alex. Trust me, if there was money lying around here, I'd have found it and spent it by now. Someone other than yours truly would be scraping and painting."

"Have you been looking?"

"Looking for what? Or where?" she chided.

He shooed her away from the front of the stove. "Well, I can't believe you would just open up your house—not to mention Thomas's desk, his *notes,* for cripes's sake—to a stranger."

"Alex, we are talking about notes that a man used fifty years ago to write a series of children's books, not detailed instructions on locating the Holy Grail. We are talking about bits and pieces of papers with little half-sentences or whatever. I think it is enormously touching that Drew is so interested in his grandfather's stories."

"Abby, there was a big magazine article a few years back about Thomas . . ."

She waved him aside with a sweep of one hand. "I know, I know. Some people think maybe Thomas gave clues to finding real treasures in his books. I've heard it before. And I think it's nonsense. Now, it makes sense that if he located something he could not get to—like that sunken ship he found back in the thirties but which was only raised a few years ago—he would have had to leave it. But if you read the books, which I have done, incidentally, you'd know that accessibility was not a problem in ninety percent of the places and things he wrote about. Most of the 'adventures' led to places that were, in fact, accessible—though not without some danger. I mean, otherwise, they wouldn't have been adventures, right?"

"So what are you trying to say?"

"Only that if Thomas knew how to find these so-called treasures, don't you think *he* would have done it? I mean, do you really think he went to all the trouble of tracking down these treasures for the sole purpose of leaving clues for *other* people to follow, instead of doing it himself?"

"How do you know he didn't find the things he wrote about?"

"Where are they, then?" Her fists sought her hips with an air of defiance. "Where are these wonderful things he wrote about, these fabled antiquities you are so certain Drew is plotting to find?"

"I don't know. Maybe they're in your basement. Or your attic. Thomas could have buried it all under the front porch for all I know."

"Why would he do something like that? Why would anybody risk his life to go find something only so that he could take it home and bury it, like a dog buries a bone?"

"Abby, I don't know. But neither do you. And my guess is that Drew is betting that the stories are true. If he can get his hands on Thomas's notes and those notes are legitimate, his little masquerade would be worth every minute he puts into it, wouldn't you say?"

"Alex, this interrogation is starting to get on my nerves. I don't know what your problem is with Drew, and why you are so intent upon finding some nefarious motive where none exists, but I have no problem with him, and, quite frankly, that's all that matters, isn't it?"

"In other words, 'Butt out, Kane, this is none of your business.' Well, Miz Abigail, do forgive me if I seem to have forgotten my place." He tossed the eggshells into the trash with a vicious and well-aimed pitch. "And I do thank you for that well-needed reminder that I am, after all, just the handyman. I promise not to interfere with *your* business again."

"Alex, you are being ridiculous. It's not necessary to . . ."

"Umm, something smells just lovely, Alexander." Belle opened the door just enough to poke her diminutive nose in the direction of the morning's offerings. "I do adore French toast. Alexander, do you remember how your grandfather always made French toast on Sunday mornings? But of course you do, dear. Is the water ready for tea?"

"Almost, Gran. Why don't you go sit at the table and chat

with Abby while I fix it for you? It'll only be a minute." Alex glared meaningfully at Abby.

"Fine. I will go sit with your grandmother while you . . ."

"While I prepare your breakfast, Miz Abigail. After all, that was the deal."

"Alex, you are being an absolute jerk."

He prepared Belle's tea to the proper degree of amber, then, without another word, pushed past Abby to deliver the cup to his grandmother, who was already seated in the morning room awaiting her breakfast.

Now, if that doesn't beat all. Abby shook her head angrily. *What difference could it possibly make to Alex if Drew is or isn't a Cassidy?*

And just what, she wondered, *is eating Alex Kane?*

"I do not recall that you are color-blind," Naomi said pointedly on Monday afternoon after listening to Abby's recitation of the weekend's events. She leaned against the wooden frame of Abby's front door, her dark green vinyl poncho glistening with the large drops of water that ran in rapid streams to puddle at her feet. She had braved the sudden storm to bring Abby the book that had kept her up reading till the early hours of the morning, a "yummy romantic suspense that I guarantee you will not be able to put down."

"I'm not."

"Abby, that man is turning green right under your nose, and you don't even see it." Naomi flinched as yet another crack of thunder bellowed from the heavens.

"Alex?"

"Absolutely."

"You think he's . . ."

"Green as new grass, honey."

"Why would Alex be jealous?"

"Maybe he doesn't like the thought of Drew hanging around here." Naomi attempted to squeeze some excess water from her tangled hair, which was beginning to look more and more like Brillo.

"Drew doesn't hang around here. Saturday was only the second time he was here."

"Does Alex know that? And you greeted Drew like he was the dearest of friends. I saw you from my front lawn, Abby. You looked like you were mighty glad to see him."

"Well, I was. I was happy that he felt comfortable enough here to take me up on my invitation to come back. I know what it's like to feel disjointed, to feel like you have no one. I have been where Drew is, Naomi. I want him to know that he doesn't have to feel that way anymore. That he has family . . ."

"Girl, you may be moving way too fast."

"What do you mean?"

"You don't know anything about this man."

"Good grief, you sound just like Alex. He thinks Drew is an impostor."

"Maybe he is, and maybe he's not. Let's assume that he is Thomas's grandson. That alone doesn't automatically make him a good person." She raised a hand to silence Abby's protest. "You hear me out. He may be a good guy, he may not. The fact is that neither you nor I nor Alex nor Belle knows one way or another. Time will tell what's what. In the meantime, certainly, be pleasant to him, leave the welcome mat out. But don't start handing over any of the Cassidy family silver, you know what I mean?"

Abby nodded. "Naomi, do you realize you're the first person who has had anything to say on the subject who has made sense? Belle cannot be objective, and Alex is being positively obnoxious."

"Jealousy will do that." Naomi nodded, a satisfied grin crossing her face.

"You really think that's it?"

"There is not a doubt in my mind. Abby, those two were circling each other like a couple of suspicious old dogs. I mean, it was all I could do not to stand at the end of my driveway and yell, 'Why don't you two just sniff each other's butt and get it over with?'" Naomi grinned.

"But, Naomi," Abby said when she had stopped laughing

at the image Naomi had conjured up, "why would it matter to Alex? He has Melissa."

"Umm, well, we don't know what he's got going with her, now, do we? He's been spending a lot of time in Primrose these past few weeks, and Melissa has been nowhere in sight."

"Alex said she's busy with the preparations for her sister's wedding."

"And just when is that little event to take place, do you know?"

"In two weeks."

"Well, I guess after that, we should get a pretty good idea of just where Miss Melissa stands."

"What do you mean?"

Naomi grinned over her shoulder as she opened her umbrella and started down the steps. "She'll either be here with him in three weeks, or she won't."

✦27✦

"Come on, Abby. Let's take a walk out back and see what we can do about resurrecting Leila's garden. It's a gorgeous day, much too wonderful to waste indoors, and, besides, you've been breathing too much stale air and plaster dust for far too long." Naomi stood and stretched out her stiff leg. Grabbing an old sweater from a hook by the kitchen door and tossing it to Abby, she pointed toward the backyard. "I, for one, cannot wait to see what is lurking under the vines and the weeds." She followed Abby through the doorway and down the steps. "I do know that at one time, Miz Cassidy's garden was the talk of Primrose."

Naomi led the way down the worn path that bisected the immense yard.

"Oh, look." She knelt and, beckoning Abby to join her,

gently nudged aside some green leafy things growing in what had once been Leila's prized perennial bed.

"What am I looking at?" Abby frowned.

"Old-fashioned geranium." Naomi fingered leaves of green filigree. "Beautiful. It's a wonder they survived all these weeds and the overgrowth of clematis and morning glory and sweet pea that you have here, not to mention the plantain and the dandelions. What a mess. Ooh, look here. Lily of the valley. Purple violets. Some old roses. What's this . . . shasta daisies, maybe? And oh, Lord, peonies. Abby, you have to get these uncovered. The vines must be two or three feet thick over these peonies. It's a wonder they haven't been choked to death down there."

On and on Naomi went, from one bed to another, carefully parting the weeds, seeking out the remnants of Leila's garden, punctuating her survey from time to time with "Wow! Columbine!" or "Rose campion, thick as grass!" Abby trailed behind, trying to share Naomi's enthusiasm, attempting to distinguish the treasures from the trash and memorize the names and foliage of the specimens displayed before her.

"I'll never remember all this," Abby finally said with a sigh.

"Of course you will," Naomi assured her. "Once everything blooms and you can see the flowers, you'll remember. Look here, Abby, this must have been Leila's herb garden."

Naomi tugged at the thick web of vines that grew atop the entire bed along the right side of the path.

"Leila must have loved lavender. Why, there is an absolute mass of it!" Naomi exclaimed.

"Lavender was Aunt Leila's favorite fragrance," Abby told her. "She wore it as perfume, scented her drawers and all the closets with it—even the bed linens and the tablecloths. She had sprigs of it in the trunks in the attic and the clothes in storage. The scent still lingers in her bedroom and her sitting room. Why, sometimes, I even imagine I catch a whiff of it here and there throughout the house."

"This will be absolute heaven when it blooms." Naomi

beamed. "Umm, just think of the potpourri you can make, with all this lavender and the roses you'll have after we rescue them from that canopy of clematis." Frowning, Naomi tugged at a thick vine, following its length to where it sank into the earth at the root. "Honestly, for something so fragrant, this stuff sure is a pain in the neck."

"What is it?"

"Honeysuckle. It is all wrapped around everything and everywhere and all intermingled with the clematis and the morning glory and sweet pea." She stood and shook her head. "It is like vine-o-rama out here. It will take us forever to sort this stuff out."

"Us?" Abby asked hopefully.

"With all this wonderful stuff"—Naomi waved her arm in a sweeping gesture—"waiting to be uncovered, do you honestly think I would turn an amateur like yourself loose to work out here alone? You, who do not know dandelion from delphinium, will be closely supervised, at least until you pass the first and most basic identification test."

Abby laughed and followed behind Naomi, who was clearly in her glory.

"I cannot get over the variety of herbs, Abby. Anise, lemon balm, chamomile, red sage, rosemary, echinacea," Naomi whispered as she uncovered yet another leafy plant. "Abby, do you think Miz Cassidy may have been an herbalist?"

"Well, obviously, she grew herbs . . ."

"I think she may have grown them to use for medicinal purposes. I can't think of one other reason why she would have this combination of plants, if she wasn't into natural healing." Naomi nodded slowly, a tiny smile just starting at the corners of her mouth. "Wouldn't that just beat all?"

"Well, I know she always used the herbs from her garden for seasoning—basil, dill, rosemary . . ."

"And teas? Didn't she ever give you teas when you were sick?"

Abby sat on an old stone bench which was partially obscured by overgrown vegetation.

"I remember one summer when I had a really vile chest cold." Abby frowned, trying to recall. "She gave me some really odd-smelling hot tea to drink. She said it would take the fever down quickly."

"Well, just looking around at the variety of herbs, that tea could have been just about any one of these—yarrow, red sage, peppermint." Naomi folded her arms over her chest. "It looks like your aunt had a regular little home pharmacy here."

"Belle said Leila had some gardening journals," Abby recalled. "I should find them and see if she left any notes."

"I'll bet she did." Naomi's eyes sparkled. "And I can't wait to get my hands on them."

"Are you serious?"

"Am I ever! I am a true believer in herbal therapy."

"You mean for colds and fevers."

"I mean for just about anything that ails you."

"I wasn't aware that we had a healer in the neighborhood," Abby teased.

"It's no joke, Abby. Oh, I admit that I used to make fun of my grandmother when I was young. She always had the answer to everyone's problems in some ground-up powder in a tiny glass jar." Naomi shook her head ruefully. "All those years, I thought my grandmother had just been into the Native American thing, you know? After my accident, I learned just how powerful those powders were."

The two women walked slowly among the tangle of plants reaching out from either side of the path, Abby waiting expectantly for Naomi to continue.

"Oh, comfrey, nice." She broke her stride to lean over and touch the leaves of yet another plant. "Did I tell you I almost lost my leg to gangrene after the accident?"

"No. Oh, my God, Naomi. That must have been terrible."

"I'll tell you what was terrible." Naomi frowned at the memory. "It was terrible knowing that the doctors just sort of accepted it. 'Oh, we tried to treat it, but we've failed. Guess we'll have to take the leg off.'"

"No doctor said that!"

"Of course not, but that was the attitude. 'We can't cure it, so we'll have to cut it off.'" Naomi broke into a grin. "They did not, however, reckon on my Nana Dare showing up with her little satchel of powders and poultices."

"Your grandmother cured your gangrene?"

"Now, sugar, does *this* look like an artificial leg to you? Now, it may get stiff, and the knee sometimes locks up, but, by God, it's all mine."

"What did she use?"

"A poultice of charcoal, some herbs, whole wheat flour, God knows what else."

"And the doctors let her do this in the hospital?"

"There was no way they were going to stop her." Naomi chuckled. "Of course, when my leg started to improve, they took the credit for the cure. But I knew what saved my leg. And let me tell you, as soon as I started to come around, I sat down with my grandmother and picked her brain, wrote down everything she could tell me. What plants for what ailments. What for teas, what for ointments. What parts to use, what to grind into powders. I could write a book, Abby." She brightened. "I *should* write a book."

"You really believe in all of this, don't you?"

"Abigail, what were the gifts brought to the Christ child by the Magi? Gold, frankincense, and what?" Naomi tapped her foot impatiently on the hard dirt path. "Diamonds? Sapphires? No, my dear, it was much more valuable. Gold, frankincense, and *myrrh.*"

"What is myrrh, anyway?"

"It's a gum resin, actually. And a natural antiseptic, for one thing. Useful in treating everything from gum disease to infection." She laughed and added, "They didn't call them wise men for nothing, Abby."

"Well, I'm intrigued. And the first thing I will do after lunch is find that journal of Aunt Leila's and see if your theory is correct."

"Which you will, of course, promptly share with your best friend." Naomi draped a casual arm over Abby's shoulder as they walked to the side of the house. "I guess Miz Cassidy didn't much practice her little hobby those last few years, but I sure wish I'd known about this while she was still alive. I'd have loved to talk with her about it. I'd love to know, for one thing, who her teacher was."

"Aunt Leila probably learned from her mother." Abby paused at the edge of the garden and thought of the elegant woman whose portrait hung in the parlor. "Or maybe from her grandmother, who was a full-blooded Cherokee. And that whole side of the family—the Dunhams, the Hollisters—all lived out in Montana in the middle of *nowhere.*" Abby recalled her trips out west as a child, and her fascination with the ranch and the endless valley her cousins called home.

"Well, right there you have the ways and the means and the need," Naomi said. "Your—what would she be, great-great-grandmother?—would have been familiar from an early age with the healing properties of plants. And being in an isolated area like that, where traditional medical treatment must have been almost impossible to get, there would have been times when the survival of her family would depend on her expertise—colds, flus, fevers, not to mention snakebite, bone fractures . . ." Naomi looked at her watch and frowned. "Too bad it's so late, or I could help you look. I'm going to have to pick up Meredy in about fifteen minutes at school, and from there, I have to run on out to my sister's to pick up Sam. He's been playing with my nephew this morning, and I guess he'll be about ready to come home and have his nap by now. But I'll be home later this afternoon. Give me a call if you find Leila's journal. And don't do anything in the garden—and I mean *not one thing*—until I can come back to work with you. You don't know what you've got there, so leave it alone until I can help you to sort it out."

"Belle," Abby asked over lunch, "you wouldn't happen to know where Aunt Leila kept her garden journal, would you?"

"I believe she used to keep it in her sitting room. The one off her bedroom. Probably on or in that table in the alcove." Belle put her soup spoon down and eyed Abby curiously. "Thinking about taking up gardening, are you?"

"I'm thinking of cleaning up that mess out back," Abby told her. "If what I have left resembles a garden, I think we'll be lucky."

The scent of lavender was particularly strong in Leila's sitting room. Odd, Abby mused, how at different times the scent was stronger or weaker. Maybe it had something to do with the temperature of the air.

She found the journal, a thick notebook with a heavy dark green leather cover, on a small table next to Aunt Leila's reading chair. Abby sat down and carefully thumbed through its yellowed pages. She only needed to read a few entries to realize that Naomi had been right. Aunt Leila had had a thorough knowledge of herbs and their medicinal properties. For each plant, Leila had drawn a sketch of the leaves and flowers and, in her small, precise script, had jotted down the usable parts of the plant and how to use it to treat which ailment. Fascinated after having read but a few pages, Abby decided to take the notebook outside to see if she could identify any of the plants from the carefully drawn pictures.

Because of the dense growth around the herb bed, Abby had to pull some weeds—she hoped they were only weeds—before she could test her new knowledge. Leila's sketches were, she found, accurate to the most minute detail, and Abby had no difficulty distinguishing between the geranium and the valerian, the lobelia and the tansy, which grew in a huge clump covered with morning glory. Abby put the book down on the bench and proceeded to extract the vines from the tall, leafy stalks of the herb. Before she knew it, she had spent the better part of the afternoon carefully cleaning up first one section, then another, of Aunt Leila's herb garden.

The lengthening shadows from the pines told her that the day had, for the most part, passed. She chucked the unwanted greenery into the trash, then walked back to the stone bench to retrieve the notebook. She sat for a second to survey the yard, her mind's eye seeing things as they had been, so many years ago, when tending the beds had been Leila's most welcomed task and the results of her labors brought joy to all who strolled the old brick paths.

It could be beautiful again. It might even be fun. And, if nothing else, surely the restored garden would enhance the value of the property when selling time came around. She'd read somewhere that most real estate purchases were made first on an emotional level. Who, she mused, could resist such a lovingly renovated house, one that boasted so lovely a garden?

For the first time, she tried to picture what the new owners might be like. She prayed the new mistress would not be a pert little blond thing with a turned-up nose.

◆28◆

"Abby, for crying out loud, what did you do?" Having responded to Abby's frantic phone call just as the supper hour concluded, Naomi now stood, hands on her hips, before the chair in which a miserable Abby sat and scratched at her burning arms and legs and everywhere the burning itch had spread like wildfire. "You were weeding in the herb bed, weren't you?" The question bore the distinct ring of an accusation.

"And you had your face in the tansy." Naomi leaned over and peered at Abby's lips, which had swollen to twice their normal size. "Didn't I tell you to leave that bed alone until I could work with you?"

Abby nodded in the affirmative. "I thought it was because you were afraid I'd weed out the wrong things," Abby wailed, "but I found Aunt Leila's book and used the pictures as a guide. I only pulled out the grass and the dandelions."

"And stirred up the chiggers, by the looks of your neck and arms."

"Chiggers?"

"The scourge of the Southern gardener," Naomi told her. "Little red bugs—mites, actually—that hatch in the ground and wait for some unsuspecting host to come along and offer them dinner. That's what raised those itchy welts all over you. Burn like nobody's business, don't they?"

"How do I get rid of them?"

"They'll drop off when they've had their fill."

"Oh, that's encouraging. So, meanwhile, I just sit here and play lunch counter to a flock of bugs I can't even see."

"Go take a shower, then rub this on the welts." Naomi handed Abby a dark blue glass jar half-filled with a pleasant-smelling ointment. "My, you do have a lot of them, don't you?"

"Do I put this on my lips, too?"

"No, sugar. You owe your fat lips to sticking your face into the tansy. If you are one of the unfortunate ones who are sensitive to it—and, obviously, you are—it can cause a nasty contact dermatitis. I'll have to bring you something special for that. In the meantime, run up and get out of those clothes, and take a warm shower. Dab the bites with the aloe"—she pointed to the jar—"after you have dried off. I'll be back in half an hour, and we'll try to work on those lips."

The warm water felt good, but Abby emerged from the shower every bit as itchy as she was when she went in. The light gel Naomi had given her did, however, soothe the sting. She put on a nightshirt and went downstairs to wait for Naomi's return.

"I will never forget the one and only time I got that close to tansy," Naomi told her as she put a tea kettle of water on the stove to boil. "My bottom lip blew up so big, I scared the bejesus out of Meredy. She thought I looked like a circus clown."

"Why would anyone grow that stuff if it does this to you?"

"Everyone doesn't react to it. Now, my sister can go all day with her face right in it and never have a problem. Of course, she doesn't get poison ivy, either, now that I think about it."

"Well, my lips are *throbbing,* so whatever cream you brought with you, give it to me now, please," Abby begged, "and we'll worry about making tea later."

"Abby, I am not making tea. I am boiling water to make an infusion." Naomi pulled an envelope out of the pocket of her jeans and dumped some gold and green dust into a bowl.

"Oh, wait, let me guess. An herbal cure?" Abby looked horrified. "Thanks, but no thanks. I think I've had enough close encounters with the plant world for one day."

"Abby, there is only one treatment I know of for the reaction you have had, and it's in this bowl." Naomi tapped the blue and white pottery bowl with her index finger.

"I think I need a dermatologist."

"Abby, you need what's in this bowl."

"What is it?" Abby sniffed suspiciously.

"Myrrh and golden seal."

"Of course. The miracle drugs for the next millennium."

"Scoff now if you must." Naomi poured boiling water into the bowl, then added cold tap water to cool it down. "But you'll thank me in the morning."

"If I live till morning," Abby muttered. "If I haven't scratched myself to shreds clawing at the chigger bites. Or ripped my bottom lip right off my face."

"Are you finished whining, Abigail?" Naomi asked with all the patience of a mother of two small children.

"I guess." Abby grunted. "What are you going to do with that stuff?"

"First, we make a compress." Naomi dipped a cotton pad into the liquid.

"And then what?" Abby asked, her head tilted back as Naomi spread the warm, soothing compress on her hugely swollen bottom lip.

"Then you drink what's left over."

"Ugh!" Abby groaned at the thought of swallowing the watery, pea-green substance.

"Trust me." Naomi laughed at the face Abby made. "It

works. I swear it does. You'll feel one hundred percent better in the morning."

And actually, she did. Although Abby's bottom lip was still swollen, the compresses she made with Naomi's herbal powder soothed the discomfort. And the chigger bites, while still a distinct presence, had lost a lot of their sting with the application of the aloe gel.

"I told you you'd thank me in the morning." Naomi chuckled as she placed a peace offering of still warm banana bread on Abby's kitchen table.

"I can't believe how much better I feel," Abby admitted. "But I also can't understand how—or, for that matter, why—anyone gardens around here, with those damned little bugs lurking in the leaves."

"Chiggers lurk in the dirt, actually. Before you venture out into the garden again, cover yourself with this." Naomi handed Abby a plastic bottle of bath oil spray. "And I mean *cover* yourself. That should take care of the chiggers. And as far as the tansy is concerned, now that you know how you react to it, keep your face out it. Once you know what to avoid, you can garden to your heart's content and not have to worry."

"I think my heart would be more content if I stuck to the inside jobs."

"Nonsense. You'll learn how to protect yourself, and you'll go about your business."

"I don't know, Naomi. I'm starting to think if God had wanted me to garden, he wouldn't have had me living in cities all these years."

Naomi laughed. "As soon as the swelling goes down and your bottom lip returns to its normal size, you'll forget all about it."

"I doubt it. And how long before you think this will go away?"

"The swelling? A few days."

"A few days?" Abby bellowed. "It's Thursday. Alex will be here tomorrow night."

"Sorry, sugar. Just keep using the compresses . . ."

"I'll bet if I called a dermotologist . . ."

"It would take you a week to get an appointment, and he'd charge you next week's grocery money to tell you that you've had an allergic reaction, topical in nature, to avoid contact with the subject plant . . ."

"Okay, okay," Abby grumbled. "But I should report you for practicing medicine without a license."

"What's wrong with your face?" was the first thing Alex said when Abby opened the front door on Friday night.

"I had a little run-in with some unfriendly specimens in Aunt Leila's herb garden," she muttered, tucking her chin into her chest to obscure, as much as was possible, her reddened neck and cheeks and her still swollen lips.

Certain she resembled Quasimodo, Abby resolved to stay out of Alex's line of vision as much as possible for the weekend—or at least until the swelling of her mouth subsided somewhat. She ate dinner with her head down and made herself an extra-early breakfast so she wouldn't have to face him across the table. She would skip lunch, she told herself. Then, maybe by dinner, the swelling would be that much less apparent.

Abby had dragged the ladder into the alcove in the bedroom where she'd been working for the past week and set up to scrape the section of wall above and around the windows, the last bit of scraping in this particular room. Naomi had been exactly right, she thought. The ivory she had suggested would just perfectly reflect the light, and when the sun began to set . . .

The *tap-tap-tap* on the window, somewhere around her midsection as she stood upon the ladder, drew her attention downward. She leaned over and found herself face to face with Alex, who, atop his own ladder, was preparing to scrap the frayed paint from the outside the window frames.

"Hi." He grinned. "Missed you at lunch."

"I wasn't hungry." She pretended to concentrate on the business of spraying water on the last bit of paper clinging to the wall.

"Hey, Ab."

"What?" She refused to look at him.

"Nice lips."

Abby lowered the spray bottle and shot through the screen squarely into his laughing eyes.

It had been an agonizing weekend, start to finish, she later confided to Naomi. Alex had progressed from being merely annoying on Saturday afternoon to being sarcastic on Saturday evening to being a downright pain in the butt by Sunday morning. He had seemed to latch on to the Drew thing, as Abby thought of it, and would no sooner let go than Mrs. Lawrence's boxer would have dropped the Marshalls' cat. For the first time since returning to Primrose, Abby had been glad to see his car pull out of the driveway to head back to Hampton.

"Alexander called from the airport while you were in the shower," Belle said pointedly as Abby set the table for dinner on Thursday evening. "He was on his way to Atlanta. For what's-her-name's sister's wedding."

"That's nice." Abby shrugged, and Belle merely glared at her in return.

Abby insisted to herself that she was, in fact, *glad* he would not be there to torment her that weekend. But as the day wore on, and Thursday slid into Friday, and Friday night approached Saturday morning, she found herself dwelling more and more on the goings-on in Georgia.

Unable to sleep, Abby grudgingly got out of bed to look for a book she'd been reading earlier in the week. After climbing back into bed, she plumped the pillows up behind her and tried to snuggle into the mattress to make a cozy reading spot. Before too long, she realized, she had made herself all too cozy. Her eyes fluttered helplessly, and she nodded off to sleep. Soon some perversity of her subconscious had transported her, to her horror, smack into the wedding reception, where she, invisible, could view the lavish festivities without being seen. It was, she realized, just like being the proverbial fly on the wall.

She could see them at the wedding reception, in the grand ballroom of some Southern manse completely decorated in white for the occasion. A thin, white, ghostly mist swirled around the scene. The tables were all adorned in white lace cloths which draped luxuriously onto the thick white carpet beneath the feet of the party-goers. Tall white centerpieces—lilies and stephanotis and roses—graced every table, and all the guests were wearing white. Among white-garbed relatives, a beaming Melissa wound her way, snaking through the crowd with a smiling Alex in tow. Her low-cut gown of white satin was buoyed by rings of hooped slips. All the relatives expressed their approval of Melissa's catch by patting Alex on the back and stuffing large legal-sized envelopes into his white leather briefcase. Though no one spoke, it was clear from the smiling faces that the entire gathering was witnessing the silent announcement that Melissa and Alex's wedding would be the next cause for such a gathering. The happy couple seemed to float in slow motion, and Abby could see every little crease on his face— the laugh lines around his eyes and mouth, the little valleys that ran across his forehead and deepened when he slipped into thought.

Alex turned his head slightly as if looking into the lens of a camera, gazing past Melissa, past the crowd pressing in on him and his intended, to peer with piercing, deliberate eyes into Abby's own, mocking her with a grim satisfaction. Soon, Melissa and the others spotted her, and, with open mouths from which no sound was uttered, like watching a television movie with the sound off, they all turned to Abby, who now was, in fact, a fly on the wall, and began to swat at her with flaying arms, driving her up toward the ceiling and through the first open window.

She awoke with a start, her heart pounding and her body in a sweat of anger, the sheets tightly clenched and twisted in her fisted hands.

"*Damn you* anyway, Alex," she growled to the darkness, and she turned over fiercely, punching her pillow and wishing it was his face.

She tossed miserably for the next hour, and when it was clear that there would be no more sleep that night, she got out of bed. She opened the window overlooking the back-yard and leaned out, taking the still air into her lungs. In the moonlight, she could see the outline of the garden she would bring back to life, picturing it in June with roses winding over the fences and the flower beds alive with color. The image soothed her, as did the moment's whiff of lavender that drifted into her room through the open window.

She rested both arms on the sill and watched as yesterday and tomorrow met in the briefest of passings before merging into the new day. The moon stood large and proud in the predawn sky, the sun still only the merest promise below the horizon. All below was still and silent as Primrose lay tucked in a snug wrap of predawn sleepiness. The thought of being here, in this house, in this town—miserable though she might be at this moment—comforted her. She would rather be miserable in Primrose, she acknowledged as she climbed back into her bed, than anywhere else on earth. There was no other place where anyone cared if she hurt or if she laughed, if she succeeded in a task or failed. There were no hands that reached to help her but those here in Primrose. Belle and Naomi cared deeply for her, and she for them. Even the house seemed to welcome her every time she returned from even the shortest errand. She drew the blankets up as if to hide from the very dearness of it all.

For the first time in ten years, Abby felt at home. That it all felt so comfortable, so right, filled her with the greatest sense of peace and the most bittersweet sense of belonging. How, she wondered, would she say good-bye, once the time came, to those who had come to mean so much?

◆29◆

The sound of the car door drew Abby's attention from the thin line of ivory paint she had just traced around the ceiling in the alcove. She poked her head out the window just as Drew rounded the back of the dark blue sedan parked in front of the house. In spite of the fact that company was the last thing she wanted, she did her best to put a trace of cheer in her voice as she called down a greeting.

He stood on the grassy strip between the street and the sidewalk, shaded his eyes from the mid-afternoon sun with his right hand, and looked up to follow her voice and locate which of the many windows she occupied.

"I'll be right down," she told him.

After lining her tools up across the shelf at the top of the ladder, Abby wiped her hands on a paint rag and rested her brush carefully across the top of the can. She bounced down the steps and out the front door.

"This is a nice surprise," she said with a smile, realizing she did, in fact mean it.

"Surprise?" he asked. "Does that mean that Belle forgot to tell you I called?"

"You spoke with Belle?"

"Yes. Last evening. She said you were outside with Naomi, and I told her not to bother to call you in but to let you know that I wanted to stop by and take you to dinner tonight. I left a number at my hotel room for you to call if you were unable to make it. When I didn't hear from you, I assumed that it was a go." He was clearly embarrassed. "I guess she just forgot to tell you."

"If Belle forgot, it was by choice."

Drew laughed good-naturedly. "Well, some people do become a bit absentminded when they get to a certain age."

"Belle's absentmindedness appears to be strictly at her convenience," Abby grumbled, "but it's kind of you to stick up for her. Particularly when you've driven all the way out here and I'm a mess."

"Well, how long could it take to clean up? Would an hour be enough?"

"That would be perfect. Are you sure?"

"Positive. It's not a problem. As a matter of fact, I'll use the time to take a drive around and see if I can find a likely spot for dinner. Unless, of course, you have a favorite place."

"Please." She laughed. "The only 'dining out' spot I've

seen since I moved here is the Primrose Café. But Naomi
mentioned a restaurant out on the Point—I could call her
and get the name of it if you like."

"I've some time to kill." He shrugged. "I'll just drive out
and see if we need reservations."

"Sounds great." Abby smiled. "I'll see you in an hour."

She took the steps two at a time and hurried into the
house. First, she called Naomi and told her she'd be out that
evening and Belle would be home alone for a few hours.
Then Abby went into the kitchen, prepared dinner for Belle,
and proceeded to serve her in the morning room.

"Aren't you joining me, Abigail?" Belle asked.

"Now, Belle," Abby said sweetly as she plumped the
pillow behind the tiny woman's back, "you know I'm
having dinner with Drew tonight. Don't you remember, we
talked about it last night?"

"Why, no, I don't recall . . ." Soft tinges of pink spread
slowly across Belle's cheeks as she realized she had been
caught.

"Belle Matthews, you should thank your lucky stars that
your memory is as good as it is," Abby reproved the older
woman.

"Whatever do you mean, Abigail?" Belle sniffed indignantly, rapidly recovering, Abby noted with a tiny smile,
from her momentary embarrassment.

"You know perfectly well what I mean. Your mind is as
sharp as a tack, and you should be grateful, instead of
slipping into your dotty old lady routine whenever it suits
you."

"I am a dotty old lady." Belle's chin notched a tad higher.
"I'll be ninety years old in August. I'm entitled . . ."

"Belle, I am closer to being dotty than you are." Abby
leaned down to gaze into Belle's clear blue eyes. "I would
appreciate getting my phone messages. However, in the
event that your mind is faltering, as you sometimes claim it
to be, I'll leave a pen and pad of paper by the phone, so you
can write down who called and their number. And in the
meantime, I'm going up to take a shower."

"Abigail . . ." Belle hesitated, as if debating with herself, then simply added, "Have a nice dinner."

"Why, thank you, Belle. I'm sure I will." Abby smiled and, realizing she was now down to half an hour before Drew returned for her, sprinted up the steps.

"Oh, dear." Belle exhaled soundly. "This isn't at all what we'd planned. Mercy me, Leila, things would appear to be drifting a bit off course . . ."

It took Abby the full thirty minutes and a few more to get the paint off her skin and out of her hair, but she managed to be dressed and ready to go at six-thirty, when she heard Drew's car pull up and park on the quiet street. She ran down the steps, kissed Belle good-bye, laughing as Belle's eyebrows raised when she surveyed the short skirt Abby had chosen to wear, and met Drew on the porch just as he was about to ring the doorbell.

"Wow, don't you look great!" he exclaimed as she stepped out onto the porch.

"Amazing what a little soap and water will do, isn't it?" She laughed as she locked the front door behind her.

Drew fell in step with her on the sidewalk. "Abby, I never realized you had legs. You shouldn't keep them hidden in those baggy jeans all the time."

Abby laughed, blushing in spite of herself, trying to recall the last time anyone had complimented her on her appearance. Alex, it occurred to her, had called her beautiful not so very long ago, but, of course, that had been part of his chastisement regarding Drew, so she was certain it didn't count. Still, he had said "beautiful" . . .

". . . and the view is beautiful," Drew was saying.

"What?"

"I said, I stopped at the Point—that's the name of the restaurant—and reserved a table with a beautiful view of the Sound," Drew repeated.

"Oh. It sounds wonderful."

They rode in the silence that accompanies new relationships until the car turned onto Point Road, which followed the curve of the water's edge from the outskirts of Primrose to the place where the river met the Albemarle Sound. The boaters, drawn by the clear skies and warm breezes of an early spring day, sailed or sped past them on their left, their lights blinking like so many fireflies over the darkening carpet of water upon which they floated.

Before long, Abby and Drew were being led to their table overlooking the cove, from which they admired many of the same boats, some of which were tying up at the dock provided outside the restaurant and unloading their small crews to dine at the casual tables under the pavilion next to the dock. The outside area was defined by strings of multicolored lights that led from the waterfront to the tables, much the way balloons would decorate a children's party. The tables themselves wore jaunty red cloths in keeping with the informality of the outdoor dining room. Abby noticed that many of the boaters seemed to know one another, and a large group had gathered around the outside bar, where they ordered drinks in tall plastic tumblers, munched salsa and tortilla chips, and swayed in time with the reggae band that was just warming up.

Inside, in the more formal dining room, Drew and Abby scanned the menu, eyeing the many seafood specialties. At the recommendation of the friendly waitress, they ordered soft-shell crabs ("Just in about two hours ago," she assured them) and sat watching as the last elongated fingers of the sun's glow painted the orange of the horizon with thick purple swirls.

"What a treat this is," Abby said brightly as their food was served by the perky waitress. "To have a night out. Eating lovely food and wearing something other than my painting clothes."

"I'm glad you're enjoying it." Drew smiled.

"I am," she told him, and meant it. It *did* feel good to put on pretty clothes and go someplace in the company of a good-looking, pleasant man who was obviously happy to share her company.

"Well, I was hoping to have some time to just sit and talk

with you, Abby," he said. "I wanted to get to know you better."

"Why don't you tell me about yourself?" Abby poked at her salad with her fork in search of the mushrooms she suspected lurked beneath the curly lettuce.

"Well, I don't know that that's a very interesting story." He looked slightly uncomfortable and shifted in his seat.

"Where did you grow up?"

"I grew up in New Jersey. Center of the state. Plainsboro," he told her. "It used to be all farms, for as far as you could see, when I was a boy. Now it's all housing developments and office complexes and shopping malls."

"That's progress for you."

"Much more progress in that area, and they'll have to think up a new state nickname," he told her, "because it won't be the Garden State anymore."

"Did you go to school in the area?" Abby asked, as much out of curiosity as to keep the conversation moving.

"For a while." He paused briefly, his eyes flickering as if distracted by something on the opposite side of the room. "Before my mother remarried and moved to Boston."

"Did you move with her?"

"No. Her new husband had no interest in raising someone else's son. I went into foster care. The first of several go-arounds with the social service system." He tried to smile, but his mouth seemed to tighten into a straight line.

"That must have made a difficult first few years for you. Especially since you were an only child. Having a brother or sister might have made it easier." She looked across the table, and he wore the look of one who was about to speak. When he did not, she asked, "Were you going to say something?"

"Ah . . . no. I mean, yes . . . here's the waitress with our dinners."

Abby leaned back in her chair, wondering what he was really going to say.

"In any event"—she shrugged it off and continued on her own line of thought—"I often wish that I had had someone—a sister, a brother. I think it would have helped me so much to have had someone when my parents died."

"It is tough to be alone when your world is falling apart." He nodded grimly.

"How old were you when you lost your father?" Abby asked.

"Three. That was when we came to Primrose. After my father died. I guess my mother felt there was nowhere else for her to turn. She said that my father used to talk about how his grandfather was a wealthy man who lived in a big house near the water. I guess she figured she'd try to track him down and see what she could get out of him."

He paused for a moment as if collecting his thoughts. "I remember walking in through that grand front door. The house looked like a palace to me. My mother sat me down on a wooden seat with mirrors all around it. We didn't stay real long . . ." He appeared to struggle with some thought or other he wasn't sure he could share. Whatever it was, it flickered across his face and disappeared as quickly as it had come.

"Not too long after that, my mother remarried for the first time. That didn't work out so well, so she divorced him and married someone else. My momma was a bit of a rolling stone," he said pointedly, as if apologizing for his background. "She seemed to specialize in fast-talking men and haphazard parenting."

"It must have been hard for you to deal with so many changes at so young an age," she said thoughtfully.

"It would have been easier if she had been a little more stable, and a little less indifferent." Drew's voice bore a thinly disguised trace of sadness. "My mother was the sort who bored very easily. Mostly, she was bored with me. One minute I'd be talking to her, telling her about something that happened at school that day, she'd even look like she was listening. Then she'd turn me off like she'd just turned off the TV. She'd pick up the phone and make a call or just walk out of the room, leave me in the middle of a sentence to find something more interesting to do. So one minute, I'd think I had her attention, then the next, I'd know it was all an act, that she was only pretending to listen because she thought she had to. Growing up, I never had her attention for one entire conversation, not one time in my life. The rest of it I could deal with—the moving around, her changing her men the way some women change their shoes, even being shipped in and out of foster homes. But I never got used to her indifference toward me."

"But she must have loved you, Drew. Otherwise, she'd have given you up for adoption, or tried to pass you off to a relative." Abby tried to rationalize. How could any woman not love her child, regardless of what else was going on in her life?

"I think that's why she brought me to Primrose after my father died."

"What do you mean?"

"I think she tried to dump me on my grandfather, but obviously, he didn't want me, either. Maybe he just didn't feel up to raising a child. Or maybe his wife didn't want to be reminded that he'd had an affair which had resulted in a child . . ."

"Drew, I cannot believe that Leila would have turned you away. I simply do not accept that." Abby put her fork down quietly. "If you had showed up at her door, she would have taken you in."

"You think she would have taken in her husband's illegitimate grandson?"

"Yes. And from what I know of Thomas, I can't understand why he would not have welcomed you with open arms."

"Well, all I know is what my mother told me."

"Which was?"

"That she was given money to leave and not to come back. And, frankly, that probably satisfied my mother at the time."

"It just sounds so incongruous with everything else I knew of them." Abby shook her head. "But what about your mother's family?"

"I never met any of them, either. I think she was originally from Omaha, someplace like that . . . in any event, it never mattered."

"I think it mattered very much." She could have bitten her tongue. "I'm sorry, Drew . . ."

"Don't be. It's the truth, of course. It did matter very much. And I guess that's why now it means so much to me to be able to see Thomas's things . . . to read his books, to sit where he sat and read the words he wrote. It's the only tangible evidence that I had a family. That I came from someplace. Whether he wanted to share that place with me or not."

She watched his face as he turned his gaze to the water and stared out at the boat whose sails were being readied for a trip back across the Sound. With Drew, it seemed to Abby, there was always something underneath the surface, just waiting to be revealed. She wondered if the words that seemed always to stick in his throat would ever be spoken.

Abby's gaze drifted down to the deck area, which had been brightly illuminated with lanterns around the perimeter, and noticed a woman standing at the top of the steps, staring up to where they sat.

"Drew." Abby touched his arm to get his attention. "I think that woman is trying to get your attention."

"What woman?" He frowned.

"There . . . at the end of the deck. She's wearing a red-and-white shirt and red pants . . . the blonde." Abby all but pointed the woman out with a finger, but Drew still seemed confused. "Drew . . . the blonde in the red-and-white shirt. She's the only person dressed in red and white on the deck. Dark glasses. Straw hat . . ."

"Well, she's gone now." He shrugged. "I can't imagine who I'd know down here, though."

Abby looked down toward where the woman had stood. "She certainly looked like she knew you."

"Well, they say that everyone looks like someone." He tossed it off as if it was of no consequence.

"I don't know that I'd be so quick to pass her by," Abby teased. "She looked very pretty, from what I could see."

He shrugged off the blonde and returned his attention to his meal.

The drive back to Primrose was quiet. Drew turned on the radio and found only static. Abby offered to find music for him, being more familiar with the local stations.

"Rock or country?" she asked.

"Ummm . . . country's fine."

She turned the dial to her favorite country station. Chet Atkins was singing a thoughtful ballad and cleanly picking the steel strings of his guitar, his voice just smooth enough, just husky enough. Abby leaned her head back and hummed along.

"From everything that you've told me about your aunt, I wish they had taken me in. I think I would have liked growing up in Primrose," he said wistfully.

"We would have had fun in the summers. The three of us." Even as she spoke, Abby wondered how the presence of a third party—and another boy, at that—would have changed things. If Alex had had a choice between bike riding with her or with another boy, which would he have chosen?

"Three of us?"

"Alex spent the summers here, too. With Belle."

"I see. So you two really go back a way, don't you?"

"I guess I've known him for about twenty years."

"That explains it."

"Explains what?"

"Oh, he just had this look of . . . I guess *possessiveness* is as good a word as any, when I met him a few weeks ago. Maybe he was just being protective of an old friend."

"I'm sure it was nothing more than that," Abby said more stiffly than she had intended.

He pulled in front of her house and turned off the engine. It was still and quiet on Cove Road, and the only lights on were the ones in Naomi's kitchen and the street lights at the very end of the road.

"This was the best birthday dinner I've had in many years," he told her as he walked to the porch with his hand on her elbow.

"Is today your birthday?"

"Actually, it's Wednesday, but I figured on this being my celebration."

"If I'd known, I'd have baked you a birthday cake," she told him.

"I can't remember the last time someone did that for me," he noted.

"Then you'll have to come back and let me make dinner for you on Wednesday night, and you'll have a proper birthday," she insisted. "We'll see if we can make up for the birthday parties you did not have here when you were little."

"Abby, you don't have to do that. I mean, I appreciate the thought, but . . ."

"No 'buts.' Is seven okay? And can you make it back? I mean, with your business schedule and all."

"It'll fit in just fine, Abby, but don't you think maybe you should discuss this with Belle?"

"No, I do not. Belle will have to learn to live with it."

"I just don't want to be the source of tension between you," he said as he took the key to the front door and stepped forward to slip it into the lock. "Look, Abby," he whispered, and pointed to the stand of pines off to the left of the house. "There's an owl . . . see it, there, toward the top branches?"

Abby walked to the edge of the porch and peered upward. "No, I don't see it. Where are you looking?"

He came up behind her and turned her slightly in the direction of the street. "There . . . do you see it now?"

"No, I don't see anything. Are you sure?"

"Sure. He's right there . . . well, wait now, from this angle, I can't tell for sure if that is an owl or the way the branches are sticking up."

"I think you're seeing things," she teased.

"I could have sworn." He shrugged, slid the key into the lock, and quietly swung the door open. "I guess I'll see you on Wednesday. If you're sure . . ."

"I am positive. Look at it this way," she said as she stepped into the dimly lit hallway, "with any luck, I'll be able to sell this house long before your birthday comes around again. This could very well be your last chance to celebrate a birthday in this house. I'd take it while I could, if I were you."

"Okay." He laughed. "I get the picture. And I'll be here promptly at seven."

"Great." On impulse, Abby reached up and gave him a sisterly peck on the cheek. "I'll see you then," she called over her shoulder, and closed the front door, unaware that he remained standing on the front porch, watching her through the door's glass panels as she walked to the back of the house.

And he, in turn, could not have known that just as he stood watching Abby, so he was being observed from somewhere in the shadows of the ancient shrubs that huddled close to the house and offered shelter to those who would prefer to remain unseen.

✦ 30 ✦

"I want you to know that I do not approve of this, Abigail," Belle pronounced with all the haughtiness she could muster.

"Belle, I am sorry. But I am having a birthday dinner for Drew here on Wednesday night, and that is that."

The sound of the ringing front doorbell ended the discussion, as far as Abby was concerned. Through the glass panels, Abby could see a tall, dark-haired woman standing at the top of the porch steps with her back to the house and her hands on her hips, as if taking in the scenery. Abby unlocked the door and swung it aside.

"Yes?" she asked. "May I help you?"

"Abby?" the visitor asked tentatively as she turned toward the opening door and removed her sunglasses.

"Susannah?" Abby stepped onto the porch, barely able to believe her eyes.

"Yes. I hope you don't mind. You said to come anytime. We were on our way back from Disney World, and I thought since we were this close . . ."

"But absolutely. I'm so happy to see you, Sunny. It's been years . . . God, twelve at the very least." Abby gave a welcoming hug to her favorite cousin. "Please come in, Sunny."

"Well, I have to get Lilly out of the car first." She smiled and walked to where she had left her sporty little Mercedes at the end of the driveway.

A curious Abby followed and watched as Susannah opened the door and gently nudged the shoulder of a sleeping child.

"Sunny, I wasn't aware that you had a child," Abby said quietly as she peered into the car just as a little girl, with hair and eyes like coal and skin the color of walnuts, woke up.

"Well, actually, I haven't been a mom for all that long." Sunny knelt down and whispered something to the little girl, who smiled and stretched, arms high above her, before getting out of the front seat.

"Hello, Aunt Abigail," the child said in careful, clipped words with a hint of a British accent.

"Well, hello." Abby smiled as the girl grinned shyly and took the hand Abby held out to her. "And what is your name, might I ask?"

"Lilly Claire Hollister-Ross," she said solemnly.

"That is a lot of name for a small girl," Abby noted.

"Mommy said I'll grow into it," Lilly replied earnestly.

"I've no doubt you will." Abby suppressed a smile. "Would you like to come in and meet Belle and Meri Puppins?"

"Are they your children?"

"Sometimes I wonder. No, Belle is my friend, and Meri Puppins is her dog."

Lilly poked cautiously into the front hallway and waited until her mother caught up with her before venturing further into the quiet house.

"Come this way, Lilly." Abby gestured.

"Belle, we have some unexpected company," Abby announced from the doorway.

Belle turned with a somewhat unwelcoming look on her face, as if the visitor would be the last person on earth she'd want to see. When she saw the well-dressed young woman and child in the doorway, she brightened somewhat.

"Belle Matthews, this is my cousin, Susannah Hollister. You might remember her as part of that wild and woolly crew from Montana that occasionally descended upon Aunt Leila for a visit."

"Of course, dear. Susannah's mother, Catherine, was your mother's sister, if I recall correctly." Belle beamed at the newcomer.

"You've quite a memory, Mrs. Matthews," Sunny told her.

"Doesn't she, though?" Abby could not help but add.

Ignoring Abby's barb, Belle motioned for Susannah to be seated on the small wicker sofa opposite Belle's own chair. "What brings you to Primrose, Susannah?"

"Abby invited me to come when I could arrange it." Sunny sat as she had been directed to do and motioned for the tiny girl to follow her. "We've been in Florida, at Disney World."

"Well, hello there." Belle was startled at the unexpected sight of a child in the doorway.

"Lilly, please say hello to Mrs. Matthews." Sunny prodded the child to remember her manners.

"Hello," Lilly whispered shyly, her eyes never leaving the ball of fur draped across Belle's lap.

"Meri, do go make friends with Lilly," Belle told the dog, who promptly hopped from the lap of her mistress to investigate their visitor with curious sniffs.

"Let me get something cool for you to drink," Abby offered, "and then we can sit and visit. I'm so delighted that you're here, Sunny."

"Now, Lilly." Belle leaned forward slightly. "Tell me all about Disney World. I've seen it on TV, of course, but I've never been. So tell me what you saw there . . ."

Lilly relaxed and began an animated recitation.

"I think I'll help Abby." Sunny laughed and followed Abby's path to the kitchen.

"You didn't mention Lilly in your letter," Abby said as she removed ice from the freezer.

"We're still in the process of adopting her . . . at least, I am." Sunny frowned and took the glass of iced tea Abby held out to her. "Better put Lilly's in a cup. She'll never drink all that."

Abby reached into the cupboard for a cup and eyed Sunny curiously. "Sounds like there's a story there."

"There is." Sunny nodded and gazed out the back window. "I always loved this house, the view from the back, out over the river . . . can we walk out back?"

"Sure. Do you want to see if Lilly wants to come? Or do you think she'd rather have a snack first?"

"Snacks will do it every time," Sunny told her. "Do you have a cookie or two?"

"I do." Abby pulled an old cookie tin from the pantry shelf and popped open the lid. She handed the tin to Sunny to make her selection.

"I'll be right back," Sunny promised, taking the cup of milk and the cookies into the morning room.

"Lilly would rather stay with Mrs. Matthews and the dog," Sunny announced as she took her own drink and followed Abby out the back door. Draping an arm over her cousin's shoulder, she sighed. "Oh, Abby, it's so good to be here again. You don't know how many times over the years I've thought about Aunt Leila and this house and you. It makes me feel more settled just to be here."

As they walked toward the river, Sunny admired Abby's fledgling efforts to restore Leila's garden, and she exclaimed over the view of the river. "Just like I remembered it," she marveled. "Isn't a wonder, how little things have changed?"

"Bring me up to date," Abby said as they seated themselves at the edge of the dock. "What have you been doing with yourself, besides adopting a beautiful little girl?"

"She is just so precious, isn't she?" Sunny beamed. "I just couldn't *not* keep her, Abby. From the minute they brought her off the plane, I just knew she was meant to be my daughter. And nothing or no one is going to interfere with me adopting her."

Abby looked at her cousin quizzically.

"Justin—my husband—had agreed to adopt a child. We'd been married for six years, and it didn't look like we'd ever have a family. I'd read about this international agency that placed children privately, called them, and went through the whole process. Justin really could not have cared less, but he agreed to do this because I wanted it so badly. He turned on the charm for the social workers, and we were approved. Right about that time, there was a greater availability of children from Romania, and he agreed to adopt one of those cute little blond curly-haired baby boys whose pictures are always on the first page of the adoption books. That's what he wanted, that's what he asked for, and that's what he expected to get. Lilly, you might have noticed, is neither blond, Romanian, nor male."

"I noticed. She's, what, I'd guess Indian, Pakistani?"

"Indian," Sunny said. "Lilly was found in an alley in New Delhi, sitting alongside the body of her mother, who had died after giving birth to Lilly's baby sister right there in the alley. A Western photographer found them and took them to the local orphanage. The baby sister, being a newborn, was placed with a family right away and shipped off to her new home in Los Angeles. Lilly, however, was older—she was around two at the time—and therefore less desirable, plus she had some serious health problems."

"How old is she now?"

"We think between four and five, but we're not exactly sure. No one ever came forward to claim her or her sister— or her mother's body, for that matter." Sunny sipped at her tea. "She spent almost two years at the orphanage—that's where she learned to speak English before she came to us. The sisters at the orphanage were British."

"She must be bright to have learned the language so quickly."

"She is very bright," Sunny said proudly. "And now that

we are on the road to clearing up some other problems she has had—a severe infestation of intestinal parasites, for one—I think the sky's the limit for Miss Lilly. And Justin be damned."

"I take it Justin hasn't taken to Lilly."

"He has never held her, has never addressed her by name. He was in such shock when he saw her that first time—'Really, Susannah, you can't be serious about keeping her. Tell them to take her back.'" Sunny's voice dipped a few octaves to mimic her husband. "As if she was an ill-fitting pair of shoes or drapes done in the wrong color. And that was what it was, you know." Sunny's crystal-blue eyes looked straight into Abby's without blinking, without apology for her bluntness. "Lilly is unacceptably dark-skinned as far as Justin is concerned."

"Sunny, I am so sorry." Abby put an arm around her cousin's shoulder.

"Believe me, so am I. I took this trip with her to try to sort things out. You know, things between Justin and me have been rocky for the past several years. For a while, we looked past it because of the business—we own a business that makes specialty software for computers. Then I thought maybe if we had a child, things would be better—you know, I've always wanted a huge family and just assumed that I'd have a bunch of children, like my mother did. We went through all the infertility testing, and they couldn't find anything wrong with me—Justin, of course, refused to go through the regimen. I didn't mind so much, I have no problems with adopting. But Justin has a problem with Lilly, that's for sure."

"What are you going to do?"

"Well, the purpose of this little trip was not just to take Lilly to see Mickey and Minnie. I needed time to sort out what I feel and what I want. I want Lilly. I do not want to be married to a man who cannot love a child simply because she doesn't look the way he expected her to look."

"You'd divorce your husband because of Lilly?"

"In a New York minute. But it's not just because of Lilly. It's been a long time coming. I think I just didn't want to see it. I've had lots of time these past few weeks to take a serious look at the situation and put things into perspective. I've already called my lawyer with the deal I want to offer Justin. My lawyer feels it's too generous, but if it gets me what I want, I don't care."

"Sunny, do you think you might be moving a little too quickly?"

"Not at all. Justin can buy out my share of the business at current value—which is a great deal for Justin, since I started the company with my money and my ideas—and all he has to do is act like a loving father for the social workers when they do their final visit next week, and show up to sign the adoption papers for the judge. Then he gets to keep the business and the house, and I will take my daughter and quietly leave Connecticut."

"Where will you go?"

"I haven't the faintest idea." Sunny smiled. "I'm actually looking forward to finding someplace new to start over. Maybe I'll start another business, who knows? I think it's great to be able to start your life over. I mean, look at you. You've left the craziness of corporate America behind, and you have all this." Sunny spread her arms wide. "You are the luckiest person I know. You have this incredible house in this wonderful town, you have the peace and quiet and easy lifestyle that most folks would kill for."

"Are you crazy?" Abby turned an incredulous face toward her cousin. "I have no job, no income, and I'm working my fingers to the bone renovating this white elephant which I may or may not be able to sell."

"Abigail McKenna!" Sunny's incredulity matched Abby's own. "How could you even consider selling this place?"

"Come with me, and I'll show you. Then you can tell me again how lucky I am."

They checked in on Lilly and Belle, who were happily chatting away, and Abby gave Sunny the "construction tour." They had gone through the entire house and around the outside, full circle around the house.

"I think you are the crazy one," Sunny insisted as they stood on the front sidewalk looking back at the house.

"It's taking all my time and all my money," Abby lamented. "I can't afford to keep this house. Even if I could find a job around here, I couldn't support a house this size."

"Then put the house to work for you."

"What?"

"Abby, this house screams 'B & B.'"

Abby looked at her blankly.

"Bed and breakfast," Sunny explained.

"I know what it means," Abby told her crankily. "I just don't see myself in the role of an innkeeper."

"Why not? You have the facilities. It's perfect. And the location is just wonderful. Why, once you get the painting done and the outside cleaned up, you can have garden parties and rebuild the dock and have a few small boats . . ."

"I don't want to be an innkeeper. I want to be a financial analyst."

"Well, then, that's your choice, of course. You certainly know your own mind. I'm sorry if I stuck my two cents in, Abby," Sunny said softly. "Since you said things were so tight, I was just trying to think of a way you could use what you have to keep going. And since you don't seem to have much more than this house right now, it seemed like the logical place to start. But I'm sure you know what's best for you."

"I do."

"Good." Sunny smiled. "Then let's go see what Lilly and Mrs. Matthews are up to."

Sunny started up the steps and was halfway across the porch when she realized that Abby had not accompanied her. She looked back over her shoulder to see her cousin standing on the front lawn, gazing up at her house in deep thought. When she realized that Sunny was watching her, Abby shook her head and repeated, "I have absolutely no interest in being an innkeeper. None at all."

Sunny just smiled and held open the door until Abby joined her in the doorway. As she led the way to the morning room, Abby fought off the sudden vision of how welcoming the entrance hall could be with bowls of flowers from the garden gracing highly polished tables in summer and garlands of pine winding up the balusters in winter.

✦ 31 ✦

"This has been so pleasant, Susannah," Belle said with obvious satisfaction. "How lovely to have your company after all these years. And what a well-behaved young lady you have there."

"I think she's simply too tired to act up." Sunny smiled and stroked the dark hair of the child curled up on her lap, a gray bunny clutched in her hands and her eyes half closed.

"Your room is ready, Sunny," Abby told her as she came into the dining room where Belle and Sunny had sat talking around the table after a dinner of chicken pot pie, salad, and the carrot cake they had made together that afternoon. "Second door on the left past the top of the steps. The bathroom is clean, and the towels are fresh, if you can overlook the ancient fixtures and the total lack of decor. I'm afraid I haven't done much with the baths as yet."

"Abby, for heaven's sake, will you stop apologizing? I think it's wonderful that you've offered to put us up for a few nights. Please don't for a second feel that you have to make excuses for the accommodations. It's a treat to stay in so handsome a house after being in motels for the past few weeks. I'm sure everything will be fine."

And everything had been just exactly that, Sunny assured Abby in the morning. "We slept like logs, Abby. Beds that comfy should be outlawed as promoting sloth. I could never get out of a bed like that in the morning for something as mundane as going to work. And the bath is lovely, I don't know what you were worried about."

"Well, the paint is peeling, and the paper is faded . . ."

"Oh, for crying out loud," Sunny scoffed, "that's part of the charm of an old house."

"Once Alex gets the pipes replaced and the plumbing repaired, I'll feel a little better about offering it to guests." She realized what she had said. "Not that I plan on having any. Guests, that is. I meant showing it to prospective buyers. For *their* guests."

"Umm." Sunny bit off a piece of warm buttermilk biscuit which Abby had just minutes earlier removed from the oven for breakfast. "These are heaven. I haven't had a breakfast this good since the last time I stayed here, in 1984, it must have been. These taste just the way I remember Aunt Leila's."

"They should. It's her recipe." Abby grinned.

Sunny buttered a biscuit and placed it before Lilly. "Wait till you taste this, Sweet Pea. Do you want some jam? Abby has some . . . let's see, cherry?"

"Sour cherry. Naomi made it," Abby explained. "Our neighbor across the street. She's in Belle's old house. You'll probably meet her later. She's a good friend."

Later, while Belle entertained Lilly in the morning room with stories of vacations she had taken once as a small girl to the "wilds of West Virginia to visit a maiden aunt," Abby and Sunny took their second cups of coffee onto the back porch to enjoy the morning breeze. Before too long, they were joined by Naomi and Meredy, out for an early-morning stroll to the river.

Abby went in to get Lilly, who was close to Meredy's age. The two little girls eyed each other shyly, albeit with great interest. Finally, Meredy asked, "I know where there's some baby turtles. Just hatched. Wanna see?"

Lilly looked to Sunny for approval, and the children took off to the river with instructions about how far they were permitted to go ringing in their ears.

The three women gravitated toward the garden, and by ten A.M., they had weeded the perennial bed (properly protected from chiggers, of course), picked out the paint colors for the bath off the bedroom Sunny had slept in, and planned Drew's birthday celebration. By noon, Lilly and

Meredy were best friends, and Abby and Sunny had scoured the attic for something special of Thomas's to give Drew for a birthday present. In an old trunk, they found what was reportedly the hat a very young Thomas Cassidy had worn when he accompanied Teddy Roosevelt on the ride up San Juan Hill, and they decided that the cap of gray wool felt was exactly right. By two o'clock, Lilly was playing in Meredy's yard, and Abby and Sunny were seated in the bank vault.

"Wait till you see," Abby said as she withdrew the black velvet cases from the box and handed them to her cousin, who was the rightful owner of a good deal of the contents of the box.

"Oh, my sweet heaven, as Gramma Sarah used to say." Sunny whistled a long, low sigh of admiration. "These are the sapphires Serena wears in the portrait. God, Abby, they're magnificent. Here, help me fasten the necklace. I want to feel these babies on my skin."

Abby laughed and aided Sunny, then fished in her purse for the hand mirror she had brought for just this purpose.

"Abby, you thought of everything." Sunny grinned. "Oh, my, Abby, did you ever see anything so blue in your life?"

"Not that color blue," Abby conceded, and she watched as Sunny fitted the earrings to her ears and slipped the ring upon her finger. "I took one of the rings"—she pointed to the sapphires—"home with me, before I knew it had been left to you. Remind me to give it to you."

"And last, the bracelet . . ." Sunny appeared to have barely heard. "Oh, God, but they're handsome. Fit for a queen. Let's see what else we have here. Ah, the amethysts . . . do you know that Aunt Leila and I shared a February birthday? Valentine's Day, the fourteenth. She always told me that someday she'd have something special for me, because we shared that birthday. I never in a million years could have imagined all this." Sunny nodded slowly, turning the purple stones over and over in her hands. "Beautiful, aren't they?"

"Belle told me that Thomas gave them to Leila on their wedding day."

"Then that makes them all the more special, doesn't it?"

"Oh, here." Abby reached into the box and pulled out the last envelope. "There's one more, and wait till you see . . ."

"Oh, wow." Sunny's eyes widened. "Good Lord, Abby, I've never seen anything like this outside a museum." Sunny lifted the gold necklace from the table and held it up to the light. "It's the single most exquisite piece of jewelry I have ever seen in my life. Look, Ab, there's little figures on the leaves. It's hard to tell what they are . . . some kind of animal with a funny head, maybe?"

"I can't tell, either." Abby shook her head. "But it is pretty incredible."

"Now, where," Sunny puzzled as she fingered the long golden leaves, "would you buy something like this?"

"I don't think it was a purchased piece." Abby chose her words carefully. "I think Thomas discovered it on one of his forays. Belle told me that Thomas had given it to Leila as a symbol that he loved her more than the life he led before they married. I think this may have been something Thomas found . . ."

". . . on the last trip he'd taken before he met her. Did you ever hear of anything so romantic?" Sunny placed it on the table between them to study it. "Do we know where he'd gone, that last time?"

"Belle said someplace in Asia. One of the countries that ended with a '-stan,' she said once."

"We should try to figure out which one," Sunny said, adding reluctantly, "because maybe it should go back. It's obviously rare and probably belongs in a museum. I love it, and I love that Aunt Leila wanted me to have it, but it really isn't the kind of thing you keep."

"That's very noble of you," Abby told her.

"Not as noble as you telling me about these things when you could so easily have kept them," Sunny said bluntly. "Especially since you need the money right now. No one would ever have known, Abby."

"Aunt Leila obviously wanted you to have them, and she trusted that I would give them to you," Abby said simply.

"Well, if you don't mind, I would like to leave it all right where it is. At least until my divorce is finalized. It would be just like Justin to want me to sell it and throw the money into the common pot to be split up, and I have no inclination to sell or to share."

"I don't mind at all." Abby shrugged. "At least you'll know where they are and that they are safe."

"And maybe between now and the time I decide to take them, we'll have figured out where the necklace came from." Sunny slipped everything back into the folders and packed the metal box. "Did Thomas leave any notes we could look at?"

"Yes, but even better . . ."

"Of course, his books!" Sunny exclaimed.

"I've looked through them," Abby told her, "but there was nothing that referred to anything like this. There may be other books I haven't found, or there may be something in his notes. You ready to leave?"

"Yes." Sunny handed the box to Abby to put away. As she did so, the light danced from the purple stone on her right ring finger. "Oh, I forgot to take off this ring. Well, you know what? I think I'll just take this one piece with me. I do love it."

They stopped at Foster's to pick up something for dinner. "The sea trout is fresh this mornin', Abby," Young Foster assured them. "Dan Bridges caught these hisself out off the Point, brought them in by ten, all cleaned and ready to go."

After a short stroll around the center of town, they loaded their purchases into Sunny's car and took the long way back to Cove Road, so that Sunny could drive past the town green. Abby leaned back against the soft tan leather seat and closed her eyes.

Monday was almost over, and Abby had made it through. Alex would be on his way back from Atlanta, and whatever had happened between him and Melissa over the past four days was done. She wondered if the next time she saw him, he'd be announcing his engagement. The very thought of it stabbed at her until she could barely breathe. Thank God she'd been smart enough to keep her feelings to herself. Imagine how much worse she'd be feeling if Alex knew . . .

She opened her eyes as she felt the car slow down to pull into the drive.

"Looks like you have company, Abby," Sunny told her. "Know anyone who has a red Saab convertible?"

The owner of the Saab was found in the morning room with his grandmother and two little girls who laughed as he held a piece of cookie just inches above Meri P's nose to entice her into "dancing" halfway across the room on delicate hind legs with all the grace of a tiny ballerina. The owner of the Saab was totally charming to Sunny, whom he remembered and welcomed warmly. The owner of the Saab followed Abby into the kitchen while she prepared the fish for the oven.

"So"—he cleared his throat—"how'd things go this weekend?"

"Fine. Everything was fine," Abby said without looking at him. *And I should be asking you that question,* she thought.

"Were you all right? I mean, were you able to work? On the bathroom, I mean. Since I hadn't really finished up in there . . ."

"I wasn't working on the bathroom." She turned the dial on the oven to set the temperature. "I was working on the side bedroom."

"I thought you finished that last week."

"Not quite. I had a little bit more painting to do."

He nodded as if in deep thought. "Well, I guess next weekend, I'll finish the bath, and then you can paint in there. If you want to. Paint, that is."

Abby put the fish into the pan and seasoned it. *Why doesn't he just say it and get it over with?*

Alex cleared his throat again, then poured a glass of water. He leaned back against the sink and sloshed the contents of the glass around absentmindedly. Finally, Abby could stand it no longer.

"Alex, you obviously have something to say to me, so would you please either say it or get out of my kitchen?"

He set the glass on the counter and folded his arms, and

indecision seemed to prod at him. Finally, he said evenly, "I was just wondering if I could stay for dinner."

As if we would have refused to feed him, she later grumbled to herself as she finished the cleanup in the kitchen. In her distracted state, she had sloshed soapy water onto the front of her long denim jumper and forgotten to pull up the sleeves of the T-shirt she wore under it. Exasperated with herself, she dabbed at the front of her skirt with the end of a towel.

Sunny had taken a sleepy Lilly to her bed, and Belle had gone up to her room an hour ago, but Alex had taken his coffee to the back porch, where he sat on the rocker, obviously deep in thought. After dinner, he had brought Abby's radio downstairs, and now the sweet strains of a country tune wafted through the back window along with honeysuckle-scented breezes.

Abby poked her head out the back door. "If you're planning on staying over, I'll put clean sheets out for you."

"Come sit and talk to me for a few minutes first," he asked softly.

Warily, she came outside and paused before sitting on the step, about three feet from his chair. In the dim light, she could barely see his features, but she knew them by heart. She waited, knowing that whatever it was that he wanted to say would be said now. Abby steeled herself for the worst as she leaned against the railing. He rocked rhythmically in time with the ballad on the radio.

Finally, he said, "Do you remember my grandfather, Ab?"

"Granger? Of course."

"Seeing that big fish at dinner made me think of all the times he took me fishing when I was little, before he got sick. Gran used to pack this huge lunch for us and make us wear straw hats to keep the sun off our faces. You'd have thought we were taking a charter out into the ocean instead of taking that little whaler of his out into the Sound."

In the dark, she could sense his smile, and she smiled, too, remembering Belle's husband. Granger was a dear man, one who had doted on Alex and worshipped the ground his

diminutive wife walked on. The epitome of the true Southern gentleman, Granger Matthews had always had a kind
word for everyone he met. In Abby's mind's eye, she would
forever see the man trudging to the river's edge in the
earliest hours of the day, clad in a crisp red-and-white shirt,
a fishing rod in one hand and a tackle box in the other—and
Alex by his side. The business of the town's banking could
always wait, it seemed, where Alex and fishing were concerned.

"I remember a couple of times, when I was about eight or
nine, he took me to the Outer Banks to surf-fish. No matter
how hard I tried, I could not get that damned line out into
the ocean, but one quick flick of his wrist would send that
hook twenty feet or better from the shore.

"And we never took bait. Grampa always said the best
bait was waiting for us right there in the sea. First, he'd
catch spots offshore—shiny little fish with a dark spot—
and use them to bait his hook, then he'd set about the task
of some serious fishing. One time, he decided we'd camp
out there on the beach. He'd caught a big sea bass that day
and cooked it over an open fire right there, fifteen feet from
the ocean. You know, I've eaten in some of the finest
restaurants in the world over the past few years, but I've
never had a meal I enjoyed more than I enjoyed that fish.
And we stayed right there on the sand that night, in sleeping
bags, under the stars, with the surf pounding away and the
smell of salt so thick in the air." He paused, as if seeing it all
in his mind, then he laughed softly. "I didn't get a wink of
sleep for worrying that those damned little crabs that scurry
around the sand at night would get into my sleeping bag and
bite their way out."

"Ghost crabs." Abby nodded to the dark. "That's what
we used to call them."

"It's funny, isn't it, how some things stay hidden inside
you for so long, and then, in less than a heartbeat, some one
little thing will bring back a memory so powerful it can
knock the wind from your lungs as cleanly as a fist to the
chest?"

She nodded, then realized that he probably had not seen

the gesture, there in the dark, but she knew it did not matter. A few minutes passed before he spoke again.

"My grandfather was the finest man I ever knew," he told her. "He was what I wanted to be when I grew up. He was everything I would ever need to be."

Abby could feel the stillness settle around them.

"I had almost forgotten how much I loved him." Alex spoke just barely above a whisper, his voice cracking just the slightest bit. In the dim light from the kitchen, his face appeared to shine with a soft, wet glow.

Swallowing the sudden lump in her own throat, Abby rose quietly to return to the house to give Alex a few moments to mourn the man he had loved so dearly. As she opened the door, he called her name.

"Yes?" She replied.

"I'm sorry I argued with you last week. About Drew."

She stood in the doorway for a long minute. "I'll leave your sheets on the end of your bed."

"Abby?"

"What?"

"Listen." He turned the radio up. "Isn't this is one of your favorites?"

Patsy Cline. "Crazy."

"Yes."

"Dance with me." He stood up, walked slowly toward her, and held out his hand.

"Here? On the porch?"

"No. Out there. On the grass."

"I'm not wearing shoes."

"I'll carry you."

As easily as Sunny would lift Lilly, Alex picked her up and carried her to the grassy area between the house and the garden. Lowering her body until her feet touched the ground, he wrapped one strong arm around her and slowly pulled her as close to him as she could get. He hummed with his lips at the side of her head as he led her around the moonlit yard in a sort of waltz. Abby's toes skimmed the carpet of new grass, damp with the evening dew, and her head spun as if she had polished off the entire bottle of dinner wine on her own. If she stood on tiptoe, her head rested on his hard chest just below his shoulders. They swayed in the shadows of the pines and the rose arbor, the thick scent of honeysuckle perfuming the air and the gentle *whoooo* of an owl punctuating Patsy's vocals. Pine needles pricked softly at the soles of her bare feet as she looked up into Alex's face, but she knew that her life had never held a moment of more pure romance.

Melissa be damned.

Abby reached her left hand up behind his neck and drew his face down to hers. He leaned slightly forward to meet her mouth and seemed to all but devour her with a kiss that had been years in the waiting. His lips were soft and warm, and the kiss was hard and hot. Abby's head began to buzz loudly like a disturbed hive, and her toes were curling at the ends of her bare feet.

For a very long moment, Abby thought perhaps he had drawn her very soul through his mouth and breathed it out again. She knew she was still alive because her toes were damp and cold in the wet grass—all other systems seemed to have momentarily shut down—but she wasn't aware of having inhaled anytime recently. He tasted exactly the way she remembered, and his kisses were the same as the kisses that had haunted her for the past ten years. The only kisses that had ever turned her inside out. The same ones that years ago had fanned a living flame that had never been extinguished and had never burned for anyone else.

He kissed her eyes, and he kissed her mouth, and he kissed her chin, and he kissed her throat, and she knew if he kissed any lower, she'd be lost forever. When his lips traced a line down her throat to her collarbone, she knew it was all over.

He whispered her name into her throat, and her name became an invocation for everything that was necessary to sustain life on this planet. All she could do was to redirect his mouth to hers, knowing that if she didn't return his kisses, she would die right there in Leila's backyard, with pine needles stuck in her feet and the sweet trace of honeysuckle flooding her senses. Every inch of her body began to smolder and melt into his. Somewhere in the back of her mind, a faint alarm tried to sound, but she muffled its warning and blocked it out. She did not want to hear, did not want to know, did not want to feel anything other than Alex. After all these years, the hunger had been growing. Now that she could feed, she would.

He lifted her from the ground, and she felt her legs wrap around his hips as if they possessed a life of their own. She knew that if ever there would be a moment in her life when she would lose her head, it would be here and now.

"Abby . . ." He sighed into her ear, her hair, her throat. "I can't stand it anymore . . ."

"Neither can I," she whispered.

"I've wanted you since I was sixteen years old."

"Seventeen," she corrected him. "You were seventeen that year. I was sixteen."

"It started the year before that," he said between kisses on her neck. "I was afraid to let you know."

"So where do we go from here?"

The question seemed to throw him momentarily off guard. He looked toward the house, where his grandmother and her cousin and daughter lay sleeping. Maybe.

"Back to where it all began." The smile spread slowly, and he lifted her completely off the ground and began to walk toward the river.

She felt deliciously light-headed, and wanted nothing as much as she wanted to hold that feeling and let it continue to enfold her. She prayed that nothing would spoil the mood or the moment or the feeling of how right it was, how right it had always been between them.

"Where are you going?"

"To the carriage house, of course." He grinned. "To finish what we started half a lifetime ago."

She giggled into his neck, and he laughed as he stumbled along the worn path. There had been no need to ask or any need to grant permission. This night had been a long time in coming for both of them. It had never been a question of if but merely of when. They had always belonged together and, deep in their souls, had always known exactly that.

Whatever it was that had brought him to recognize this fact did not seem at that moment to be of any consequence. He walked along the dock in the moonlight and, with his right hand, pulled open the door. He had been prepared to have to tug on it, and the ease of its opening sent him back a step or two.

With the ease of a dancer, he stepped into the dark carriage house and let the moonlight lead the way, as he had done many times so long ago. He set her feet upon the ladder's wooden rungs and, with one hand on her hip, guided her from behind up the steps to the loft. Halfway up, her foot missed a step, and she slipped back against him. He held her there for a long moment, absorbing her nearness. His lips found the back of her neck, and his left hand dragged slowly down the length of her, feeling every inch of her from the base of her throat to her thigh.

"Alex." She gasped. "We have to get off the ladder . . ."

He pushed her up the remaining stairs, then tumbled onto her as she lay back in the old straw. He covered her with his body, and she stretched out and arched her back to blend into him.

"We are a terrible fit," she whispered, noting that her body was at least a foot shorter than his.

"The fit will be just fine," he assured her.

He slipped a hand up under her skirt and slid it to the top of her thigh, then back to her knee.

"You always had the best legs," he told her. "I swear, that last summer, every time I closed my eyes, all I could see were your perfect legs."

His hand slid farther up under her loose skirt, caressing her skin as if all the bits and pieces belonged to him, as if all were parts of himself, until her breath caught in her throat and threatened to strangle her. She was aroused to distraction, and, almost unconsciously, she made a cradle with her hips and eased him into the opening.

"Ah, Ab," he whispered gently, his breath soft against her skin, "it seems like I've waited all my life for you."

"The wait is over." She touched his lips with her fingertips. "For both of us."

There was no more talk, no more reminiscing. She tugged on the waist of his jeans with a wordless demand, and he acquiesced and followed where she led him. He slid into her warmth and was swallowed whole by it, and she by him, and, by dawn, the longing of ten long years had been sated and renewed and had grown into a fire that they both instinctively knew would never be extinguished.

✦32✦

Abby had, she was certain, passed beyond mortal existence and entered paradise right through the front gates. It seemed that a lifetime had passed while she had floated and swirled and waltzed to a melody only she could hear. When the time came for her to return to this earth, she did so grudgingly. She lay inside the cove of Alex's arms and listened to his heart's attempts to regulate its rhythm. There were no words to be spoken, no sound to break the spell that had wound, as delicately as a dream, to bind them. They lay in sheltered silence amid the faint smell of old straw and the honeysuckle that covered the back of the old building, their eyes closed as if in slumber, though neither of them slept.

Abby could feel the sunrise before she opened her eyes to peer through the dirt-smeared window to her left. Soon, Alex had turned to gaze out, watching the new day spread its purple and gold streaks behind the trees on the bank of the river. The early morning burned with promise, and when Abby could put it off no longer, she nudged him.

"It's dawn," she told him.

"I know."

"We can't stay here all day."

"We can't?"

" 'Fraid not."

"Hmmmm." He sighed and snuggled in a little closer.

"Alex." She nuzzled his face. "Belle will be looking for

me soon, and I suspect that sooner or later, someone from your office will be looking for you." She dared not put a face on that someone.

"You're right." He yawned and stretched. "I have to be in court by eleven. I will really have to fly to get there."

The thought of his real world, his life apart from Primrose and its obligations that had nothing to do with her—and everything to do with someone else—brought Abby back to reality with an unpleasant thud. Reluctantly, she prodded him until their clothes were on straight and she could inch him toward the ladder, where they descended to a reality that bore no resemblance to anything that had passed between them during the hours they spent in the loft. They went out through the old stable area, through the back door of the carriage house into the new day.

Alex stopped on the dock to soak up the morning dew and to drink in the sweetness of the dawn. He drew Abby to him with one arm, the hand of which caressed her neck through the tumble of curls that danced like unruly demons around her face and neck and shoulders. Overhead, a large crow scolded them, setting off a chorus of cackles from the pines. Alex laughed and led her toward the walk. He lifted Abby when she stepped on a loose nail and cried out, and he carried her to the back of the house, where the radio still played on the porch. Alex turned it off as he stood Abby on the top step.

She draped her arms loosely around his neck, and he placed both hands on the sides of her face and drew her close, kissing her mouth.

"Go in now," he told her, "and get some sleep."

"This is actually the time I usually get up." She stroked his hair.

"I will be tied up all this week," he said. "I am trying a case that should be over by tomorrow, but then I will be in Providence probably right through late Friday afternoon. I should be back here by Saturday morning to resume my duties as handyman-love slave. Can I bring you anything from Rhode Island?"

"Just you," she whispered.

"You can bet on that." He kissed her, and for a fleeting minute, all was very right with the world.

"Abby," he said, looking down into her eyes, "I want you to know that, all these years since that last summer I spent here with you, I never kissed a woman who did not have your face. I have never made love to anyone who wasn't *you.*"

He lifted their intertwined hands to his face and kissed her fingers before kissing her mouth, then the tip of her nose.

"I'll see you this weekend," he said, and she nodded and watched from the top step as he followed the dirt path to his car. "Get some sleep," he said before he got into the sporty red machine and turned on the engine.

She waved as he backed down the drive, and he was long gone before she moved from the spot where she had stood when he kissed her good-bye.

Abby hummed softly as she locked the back door and turned off the kitchen light. On bare feet, she half-pirouetted into the front hallway, then padded up the steps to her room. She tiptoed into the room and sat on her bed, still dressed. She pulled the old quilt up around her. In a dreamlike state, she sank back against the pillow for the better part of an hour, her mind almost as blank as the expression on her face. Her senses remained stunned, her body still soft and languid, still bearing Alex's scent and his touch.

"I never kissed a woman who did not have your face," he had told her with the solemnity of an oath. "I have never made love to anyone who wasn't *you.*"

With a prickly dart of suspicion in her heart, she wondered if "anyone" included Melissa.

Abby slept for a little more than an hour before the shrieks of the squirrels romping in the upper limbs of the sweet gum tree woke her. She stretched and hugged herself, still savoring the lingering sense of awe that had slipped in around her the night before and declined all opportunity to leave. The night had been magic, and every breath she had taken since the moment she stepped into his arms had been blessed with the sweet inevitability of loving Alex Kane. She loosened the cocoon she had made of her quilt, pushed her feet and legs beyond the fabric, and sat up, scrunching her fingers into her hair to untangle the curled reddish loops. She drew her knees up and wrapped her arms around them, picturing in her mind the way it had all unfolded, and she smiled. It had all been so right.

She picked at a loose thread on her sleeve, and her smile faded as the realization crept upon her that her life would never be the same. Alex had felt it, too, she was certain. What she did not know was whether in Alex's eyes the night in the carriage house marked a beginning, or if it signified nothing more than the fruition of an adolescent fantasy, the closing of a door too long left open.

And where from here? she wondered.

Where indeed?

"Abby? Abby, have you heard even one word I've said?" Naomi stood on the dirt path, her hands on her hips and a bemused smile on her face. "I said, the Loch Ness monster has surfaced down there near the dock. CBS and CNN have both called. They'll be here by suppertime. 'Hard Copy' will arrive in time for dessert."

"Yes." Abby nodded absentmindedly as she pulled the next section of errant plant life from the old perennial bed Sunny had started working on before taking Lilly and Sam to the library for story hour. "Okay."

"Abigail McKenna, where are you?" Naomi asked, more gently this time.

"What? Oh. I was just thinking about . . . about what to make for dinner."

Naomi laughed. "Nice try."

"What do you mean?"

"Abby, we both know that Sunny is making dinner tonight, which is just as well, since rumor has it that over the past two days, your culinary talents seem to have mysteriously deserted you."

Abby stared at her friend, as if demanding an explanation.

"Let's see, now, last night, you overcooked the pasta by ten minutes. Leather spaghetti, I heard it referred to. Then, this morning, the specialty of the house was, I believe, broiled grapefruit. Or was that charbroiled?" Naomi was fighting a grin. "Of course, this is all rumor and supposition . . ."

"Okay, so my timing is off." Abby shrugged.

"Oh, my ass, Abigail."

Abby sat back on the grass and looked up at her friend. "I admit, I'm distracted."

Naomi looked down into the eyes of the friend she had come to hold so dear in so short a time. "Are you ready to talk about it?"

"Almost."

"I'm here, sugar, whenever you need me."

"I know you are," Abby said with an easy confidence that still came as a surprise to her. "And I love you for it. It's just that right now, I need to sort some things out."

"Whenever you are ready, Abby." Naomi kissed the palm of her own hand, then touched her palm to the top of Abby's head. "The road to my house is a very short one."

Abby watched as Naomi disappeared around the side of the house, limping a bit more than normal. *She does too much,* Abby told herself as she gathered up the discarded weeds to throw on the compost pile Sunny had suggested she start near the far right side of the yard.

Sitting on the old wooden bench she and Sunny had dragged from the carriage house that morning, Abby popped the top off the plastic bottle she'd earlier filled with ice water and took a long drink, then leaned back to look around the garden. She needed to plant bulbs, she told herself, so that next spring, the beds would be ablaze with color, like Naomi's were, like half the gardens in Primrose were. Butter-yellow daffodils and tulips of red and pink, of gold and purple, and hyacinth for fragrance, and . . . *Oh, damn. I'm beginning to think like a person who intends to stay.*

Abby went inside the house and washed the dark soil from her hands. With an air of purpose, she went to her room and took the envelope from her desk, then skipped down the steps and unlocked the front door. She was just in time for the postman. They made small talk, he gave her the day's mail, and she handed him, after just the slightest hesitation, the résumé that only the day before, the head-hunter in Dallas had asked her to mail.

She went back inside and checked the birthday cake she had made for Drew. True, she had been absentminded these past few days. She was grateful that Drew's cake had neither flopped nor burned. She sensed that this birthday dinner was somehow more important to him than she had appreciated, and she wanted to make it a nice evening for him. She might be an emotional jumble this week, but Drew, by gum, would have his birthday dinner in Thomas Cassidy's house.

"Abby, that's about the best-looking birthday cake I ever saw," Sunny told her. "Certainly prettier than the one that Justin got for my last birthday. Or any other birthday, now that I think of it."

"You don't think it's *too* pretty, do you? I mean, for a man?" Abby frowned. "You don't think the violets are too much?"

Sunny stood back and studied the chocolate confection with the candied violets gathered slightly to one side to leave room for the candles.

"No, I don't. It's a wonderful cake, and Drew will love it."

Which he did, he exclaimed, when she brought it to the table after a dinner consisting of chicken in wine with pineapples and water chestnuts over wild rice.

"Abby, this is so wonderful," he told her, with sincerity so absolute that even Belle appeared to soften. "I never had a more special birthday. A terrific dinner, warm company, even balloons. How do I thank you?"

"My mother always said that all birthdays were special." Abby smiled. "I'm happy that we are able to share this one with you. And you may thank Lilly for the balloons—she thought that tying them to the backs of the chairs would be festive."

"Can we sing now?" Lilly, who had had her eye on the cake all afternoon, asked wistfully.

"I'll get some matches." Abby went into the kitchen to search for a source of candle ignition.

"I'll bet you had a big cake on your birthday, Lilly," Drew said.

"I haven't had one yet," she told him.

Puzzled, he looked to Susannah.

"We don't know when Lilly was born," she told him, "and we just haven't gotten around to choosing a day."

Drew pushed his chair back from the table and beckoned to the child. Lilly went to him and climbed onto his lap without hesitation.

"Lilly, I would be very honored to share my birthday with you," Drew said quietly.

Lilly seemed to think it over, one eye on the cake.

"The birthday cake, too?" she asked. "And the balloons?"

"Absolutely. You cannot have a proper birthday without a birthday cake and lots of balloons. I learned that today, and I believe it to be true."

Lilly looked expectantly at her mother, who was busy swallowing back a lump roughly the size of Delaware. Sunny nodded.

"Then it is settled," Drew told the child. "Today is officially Lilly's birthday."

Lilly beamed and sat up just a wee bit straighter, feeling suddenly the importance of being a birthday girl.

"And here are the candles," Abby said solemnly, sensing that a matter of some weight had just been decreed. "Shall we do three for Drew—Drew, since you're thirty-something, that's one per decade—and five candles for Lilly, since she hasn't had the opportunity to blow out birthday candles before? How's that?"

Abby lit the eight candles and watched the delighted child make a wish before blowing them out with Drew's assistance.

Abby placed the box holding Drew's present in front of him.

"Sunny and I tried to think of something to give you that

would be special," she told him, "something that would be meaningful to you and . . . well, open it and see what you think."

"Now, I know what you are thinking." Sunny chuckled as Drew opened the box and peered in. "You are thinking, 'How could they have known that an old woolen cap was exactly what I've been hoping for?'"

"It was Thomas's," Abby told Drew. "He wore it back in his Roughrider days."

"You couldn't mean, as in Teddy Roosevelt?"

"So the story goes." Abby smiled. "Sunny and I both thought you'd appreciate it."

"I think it's incredible." He shook his head as he gingerly removed the old gray felt cap. "This is wonderful. It truly is. I don't know how to thank you. I am honestly overwhelmed."

"Well, we like to think that Thomas would be pleased." Abby smiled. "And, Lilly, I apologize for not having a present for you. But I promise that tomorrow, we will go up into the attic and see what there might be for a girl your size. Would you like that?"

Lilly, whose mouth was still oozing chocolate butter cream, nodded happily.

"I will have to send something to you," Drew told the child, "since I have no present to give you today."

"Are you kidding? What you have given her is priceless, Drew," Sunny told him in a quivering voice. "You've given her something she will never forget. And neither will I."

Sunny wiped her daughter's mouth with her napkin and instructed her to say her good nights. "Birthday or no, it's still past your bedtime," Sunny reminded her.

"Drew," Sunny whispered as she kissed his cheek, "that was one of the kindest gestures I've ever witnessed. Thank you."

Even Belle, who had been, for the most part, silent all evening, seemed to pause briefly behind Drew's chair, almost as if she were about to touch him, though she did not.

"Good night," Belle said stiffly from the doorway.

Nor did Belle, Abby noted with curiosity, make eye contact with anyone before turning her back and making her way to the front hallway.

"It is late," Drew told her. "I really should go."

"I'll walk you out." Abby retrieved his jacket from the hall, and together they walked out onto the front porch.

"I cannot thank you enough for everything you have given me," Drew told her. "You've given me the first true sense of family I've ever had. You've made me feel as if I belong someplace."

"You do." She hugged him.

"If I could have picked someone to be the sister I never had, it would have been you." He kissed her forehead.

"I will accept that as the high compliment I believe it to be." She smiled.

Abby waved to him from the porch and watched as his car drove slowly up Cove Road. She caught a shooting star and immediately made a wish. She sighed deeply and thanked the stars and the heavens for all the many blessings of her life. She, too, had found family in Primrose, had found where she belonged, and was happy to share that with Drew.

And then there was Alex. Abby hugged herself with joy, dazzled by the miracle and grateful to her core for having been granted so precious a gift, a gift that, with the very best of luck, they would continue to give to each other for a lifetime and beyond.

"Abby, look here." Sunny came into the room where Abby was working, carrying a long white florist's box. "Someone has sent you flowers, and, unless I'm mistaken, they're roses."

They were indeed roses, one dozen long-stemmed red roses. Certain they were from Alex, Abby slid a finger under the envelope flap, taking the card to the window to read the note to herself.

"Oh," she exclaimed, "they're from Drew. 'Thank you for the most wonderful night of my life. Love, Drew.' Is that sweet?"

"It is, and so is he." Sunny nodded enthusiastically. "He was so sweet to Lilly last night, I could not wait to get upstairs and have myself a good cry. If Justin could show just a fraction of the caring that Drew showed, I wouldn't be divorcing him. But, Abby, was it my imagination, or did Belle seem to be a bit cool to Drew?"

"A bit cool?" Abby snorted. "That's an understatement. Belle is convinced that he is an impostor who is up to no good."

"Why?"

"I haven't the faintest idea, Sunny. I swear, I do not. But I have to take him on his word."

"Well, you won't get any arguments from me," Sunny told her, "because I would defend that man to the death."

"Good. Then you won't mind if I ask him to join us for the town fair on Sunday. Naomi told me about it. There will be games for the kids, and all the churches will have craft booths and food booths and all sorts of stuff."

"Well, we had planned to leave on Saturday." Sunny leaned back against the door. "As pleasant as this has been, I think we have imposed on your hospitality long enough."

"Don't be ridiculous." Abby started back up her ladder. "I have enjoyed every minute of it." Reaching the top step, Abby looked down on Sunny and smiled. "You know, I'd forgotten how much I liked you when we were kids. I like you even more now that we're grown up. You are welcome to stay as long as you like."

"I appreciate that, Abby. I've always felt at peace here."

"Then take it while you can get it," Abby told her as she opened the can of paint on the top shelf. "This time next year, the house will be home to someone else's family."

Sunny stared at her for a long minute, then picked up the box of flowers.

"I'll put these in water for you. Would you like to keep the card?"

"Yes. Thanks."

The threat of the sale of the house hung between them, and even as Sunny went down the steps to the first floor,

Abby regretted having brought it up so abruptly, knowing how the very thought of letting the house pass from the family had upset Sunny. With a sigh, Abby snapped the cover back onto the paint can and slowly came back down the ladder. She leaned out the window, her gaze trailing to the carriage house, where she had learned the taste and feel of love. Directly below her, Leila's garden began its stretch to the back of the property. She and Sunny, under Naomi's direction, had worked a few hours each night. The herb beds looked liberated—from the second floor, Abby could smell the lavender as clearly as if Leila stood beside her. Sunny had spent the past few mornings cleaning out the rose beds, and Naomi had gotten Colin to drive his little tractor over to till the soil between the back fence and the dock to put in the vegetable garden Naomi insisted Abby had to have. The newly uncovered bricks formed a path through the yard as they had in days past, and the birdbath, cleaned and repaired by Naomi, welcomed the songbirds back.

In spite of her best efforts to maintain the tunnel vision that goaded her back toward the corporate world, Abby knew with certainty that the tapestry of her life could not be completed anywhere else. The faces woven in silk were Belle's and Naomi's, Colin's and their children's, Young Foster's and Pete Phelps's and Steve the mailman's.

And at the center of it, still, after all these years, was Alex.

✦ 33 ✦

"This is fabulous." Sunny laughed with all the glee of a young girl as she backed out of the driveway at Thirty-five Cove Road and headed the car in the direction of the interstate. "I think we both need to follow our impulses a little more frequently, don't you?"

Abby could have told her that she'd done just exactly that a bit earlier in the week, but kiss-and-tell had never been her style.

"I haven't been to the Outer Banks since I was fourteen or fifteen years old," Sunny continued. "Remember, that year we all came out for two weeks—*all* the Dunham cousins and *all* us Hollisters? I thought Aunt Leila handled it quite well, though, didn't you?"

Abby laughed out loud. Aunt Leila had handled it by suggesting that the combined families rent two beachfront properties. All the boys stayed with the Dunham parents in one, the girls in the Hollister house with Sunny's parents. Leila divided her time between them for the two weeks they stayed in Kill Devil Hills.

"And how wonderful of Naomi to offer to stay with Lilly and Belle. She is a most remarkable woman, Abby. You are so fortunate to have such a friend. She is one in a million."

"That she is," Abby readily agreed.

Naomi had not only offered to stay with Lilly and Belle, she had insisted, saying, "Colin is working all night, and Sam is staying at my sister's overnight anyway. And, besides, it's time Miz Matthews learned how to play Candyland. You two go have an overnight out to the beach, and enjoy yourselves. Abby, you need to get away from this house for a few hours, and the beach is sure the place to be when you need some downtime."

Abby had called ahead and booked a double room at the Holiday Inn on the beach in Nag's Head. The room opened onto a balcony which overlooked the beach and the ocean just a stone's throw away. They checked in around two and slung their hastily packed bags onto the bed. As eager to see the ocean as a pair of eight-year-olds, they ran down the steps and through the deserted lobby to the doors that opened onto a wooden walkway which they followed down to the beach. Sitting on the bottom step of a short flight of stairs leading directly onto the sand, they hastily untied their sneakers with fingers excited by the remembered feel of long-ago sand between their toes.

The sand was cool in the April sun, and, without making a shared decision to do so, Abby and Sunny both spontaneously broke into a gentle trot, first toward the ocean, then parallel to it as they followed the water line. The sand washed over by the ocean was cold and the water bracing, but they ran with the delight of children too long kept from the sea. In silence, they ran, Abby puffing along, her short legs no stride-for-stride match for Sunny's longer ones, until Abby could not take another step. She dropped off the pace, then stood by the water's edge, her hands resting on her hips, and let the chilly waves plant icy kisses on her toes while she sought to fill her lungs with the salt air. When her breathing had regulated somewhat, she plopped herself onto the beach well beyond the tide line and leaned back on her elbows. Looking to her left, Abby could see Sunny still moving down the beach on long, muscular legs that churned, propelling her lithe body along the sand.

Life changes were in the wind, Abby reflected, and decisions made now would guide the course of the rest of her life. Heady stuff. She sighed, welcoming these moments when she could gaze out at the sea and, without distraction, weigh her choices.

Soon, movement from her left drew her attention, and she turned to watch her cousin approach. Sunny's black hair swarmed around her face with every stride, reminding Abby of a shampoo commercial in which a hopelessly beautiful woman ran, in slow motion, into the arms of an equally beautiful man. Only, for Sunny, the beautiful man was fading from the picture. Abby wondered what it was like to love a child so much that you would be willing to give up everything in your world just to make things right for a tiny stranger—and what kind of a man would reject a child for such superficial reasons, would risk losing a woman such as Sunny for any reason.

"Oh, God, I'm feeling old," Sunny groaned as she flopped onto the sand next to Abby. "I can't remember the last time I ran that far."

"How far do you think you went?"

"Not near as far as it feels." Sunny smiled. "I used to run every morning. I'm not one of these people who can do things sporadically, you know. If I run, I run every day. Or I don't run at all."

"How far did you go each day?"

"Just four miles."

"Four miles is not 'just,' Sunny. That's a good distance."

"It was just right for me. I'd like to get back into that. Maybe when Lilly and I get settled, I can get back into a routine again." Sunny drew up her knees to wrap her arms around her legs. She inhaled deeply several times to fill her lungs with the cool salt air. "God, that smells good. Doesn't it almost feel like if you close your eyes, we'd be fifteen again?"

"Oh, God," Abby groaned. "About the last thing I would want."

"Me, too." Sunny laughed. "One stroll through the garden of adolescence was enough for me, thank you."

"I couldn't bear it, going through those years again," Abby said somberly.

"God knows you had a rougher time than most of us. You know, when my mom got the call that your mother had been killed in that plane crash, she fainted. It was the only time I ever saw my mother so overcome by something that she just chose to shut down. She had always thought her sister was one of the immortals, she said. That Charlotte's life force was so strong, it could defy the heavens, and she could live forever. I don't think anyone in the family took her death as hard as my mother did."

"She stayed with me for a week," Abby reminded her. "After the rest of you went home, Aunt Catherine stayed. She told me things about my mother that I never knew. About what a daredevil she had been as a girl. About how she liked to break the wild horses on the ranch. How she once shot a rattlesnake that had somehow gotten into Gramma Sarah's laundry basket one day when Gramma was out hanging up the wash. My mother shot it with Grampa's rifle, splattered it in pieces right there in the basket. Gramma was furious that my mother had ruined the entire family's supply of underwear."

They laughed at the thought of their grandmother scolding her daughter and shaking bits of rattlesnake from the week's wash.

"Your mother had invited me to come stay on the ranch after that, did you know?" Abby asked.

"Of course." Sunny nodded.

"I thought it was really sweet. But I had school in Philadelphia. And besides," Abby confessed, "I always felt so out of place out there. When I was thirteen, we went out to stay with Gramma Dunham for a couple of weeks, and I thought I'd woken up in a foreign country. All of you swinging saddles onto your horses as easily as you tied your shoes. I never felt so incompetent in my life. Trevor saddled up that white horse for me, and I knew I had to get on it . . ."

"And then Trevor smacked its rump, and that horse took off out of the corral with you hanging on for your life."

"I thought that beast was going to drag me to the highest peak overlooking the ranch, stop dead at the edge, pitch me over her head as neatly as you please, and dump me in the gully, just like you see on cartoons."

"I never did see a face whiter than yours was when we caught up with you." Sunny grinned. "But my brother paid dearly for that little stunt. My dad didn't go for practical jokes that could end in someone being hurt. He made Trevor muck the stables every day for a month. But I'd say you had the last laugh anyway, when we were out here two years later."

"What do you mean?"

"Remember the first day we were all in the ocean—all of us—and my brother Schyler saw those dark fins not twenty feet from where we were . . ."

"And you all took off like crazy people, couldn't get to the shore fast enough."

"And we were all on the beach, jumping up and down, yelling for you to get out of the water, and Clay Dunham swam out to get you."

"I could not understand why you all panicked so at the sight of a couple of dolphins."

"Which we all thought were vicious, man-eating sharks. We still tease Sky about that—it was days before he'd even come onto the beach again. And we all thought you were so cool, Abby, standing there waist-deep in water while those huge things were closing in on you."

Abby smiled and pointed out toward the ocean. "Straight out," she told Sunny, "about fifteen yards from shore."

The gunmetal-gray dorsal fins split the crown of the waves as first one, then two, then two more dolphins flipped themselves above the surface of the ocean and for a split second seemed to dance upon the crest, a conga line of slapping tails and curved bodies in a nearly straight line across the horizon.

"Wow!" Sunny jumped up and ran to the water's edge, where she hopped up and down with all the exuberance of a child. "Oh, aren't they just so magnificent!"

They watched the silent ballet until the dolphins had moved farther down the beach, where their antics drew the attention of a couple who strolled arm in arm along the sand.

"Sunny, don't tell me you don't have dolphins off the shores of Connecticut." Abby had followed her to the shore.

"I'll tell you the truth, I spend so much time at work, I couldn't tell you if we do or if we don't. But that is going to change." Determination set into her jaw line. "No more working seven days a week for this woman. Uh-uh." She shook her head.

"You, too?" Abby thought back to her days at White-Edwards.

"You know, we have done it for eight years, Justin and I have. I started that business right out of college with money from my Aunt Hallie on my father's side." She shook her head. "But that business became bigger than me, bigger than Justin, bigger than anyone. I'm ashamed to tell you that it took Lilly's arrival to show me how foolish that all is. I'll never do that again."

"Well, sometimes you have to do that to earn a living."
Abby shrugged.

"You can earn a living without letting your life pass you
by. Justin is welcome to the business. I want to spend time
with Lilly and learn to be a mom."

"You're very lucky to have such options."

"Don't I know it? But I won't take that much time off. I'll
find something I want to do. It just won't be something that
will take over my life."

"Look, Sun." Abby pointed skyward. "Pelicans."

The brown birds, following their leader on their endless
primeval flight pattern—*flap-flap-flap-glide, flap-flap-flap-
glide*—skimmed above the ocean just inches from its surface.

"The first time I saw them, I thought they were pterodac-
tyls." Sunny grinned.

"So did I."

"Let's go back to our room and clean up and go out to eat.
My treat." Sunny swung an affectionate arm over her
cousin's shoulder. "There has to be at least one wonderful
seafood restaurant out here on the island. I want a fabulous
dinner and good wine and a totally decadent dessert. And
maybe even champagne," Sunny said as they headed back
up the beach to their distant hotel. "I want to celebrate
tonight. I want to celebrate Lilly and celebrate my favorite
cousin and drink to the changes ahead."

"You feel it, too?" Abby asked as they gathered up their
discarded sneakers.

"I have since I pulled into the drive on Cove Road."
Sunny nodded. "And I aim to welcome them in style."

They found their restaurant on almost the exact opposite
side of the island. The Windmill stood looking over the
Sound, its namesake but several feet from the shore. Midway through dinner, a storm rolled in from the ocean,
taking Abby and Sunny by surprise. The locals, however,
appeared hardly to notice that angry waves threw themselves over the bulkhead and raced toward the far end of the
parking lot. Rain came down in torrents, splashing at the

MARIAH STEWART

wide windows overlooking the water with the fury of a demon. Abby had never seen such rain. The darkness was sudden and complete, the Sound obliterated by the totality of the storm.

"Were they predicting a hurricane?" Abby asked the waitress, trying to sound blasé.

"Oh, no. This is just a little storm," the blond waitress assured them. "It'll be gone before your dinner even gets to your table."

And so it was, the storm clouds passing as quickly as they had arrived. Within minutes, the Sound was bathed in light, the sun beginning its drop into the purple and orange arms of the horizon.

The waitress uncorked the champagne, and a smiling Sunny filled the two fluted glasses.

"To you and to Lilly," Abby proposed.

"And to you and Alex," Sunny responded without missing a beat.

"Is it that obvious?" Abby looked chagrined.

"Totally. But it's too marvelous, don't you think? I always knew he was yours. Even when I was fifteen and thought he was just the cutest thing I'd ever seen."

"You didn't."

"I did. And here you are, together at last. You know, Gramma Sarah always said that one door didn't close that another didn't open, and I guess, once again, she was proven right."

"What do you mean?"

"Abby, just look at you. You lost your job and came down here and found him again. What could be more perfect than that?"

"Well, it could be a *lot* more perfect. I still don't know where I'm going from here. And, certainly, there's been no commitment made. I mean, as far as I know, he's still involved with another woman."

"You're kidding."

Abby slowly shook her head.

"What's the status of that?"

266

"I don't know."

"Don't you think you'd better find out?"

"Yes." Abby nodded, resolving to do just exactly that, at the earliest possible opportunity.

·34·

Abby was alone in the kitchen when the Saab pulled into the driveway. She peered through the curtains just as Alex got out of the car, slung his overnight bag over one shoulder, and hoisted a grocery bag from the trunk with his free hand. With two long strides, he had crossed the drive and reached the lawn. She watched him with a longing so real her insides began to ache. He paused in the yard to look down toward the river, then turned toward the house. He stopped for another moment and appeared to admire the work they had done that week.

Abby unlatched the door, and, at the sound of the lock turning, he grinned and quickened his stride. She had wondered if he would be as hungry for her as she was for him. She need not have worried.

"I missed you," he said between kisses that sent her world spinning. "If the jury had come back earlier, I'd have been here last night."

She pulled him into the house, and he dropped his bag at his feet and used both hands to lift her onto the counter, where he set her down and kissed her senseless. So senseless that she did not hear Belle's footfall on the steps until he had set her back on her feet, with her wondering why he had stopped.

"I want to tell Gran I'm here"—he kissed the tip of her nose—"so she doesn't get a start when she comes in."

Abby leaned hard on the counter, trying to regulate her breathing and convince her legs that they could, in fact, hold her up. She would make coffee, that's what she would do. And tea, of course, for Belle . . .

He swung the door open hard, and it crashed sharply into the wall behind. In his hand, he held what appeared to be a business card, and his face held a fury so dark that she involuntarily backed away from its intensity.

"Thank you . . . for the most wonderful . . . night . . . of . . . my . . . life?" he read with caustic incredulity, deliberate emphasis on each word.

"Alex, that's from Drew." She dismissed the importance of the note with a wave of her hand.

"I'd say you've been a very busy girl this week." His eyes narrowed dangerously.

"Alex, that's the card that came with flowers that Drew sent to me because . . ."

"Oh, I think I can figure out why he sent them." His snort of disbelief shot through her.

"Alex, you can't think for a minute . . ." She laughed.

He slammed past her, out the door, and into the yard to his car.

"If this isn't the stupidest thing . . ." Abby muttered, then followed him down the driveway.

"Alex, where are you going?"

He glowered from behind dangerously dark eyes but did not break stride.

"Alex, this is ridiculous . . . where are you going?"

"Fishing!" he fairly shouted.

"Alex, don't you want to know . . . ?"

"I *know* what constitutes a wonderful night," he growled, "and I do not want to know if *his* wonderful night"—he opened the door of the Saab—"was more wonderful"—he slid into the front seat—"than *mine!*"

"Oh, for pity's sake, Alex." Abby's hands flew to her hips. "This is the most absurd . . ."

He had not heard a word. The Saab peeled back down the drive and halfway up Cove Road before she could finish her sentence.

She stood staring at the empty driveway, unable to believe

that he had left. The shaft of pain that welled inside her touched every bit of her, every muscle and every nerve. She had no idea how long she stood there before she realized she was crying. She walked to the dock and plunked herself down loudly, where she could wail and not be heard by anyone other than the occasional passing duck or curious magpie. She cried until she choked, stopped long enough to catch her breath, then cried some more. After all these years of wanting him, all these years of waiting for the miracle that would bring the only man she had ever loved back into her life, to lose him so quickly and so foolishly was more than she could bear.

She had the hiccups and knew that a long, tall glass of water was the only cure. Reluctantly—she hadn't quite finished feeling sorry for herself—she wiped her face on her shirt and returned to the house.

"Where did Alexander go?" Belle asked as Abby passed through the back door.

"He said he was going fishing." Abby turned her face, hoping that Belle had not noticed that her eyes were puffy almost to the point of being narrow slits in her face and that her face was blotchy and streaked. It was, she knew, too much to ask.

Belle pondered Abby's response, then nodded as if she understood completely, before tottering off to watch her Saturday morning movie.

"The Mad Miss Manton," Belle explained as she hurried to the morning room. Meri P., who had paused for a quick drink from her water bowl, scurried to catch up. "Barbara Stanwyck. Henry Fonda. Two of my favorites. Leila's, too, as I recall."

Abby sighed, a long, loud sigh of woe. Tapping her fingers on the counter, she debated her options for the rest of the day. She could (A) wallow in misery and spend the day bemoaning her fate, or (B) find something constructive to do. Common sense won out, and she went upstairs to paint. No reason why she couldn't be heartbroken and constructive at the same time.

After an hour, during which time she had painted one wall yellow in a room in which she had, only earlier in the week, painted the other three walls blue, Abby gave up. She heard Sunny and Lilly come in from Naomi's, but, not wanting any company, she went to her bedroom, where she hid by snuggling into her quilt and curling up in a ball. She slept until Sunny sent Lilly to get her for dinner, which was a relatively quiet affair. Abby turned in around nine and tucked herself into bed with a romance novel she'd borrowed from Naomi. As least someone would be living happily after, she thought as she settled in to read.

At ten-thirty, she put the book facedown on the bed beside her. The heroine's efforts at winning back the man she loved were proving to be more than Abby could take. The last seduction scene had been hotter than anything Abby had ever seen in print. Though not hotter, she recalled, than the scene in the carriage house on Monday night. How, Abby wondered, could Alex walk away from her after the hours they had spent loving each other so completely?

He hadn't walked, she reminded herself, he had run.

More exactly, he had peeled out of the driveway in a jealous snit. Naomi had been right.

Abby swung her legs over the side of the bed and dangled her toes just inches over the carpet, trying to digest this fact. On the one hand, she thought, it meant that he did, in fact, care for her, enough that he did not want her to be with anyone else—not that she had been, of course. But, on the other hand, there was still Melissa, and apparently that was okay as far as he was concerned. He could spend four days in a distant city with another woman, but she, Abby, could not have a friendship with another man. And that simply wouldn't do. As much as Abby loved him, there were certain things she could not accept. Playing by the old double standard was one of them.

Tomorrow, she would go to Hampton and ring his doorbell and tell him exactly how she felt. She would tell him . . .

The sound of tires crunching in the driveway made her sit

straight up in bed. Without looking, she knew it was Alex. On tiptoes, she crept into the darkened hall and down the dark steps in her nightshirt. After unlocking the back door, she flew into the yard. At the corner of the house, she caught herself and forced herself to slow down. Remembering the cool attitude of the heroine in the book when she had to face down the hero, Abby smoothed back her hair and cleared her throat.

She picked her way carefully along the path—*damn, when would she learn to put something on her feet?*—to the car, where he still sat behind the wheel. Abby opened the driver's-side door.

"I guess you came back to apologize to me," she said.

He scowled and tried to grab the door handle to shut her out, but she leaned against the door to prevent him from doing so.

"You want to say you're sorry for jumping to conclusions."

"Ha!"

"And for assuming that something was going on between Drew and me. And you didn't like it, even though you have something going on with someone else. But that's okay. It's the old double standard. Well, it's not okay. What's good for the goose is good for the gander."

"What are you talking about?"

"I'm talking about how you think it's okay for a man to have something going on with two women at the same time, but boy, oh boy, if you even *suspect* that a woman has something going with two men, well, then, that's a whole 'nother ball game . . ."

"Abby."

"A horse of a different color . . ."

"Abby."

"The pot calling the kettle black . . ."

"Abby, shut up."

She did.

"I do not think it's *okay* to have 'something going' with two different people at the same time. Makes no difference, man or woman, the rules are the same. How can you give

271

everything to more than one person? I know I don't have that kind of energy."

"I see."

"Good. I need to know that you understand."

"I understand perfectly."

"Well?" He seemed to be waiting for her to tell him something.

"Well what? I understand. I understand that you are telling me that she was in your life before I came back and that . . ."

"Abby, who are you talking about?"

"Melissa, of course."

"Why?"

"Why? Because she's your . . . your . . ."

"She's my coworker."

"Your coworker?" Abby stared at him dumbly.

"Abby, you knew that."

"But I thought that you . . . that she . . ."

"Abby, as far as I'm concerned, Melissa is a friend. I have absolutely no interest in her in any other way."

"But she . . . I mean, it's obvious that she . . ."

"She knows how I feel."

"You sure?"

"Positive."

"How can you be so sure?"

"I told her."

"When?"

"Last Saturday night. After the wedding."

"Saturday night? That was before . . . before we . . ." She gestured lamely toward the carriage house.

"Yes."

"I see." Abby cleared her throat.

"I'm glad that you do. So you can understand how I feel about you and Drew."

"Alex, there is no 'me and Drew.' He's my friend, maybe more like a long-lost cousin, or maybe almost like the brother I never had."

"What about the 'best night of his life'?"

"Wednesday was his birthday. I had a birthday dinner for him. And I baked a birthday cake. It's something he never had. He had a terrible childhood, Alex. I was just trying to maybe help make up for some unhappy times in his life."

"And you really think that Drew looks on you as a sister?"

"I know he does. Why is that so difficult for you to understand?"

"Because I cannot understand how any man could know you and not be hopelessly in love with you. Like I am. Like I have always been."

His confession was so unexpected that his words all but struck her dumb.

"Abby."

"What?"

"What are you wearing under that . . ." He motioned to her nightshirt.

"Nothing." Her eyes widened innocently.

"Nothing at all?" He swallowed hard.

"Nope." She leaned back against the car door. "Nary a stitch."

"I see." He nodded almost grimly.

"The bed's made up in your room," she told him.

"I like that room," he said without looking at her. "I like that bed."

"It has a real feather mattress, did you know that?" she asked nonchalantly.

"No. I wasn't aware of that." He swung his legs out of the car, and she took a step back away from the door.

Alex closed the car door behind him and locked it. In the dark, Abby smiled as she backed toward the house slowly, knowing he would follow her.

As she turned to open the back door, she felt his hands on her waist, and she turned with her mouth half opened to him, no longer able to play the game. She was both devoured and devouring, and she thought her heart had beaten itself into such a frenzy that it would just spin out of her chest. Alex was all at once in her and through her and around her. She felt his hands under her nightshirt, caressing her bare skin, and then she felt the clapboard of the house on her bare back and knew they would be in serious trouble if they didn't get into the house soon. Very soon.

He lifted her with one hand and opened the back door with the other. When they had crossed the threshold into the kitchen, he said, "Isn't it your turn to carry me?"

"If you are waiting for me to carry you up the steps, it will be a very long night." She laughed and took his hand and led him to the stairwell. "You could, of course, follow me."

"Or you could follow me."

"Someone wrote a song like that . . ."

"Phil Collins. 'Follow Me, Follow You.'"

"I thought it was 'Follow You, Follow Me.'" She pondered.

"Whichever." He dismissed its importance as they did, in fact, follow each other up the long staircase, circling each other on the steps like cats, then tiptoeing like ghosts down the hallway.

Abby quietly opened the door to the room she had prepared for him in the front of the house. The moonlight spilled across the antique bed with the high head and foot boards and the puffy feather mattress. As quietly as it had been opened, the door closed behind them. Abby tugged at the buttons of his shirt impatiently. Alex grabbed her hands to still them.

"Not until you say the magic words," he told her solemnly.

"Please?" She frowned. "You want me to say 'please'? Now, there's a real mood breaker for you . . ."

"No." He laughed. "I want you to tell me."

"Tell you?" She eased her fingers from his grasp and continued to unbutton his shirt, this time without his interference. "Tell you that I love you? That you are the only dream that I've ever had? That all I ever wanted was . . ."

Whatever it had been that was all Abby had ever wanted would have to wait, because he could not. And by the time the moon had passed the rising sun on its way to the dawn, even Abby wasn't certain of what she had been about to say. Not that it mattered. By that time, every dream she had ever had had become her reality, and every promise that could be made had been pledged. By the time Sunday dawned over Primrose, there was nothing left to wish for. Everything that mattered was hers.

It was late when Abby awoke, almost eight A.M. according to the clock on the bedroom mantel. Certain that Belle would be wondering where she was, Abby tried to ease herself out of bed without waking Alex. Just as she was about to lift herself off the side of the mattress, a hand wrapped like a steel band around her wrist.

"And where do you think you are going?" Alex whispered.

"Downstairs." She leaned back across the bed to kiss his chin. "To make breakfast."

"That's my job," he reminded her with mock indignation. "I am the Sunday morning breakfast guy around here."

"Then you had better get yourself up, dressed, and into the kitchen." She pulled the nightshirt she had discarded the night before over her head. "And take care of business."

"What's the big hurry?" He yawned and covered his mouth with the back of his hand. "Gran's probably already had her tea . . ."

"And Sunny has already made the coffee. But we—that is, Sunny and I—invited Drew to come to the town fair with us today, and he will be here in an hour."

Alex groaned.

"Don't you dare." She looked over her shoulder. "You are going to make every effort to be his friend, Alex."

"Fine. I'll make a few extra waffles."

"That's what I want to hear." She blew him a kiss from the doorway, but that being a totally unsatisfactory beginning to what she felt would be a glorious day, she plunked herself on his side of the bed and cuddled up to him just long enough to kiss him soundly and tell him, "You will like Drew, I promise you will. But you have to give him a chance."

"Okay. I will be his friend. I will be his best friend. I will be like a brother to him, if it makes you happy." Alex sighed. "Now, get back to your room and dress yourself properly, or no one will have waffles this morning."

✦ 35 ✦

"This was a stroke of genius," Alex acknowledged as they removed the wheelchair from the trunk of Drew's car.

"Well, I sure hope that Miz Matthews thinks so." Drew sighed. "I hope she's not insulted. But she had mentioned that she hadn't been to a town fair in so many years, and she sounded sort of wistful about it, you know?"

"I think it's perfect," Alex told him. "There is no way that my grandmother could walk all the way into town and walk around all afternoon. This way, she'll be able to go and see everything and everyone and not have to worry about getting tired or tripping over someone else's big feet."

"I hope she sees it that way." Drew grimaced as he carried the chair to the foot of the porch steps and placed it on the grass. "I'm almost afraid to tell her."

"You stay right there." Alex bounded up the front steps. "I'll go get her and bring her out."

Halfway through the door, Alex paused and turned back to Drew. "Thanks, Drew. This was very thoughtful."

Drew nodded. He seemed to be holding his breath until Alex returned with Belle, who at first appeared taken aback that anyone would think she would need such assistance. But Alex sweet-talked her into sitting in it and letting him take her for a ride. In the end, it hadn't taken much to convince Belle that the wheelchair was the only way she'd be getting into Primrose proper that day, cars being banned from the center of town for the fair.

"Thank you, Alexander." She reached for her grandson to lean down so that she could kiss his cheek. "How very kind. How very thoughtful."

"Thank Drew, Gran," Alex told her. "He brought it for you."

"Did he, now?" Belle exclaimed, and she turned to look up at Drew from where she sat in her rented conveyance.

Drew sat on the bottom step and watched the old woman as she turned the wheels to spin the chair slowly in his direction.

"Thank you, young man," she said softly. "I appreciate your kindness."

"It's my pleasure, Miz Matthews," he told her. "Didn't seem right to go off to celebrate Primrose and leave you behind."

"Would you mind pushing me for a block or so, Drew?"

"My privilege." He nodded.

"Now, where is Abigail?" Belle gestured to Alex. "Could you please tell her and Sunny to come along? I can't wait to get to the fair, now that I know I am going. Oh, yes, indeed." Her eyes shone as she looked up at the two young men who stood by her chair. "This will be a *very* fine day."

"Which committee are you signing up for?" Naomi peered over Abby's shoulder at the booth set up to attract new members and volunteers for the Friends of Primrose, the budding civic association that had become Naomi's latest project.

"I shouldn't sign up for anything," Abby replied, "since my stay in Primrose is uncertain."

"Honey, *everybody's* stay is uncertain, if you know what I mean." Naomi's eyes twinkled as she handed Abby the pen and pointed to a sheet of looseleaf paper. "I would definitely consider the garden tour if I were you, Abby. Another month or so, and we'll have that place looking near as good as it did when Miz Cassidy tended it. What do you say?

What are the chances of you finding a job and selling the house before two months have passed?"

Abby signed her name on the line.

"You sure have had some interesting houseguests this week." Naomi grinned, observing both Alex and Drew in conversation over by the table that sought recruits for the planned Civil War reenactment that fall.

"You don't know the half of it." Abby laughed.

"Everyone appears to be getting along."

"I made Alex promise he'd make an honest attempt to get to know Drew before passing judgment," Abby told her, "and, so far, I have to say that they have been very cordial to each other."

"That's good."

"And Drew made points with everyone by having the foresight to rent a wheelchair for Belle so that she could come to the fair." Abby nodded toward where Belle sat in the shade of a sweet gum, surrounded by a number of old friends and acquaintances who were obviously pleased with her company.

"Is that just the sweetest thing?" Naomi sat in the folding chair Colin had insisted she bring with her so that she could occasionally take the pressure off her leg. "There are many times when I could use one of those things myself. Come to think of it, we have one in the attic. I used it for a long while after my accident. Why, we could get it down, and Miz Matthews could have use of it whenever."

"Mommy, look." A beaming Meredy zipped up to them and unrolled a sort of white felt banner. She held it up for her mother and Abby to see. "It's a picture of me and Lilly right on this fabric. Lilly got one, too. There's a man with a special kind of camera over there."

"Friends forever," the banner declared in bright red, fuzzy letters right under the smiling faces of the two little girls.

"If that isn't the cutest thing," Naomi declared solemnly. "And don't you have the perfect spot for it right there between those two big windows in your room."

Meredy nodded happily and handed the banner to her mother to hold.

"Now, where are you off to, Meredy?"

"Susannah said we could go on the pony rides over at Foster's."

"Don't wander off, sugar," Naomi called to her daughter's back as Meredy sprinted in the direction of Foster's store. "Honestly, that child will give me heart failure one of these days. She just *goes*, without giving thought to where or whatever."

"I think she's safe, Naomi. She's already caught up with Sunny, and Colin is here." Abby nodded toward the center of the street, where Colin and two other members of Primrose's police force conferred.

"I know she's safe, Abby. I just like to know where she *is*."

"We'll all keep an eye on her," Abby assured her, "so go ahead and sign up that crew that just wandered over to the table. Give them your 'Primrose needs you' speech. The one you give me every chance you get."

"Primrose does need you, Abby." Naomi tossed the words over her shoulder as she approached the three couples who had stopped to study the display of old photographs depicting Primrose in its heyday. "Almost as much as you need Primrose."

I'm beginning to think she may be right, Abby admitted to herself as she turned away toward the crowded street. *For all the good it will do me.*

She wandered toward the Civil War displays where she had last seen Alex and Drew. The size of the crowd was increasing steadily, the churches having opened their doors to spill their congregations out onto the streets of Primrose to show their civic pride. Abby strolled over toward the town green, where table after table of jams and breads, jars of piccalilli and pickled cauliflower, painted wooden garden ornaments, hats adorned with dried flowers, beaded jewelry, and mounded rounds of sweet potato pies and lemon pound cakes stretched from sidewalk to sidewalk.

Abby paused before the display of wooden toys and ran a small train on smooth wooden wheels back and forth across the front of the table. Hand-carved animals guarded a small cottage around which seven carved men stood. In the doorway stood a woman in a long dress. Snow White and the Seven Dwarfs, their cozy home in the woods, and their tiny animal friends, all painstakingly crafted from lengths of wood that were burnished and polished and stained naturally so that the characters from the children's fairy tale became works of art. On one side of the table stood a chess set with fairy-tale characters in place of the usual figures. Abby marveled as she lifted Beauty and the Beast to admire the cleverness and skill of the craftsman who had first envisioned and then created such fine and tiny sculptures. Turning from the table to seek out Alex, wanting to show him these tiny works of art, she collided with a young blond woman whose mind was obviously elsewhere.

"Oh!" Abby exclaimed as her elbow knocked the woman's purse to the ground. Bending to retrieve it, Abby attempted to apologize, but the woman merely snatched up the purse and hurried on, leaving the heavy scent of her perfume hanging like a curtain between Abby and the table of wooden ornaments.

Gardenia. Abby unconsciously identified the fragrance and, spotting Alex and Drew at that precise moment, waved them over.

"You have to see what this man has done with wood," she told them both. "The most incredibly intricate carvings you could imagine. Can you imagine what stores in the cities would charge for something of this quality and design?"

Alex turned over the white tag, which bore a ridiculously low price.

"Five times what he is asking." Drew nodded.

"At least," Alex agreed as he inspected one of the Dwarfs. "Sleepy, I believe," he told Abby.

Something plunked onto her head, and she reached her hands upward to feel the floppy straw brim of the hat that had landed on her head. Laughing, she removed it and turned at the sound of girlish laughter. Meredy and Lilly giggled as Abby held the hat out before her.

"The girls and I agreed it was you," Sunny said, "so we had to have it. You need to cover that fair skin of yours when you are working outside."

"This is definitely a Primrose gardening hat," Abby agreed, and she plunked it back upon her head. "Thank you so much."

"It looks great on you," Alex told her as he straightened the brim.

"Meredy and Lilly are ready for lunch. How 'bout joining us? There are certainly plenty of choices." Sunny gazed around at the various vendors. "What are we in the mood for? I see Miz Matthews has already found some friends to dine with."

"Those are ladies from her church," Abby noted, following Sunny's gaze to the opposite side of the square, where Belle sat at a table with several other white-haired ladies and gentlemen, all seeming to be enjoying the lunches they removed from the white cardboard cartons being served by the minister's wife, "and it appears that she is having one heck of a good time."

"Well, the Primrose Café gets my vote," Alex said. "They have tables set up out under the tree, so you can have some fresh air and gentle breezes with your hushpuppies and barbecue."

"Sounds good to me." Abby nodded. "Drew, is that okay with you?"

"What?" Drew asked.

"I said, is the Primrose Café all right with you for lunch?"

"Oh, sure. Look, you all go on over. I'll join you in a few minutes." Drew appeared to be looking beyond the small group to someplace over near the bandstand.

"We'll wait for you if there's something you want to see," Abby told him.

"No. You go ahead and get a table. I just want to take a quick look at the used books."

"Okay." Abby shrugged and, taking two long strides, caught up with Alex and Sunny, who had already taken off to keep up with the little girls, who were excitedly planning their after-lunch pony rides. Rounding the corner of the café, Abby glanced back over her shoulder and sought Drew's form in the crowd. She stopped and searched the small gathering in front of the used-book table, then glanced up and down the concourse formed by the tables running along either side of the green, but he was nowhere to be seen. Just as she was about to turn back, she saw him, just to the left of the bandstand, just at the moment when he was joined by a young blond woman in a short denim skirt and a cropped flowered sweater, the same woman Abby had collided with earlier.

As Abby watched, the woman reached behind her and pulled the ribbon from her hair, which spilled in a golden river around her face and shoulders. There appeared to be some conversation, then, abruptly, the woman's hands were firmly planted on her hips, and, judging from the movements of her head, she had words for Drew that were obviously not ones that would be exchanged with a stranger. His gestures were those of protest, Abby thought, as she observed the strange scene.

Now, why wouldn't he tell us he had a friend here? she wondered, as Alex stepped back around the corner and grabbed her by the hand.

"Come on, pokey. We got the last table in the shade," he told her, oblivious to the fact that her attention was focused elsewhere.

And where have I seen her before?

"Mommy, I'm so tired," Lilly whined, her little lower lip jutting out just the tiniest bit. "Can't you carry me?"

"My arms are full, sugar," Sunny told her, "with all the fun things we bought today."

"Come here, Lilly." Drew opened his arms, and Lilly walked into them. He swung her onto his shoulders and moved to the head of the little procession that headed wearily toward Cove Road.

"Look, Meredy, I'm riding!" Lilly called down to her friend.

"I think I'm too big to ride," Meredy told her.

"I don't think so." Alex laughed and hoisted her atop his own shoulders so that both little girls could ride back to Cove Road.

Abby sidled next to Alex, and he smiled down at her, stepping to the side of the walkway to permit Naomi, who was pushing Belle's wheelchair, to pass them. With one hand, he supported Meredy. His free hand sought Abby's own.

"Well, I think that's an absolutely brilliant idea, Miz Matthews." Naomi winked at Abby as she passed by. "And I would hope that you would be the first of the senior members of Primrose to offer to preserve your recollections on tape. Now, who else do you think might have some interesting tales to tell?"

"Wasn't this a great day?" Alex sighed and squeezed Abby's hand.

"A great day," she agreed, and she leaned against him as they strolled slowly. "Can you remember the last time you saw Belle so perfectly happy?"

"No, I cannot," he said. "And I can't remember the last time I was this happy, Abby. Maybe not since I was a kid. But then again, being in Primrose always brought out the best in me."

"Who was that older gentleman you were talking to over by the reenactment booth?"

"Oh, you mean Professor Weston." Alex grinned. "He is a retired professor of history from the University of Richmond. He's into Civil War battle reenactments and serves as a consultant to a number of different groups. He's really concerned with historical accuracy. Interesting fellow."

"You're talking about Professor Weston?" Drew dropped back behind Sunny and addressed Alex. "Are you considering joining the battle group?"

"I don't know." Alex shrugged. "On the one hand, it sounds like fun. On the other, I don't have any Southern sympathies, so I don't know how uncomfortable I'm willing to make myself for the sake of recreating battles I don't really care too much about."

"You watch yourself there, Mr. Kane," his grandmother called over her shoulder. "In some parts of town, that sort of talk is near blasphemy."

Abby stifled a giggle, and Alex and Drew exchanged a bemused glance, before Drew's eyes lighted on Abby and he realized that she and Alex were holding hands that swung between them with casual intimacy. With a brief glance at Alex, Drew turned back and caught up with Sunny just as they approached their destination. The two little girls were swung to the ground almost simultaneously, where they compared notes about their rides and went giggling onto the front porch.

"Drew, I have to thank you for finding a way to include me in this most remarkable day." Belle patted his arm and smiled. "I saw so many folks today, and so many things. What a pleasure to see the center of town from something other than the occasional car window. Your thoughtfulness gave me a freedom I haven't experienced in many years. I don't know how to thank you."

"Why, I believe you just did, Miz Matthews." Drew offered his hand to assist her out of the chair.

"Call me Belle," she told him as she accepted his hand. "Now, you will be joining us for dinner?"

"No, I'm afraid I need to be going," Drew told her. "I have a sales meeting early tomorrow morning."

"Well, then, we'll say good-bye here." Sunny kissed his cheek as she breezed past, being dragged by Lilly, who had loudly claimed to be in need of the bathroom.

"As will I." Abby waved from the top of the steps, where she was assisting Belle into the house.

"Well, it was a fun day." Alex offered his hand to Drew. "I'm really glad you joined us."

"So am I." Drew nodded and hesitated slightly as he turned toward his car.

"What?" Alex asked, sensing the unasked question.

"Well, it's . . ." Drew laughed self-consciously. "About Abby."

"What about Abby?"

"Look, I don't like to intrude into anyone else's life . . ."

Drew ran his fingers through his hair as if debating whether or not to continue. "I mean, it's something I never do . . ."

"Stick to that, and you'll be right one hundred percent of the time." Alex folded his arms across his chest, almost challenging Drew to continue. Which he did.

"I don't want to sound like I'm her father or something, and I don't want this to sound as if I'm asking you what your intentions are toward her . . ."

"But you are."

"I guess I am." Drew shrugged. "Abby is very special to me, Alex. I've never known a woman like her."

"Neither have I."

"What I mean is, she means a lot to me, Alex. She's like the first bit of family I've had in a very long time."

"And?"

"And I don't want her hurt. By anyone."

"So what are you saying?"

"I know she cares about you. I guess I just need to know that you . . . that . . ." He struggled with his words almost sheepishly.

"That my intentions are honorable?"

"Something like that."

"I see." Alex nodded slowly.

"Well?" Drew waited.

"Well, I don't think you—or Abby—need to worry about my intentions." Alex rubbed his chin. "But it does make me wonder if I will have to ask you for her hand."

"I think she can speak for herself when it comes to that."

"And will, if I know Abby."

They exchanged knowing glances.

"I guess I better be on my way." Drew turned toward his car.

"Thanks, Drew," Alex called to his back. "For what you did for Gran. And for letting me know how much you care about Abby."

Drew turned and gave Alex a sort of semi-salute as he got into the car.

Abby stood on the front porch and leaned over the railing, watching Alex as he watched Drew drive away. He put his hands on his denimed hips and seemed to inhale deeply as he turned and saw her half hidden by a massive rhododendron.

"How long have you been standing there?" he asked.

"Long enough to hear you and Drew discussing your relationship with me."

"And?"

"And I think it's really sweet that he cares enough to feel as if he wants to sort of look out for me."

"I can look out for you."

"I know that. But this is different. It tells me that he feels . . . oh, I don't know, *honor*-bound, maybe, to keep an eye on things. It's sweet, Alex." Her eyes twinkled, and she pulled a dead flower bud off the shrub and tossed it at him. "I saw you talking with him today—talking and laughing like old friends. Admit you were wrong about him. Admit that you like him."

Before he could respond, Belle appeared in the doorway, her eyes filled with panic and tears even as she opened the door.

"Alexander! Abigail!" she called. "Meri Puppins is missing!"

"Belle, how could she be missing? She was in the front hall when we left this morning." Abby turned and saw the full measure of Belle's disturbance. "She has to be in the house, Belle, there was no one here to have let her out. Come on, Alex, we have a naughty puppy to find."

◆ 36 ◆

"I can't believe this." Abby threw up her hands in a gesture of incredulity. "There is no way that dog could have gotten out of this house. Where could she be? We've looked everywhere."

"It is pretty strange." Alex leaned back against the

kitchen counter and rubbed his chin. "The only thing I can think of is that somehow, one of the doors had to have been opened while we went out."

"The doors were all locked, Alex. No one has a key except for me. And Naomi."

"All the same, I can't see any other way the dog could have gotten out. We've checked all the closets . . . every place the dog could hide if she wanted to. Could someone have come in through a window and let the dog out when they left by a door?"

"The doors all have dead bolts. You'd need the key even to get out," she reminded him.

"Let me take another look and see if we missed anything."

Alex went, one more time, from room to room, but there were no signs that a break-in had occurred.

"I'm stumped. I give up." Alex shrugged his shoulders as he met up with Abby in the front hallway.

"I think we should call Colin."

"Good thinking. Even though nothing seems to be missing except for the dog . . ."

"I haven't really looked to see if anything is missing," Abby said as she headed for the dining room, the site of the only real valuables in the house, "but I will now."

"Wait till Colin gets here," Alex told her, "in case there are fingerprints."

"Well, of course there are fingerprints," Abby said. "Yours. Mine. Sunny's. Drew's. Belle's."

Colin agreed that fingerprints were always a good place to start when there has been a theft—and a heartbroken Belle insisted that her dog had in fact been shanghaied. While Colin lifted prints from the dining room, Abby and Sunny searched the second floor.

A mystified Abby came back into the kitchen and told Alex, "I just cannot figure this out. How can a dog just disappear into thin air?"

"It really is bizarre, isn't it?" He shook his head.

"Abby?" Colin stuck his blond head in through the

kitchen door. "Can we get all your prints so that we can do some comparison?"

"Sure, Colin." Abby tried to smile. "We're all here—except Naomi and Drew."

"Where is Drew?" Colin stepped into the room.

"He said he had a sales meeting early in the morning, so he left right after the fair."

"This is so strange, Abby. There is no sign of breaking and entering, no sign that anyone has even been here who shouldn't be. Except for the fact that the dog is missing." Colin scratched his head. "And you are positive that you locked the house? And that the dog did not scoot out of the house when you all left?"

"Absolutely. We all left by the front door. If the dog had come out, she would have stayed right by Belle. She would not have taken off."

"Don't know quite how to write this one up, folks." Colin leaned his elbow on the stairwell's carved banister. "We have an apparent theft with no signs of breaking into a locked house, and nothing is missing except that little dog."

"That little dog, my traveler's checks, and my amethyst ring," Sunny announced from the doorway.

"What?" Abby exploded.

"My ring—the one Aunt Leila left me, the one we got out of the safe deposit box—and my traveler's checks are gone. I almost didn't even look in my suitcase," Sunny grumbled. "But there's something odd in my room . . ."

"Show me." Colin motioned for Sunny to lead the way.

". . . almost as if something heavy had been set upon it," Sunny was saying as she pointed to the quilt that covered her bed and the flat, rectangular depression that appeared on one side toward the footboard. "And then I noticed that the suitcase was open. I had zipped it up this morning."

"So it would appear that the person or persons placed the closed suitcase on the bed, making that indentation in the feather mattress," Colin concluded, "then proceeded to go through the contents until they found your checks and your ring. I'll need a good description of the ring, and I'll also need you to go through your things one more time to make sure that there's nothing else missing."

"Sunny, I feel so bad. I cannot apologize enough for what has happened." Abby leaned back against the radiator.

"Abby, don't be silly. It's certainly not your fault." Sunny's nose began to twitch. "Oh, dear, I'm going to . . . *ahhchoo!* Excuse me, but . . . *ahhchoo!*"

"Sunny, are you all right?" Abby asked, handing her cousin a box of tissues after the fifth major sneeze.

"I'm afraid that someone's wearing aftershave or perfume that's bothering me. Certain fragrances very often make me . . . *ahhchoo!* . . . sneeze, and I could smell just the trace of something when I came up the steps . . . *ahhchoo!*"

"Colin, are you wearing aftershave?" Abby asked.

"No."

"Well, I'm not wearing perfume, nor is Sunny. Alex doesn't wear aftershave at all."

"Can you identify the scent, Sunny?" Colin asked.

"Some sort of flowers, heavy-scented."

"I didn't know that you had such a sensitivity," Abby said. "How have you managed in this house with all the lavender Aunt Leila left around?"

"For some reason, natural herbal scents don't bother me, but heavily concentrated florals in perfumes do." She shrugged.

"Well, maybe whoever was in here was wearing a flowery perfume." Colin nodded. "Can you sketch the ring for me?"

"Sure. It was a very simple gold setting, but it was an immense stone." Sunny shook her head. "Damn! I hadn't even really gotten to wear it but once or twice. Damn!"

"Well, we'll see what we can do about getting it back for you." Colin patted her on the back. "Now, come downstairs and draw us a picture of the ring, and we'll get the reports made out."

"Colin." Abby spoke up. "A woman bumped into me today at the fair. She wore a very pronounced perfume."

"I guess it's too much to hope that you know who she was," Colin said.

"I didn't see her face," Abby replied. "But Drew knows her. I saw him talking to her right before lunch. There was something familiar about her, but I just can't place her."

"Oh?" Colin's eyebrows rose. "Well, then, let's get Drew on the phone and find out who his friend is."

"He's on his way to a sales conference."

"Did he say where the conference is?" Colin asked.

"I think he said Williamsburg."

"I have a friend in the Williamsburg P.D. I'll give him a call, and we'll track Drew down. Now, Sunny, let's see about that sketch."

"Abby, if there was any way I could get out of this trial tomorrow morning, I'd do it," Alex said as he reached his hand through his car window to bring her face close for one more kiss good-bye. "I do not like leaving with all this going on."

"It's okay." She kissed his nose. "We'll be fine. And Colin is right across the street."

"Well, I want you to call the office and leave word if anything happens." He put the car in gear. "And I'll give you a call tomorrow night."

She stepped back from the side of the car as he began to drift slowly backward.

"Do you think Gran will be all right?" he asked.

"I think she'll be better if we find Meri P."

"Maybe some signs around town?"

"First thing in the morning. And I'll call the SPCA, the local vets . . ."

"Good idea. That little dog means a lot to my grandmother."

"I know. We'll do our best. Oh, and Alex?"

He stopped the car.

"Good luck tomorrow. With your case."

"Thanks, Ab." He reached out a hand and clasped the back of her neck gently, drawing her to him for one last deep kiss to hold them both until Friday night.

Abby closed up the house and started her nightly ritual of turning off the lights. Sunny and Lilly had already turned in, but Belle had insisted on waiting just a little longer to see if Meri would come home. Abby helped her up the steps around eleven and placated the woman slightly by describing all the means she would try the next day to find the dog.

"She's been dognapped." Belle wiped the tears from her face. "I just know she has. Whoever broke into the house just fell in love with that dog and had to take her. Oh, Abigail, pray that this . . . this person will take good care of her. Though, of course, one who breaks into houses to rob them can't be counted on to give a dog like Meri the manner of care she is accustomed to."

"We will find her," Abby told Belle firmly as she turned on the old woman's bedroom light for her. "You'll see. We'll pull out all the stops."

"I do so hope you are right, dear. Meri is like a very dear and special friend to me. I have loved that little dog since the day Naomi brought her to me." Belle removed her sweater and folded it neatly before placing it on a small yellow-and-green print slipper chair near the door. "And it is so very wonderful to find someone new to love, Abby. At any age, at any stage of your life, it's always unexpected, you know. But it's always glorious to have a special someone who loves you, who brightens up when you enter the room . . . even if that special someone is only a dog. What I learned from that little dog is that life can still hold surprises, Abigail, even at my age. And that if I'm still young enough to feel that sort of joy in the company of so small a creature, then perhaps I'm not so very old after all."

Belle turned sorrowful eyes on Abby. "I do miss her already, Abigail. And I am worried about her."

"I know you are, Belle. We'll do our best. I promise."

Belle nodded and dabbed her eyes as Abby kissed her softly on the cheek and left the room. She had planned on trying to probe—subtly, of course—Abby's growing relationship with Alex but had no heart for a discussion on something so important as their future. Belle sighed as she closed her bedroom door. It could wait till tomorrow or the next day. Or the next.

* * *

"How's Gran?" Alex asked for the third day in a row when he called on Wednesday evening.

"Not well at all, I'm afraid," Abby told him. "I'm thinking about giving her doctor a call, Alex. She is listless, distracted, hardly eating . . ."

"She is mourning the loss of someone she loved," he said softly.

"It's more than that, Alex. Belle insists she hears the dog crying."

"What do you mean?" he asked warily.

"I mean, she'll call me into the morning room and say, 'Abigail, can't you hear her? I hear Meri whimpering.' Then she gets up and proceeds for the eight-hundredth time to look behind the furniture." Abby sighed deeply. "I'm really worried, Alex."

"Go ahead and call the doctor first thing in the morning. This doesn't sound good." Alex sounded worried. "If she is starting to hallucinate . . ."

"Alex, she is so adamant that I've even thought once or twice that *I* heard the dog. But, of course, it was the wind. We had a storm yesterday and another one today."

"Well, if you could call her doctor, I'd appreciate it. I'd call myself, but I'll be in court again tomorrow."

"How is that going?" Abby tugged the phone line into the morning room, stretching the cord as far as it would go so that she could curl up on the love seat.

"It's actually going quite well," he said hesitantly. "I expect we will win the case."

"'But'?" she asked. "I hear a definite 'but' there."

"We'll win because our client has more money to defend the case than the plaintiff has to pursue us. He can't afford the caliber of experts that we have. He can't afford a panel of high-priced lawyers. He can't afford all that it would take to prove that our client's product was responsible for his son's death."

"That's a very sad commentary on our legal system."

"I see it every day of my life." He seemed to shrug through the phone.

"But I guess winning is everything, right?"

"It's the only thing, as Vince Lombardi once said. Sometimes I think maybe I'm . . ." He stopped in mid-thought.

"You're what?"

"Nothing. This is where the money is, defending the big corporations." He laughed, but to Abby, it had sounded forced. "Not exactly what I thought I'd be doing when I first entered law school. I always thought I'd be the defender of the little guy."

"I remember," she said softly. "You were going to hang out your shingle right up there on Main Street and take care of Primrose's legal business in the morning and fish in the afternoon."

"Actually, it was the other way around." He laughed again, but this time it was natural. "Fish in the morning and practice law in the afternoon." There was an overlong silence, then he said, "Unfortunately, there's no money in that kind of lifestyle."

"Small-town lawyers do get paid, don't they?"

"Not like they do in this firm. I'll bet I make in one day what old . . . what was Leila's attorney's name?"

"Tillman."

"What old Tillman makes in a week. Maybe two weeks."

"Well, I guess that's the bottom line."

"Absolutely. I worked hard to get where I am in this firm," he said, although Abby was uncertain if he was telling her or convincing himself. "I have a great future here. I'll be offered a partnership soon, I expect. Maybe my own branch office."

"Where would that be?"

"Who knows? The point is, I worked hard through law school, and I've worked my butt off since I got out—sixteen-hour workdays are not unusual for me—but I'm lucky to have the type of opportunity that a firm like this can offer. And I mean to take advantage of everything they send my way."

"Well, I do know what that's like," she admitted. "I know what it's like to work harder than anyone else, to want to be the best at what you do. I've always done the same thing. I always had that drive." Even as she spoke the words, her lack of fervor lent a quiet protest to the sentiment.

Of course, she had always felt that way. Of course, she would again. She still had résumés out there. Her corporate life was not over. Alex wasn't the only one who'd be going places. She'd be back on track soon enough.

And when she got back on track, she would leave Primrose behind. It would mean leaving Alex behind as well. Though he obviously had his own plans, too. His own agenda included making partner and eventually heading up one of the branch offices. Unless the fates would decree at some future time that they would end up in the same city at the same time, they would part company when Abby got a job or Alex made partner. Until then, he was hers, and she was his.

She had survived losing him once before and would survive it again, she assured herself, but this time she would have memories to last a lifetime. Memories enough to live on. He would be back on Friday night, and there would be more memories to make to warm her through some future time when the only love in her life would be found in the images of these very days and nights in Primrose.

◆37◆

"Abby, I hate to leave you to deal with all this," Sunny said as she tucked Lilly's Minnie Mouse suitcase into the trunk of her Mercedes.

"Don't be ridiculous. You've been wonderful. I don't know what I would have done without you and Lilly these past few days. Sunny, I can't tell you how terrible I feel about your ring."

"Abby, don't." Sunny hugged her. "We've gone over that

enough times. It wasn't your fault, and I don't want you feeling guilty about it. Besides, it would appear that Belle's loss is actually greater than mine. I sure hope the doctor is right."

Susannah slid behind the wheel of her car, and Abby closed the door. They had all said their good-byes in the morning room, and the business of getting in the car and actually going was almost anticlimactic.

"Come back again," Abby told them as Sunny turned the key in the ignition.

"We will, won't we, sugar?"

Lilly nodded enthusiastically.

"Good luck next week," Abby called as the car began its descent back down the drive. "Let me know how it goes."

Abby watched the little sports car as it rounded the curve toward the end of Cove Road and disappeared someplace past the old Lawrence house. She kicked a stone with the toe of her sneaker and sighed. She would miss Sunny and Lilly. They had almost seemed to belong here, as they, too, had been woven into the tapestry of all she loved best—all she would miss most—of Primrose. She hoped that Justin would keep his word and be pleasant when they appeared in court the following week to formalize Lilly's adoption.

The front door needs something, she noted as she walked back toward the house. Something to make the house appear less foreboding. She frowned as she crossed the porch and entered the hall. Of course, the inhospitable appearance hadn't deterred their burglar one bit. *Damn whoever it was,* she silently cursed. *Damn them for taking Meri and creating such heartbreak for a dear old woman.*

"Let her grieve," the doctor had told Abby when she called him on Monday morning and explained what had occurred. "She has lost something that was vitally important to her. Just let her mourn her loss, Miz McKenna. Of course, if she still appears despondent in another week or so, give me a call back."

On the phone the previous night, Alex had suggested buying Belle a puppy, but Abby felt it was perhaps too soon.

Belle wasn't ready to concede that her beloved pet was gone for good. The doctor was right. Belle needed time to mourn the loss of her friend.

"Abigail! Come quickly!" Belle called from the morning room.

"Belle, what is it?" Abby raced into the room to find Belle standing near the fireplace wall.

"I hear Meri," Belle told her with frantic eyes.

"Oh, Belle." Abby sighed sadly. "Oh, Bell, Meri isn't here."

Belle pointed a finger slightly crooked with arthritis in Abby's direction. "I tell you, I hear her."

"Belle, if you hear her, then why can't we see her?" Abby asked gently. "Belle, the doctor said you think you hear her because you want so badly to have her back."

"Dr. Ellrick is a fool. I know what I know, Abigail," Belle said sternly, 'and I know that I hear my dog."

"How about I make us some tea, and we sit down and we discuss . . ." Abby stopped mid-speech.

There *was* a sound.

"You hear her, too, don't you?" Belle said triumphantly.

"I . . . I hear something. I do. But where is it coming from?" Abby turned her head this way and that, trying to discern the direction from which the faint whimpering sound was coming.

"I've been trying to figure that out all week." Belle glared. "While you and everyone else were insisting that I wasn't hearing anything."

"Hush." Abby waved a hand in Belle's direction as she pressed the power button on the remote control to turn off the television.

Standing in the middle of the room, Abby strained her ears and concentrated on the barely audible cry.

"Meri?" Abby called softly, then louder. "Meri P.?"

A muffled bark from someplace far away answered her.

"Oh, my stars!" Belle exclaimed. "She *is* here!"

"But where?" A puzzled Abby shook her head. "It almost sounds as if she's in the walls someplace."

"But, of course, Abigail, that's exactly where she is." Belle beamed.

"How could she get into the walls?" Abby began to feel along the wall near the fireplace, where Belle had been standing when Abby had first entered the room. "Belle, do you suppose there is some passageway . . ."

"I know there is. Unfortunately, I do not know exactly where it comes out in this house." Belle's eyes shone with the joy of finding Meri. "I know that there is a passage from someplace in the carriage house into this house. It leads to a tunnel that runs under Cove Road into my old house."

"The Underground Railroad?"

"Exactly so. People would be brought up this far by river and, from the river, would come through the back of the Cassidys' carriage house. There was a tunnel from there into this house, and from here to the house across the street. Sometimes people who'd been brought up this far north by other means would go the reverse route, from the house across the street to this one to the river, depending on which route was the safest at any given time."

"You don't know where in the carriage house?"

"No, but I know where it comes out over there." Belle motioned across the road with her head. "Josie used to hide there sometimes."

"Where?"

"Under the stairwell in the back hallway is a closet. Along the back wall of the closet is a loose floorboard. Pull up the board, and the last panel on the right side will slide away. It's not a real big space until you get inside, as I recall. I mean, you have to sort of crawl in, but, once inside, you can stand up."

Abby was already on the phone to Naomi.

"She's bringing the kids over here to stay with you," Abby told Belle. "Naomi doesn't want the kids to know about this just yet."

"Don't you think she should call Colin?"

"She's doing that. He'll meet us there."

Naomi was at the door in a flash, her eyes sparkling with anticipation, her children in tow. She planted Sam and

Meredy in the morning room with Belle—"Y'all just sit here and keep Miz Matthews company for a few minutes while Mommy and Abby look for something"—and the two excited women made a beeline for Naomi's house.

"Did you call Colin?" Abby asked as they flew up the front steps.

"Yes, but he's on the road. I left a message for him to call home as soon as he gets the chance." Naomi closed the front door behind them and practically ran to the back hallway off the kitchen. "I cannot believe what a dunce I am not to have thought of the tunnels. Anyone who grew up around here knows about them."

Naomi unlatched the closet door with excited fingers. "Help me get this stuff out, Abby. I swear, I am such a damned pack rat . . . well, here's my old tennis racket. I was looking for that a few weeks ago. And Lord have mercy, Colin's old hip boots. He had to buy new ones when he went duck hunting last year because we couldn't find these. Never thought to look in here . . ."

They tossed items this way and that in their haste to clear a path to the back of the deep closet.

"What am I looking for? A loose floorboard?" Abby asked.

"Yes. Right along here someplace."

Abby's fingers searched along the baseboard in the dark. "Naomi, this is silly. Go get a flashlight."

"Right. A flashlight." Naomi backed out of the narrow closet.

She was back in less than a minute with two long black-handled flashlights, one of which she handed to Abby.

"It's here. Right here," Abby whispered. "Hold the light for me while I see if I can pull this back."

"Abigail." Naomi leaned forward and whispered in Abby's ear.

"What?"

"Why are we whispering?"

"What? Oh!" She laughed. "I guess it just seems apropos, looking for secret panels in an old . . . oh!"

The side of the wall slid away to reveal a black hole.

"Give me the light." Abby put her left hand over her shoulder to take the flashlight from Naomi. In the dark, she found the switch and turned it on, sending a bright beam of light into the darkness that had opened up in front of them.

"Shouldn't we wait for Colin?" Naomi asked as Abby inched into the hole.

"One of us should, I guess."

"Oh, no you don't, Abigail McKenna." Naomi watched Abby disappear into the open wall. "If you think I am going to sit here and wait while you have an adventure, well, you are sadly mistaken."

Naomi followed Abby into the wall.

"Wow, this is something." Abby shined her light along the wall, where dozens of names had been scratched into the stone that lined the passageway on one side. "I'll bet these are the names of the escaped slaves who passed through this very spot."

"I doubt that they'd have wanted to leave such a record. More likely than not, it's the names of the town kids who made it through the tunnel. It was sort of a badge of distinction, you know, to make it through this far. Oh, my golly, would you look here," Naomi exclaimed. " 'Sharon Dare.' Looks like my sister was a little bit more of a daredevil growing up than we knew."

"Watch your step, Naomi, the landing here is a little weak." Abby sent the stream of light downward to illuminate the stairwell, which seemed to descend forever into the earth and end somewhere in darkness far below. Without thinking, she began slowly to follow the wooden pathway down. Seeing that Abby had gone exploring, Naomi fell in step behind her.

"Oh, my God, Abigail, what was that?" Naomi cringed as something fat and furry passed over her ankle.

"You probably don't want to know. Oh!" Abby shrieked as the hairless tail of something flicked at her leg.

"Don't look down at it," Naomi told her. "Maybe it's not what we think it is. Just keep going."

"How's your leg holding up on the steps?"

"Okay. If I fall, I'll just be sure to land on you."

"Please, feel free to do that . . . oh, God, Naomi, I hate spider webs . . . oh, this is creepy."

"Maybe we should wait for Colin." Naomi paused on the steps. "Nah. Keep on going, Abby. This little adventure is all ours. You know, after you've had children, your life really changes—oh, Lord, what do you suppose *that* was?— and you sort of settle into this nice, safe routine . . . did you hear that?"

"Don't think about it. We're almost to the bottom."

"Then what?"

"We'll soon find out. Oh, look, there's a sort of bunkbed-type thing. People must have stayed over here when it was too dangerous to travel." Abby flashed her light around the room which was a widened section of a long passage. A brass candle holder, its candle long since burned away, stood atop a small wooden table. Wooden bowls and tin cups were stacked on another.

"Look." Abby pointed her beam of light straight ahead to a long, narrow pathway. "This goes right under Cove Road. Right to Aunt Leila's."

She took off toward the passage with Naomi close behind. They followed the path for about three hundred feet before coming to another flight of wood steps that led upward at a steep angle.

"Almost home," Abby muttered as she started up. "Literally and figuratively."

"Wait up, Abby," Naomi pleaded. "Going up is always harder than coming down."

"Want to stop and rest your leg for a few minutes?"

"No." Naomi shook her head. "I don't want to stand in one spot that long, Abby, something's bound to crawl on me. No, I just want to slow down."

Abby held in check her natural inclination to run up the rest of the steps and slowed her pace for Naomi's sake.

"We must be inside Aunt Leila's house," Abby told her. "There can't be too much farther to go."

From deep in the darkness above them came a low growl.

"Meri?" Abby called out hopefully.

Tiny doggy toenails began to tap-dance on the wooden landing as Meri heard her name.

"Meri Puppins!" Abby laughed, and the dog barked happily. "Oh, my stars, as Belle would say, someone is going to be so happy to see you!"

Abby picked the dog up in her arms and was immediately rewarded with dog kisses on her neck, her chin, and wherever else the little dog could reach.

"Belle?" Abby called as loudly as she could. "Belle, can you hear me?"

"Yes! Yes, Abigail." Belle's reply was muffled.

"We found Meri, and she appears to be fine," Abby yelled. "Now all we have to do is find a way out of here and . . . oops!"

Abby's hand accidentally found the way out. The thick wall she leaned on opened suddenly, spilling her into the morning room, where the dog flew out of her arms and into Belle's.

"Oh, my dear little pup!" Belle crooned. "Oh, Abigail, you found her! Oh, Meri, I've missed you."

Belle fell back into her chair, her legs wobbly from emotion and tired from the strain of it all.

Sam and Meredy immediately poked their heads into the passage.

"Oh, no you don't." Naomi wagged a finger at them. "Don't even think about it."

"Mommy, you have webby things in your hair," Meredy told her.

"I don't." Naomi cringed and peered into the mirror over the mantel. 'Oh, Lordy, don't I, though. You're even worse than I am, Abby. Look at yourself."

Abby took a peek at herself and shrugged. A car door slammed outside, and Abby went to the front hall to look through the window.

"Colin's here," she told Naomi as she opened the front door and called across the street. "Colin! We're all over here. Come see what we found!"

"Abby, what happened to you?" Colin frowned as he took

in her appearance, dirty clothes and cobwebs in her hair. "Naomi! What in the world . . . ?"

"Colin, we found Miz Matthews's dog!" Naomi's eyes danced as she grabbed her husband by the arm and pulled him into the room where Belle sat with her dog on her lap.

"Hi, Daddy." Meredy came in from the kitchen carrying a pot of water, which she set on the floor next to Belle's chair, just as Belle had instructed her to do. "Mommy and Abby brought Meri out of the wall."

Colin's gaze followed Meredy's pointing finger.

He whistled long and low, then walked over and peered into the dark chamber beyond the room.

"How did you find this?"

"From our house," Naomi told him.

"What do you mean, from our house?" Colin frowned.

"Miz Matthews remembered a secret panel in our back hall closet that opened up and led to a passage that came over here . . ."

"Whoa, back up there, sweetheart."

"There's an old passage from the Underground Railroad days that links this house with the carriage house and goes under Cove Road to your house," Abby explained.

Colin took the flashlight from his wife's hand and entered the darkness, instructing the others to stay behind, telling them, "You never know what's down here."

"Oh, we have a pretty good idea." Naomi giggled.

Within twenty minutes, Colin appeared at the back door.

"There's a trap door in the stable which leads to the tunnel which leads to the house." He shook his head. "I cannot believe you two were foolish enough to go down there alone."

"You weak woman," Naomi grunted. "Me macho man."

"Knock it off, Naomi." Colin scowled. "I have never played that game with you, and you know it."

"Well, Abby and I did just fine."

"I think you and Abby were damned lucky that whoever used the tunnel to come in here on Sunday wasn't down there today when you decided to go exploring. I wish you had waited for me."

"We tried to. At least, we thought about it. But you were taking too long getting here, and the wall opened up, and we just had to go in."

Colin kissed the top of his wife's head. "Okay, let's go on home, and you can show me where it starts. Abby, you stay here and watch that the kids don't go down into the wall."

"And that no one unexpected comes out," Belle called over her shoulder.

⋆38⋆

"It sounds as if you had quite a week." Alex leaned back against the wooden garden bench where he and Abby had cozied up after breakfast. He pulled Abby back with him, so that they rested against each other on the rustic settee which Susannah had found in the carriage house. Sunny had painted it a gleaming white to surprise Abby, who had found it to be the perfect spot to sip her second cup of morning coffee and watch the birds.

"Umm," she murmured, snuggling back against his chest, her arms around his to sink closer into him, still wrapped in the early-morning glow of having Alex awaken her at dawn to love her into a new day.

"And I do agree with Colin, that you and Gran should not be here alone," he continued. "As soon as this trial is over, I will take a few weeks off and come stay with you. That is, of course, if you'll have me."

"As often as possible." She grinned in reply.

"Ah, yes, just one of the fringe benefits of playing security guard." He laughed and gave her a squeeze.

"I feel like I'm playing hooky," she told him with a sigh. "I should be upstairs working on the wainscot in the small bathroom."

"I think you can safely take an hour off here and there to relax. And what is the point of having done all this"—he waved his arm to take in the entire backyard area—"if you never sit and just enjoy the view?"

"It does look pretty good, doesn't it?" She sat up slightly so that she could see the full expanse of garden she and Sunny had worked on over the past few weeks.

"It looks wonderful," he assured her.

And it did. The old paths had been painstakingly uncovered and the bricks dug up and reset, the perennial beds cleaned up, and the herb garden restored. The first of the roses were in bud and early bloom along the fence, several long-armed branches reaching up and over the arbor where the white roses would soon bloom in concert with the red as they had so long ago. All in all, Abby thought, some of the old magic had returned, and it filled her with pride. Aunt Leila would have been pleased.

"What do you hear from Drew?" Alex asked casually.

Abby frowned. "Actually, nothing. I haven't heard from him since last weekend. He still doesn't even know about the break-in."

Alex leaned back against the hard bench and sighed, debating whether or not to tell Abby that, in trying to track Drew down to see if he could check in on her and Belle this past week, Alex had found no hotel in Williamsburg that was hosting a sales meeting for an athletic equipment company. And in checking with the colleges Drew claimed to have as clients, he discovered that no one had ever heard of a Drew Cassidy.

Maybe, Alex thought, while Abby was painting inside and he was painting the front porch, he'd slip on over across the street and ask Colin to do a little background check on old Drew. Just a precaution, Alex told himself, trying to beat down the uneasy feeling that had begun to spread. Maybe Colin could track him down and there'd be a logical explanation. For Abby's sake, Alex wanted Drew to be everything that Abby believed him to be.

But even beyond wanting to confirm Abby's faith, there was something more. Alex had, as Abby had predicted, liked Drew. While there did appear to be something guarded about the man, there was also something intrinsically decent about him. Alex found himself wanting to solve this little mystery, hoping that his earlier suspicions would be proved false.

"Well." Abby patted his arm gently before standing up and stretching. "I really do need to get to work."

Alex sighed. He liked just sitting with her, smelling the early-morning scents of honeysuckle and roses and lavender and feeling Abby's softness. He wanted to hold on to the moment, and he wanted to hold on to her. He could have stayed right there for the rest of the day and been damned happy to do so.

"Okay." He reluctantly let her go. "Help me up, and I'll get started on the front porch. But, you know, that will only take another weekend or so. If I spend a few weeks here, all of the work will be done by the end of next month."

"Most likely."

"What will you do then?"

"Contact a Realtor." Abby shrugged. "I guess that's the next logical step."

They walked in silence the rest of the way to the house, holding hands, neither one of them wanting to think about the next logical step, both of them wondering just what, after all, logic had to do with what was going on between them. They both sighed at the same time, as each considered first the other's personal agenda, then his or her own.

"I think I'll cut some flowers for the hallway," Abby said unexpectedly as they reached the back porch, and she sought out the small clippers she had left in a small basket for just such a purpose.

Knowing this was his chance to sneak a call to Colin, Alex leaned down and kissed the back of her neck. "I'll get started with that front porch railing. See you at lunch."

Alex began to dial Colin's number but was distracted by the sight of Abby strolling leisurely, basket in one hand, clippers in the other, as she followed the path into the garden. He hung up the phone without completing the number and went to the window for a better view. Mesmerized, he stared.

In old jeans and a dark green T-shirt, Abby's lithe body

moved between the rows with all the grace of a tiny dancer, the cobbled walk her stage and he her only audience. A surge of unexpected emotion flooded him to the core, and he knew with crystal certainty the most elemental of facts, the only real truth of his life. His only true agenda stood in the damp grass in bare feet, snipping stalks of butter-yellow forsythia.

Oh, he could protest as much as he wanted that the law was his love and a senior partnership his goal, but it was meaningless when taken in the context of the truth he had so recently discovered about his life.

Abby was his life, and his life was here in Primrose.

Once he accepted what he had so long ago suspected, he knew the only thing that lay between him and a lifetime of happiness was convincing Abby that this town, this house—and this man—were her destiny just as they, and she, were his.

He hoped it wouldn't take too long.

"Are you sure there isn't something you want to tell me, Abby?" Naomi arched her eyebrows and batted her eyes, all innocence and naïveté.

"I guess if I thought I could hide something from you, I was delusional at the time." Abby laughed. "Where would you like me to start?"

The two women stood in Naomi's backyard, surrounded by the flats of herbs, vegetables, and annual flowers that Naomi had started from seed in her little greenhouse. Abby had volunteered to assist in the planting, and, with the work on her own house almost completed, she was happy to have time to help her friend.

"A simple 'You were right all along' would suffice. For now, anyway."

"Ah, is that a smirk or a gloating grin I see on your face?"

"Oh, perhaps a touch of both. I can't even begin to tell you how happy I am for you both. I knew it was merely a matter of time before you realized that you were hopelessly in love and couldn't live without each other. I knew that ten years ago. I'm just happy that you found each other at last."

Naomi, ever the romantic, sighed. "And now you can live happily ever after."

"Well, I don't know about that part."

"What do you mean?"

"Well, Alex has his law practice . . ."

"Abby, he could commute if he had to, you know. It's not like Hampton is hours away."

"He may not be in Hampton for all that long. He may be transferred to another office."

"Seriously?"

"Seriously. Alex expects to be made partner. And, from what he said, that could happen anytime. Once he makes partner, he could be given his own office to open up in another city."

"Then you just have to make him understand that he belongs here."

"I can't do that, Naomi," Abby said. "Alex has to decide for himself what he wants."

"And you would stand by and let him walk out of your life again?" Naomi's eyes widened with horror. "Girl, what are you thinking?"

"I'm thinking Alex has to choose."

"I'm thinking you have lost your mind if you believe for one minute that either of you would ever be happy without the other. I'm thinking if you let him go, it will be the biggest mistake of your life."

"I'll deal with it when it happens," Abby told her. "It may not be an issue for a long time yet. Right now, it's still all very new, and I'm happy, and Alex seems happy, and that's what matters to me."

"Please do not bury your head in the sand for too long. I would hate to have to help you put that heart of yours back together when I know and you know and even Alex knows you belong together."

"Sometimes things don't work out the way they should." Abby concentrated on smoothing the soft dirt around the seedlings she placed in the ground.

"Sometimes they do," Naomi replied pointedly. "You can't always leave things to fate, Abby."

"I'll worry about it later." Abby dismissed the matter with the wave of one hand, smiling as if to assure Naomi that she did, in fact, have everything under control. "Right now, let's just concentrate on getting your garden in so that I have time to take a shower before dinner. Alex and I are taking Belle to the new mall out there off the interstate. Having your old wheelchair is a real blessing, Naomi. Thanks for the loan."

"Thanks to Drew for thinking of it."

There was a long pause before Abby confided, "We still haven't heard from him, Naomi."

"Drew?"

Abby nodded.

"He'll pop up."

"I guess so. He must have had a business trip this week." Abby shrugged.

Naomi was silent. How to tell Abby what she and Colin had learned from Alex? Or what Colin himself had determined through his law enforcement connections: that he could find no trace of the man's existence, that Drew was not, after all, who he said he was.

Abby glanced across the row and saw the tightness in the line of Naomi's mouth. She watched for several minutes while some tension played in her friend's eyes, then said, "Okay, spill it."

"Spill what?" Naomi did not look up.

"I want to know whatever it is about Drew that you know."

"What makes you think I know anything?"

"Naomi, you are absolutely the world's worst liar. Look me in the eye, and tell me that you don't know anything about Drew."

"I don't know anything about Drew." Naomi continued to stare into the dirt.

"I said, look me in the eye, and . . ."

"All right, all right," Naomi muttered. "Alex didn't want to say anything at all to you until we had exhausted all the possibilities."

" 'We'?"

"Colin is trying to track him, Abby. Some prints that Colin picked up when he dusted your house didn't match any of us, not you or me or Sunny or Belle or Alex. So Colin sent them to a friend of his in D.C. to put through the computer system, which, unfortunately, Primrose isn't hooked into. Not yet, anyway."

"And nothing came back?"

"Not as of this morning."

"What about the colleges where he . . ."

"He doesn't." Naomi held up a hand to stop Abby from completing the sentence. "He doesn't work for any company that deals with any of the colleges he told us he sold to."

"Well, just when was someone going to tell me?" Abby's eyes crackled with the anger that was rapidly building inside her. "You could have told me what you were doing." She flung a handful of deep brown soil in Alex's direction as he approached with Colin from the driveway.

Alex flashed an inquiring look in Naomi's direction. Naomi merely shrugged and said, "What can I say? Abby asked me point-blank, and I could not lie. And, besides, you should have told her yourself."

"You are absolutely right." Alex nodded as he eased himself onto the ground next to the row of green beans Abby was planting. "And I apologize to you for not telling you sooner. But I really wanted to clear it up before you even had to know. I know how you feel about Drew. Hell, I was even starting to like him myself."

"But, of course, now you can't like him anymore because you think he somehow . . ." Abby struggled with her thoughts, reluctant to put words to any of them.

"He's a liar, Abby. He lied to all of us." Alex's jaw squared.

"And I guess you feel pretty smug about that, don't you? Go ahead and say 'I told you so' and get it over with."

"Abby, I didn't want it to be true any more than you did. Yes, I admit that in the beginning I had reservations—I was suspicious about him showing up out of the blue the way he did. But there's something about Drew that is very likable once you get to know him. He was kind to Gran and very sweet to Lilly, and I really do believe he cared very much for all of you."

"I absolutely agree." Naomi struggled momentarily to rise, shifting her stiff leg slightly. "There is no question that he was growing close to you. There are some things you just can't fake, Abby."

"So what you're saying is that Drew was a fake but his feelings were genuine," Abby said sarcastically.

"Sort of. Maybe. What we're saying is we don't know who he really is or what he really wants." Colin spoke up for the first time. "But we will find out who he really is, Abby. I feel pretty certain of that."

"Until you do, could we refrain from assuming that he was a crook?" Abby stood up and dropped her trowel onto the ground. "Because that's the implication you're making."

"You have to admit that it looks pretty suspicious, Abby. At least be open-minded. Someone definitely broke into the house. And Drew—or whatever his name is—hasn't been seen since."

"Do I need to remind you that Drew was with us at the same time the house was being burglarized?"

"True. But he could have had an accomplice," Colin said gently.

The memory of Drew standing in the shadow of the bandstand, in a lively discussion with a woman, flashed through Abby's inner vision.

"Even if he had, how would they—or Drew, for that matter—have known about the tunnels? He wouldn't have known, Naomi. He didn't grow up here, like you did."

"Maybe he knows someone who did."

The slight glimpse Abby had gotten of the young blond woman stumbling into Abby at the town fair played again through her mind. There had been something vaguely familiar about her, but Abby had paid little attention to her at the time.

"Well, I think we owe it to Drew to wait for an explanation from him before we all convince ourselves that he's some slick ne'er-do-well con artist."

They all nodded, all but Abby thinking that perhaps a con artist was exactly what Drew Cassidy—by any name—was.

"I don't want him to be a bad guy," Abby muttered sullenly as she sat down on the edge of her bed and kicked off her once-white sneakers.

"I know you don't, sweetheart." Alex stood in the doorway and tried to soothe her. "And, frankly, neither do I."

"So what do we do?"

"There's nothing we can do until we hear from him."

"I'm angry with him for deceiving me."

"You have every right to be. I'm not particularly happy about that myself."

Alex clenched a fist behind his back. There were things that he, too, was anxious to discuss with Drew. Starting with the abuse of Abby's trusting heart.

"You know, we could be blowing this way out of proportion. There could very well be a logical explanation." Abby peeled off her socks and dropped them to the floor.

"I guess anything is possible. Just promise me that you will let me know if and when you hear from him."

"I will." She grabbed the hem of her shirt and was about to pull it over her head, when she looked up and asked, "Don't you think you should go and keep your grandmother company while I get cleaned up?"

"No." He shrugged casually.

"Don't you think she'll get suspicious, if both of us are up here, together, for more than ten minutes or so?"

He closed the door behind him quietly and crossed the room with deliberate and clear intent. When he reached the place where she sat, his arms pulled her to him and surrounded her like a comforting thought.

"I think Gran has already caught on," he said softly, tracing a line with his tongue along the right side of her face.

"How do you think she feels about it?" Abby tried to focus on her words as she awaited his response, knowing that if he didn't back away in, oh, the next thirty seconds or so, she wouldn't remember the question, so the answer wouldn't much matter.

"I think she is delighted." Alex's mouth seemed to swallow her whole, and her knees began to shake.

Helpless to do anything else, Abby leaned back onto her bed and drew him with her. Within seconds, her world began to buzz and glow, as he led her back to that place where he alone could take her, where nothing mattered except his mouth and his skin and his body, and where the vortex of emotion and sensation swirled around her with frightening velocity and plunged them both into orbit, each with the other at the center.

Drew's falseness, along with Belle's opinions and just about everything else on the face of the earth, seemed to drop into a vacuum somewhere and simply ceased to exist.

✦39✦

"Don't forget," Alex whispered in her ear just before kissing her good-bye in the wee hours of a gray and rainy Monday morning, "call me the minute you hear from Drew."

"I will," Abby murmured sleepily.

"I'll miss you," he said. "Every week, it seems I miss you more."

"Umm."

"I'll be out of town most of the week," he reminded her as he tucked the quilt around her shoulders, "but I'll be back on Friday night. It may be late, but I'll be here."

"Are you sure you don't want me to come downstairs and find something for you to munch on in the car?"

"Go back to sleep." He patted her hair and kissed the back of her neck. "I'll stop someplace and get coffee. That will hold me until I get to the office. I'll be fine."

"See you Friday," she mumbled into her pillow. She heard him chuckle before the door closed softly.

As tired as she was, she could not fall back to sleep. After almost a full hour of trying, she yawned mightily, then rose, groggy. A shower, she told herself. Maybe a shower would wake her up.

Feeling as if she'd been drugged, she thrust aside the flowered curtain and stepped into the pulsing stream of water whose sharp, hot needles pricked at her skin. She stood beneath the stinging drops until she felt sufficiently invigorated to face the day. Pulling back her still damp hair with a scrunchie, she slipped into a cream-colored fleecy top with long sleeves and a pair of worn but clean blue jeans. Awake now, she stretched into the new morning with pleasure as she mentally relived the hour between five and six A.M., when Alex coaxed her from sleep with gentle kisses that banished all memory of the dream she'd been having when his lips had first fallen upon her bare shoulder. She shivered at the thought of it as she bounded down the steps.

Mr. Coffee was just beginning to do his thing when Belle appeared in the doorway, Meri P. close behind.

"Good morning, Belle." Abby grinned.

"Why, yes, dear." Belle's eyes seemed to twinkle. "I believe in fact it is. Now where is that grandson of mine?"

"Alex left a while ago," Abby told her, filling the pot for Belle's tea. "He had to be in court this morning."

"Drat," Belle muttered.

"Is something wrong?"

"I just wanted a word with him, that is all. I thought perhaps it was time for us to have a chat." Belle took down her new favorite cup, which Abby and Susannah had bought for her in a gift shop in Nag's Head, and set it on the counter.

Abby's cheeks flushed red, knowing instinctively what was on Belle's mind.

"You don't need to blush, Abigail. I couldn't be more pleased." Belle beamed. "If the truth were to be told, all Leila and I ever wanted was for you and Alex to fall in love and marry and live happily ever after, right here in Primrose. And, my stars, it's going to happen after all. I don't mind telling you, Abigail, that there was a time when we—

Leila and I, that is—wondered just how we were going to go about getting you two together, but it looks as if all's well that ends well."

Abby tried to smile wanly.

"What is it, dear? Oh, do forgive me, Abigail, I don't mean to intrude into your private life. I'm just so happy that I . . . Abigail?" Belle peered closely at the young woman.

"Belle, I don't want you to set your heart on Alex and me marrying and living happily ever after."

"Why not, dear? You are in love, aren't you? I mean, it's obvious to anyone who looks at you . . ."

"Yes."

"Then what, dear?"

"Alex and I haven't discussed marriage, Belle."

"Merely a detail."

"Belle, it's more than a mere detail. Alex may be transferred to another city sometime in the near future."

"What?" Belle's eyes narrowed with this latest bit of news.

"He apparently is in consideration for an office of his own within the firm. He expects to hear anytime now."

"Alexander can have his own office. Right here in Primrose."

"I don't think it's quite the same, Belle."

"Oh, of course, a small practice here in Primrose isn't quite as good as a large practice in some far-off city, any fool knows *that.*" Belle puffed indignantly. "I don't know what is the matter with you young folks. You simply have the oddest sense of values. Why, in my day, if you loved someone, you did what you had to do to be together. And it wasn't always easy. I don't even want to tell you what I went through, waiting for Granger all those years . . ."

"But you knew you would be with him one day?"

"Yes, I did. And I never gave up. And I never took off looking for *fulfillment* in some big-city job, either."

"How did you know that you would marry him?"

"I just always knew that we belonged together. And I knew if I waited long enough, it would come to be." Belle plunked a tea bag unceremoniously into the earthenware cup. "And it did."

"Well, I'd say you were either very lucky or you were psychic."

"Whatever it was, I never doubted for a second where I belonged. I'm sad to see that neither you nor my grandson has the same sense of who you are and where you belong."

"Belle, this has nothing to do with who we are or where we belong or think we might belong."

"Then do explain to me what this *is* all about. Explain to me, Abigail, what does matter in this life. Tell me what lasts, if not love."

"Belle, it isn't just about love."

"Abigail McKenna, haven't the past ten years of your life taught you anything? Child, when you get right down to it, love is all there is. Everything else—money, property, material possessions—can vanish in the blink of an eye. But love is always inside you, Abigail. It will always be with you. No one can steal it from you or rob you of its joys. No amount of money can buy it for you, nor can it be sold on the open market. It cannot be swept away by flood or lost to fire. It is totally portable, costs nothing, but outlasts everything else you will ever possess. There is nothing else that is *yours* that cannot be taken from you. Except for your memories, of course. Even death is powerless in the face of love, Abigail. And if you do not understand this most basic of truths, then I greatly fear for your future and pray for your soul." Belle sighed heavily and, with a snap of her fingers, called Meri P. to her and left the room, her teacup in her hand and her air of indignation like a mantle about her tiny shoulders.

Abby was still mulling over Belle's impassioned words when she stepped onto the front porch to collect the day's mail. A card from Sunny and Lilly, postmarked in some little seaside resort in Maryland, was the highlight of the morning. As she passed through the hallway, the sudden shrill ring of the phone startled her. Hoping it might be Drew, she jumped on it before it could ring again.

"Ms. McKenna?" a woman's voice inquired.

"Yes?"

"Ms. McKenna, my name is Jacqueline Post. I'm with Post Associates in Dallas. I received your résumé several weeks ago . . ."

"Oh, yes."

"Ms. McKenna, we have an opening with a firm here in the Dallas-Fort Worth area that would be perfect for you," Jacqueline Post purred. Abby could hear her shuffling papers. "As a matter of fact, the company has asked that I invite you to fly down here on Thursday—at their expense, of course—for an interview. They are most anxious to meet with you. Are you available?"

"Thursday?" Abby hoped her voice did not sound as much like a squeak to the woman on the other end of the phone as it did to her own ears. Abby cleared her throat. "I think Thursday is doable."

"Wonderful. I'll have the plane tickets sent by overnight mail." Abby could hear the woman's smile through the miles of phone line. "The folks at Lance and Sherman will be very pleased."

Abby's eyebrows rose involuntarily. Lance and Sherman was a major player in the financial world. "Can you give me an idea of the salary range?"

"They'd be willing to start you at eight thousand a year more than you were making this time last year."

"Bonuses?"

"Absolutely. And a benefit package to die for. Every conceivable bell and whistle."

"Well." Abby forced an exercise of slow inhale followed by silent exhale. "Well, then. Please tell the fine folks at Lance and Sherman that I'm looking forward to Thursday."

"Wonderful. I'll send the tickets along with directions from the airport and everything else you need to know. Why not plan to stay over? We'll put you up in a hotel, and we'll have dinner, and I can show you around the city," Jacqueline Post offered.

Abby paused, wondering if she should leave Belle alone

overnight in view of the recent break-in. She declined, saying she had a commitment on Thursday evening.

"We'll do lunch, then," the headhunter said agreeably before hanging up the phone.

Oh, my stars, as Belle would say.

Abby replaced the heavy, old black telephone receiver onto its base and sat herself down on the bottom step of the front hall stairs.

A job. Not just any job. A job with a big firm. A big, stable firm. A big salary. A big future. Everything I wanted. Everything I've waited months for.

Abby waited for the reality of this longed-for moment to sink in. Waited for the surge of joy and triumph to flow through her. Waited for the exhilaration to kick in. She tapped one foot on the shiny floor of golden oak and waited.

Nothing.

I am happy, she told herself. *Of course, I am. This is exactly what I prayed for. The exact job. The exact kind of company. I'm thrilled. It just hasn't hit me yet, that's all. But it will. It will. Soon. And I'll be kicking up my heels. Just as soon as this good news sinks in . . .*

Abby walked across the street to share her good news with Naomi. She found her friend in the backyard, watering newly planted seedlings.

"Naomi, guess what?" Abby forced an excitement she still wasn't certain that she felt. "I have a job interview on Thursday. In Dallas."

Naomi looked up at her as if Abby had just sprouted a second head.

"Dallas? Why on earth would you want to go there?"

"Because that's where this job is, Naomi. Isn't it great? The headhunter just called. You're the first person I've told."

"Well, I'll just bet Belle and Alex will both be every bit as overjoyed about this as I am, Abby," Naomi pronounced evenly.

"Alex will be. He'll understand just what this means to me," Abby said defensively.

"And just what, may I ask, does this mean to you?" Naomi stood and folded her arms across her chest.

"It means I can get my life moving again, for one thing."

"Moving where, Abby? Just where is it that you want to go that you think you can only get to by way of Dallas?"

"Back into the business world. Back where I belong."

"Well, then," Naomi said with little enthusiasm, "I guess I should wish you well, Abby. If that is where you want to be, I certainly wish you all the best luck on Thursday."

"Momma, Aunt Carole is on the phone." Meredy popped her little head out the back door.

"Okay, sugar. Tell her I'll be there in a second," Naomi called to her daughter, who slammed the screen door as she ran back to the phone to deliver the message. "I guess I'll see you later. Let me know if you need a ride to the airport."

Abby stood among the long rows of fledgling sweet peas and lettuce and watched as Naomi walked, her back nearly as straight and stiff as her leg, to the back porch without a backward glance.

Damn, Abby thought to herself as the door slammed for the second time in little more than a minute. *Naomi is my best friend in this whole world. You'd think she'd be happy for me.*

With the very deepest of sighs, Abby started back home. Naomi's reaction, she knew, would be a joyful noise compared to what Belle would say. Abby was wondering if it would be possible to make it to Dallas and back without telling Belle where she was going and why, when she happened to look across the road at the house directly in front of her, and smiled in spite of herself.

Alex's paint job had worked wonders. Gone was the gloomy facade that had greeted her when she first arrived in Primrose. The shutters, half of which had been hanging sideways off the front of the house, had been repaired, repainted, and rehung. Once bland white, they now gleamed forest green against the taupe clapboard. Thin painted ribbons of terra-cotta wound around the windows to lend a touch of warmth. The front door, freshly washed down and polished to enhance the grain of the wood, stood ready to welcome rather than to repel. The newly repaired porch with its tricolored railings had been just the right finishing touch. The once overgrown shrubs had been trimmed back to enhance rather than to hide.

It looks so different now, she thought, admiring the house in its totality for the first time. *I did that. Well, with Alex's help. When I leave Primrose, at least I will know that I left this little piece of it better than I found it. At least I will have that satisfaction.*

I should start the ball rolling to sell it, she told herself. *I should stop in to see Mr. Tillman when I go into town this afternoon. He said he could refer me to a Realtor. I might as well find out what this place is worth. Now's as good a time as any. And I should find out if he can recommend an antique dealer. I will have to sell off so much of what's here.*

Abby entered the cool of the front hallway and paused before going into the music room. The grand piano would have to go. She struck a few notes. It needed tuning. She stroked the satin finish of its top, recalling how Leila had so loved it. If she closed her eyes, she could almost see her great-aunt perched on the edge of the bench, her back ramrod straight, her once-auburn hair piled atop her head as she played with the slightest of smiles upon her face. The piano had been Leila's salvation, she had once told Abby. It had been Thomas's gift to her when, after a few months far from her beloved Montana hills, Leila began to exhibit signs of homesickness. He had hired the elderly Mrs. Langston to come to the house to give Leila lessons three times a week, hoping to give his wife something new, something different to cherish in her new life. Making music was a joy, Leila had told Abby, and she had played for nearly half an hour every morning from the morning of Thomas's death until her own. She played for Thomas, she had said, songs he had loved to hear her play. It kept him near to her, she had told Abby, and was her way of letting him know that she had never forgotten who had given her this precious gift of music.

How could a price be placed upon such a piece? Abby wondered.

She wandered from room to room, wondering how much she could afford to place in storage. Surely, she could not sell Aunt Leila's dining-room set nor the Eastlake parlor set, with its tapestry upholstery (original, in mint condition), though it would fetch a handsome sum. Family portraits, large and small. China, silver, books. Needlepoint pillows worked by the patient fingers of her great-aunt or her great-great-grandmother. How could anyone other than *family* appreciate the connection between past and present generations?

Abby sat on the caned seat of Aunt Leila's desk chair and tapped her fingers on the flat surface of the old oak desk. She thought of all she had lost of herself that day so many years ago, when the auctioneer appointed by the estate had slammed his gavel to commence the sale of everything she had held dear. How could she bear to part with yet more pieces of herself?

With a sigh of confusion, she peeked in on Belle, who was resting between the morning game shows and her soaps. Abby scribbled a short note telling Belle where she'd gone, then quietly left the house. The grocery shopping, which was normally done on Thursday, would be done today. And then, if she had time, she would stop in at Tillman's office and get the name of that Realtor.

There was, she knew, no point in putting off the inevitable.

Mr. Tillman seemed pleased to see her.

"Why, Miz McKenna, it's always a pleasure," he assured her after she apologized for having stopped in without an appointment. "Don't you ever worry yourself about not having called first, my dear. I am always available to you."

"Thank you," she said as she took the seat he held out for her at one corner of the big cluttered desk.

"And may I congratulate you on the wonderful job you are doing on your home. Drove by there just last week—looks like a different house entirely. Remarkable what you've done there. The Cassidy house has always been one of Primrose's premier properties, of course, but to see it restored to its former handsomeness . . . well, you are to be applauded. As a matter of fact, I said that very thing to George Hattersly—he is the president of our town council, you may recall—when nominations were being taken for the Most Improved Property award. I was happy to throw your hat, as it were, into the ring."

"You nominated my house for an award?" In spite of her mood, Abby brightened.

"Absolutely. And between you and me, I feel certain you'll walk away with the top prize. It's the town's way of thanking the residents who do their part to raise the standards, so to speak. To improve the appearance of the town by fixing up their own little part of it."

"I'm very flattered, Mr. Tillman," Abby told him.

And she was, though why this little bit of local news gave her such pleasure, she could not say. *I mean, in the grand scheme of things, this is not quite in the same league as being offered a high-powered position with Lance and Sherman,* Abby reminded herself.

"So, tell me what I can do for you today." He folded his hands neatly atop his desk and waited.

"Well, actually, it was the house that I wanted to talk about." She took a deep breath. "You had mentioned that you were acquainted with a Realtor here in town—I forgot to write his name down . . ."

"You mean to sell the property, Miz McKenna? After all the work you have put into it?" Tillman said with barely disguised incredulity. He barely missed a beat before recovering to add, "Though, of course, that was the wise thing to do. Certainly increased the value of the house. I'm sure that you'll be able to find a buyer in no time, and at a respectable price, at that."

He leaned over and hit the intercom.

"Cerise?" He waited a second before repeating the name. "Cerise?"

"She must be in the ladies room, Mr. Tillman," a young voice responded. "Can I get something for you?"

"Thank you, Andrea, yes. Please look up Artie Snow's phone number and bring it in." He turned back to Abby.

"Artie Snow's your man. I'm sure if anyone can find a good buyer for your home . . . thank you, Andrea . . ." Tillman glanced at the piece if paper before passing it across the desk to Abby. "Now, you be sure to tell Artie I referred you." He winked.

"I certainly will." Abby rose, thanking Tillman for the information and promising to let him know when she left town.

"And Miz Matthews will be going where?" he inquired as he shook her hand.

"No decision has been made as yet." Abby tried to appear nonchalant. "I want to see how my job interview goes in Dallas."

"I'll bet you're a shoo-in." His eyes twinkled as he walked her to the door. "You keep in touch now, hear?"

After smiling to assure him that she would do just exactly that, Abby followed the long hallway to the reception area. The remnants of a scent hung in the still air, evoking a memory both elusive and certain. It seemed as familiar to Abby as its wearer, and the suspicion nagged at her. Abby tucked the paper in her pocket and headed to Foster's, where she hoped to find something to make an especially fine meal for Belle.

There would be a lot to talk about over dinner.

✦ 40 ✦

All in all, Abby reflected wryly as she gazed out the window of the plane, it hadn't gone *so* badly. Abby had told Belle she had a job interview in Dallas, and Belle had neatly folded her white linen napkin, dropped it with no small amount of ceremony onto the dinner table, looked at Abby with eyes that burned her very soul, then left the room and hadn't spoken to Abby since.

Abby knew that Belle's pain was as much despair over her own plight as it was anger with Abby for even considering leaving Primrose. Following her unsuccessful attempt to have a rational discussion with Belle, Abby had called Alex's office, hoping to catch up with him, but he'd already left for his own flight to Salt Lake City. She had hesitated about leaving a message, then declined. This was a matter that had to be dealt with in person. And she would do just that on Friday night.

There was no reason why they couldn't still see each other, she told herself as she watched the earth below grow ever more remote. Lots of people carry on long-distance relationships. And this way, they would both be doing what they wanted to do.

You are certain that this is what you want to do, aren't you? a tiny voice from within prodded.

Of course I am, Abby assured herself as she smoothed the skirt of her red linen suit, last year's power dressing.

The silk shirt, once part of her daily uniform, felt foreign on her skin, and the jacket, even though it was slightly too large for her now, seemed to constrain her arms in a way it had never done before. Her black leather pumps bound her toes like the bindings wrapped around the feet of Chinese women in the last century.

Abby had spent all of Wednesday trying to recapture her former executive image, taming her hair and patching her nails. Glancing down at her hands, she smiled. She'd never make it as a manicurist, but it was a vast improvement over the broken, unpolished nails she had before she had hit the drugstore in search of a quick cure. She hadn't looked this polished and tidily corporate in months. She wondered why it all felt so awkward.

The interview could not have gone more favorably if she herself had scripted it. The fine folks at Lance and Sherman had loved her and would, she was absolutely certain, offer her the job before a week had passed. Where, she had wondered as she rode to the airport for her return flight, was the sense of elation she had anticipated?

Her flight had been delayed for four hours by a severe thunderstorm, and she'd called Naomi to see if perhaps she could look in on Belle. Naomi had already done that, she was told, since Primrose was experiencing some pretty severe storms, too. Abby had selected a novel from the paperback rack in the airport gift shop and taken a seat to await her departure. When her flight had finally been called, she boarded the plane, took her seat, and promptly fell asleep.

The drive to Primrose from the airport seemed to take forever, the effects of the storm readily apparent on every stretch of roadway. Whole trees had fallen, and entire sections of road were washed out with floodwaters. At several points along the way, Abby had to detour and take alternative routes toward the coast. It was with great relief that she made the turn off the interstate that led to Primrose.

The storm that had already passed through must have been a nasty one, she thought as she turned onto Cove Road. It appeared that the entire town was without electricity. No streetlights illuminated the roads, nor were any lampposts lit. All was black as the deepest of nights. She eased into the drive at Number Thirty-five. Looking down toward the river, she could see nothing but the mist as dense as smoke from a deadly fire. Even the carriage house was lost from view. Abby backed the Subaru out of the drive and parked in front of the house, nearer the front door.

As quietly as she could, Abby closed the car door. All of Cove Road—all of Primrose—seemed to be wrapped in the thickest silence, as if all life had fled in the face of the storm. She tiptoed across the front porch, the key as eager for the lock as she was to get inside her house. From somewhere beyond the porch, a rustle in the shrubs set branches dancing as an owl or some other nocturnal being watched. The hairs on the back of her neck slowly stood up as her fingers fumbled with the key. She was relieved beyond words when the door pushed open without resistance, and she could leave the vague and dismal vapors behind her with whatever night creatures lurked about.

She locked the door and stepped into the darkness within, which was only slightly less menacing, she noted, than the murky blackness without. Slipping out of her shoes, she followed the wall, tracing the top of the wainscot with her fingers as she felt her way toward the steps.

"How did it go?" His soft voice came from within the dark and filled it.

She stood stock still, her shoes in her hand, then replied, "It went well."

"Did they offer you the job?"

"Not yet. But they will," Abby replied, the pronouncement confident but lacking joy.

"Will you accept it?"

"I don't seem to have any other options."

"And if you did?"

"Then I would consider them equally."

"Come here, Ab."

She followed his voice to where he sat alone in the dark, waiting for her.

"I was worried about you. It's a long drive from the airport."

"I was all right."

His hands reached for her in the dark and pulled her to him until she rested on his lap.

"Why didn't you tell me about the interview?" He stroked her hair gently.

"I tried. I called your office." She felt herself relaxing for the first time since the call from Jacqueline Post had come on Monday.

"I didn't get a message."

"I didn't leave one," she whispered into his neck.

They sat in silence for several long moments. Finally, he said, "Let's go to bed, Ab. We can talk about this and all that it means tomorrow. Right now, I am weary, as I suspect you are. Let's just go to bed."

She nodded and took his hand, and they fumbled slightly in the dark until they found their way to the steps, then climbed them one by one, hand in hand, to the top.

"Which way?" she asked.

"This way." He tugged her toward the room that had become his. "The bed is bigger, and I need to hold on to you tonight. All night."

And he did just that, until the sun rose and began to burn off the soupy fog to bring back both light and life to the dark shores of the river.

"You are very quiet this morning, Alexander," Belle said pointedly. "Are you all right?"

"I'm fine." He nodded. "Hey, the electricity is back. Great. I was beginning to think that I'd have to start my day without my morning stimulant."

Alex poured some dark brown beans into Abby's coffee grinder and turned it on. "What did you say, Gran?"

"I said, that blasted thing makes the most infernal racket."

"It does," he agreed.

"Did Abby make it home last night?"

"Yes."

Belle watched as her grandson opened the refrigerator and began to poke around inspecting its contents. "What exactly are you looking for, Alexander?"

"Stuff for sandwiches."

"Breakfast sandwiches?"

"Lunch. I thought I'd head out to the Outer Banks this morning."

"I see." Belle nodded knowingly. Matthews men always headed toward the sea when there were important thoughts to think or decisions to be made.

"Never mind." He closed the door and forced a smile in his grandmother's direction. "I'll stop at one of the little delis along the highway and pick up something."

"What would you like me to tell Abigail when she wakes up?"

"Tell her that I've gone fishing"—he kissed the tiny woman on the top of her white head—"for options."

He pulled a white sweatshirt over his denim shorts and turned toward the door. "Gran," he said as he unlocked it.

"What, dear?"

"I don't want you to worry. About anything. It's all going to work out."

"I know that, Alexander. And I'm not worried." She filled up her teapot. "But what exactly do you have in mind, dear?"

"Nothing, yet. But something will come to me. I can't lose her again, Gran."

Belle nodded and blew him a kiss. She watched from the window as he backed his car down the driveway.

"He'll think of something, Leila. We just have to be patient . . . well, dear, *all eternity* is a luxury we don't all have. Actually, I was hoping to see this worked out in this lifetime."

Belle felt the comforting cloud of faintest lavender settle around her. "Now, do come along, dear. It's *The Maid of Salem.* Claudette Colbert, Fred McMurray, 1937. And it's just about to start."

Abby had been disappointed when she awoke to find that Alex had taken off someplace, though Belle assured her that he would be back before the day was over.

It was around three-thirty when he called.

"Where are you?" she asked, the connection being somewhat unstable.

"I'm just about to leave Nag's Head."

"Did you catch anything?"

"Ah, yes. In a manner of speaking. Listen, Ab, could you please set the table in the dining room for four? You know, good china, linen cloth, the good silver. And make some of those wonderful herbed potatoes, a big salad . . ."

"Is this your way of telling me that you ran into some old friends and are bringing them home for dinner?"

"Sort of. And they're more like new friends." He paused, then added, "And, actually, they are coming for the weekend, so you'd better make sure that there are two bedrooms with made-up beds and at least one bathroom with fresh towels."

"What?"

"I said, they are staying over till tomorrow. Paying guests. Four of them."

"Four paying guests?" she repeated, certain she'd not heard correctly.

"The first patrons of the Primrose Inn will be arriving in, oh, roughly two hours."

"Have you lost your mind?"

"Sweetheart, you were looking for options. You have an option. Go for it."

"Alex, do I look like Wonder Woman? I can't turn this house into an inn in two hours. Even if I wanted to—and I'm not certain that I do—I couldn't pull this off. The house isn't ready for this type of thing."

"Of course it is. What do you think still needs to be done before it's ready?"

"I'm not ready," she protested. "I don't know how to run an inn."

"You're resourceful. You'll figure it out. Look, I'm out of change. I'll see you around five. And, Ab . . ."

"What?" she yelled.

"Make something spectacular for dessert."

"Arrgghhh!" She slammed the old receiver into its cradle with a roar.

"Paying guests. Four paying guests. He has one hell of a lot of nerve. If I wanted to run an inn, I'd do it with no prodding from him," she grumbled as she frantically ran the vacuum cleaner on the first floor, sucking up the dog hair and dust bunnies with a vengeance. Not finding Belle or Meri P. in the morning room, which, she gratefully acknowledged, she had refurbished with Sunny's assistance, she plumped the new pillows and removed a pile of newspapers.

"Damn that man, anyway," she cursed as she scrubbed new potatoes and set them aside in a pot of cold water.

She raced up the steps and checked the state of the beds. No sheets.

She flew to the linen closet and selected some fine white

cotton sheets, ancient but soft and cool to the touch, then set about the task of making up two guest rooms. "Thank God for the quilts," she muttered as she spread them upon the beds.

She pulled the curtains aside to flood the rooms with light, then ran for the vacuum cleaner. She gathered spray furniture polish and some old cloths to dust the furniture and make it shine. Puffing from the frantic exertion, she stepped back to look at the results.

Not so bad, she grudgingly admitted.

"Flowers," she said aloud. "The bedrooms should have flowers."

Abby took the steps at record speed and flew into the kitchen, where Belle had just returned from a leisurely afternoon stroll in the garden with Meri.

Belle's eyebrows rose at the sight of the young woman vigorously punching numbers into the wall phone.

"Naomi! I need your help! Alex invited people to come, and I need flowers! And salad stuff! And yes . . . yes . . . thank you . . ." Abby leaned back against the wall as she hung up the phone. "She's coming over," Abby told Belle. "She's going to help."

"Help with what, dear?" A perplexed Belle sat down on one of the kitchen chairs.

"Your grandson has turned my home into a bed-and-breakfast inn. He will be arriving in about one and a half hours with our first guests," Abby announced with her hands on her hips.

"Why . . ." Belle blinked, absorbing the news. "Why, yes. Yes, of course. How clever of him."

"Don't give him credit he doesn't deserve," Abby told her as she raced to the front door to let Naomi in. "It was Sunny's idea . . ." Her voice trailed down the hallway.

"Whosever." Belle waved a hand in the air signifying that it didn't really matter whose idea it was. It was perfect.

"Don't you think so, dear?" Belle said aloud to the empty room. *"Well, of course, but they will be, I am certain, perfectly nice strangers, or Alexander wouldn't be bringing them home. Oh, yes, this could work."* Belle's little fingers

tapped an increasingly merry tune on the enameled top of the kitchen table. *"We'll both have to do our part to help, of course. Yes."* She tilted her head as if listening to a voice only she could hear. *"Yes, this could be fun. It could, indeed . . ."*

By the time Alex pulled in the driveway, the Primrose Inn was as ready as it would ever be to receive its first guests.

Naomi had cut armfuls of flowers from her garden and had set up a workplace for herself on the back porch, where she sorted flowers and greens to grace the house and fill it with fragrance, thereby unwittingly creating the ambience for which the inn would become known. The washbasins in the guest bedrooms overflowed with dried hydrangea from Naomi's stash from the previous year, and the bedside tables highlighted vases of colorful tulips which perfectly accented the faded hues in the old quilts that covered the beds. Huge bowls of heady-scented peonies of deepest red transformed the front hallway into a cheerful reception room, and a carefully crafted centerpiece of vines and flowers and herbs graced the dining-room table.

"Dessert!" Abby cried as she nearly collapsed on the back porch railing after scrubbing down the bathrooms and setting the table. "And something for hors d'oeuvres . . ."

"Abigail, calm down." Naomi spoke serenely from the opposite side of a tall display of forsythia which she was preparing to set right outside the front door, first impressions being *so* important. "Now, you do, as I recall, know how to make a pastry shell?"

"Of course, I do."

"Then I suggest you go inside and make one. Umm, better make that two."

"Do you have any thoughts on what I might fill them with?"

"As a matter of fact, I do." Naomi grinned. "When I went back home, I took a few packages of last summer's blackberries out of the freezer. They should be ready right about the time you will need them. And I called Colin and asked him to stop at Foster's and pick up some whipping cream. So, you just go on inside there and make a crust for your blackberry tart. There's some cream cheese and a jar of homemade chutney on the counter and some herbed dip in the fridge. You can set them out with the wine—which is chilling alongside the dip—so your guests can have a few minutes to warm up for dinner."

Abby stood drop-jawed and humbled as Naomi so calmly laid out before her the agenda.

"What, by the way, is the main course?"

Abby blanched, then panicked. "I . . . I don't know. Alex just said to make potatoes and salad and dessert."

"Then he must have something else in mind. If worse comes to worst, we can run down to Foster's. He doesn't close until six." Naomi smiled brightly. "Now, go, girl. You have things to do."

"Naomi, I don't know what I'd do without you." Abby spoke with all sincerity.

"Neither do I, sugar." Naomi shook her head slowly, then smiled meaningfully. "Neither do I."

·41·

Abby was standing in her underwear, fresh from her shower, contemplating just what an innkeeper should wear, when she heard the sound of slamming car doors from below her windows.

"Damn," she whispered loudly. "Damndamndamn."

Dancing an anxious jig of sorts, she shimmied into a short denim skirt, pulled a long-sleeved ballerina-styled knit shirt with blue cornflowers over her head, and hastily slid into canvas espadrilles before fleeing down the steps, tying her hair back with dark blue ribbons as she went. Seeing her frazzled reflection in the hall mirror, she paused and took several deep breaths. It would not do for the innkeeper to appear unnerved at the sight of her guests. She resumed her steps, more slowly now, toward the front door and prepared to open it just as it swung aside.

"Oh, here she is now," Alex announced, all pleasantries as he led two couples into the front hallway. "Abby McKenna, this is Bob Conroy and his wife, Elaine, and Sue and Jeff Turner."

Abby did her best to cast a wide smile as she extended her hand to her guests. "Welcome to . . ." What had he called it? ". . . the Primrose Inn."

"This is lovely." Sue Turner, a short, slightly pudgy woman with very short red hair and too-pink lips, looked over the length of the foyer. "And I just adore your wreath."

"My wreath?" Abby frowned. *What wreath?*

"The one on the front door. I just love grapevine. So homey."

"Oh, of course. That wreath." Abby made a mental note to steal a peek at whichever of Naomi's creations she had loaned for the occasion.

"We're so glad you could accommodate us on such short notice." Bob Conroy's bald head bobbed up and down as he pumped Abby's hand.

"I ran into the Conroys and the Turners on the beach in Nag's Head," Alex told her in an offhand manner, as if this sort of thing happened every day. "The motel they were staying in lost part of its roof in the storm. They asked if I knew of a nice place to stay somewhere between the Outer Banks and Edenton."

"When Alex told us that his fiancée had just opened a B&B, well, it just seemed to be fate," Sue Conroy told Abby. "And I'm so glad he mentioned it. We'd never have found this charming little town on our own."

His fiancée?

Ignoring Abby's raised eyebrows, Alex draped an arm over her shoulder and gave it a squeeze.

"We're certain you'll enjoy your stay with us. Now, I would think you'd like to see your rooms. Abby, why don't you show your guests upstairs while I take care of the fish . . ."

"What fish?"

"The one I caught. Right before the Conroys and the Turners came down the beach, I reeled in the biggest sea bass I ever saw. It will be perfect grilled."

"We don't have a grill," she reminded him.

"Colin does."

"Ummm. Grilled sea bass." Bob smacked his lips. "I can hardly wait."

"Well, then, let me show you to your rooms, and you can get settled. We'll have dinner ready for you in half an hour." Abby beckoned the foursome to follow her up the wide stairwell.

"Ah, actually, Ab, it may take a little longer than that. See, the fish isn't cleaned yet, and you know it's been some years since I last cleaned a fish . . ."

"Why, Alex, *you're* resourceful." Abby turned on the steps with a smile that assured him that she enjoyed watching the tables turn. "You'll figure it out."

To the Conroys and the Turners, she said, "Dinner will be served at six."

It was actually closer to seven when Abby seated the guests in the large dining room. Naomi's homemade chutney, served over cream cheese with savory crackers and chilled white wine on the newly restored front porch, had been a huge hit, as had been the herbed dip. For that matter, the entire meal, she had to admit, had been pretty terrific. Alex's grilled sea bass was perfect with the herbed potatoes and the salad put together with greens from Naomi's garden. The blackberry tart was oohed and ahed over. Naomi had been right, Abby noted. One entire tart and part of the second were cheerfully devoured.

"How long have you been running your inn?" Elaine Conroy tucked a long blond strand behind one ear and peered over the top of her glasses, leaning back slightly to permit Abby to remove her dinner dishes.

"Ah, well, actually, I just inherited the property a few months ago."

"Really? Well, one would think you've been doing this

forever. Dinner was excellent. The views of the river are gorgeous. All in all, I must say that this is one of the most charming inns we've visited."

"You wouldn't happen to have any small boats for little moonlit rides on the river? Even a rowboat would do." Jeff Turner, stout and serious even as he contemplated a romantic row on the river in the moonlight, was apparently more of a middle-aged Lothario than his appearance implied.

"Not quite yet," Alex interjected before Abby could open her mouth. "We're still in the process of renovating the carriage house. Once it's done, we'll be able to bring in a few rowboats for our guests' use."

"Well, it's just all too perfectly delightful," Elaine marveled. "And you've just thought of every little thing. Those little sprigs of lavender on the bed pillows, for example. Just the right little touch."

Sprigs of lavender on the bed pillows? Another little touch of Naomi?

"Abby, how many guest rooms do you have?" Elaine continued.

"Umm, we have four double rooms that are finished." Abby mentally tallied up the work she had completed. "And several others I haven't had a chance to work on yet."

"Abby has done most of the renovations herself." Alex's pride in her accomplishment was unmistakable and genuine.

"Bob, you simply have to consider the Primrose for your managers' retreat in the fall." Elaine tapped her husband on the arm.

"Why, you're absolutely right, Elaine." He nodded. "It would be perfect. Assuming that we could use that big room out front"—he gestured toward the front parlor—"for a group meeting?"

"I'm sure we could accommodate you," Abby replied as she removed dishes to the kitchen. *Listen to me. As if I'll be in business come the fall.*

"So, tell us, when is the big day?" Sue asked, accepting a cup of freshly brewed coffee from Abby's hands.

"The big day?" Abby frowned.

"The last weekend in June," Alex told them. "Abby's mother was a June bride . . . right out there under that very rose arbor, wasn't it, Ab?"

"Yes." Abby eyed him warily. What kind of game was he playing?

"So I thought it would be special if we did the same thing." He set the tray he was holding on the end of the sideboard and waited for her to react.

"And you'll continue to run the inn after you're married?" Jeff Turner asked Abby.

She found she could not respond. She was too focused on fighting off the urge to strangle him for inventing this fantasy merely for the sake of these strangers. Particularly when the fantasy so closely resembled the dream she had sheltered for so long. How dare he stand there so calmly spouting such bald-faced lies when . . . Abby's heated brain caught up with Alex's latest pronouncement. She turned on him fiercely, ready to blow the whistle on the charade, when she realized he was speaking directly to her, his words flowing softly to her alone, as if the others had faded somehow from the room.

". . . but I will be moving my law practice here to Primrose as soon as I wrap up the case I've been working on," Alex was saying as he lifted a cup to fill it with coffee, his eyes still holding hers across the room. "I'm thinking I might renovate part of the carriage house to use as my office."

Her shaking hands set the clattering cup upon the table. This was no charade.

"Good evening." A smiling, congenial Belle—oblivious to the fact that she was abruptly breaking the spell her grandson sought to cast upon his beloved—appeared in the doorway, dressed outlandishly in a long skirt of purple, God only knew its genesis, and a multicolored shawl flung about her shoulders, incongruously draped over her prim little white blouse.

What in the world?

"Good evening," the guests all murmured somewhat uncertainly.

"This is my grandmother, Belle Matthews." Alex, too, was taken off guard.

"Now," Belle asked brightly, her dancing eyes clear evidence that she was enjoying her self-appointed role as the evening's entertainment, "who'd like to have their tea leaves read?"

A long silence followed, before Alex told her gently, "Gran, everyone had coffee."

"Oh, dear." She frowned, clearly disappointed that her efforts to make a contribution to the action were thwarted even as she was beginning to get into character.

"But I'd be happy to bring you some tea, Belle," Abby offered, "and perhaps you could sit with our guests and chat for a few minutes."

Abby turned toward the dinner table. "Belle has lived in Primrose all her life. I'm sure she would be happy to tell you anything you'd like to know about the town. Primrose, for example, was a stop on the Underground Railroad. As a matter of fact, this house and the one directly across the street, which was built by the family of Belle's late husband, were part of the network."

"Really? This very house?" Jeff Turner brightened. "That's music to the ears of a history buff like me."

"Oh, Primrose has a very rich history, as one might suspect from so old a community," Belle said as she draped the awful shawl—where had she found *that?*—over the back of her chair. "Why, this house alone has seen so much. Now, the original section of this house was built, I seem to recall, in 1790 or thereabouts. Of course, it was added onto over the years . . ."

Belle's voice trailed off as the kitchen door swung behind Abby, who ran the water for Belle's tea.

"I'd say everything is going just right," Alex announced in a whisper as he hugged Abby from behind. "Now, aren't you glad I . . . uh-oh . . ." He studied the look on Abby's face as she turned around.

"I think you have some explaining to do."

"Don't you want a June wedding, Ab? In the garden? By the arbor?"

"Alex . . ."

"I apologize for not properly asking you before I announced it to everyone else. I admit that was a little tacky." He pulled a hand through the hair that had slid onto his forehead. "But it just all seems so right, Ab. You said once that maybe you'd start your own business. I kept thinking about Sunny's suggestion. What's wrong with this as a business? You're a natural, and the house is perfect. Why go all the way to Dallas when everything you need is right here?"

"I admit the idea of turning the house into an inn has intrigued me since Sunny first suggested it. And I admit it could probably even be fun . . . although I do think we should do a little more homework before we hang out a sign. I mean, if the Board of Health finds out that we are running a restaurant without the proper inspections and permits . . ."

He laughed good-naturedly, sensing she was mere seconds away from telling him everything he wanted to hear. "I apologize for springing this all on you, but once I caught that fish and the Conroys showed up, it just all seemed so clear to me. And I really believed you'd love the idea of a B&B, once you gave it a try."

"Well, I admit that the thought of leaving Primrose, now that it's really a possibility, is making me ill. All this time, finding a job on the same level as the one I lost seemed so important to me. That's what I thought was me. Now that it's a reality, I'm not so sure. I just don't think I'm the same person who left Philadelphia back in the fall. I'm not so sure that I want to be—that I *can* be—that person again. I love this house, and I love this town. I love Belle, and I love Naomi. I've never had a friend like her, and I never will again. The thought of leaving and not having her in my daily life . . ." Abby began to sniffle.

"What about me?" Alex asked.

Abby burst into tears.

"You love me, don't you, Ab?" he asked softly.

"More than anything in this life," she sobbed.

"Don't you want to marry me?"

"It's all I ever wanted." She tried unsuccessfully to stem the flood of tears. "But look what you'd be giving up to move here. Big, high-profile cases, hefty fees . . ."

"So what?" He shrugged it off. "Abby, you're not the only one who's reevaluated things since coming back to Primrose. Being here has helped me put my feet back on the ground and brought the important things into a finer perspective. Things I thought I'd lost long ago, I've found again. I don't want to lose them for the sake of doing hack work for clients I don't really care about. I want to know the people I represent and care about whether I win for their sake, not for mine. I want to come home every night to the woman I love. Maybe sneak away from the kids every once in a while and steal on out to the carriage house. Maybe a little dance in the moonlight or a midnight swim from time to time."

"Do you love me that much? To give up everything else?"

"There is nothing else, Abby. Just you. I hadn't realized just how much was missing from my life until you came back into it. I can't let you go a second time. I need you too much." He paused before adding, "You do need me, too, don't you, Ab?"

"Yes, I need you."

"And you love me, too, don't you?"

"Yes, I love you. I've never loved anyone else."

"Then what's stopping you from saying, 'Why, yes, Alex, I will marry you. And, thank you, a June wedding in the rose arbor would be absolutely perfect.'"

"Yes, Alex, I will marry you," she recited softly. "And, thank you, a June wedding in the rose arbor would be . . ." Her words disappeared into his mouth which descended upon hers like a hungry hawk.

Her hands, which had moments earlier tugged gently on the points of his shirt collar, now held the sides of his face to hers, and she half laughed, half cried as he set her up on the wet counter where the just-rinsed dishes were stacked.

"And I trust that first thing Monday, you will call the headhunter in Dallas and tell her you've had a better offer right here in Primrose." He kissed her throat and behind her left ear.

"The best offer I ever had," she agreed, sniffing back the tears that had begun to roll down her cheeks in furious streams.

"Ab, we will be so happy, you'll see," he vowed, holding her chin in his hand.

A shrill scream from the morning room broke the spell.

The couple cuddling in the kitchen making their wedding plans exchanged a look of alarm. Abby jumped down from the counter and followed Alex down the short hall to the morning room.

"Over against the wall with the others." The young blond woman waved the pistol, gesturing for Abby and Alex to join the group in front of the fireplace wall.

The paneled wainscot stood open to the tunnel, a gaping dark blemish on the newly painted wall.

"What in the name of God?" Alex exhaled, stopping dead in his tracks inside the morning-room door.

"I'm sorry, Alexander," Belle said shakily. "I'm afraid it's my fault. The guests wanted to see the secret passage, and when I pushed in the cornerstone, the wall opened, and out she came."

"I'm not kidding, Mr. Kane. I said move," she said coolly.

"Cerise?" Abby peered closely at the young woman.

"Who is Cerise?" Alex asked.

"Tillman's secretary."

"Who is Tillman?" Bob Conroy asked.

"Aunt Leila's attorney."

"Who is Aunt Leila?" asked Elaine.

"Shut up, all of you!" Cerise yelled. "This is not a 'Moonlighting' rerun."

"All right, Cerise. What do you want?" Abby decided calm and direct was the way to go.

"I want the pearls."

"What pearls?" Abby frowned. "Aunt Leila sold her pearls to pay for new kitchen appliances."

"Not those pearls, stupid." Cerise rolled her eyes. "The Tears of the Maiden."

"Who's the maiden?" Alex asked.

"Cerise, that was a kids' book." Abby sighed, ignoring Alex in her efforts to get Cerise to leave before someone got hurt. "Thomas made it up. Those pearls do not exist."

"Oh, but they do," the woman replied, and, sticking her left hand into the pocket of her tan jacket, she withdrew a luminescent orb the size of a fat man's thumb.

The only sound in the room was that of the entire gathering sucking in its collective breath.

"Where did you get that?" Abby asked, as wide-eyed and dazzled as all the others.

"In a little hidden compartment in Thomas Cassidy's desk," she told them with a perverse sort of pride. "And now I want the rest of them."

"Cerise, this is silly." Abby shook her head. "No one knows where those pearls are, if, in fact, there are more."

"I do," Belle said evenly.

Seven heads swiveled to gaze upon the old woman.

"You do?" Abby gasped.

"Of course, I do." Belle straightened up importantly.

"Belle, if you knew where those pearls were, why didn't you tell me?" Abby asked, dumbfounded.

"Because I was afraid that if you had that much money, it wouldn't have mattered how much you could get for this house. You'd just have sold everything off right away and taken the money and left." The old woman's chin rose slightly. "And where would that have left *me*, I ask you? In a smelly old nursing home someplace, *that's* where!"

"Then why didn't *you* take the pearls and sell them? You would have had enough money to hire someone to live in with you."

"Because they weren't mine." Belle was indignant at the very thought.

"Okay, enough of this nonsense." Cerise waved the gun. "Where are the pearls?"

"They're . . ." Belle began.

"Don't, Belle," a voice spoke from the opening in the wall.

Drew Cassidy emerged from the tunnel, draped in cobwebs. "Cerise, what are you doing?"

"I am doing what I thought I could get you to do," Cerise fairly spat at him, "before you went stupid on me."

"Is that a real gun?" Drew asked.

"Of course, it's a real gun." Cerise popped her gum.

"Give it to me." He motioned to her calmly.

"Not on your life." She shook her head.

"Cerise, this is foolish." Drew tried to reason with her.

"You have the nerve to call me foolish?" Cerise's overly shadowed eyes widened. "I'll tell you what's foolish. Foolish is walking away from a fortune. You could have found it, Drew. She"—Cerise waved the gun in Abby's direction—"never would have known. It was the damned birthday party that did it, wasn't it? You weren't the same after that. One bloody birthday cake, and the whole scam's off? I don't think so."

"Is that true, Drew?" Abby asked quietly. "Was it all a scam?"

"Well, I hate to admit it, but at the very beginning, before I met you, I was intrigued by Cerise's plan." He was having trouble meeting her gaze.

"Which was?"

"To find whatever it was that Thomas had found on his trips, and to steal it," he said simply. "I'm sorry, Abby. I thought I had talked her out of it."

"Where did you meet up with *her?*" Alex frowned, nodding in the direction of the woman with the gun.

"It's a long story." Drew sighed.

"One we don't have time to listen to," Cerise snapped impatiently. "Mrs. Matthews, go get the pearls, and bring them back here. You have one minute. If you're not back, I'll . . ." She looked about the room wildly looking for a likely "or else." ". . . I'll shoot *him.*" She waved the gun at Alex.

"A minute is not a very generous amount of time"—Belle shook a finger at Cerise—"for a woman of my age."

"Just do it." Cerise was clearly becoming nervous and agitated. Abby hoped the stress wouldn't make her trigger finger twitch.

"I do not know how to apologize to you for this." A distressed Abby turned to her paying guests. Oddly, they appeared to be relaxed and smiling. "Nothing like this ever happens around here . . ."

Bob Conroy held up a hand to cut her off. "Well, *we're* certainly frightened, but we'll do as she says." He winked.

Abby stared at Bob as if he was crazed.

"Alexander, you'll have to help me to take this apart," Belle muttered from the doorway. In her hand, she held the framed picture of Leila that had stood on Thomas's desk.

"Give me that," Cerise lunged toward Belle for the frame.

In a heartbeat, a swirling mass of dark fur dashed out and sank its teeth into Cerise's ankle.

"Ow!" she shrieked, looking down for a split second. Drew stepped behind her and grabbed her wrist, knocking the small pistol to the floor.

"Oh," Bob said gallantly as he picked it up, "allow me."

"Alex, give Colin a call." Drew led Cerise to a chair and plunked her down.

"I already did that," Belle announced, "when I went into the study."

"Good thinking, Gran." Alex kissed the top of the old woman's head and led her to a chair. "Are you okay?"

"Of course, I'm okay, Alexander." Belle sniffed. "What do you take me for?"

"Gran, all the excitement . . ."

"Pooh." She dismissed him as if insulted by the suggestion, while at the same time grateful to give her quaking her legs a rest as she turned her attention to her little dog. She patted her lap, and the dog climbed aboard as if taking the place of honor at an awards banquet. "Alexander, get Meri a Milk Bone. She deserves a reward for saving the day."

Abby turned toward the Turners and the Conroys, holding out her hands helplessly. What do you say after the guests in your establishment have been held at gunpoint for twenty minutes?

"Well, what do you think, Elaine?" Bob said. "Wasn't that one of the better performances we've seen lately?"

"Performance?" Abby repeated dumbly.

"We go to these types of things all the time. Solve-the-murder dinners. Mystery weekends. Alex didn't mention that you folks would have something, but hey, that only added to the fun," Bob assured her.

"I'll say." Sue Turner laughed. "But, to tell you the truth, I can't remember seeing anyone make the entrance *she* did. Just for a split second, one might have thought it was real."

"The timing was too perfect. Gave it away." Jeff Turner turned to Abby and whispered, "Just a little advice? Next time, she shouldn't come out of the wall so quickly."

"I'll try to remember that." Abby nodded.

"So, what time's breakfast?" Bob paused in the doorway.

"Ah . . . eight-thirty," Abby replied, trying to decide which had surprised her more, Cerise's appearance with the gun or the realization that her guests thought it was the evening's entertainment.

"Perfect." He saluted her as he ushered his wife and the Turners into the hallway.

"By the way." Jeff stuck his head back through the doorway. "What was the signal for the dog?"

"What?" Abby turned to him, still in a bit of a daze.

"I didn't see anyone signal the dog. Pretty clever, whatever it was." He smiled brightly.

"Thanks."

"And, hey." Bob laughed. "The police officer is a nice touch. Adds authenticity. But you're too late." He patted Colin on the back as they passed in the hallway. "It's all over, and we already figured it out."

"Glad to hear it." Colin nodded thoughtfully, then asked Abby, "What the hell was that all about?"

"You wouldn't believe it." She shook her head and slumped onto the love seat.

"Cerise, Cerise, Cerise." Colin gently helped the woman to her feet and folded her arms behind her back. "What have you gotten yourself into this time?"

"I'm not going to say a damned thing until I see my lawyer."

"You want to give ole Horace a call? I bet he'll be hell-bent when he finds out you got yourself into another little scrape, now, won't he?" Colin guided her toward his partner, who was waiting in the hallway. "Yep, I'll bet ole Uncle Horace is going to have exactly what my wife would call an all-out hissy."

"Cerise," Drew called to her, and she flashed him a black look. "Make sure you give Colin the ring you took from Susannah's suitcase."

Cerise stuck her tongue out at him as she went through the doorway.

"How did you know about that?" Abby asked. "You left before we even knew the house had been broken into."

"Cerise called me and asked me to meet her for dinner the next night. She was wearing it," Drew said.

"How did she know about the tunnel? And how did she know about the ring?" Colin took out a small book and began to make notes.

"Cerise said when she was in high school, the kids used to sneak in and smoke cigarettes, drink beer, whatever." He sighed. "And I don't think she knew about the ring. I think she went through Sunny's things looking for whatever she could find."

"I think now would be a nice time for you to explain how you got involved with her." Abby sat on the edge of her chair and folded her arms across her chest, clearly waiting.

"I came to Primrose after I read your aunt's obituary in the newspaper," Drew began. "The widow of the adventurer Thomas Cassidy had died, leaving several grand-nieces and -nephews. I figured I could just get in line with the rest of the heirs. When I got to Primrose and started asking some questions about the estate, I was directed to Mr. Tillman. I went to his office, but he wasn't in."

"But Cerise was."

"Yeah, she sure was." He sighed. "She told me there was only one heir and that *she* was on her way down from up north to claim the estate. I am embarrassed to say it took very little for Cerise to talk me into getting into the house to look around and see if we could find any of the old treasures. We both went in a few times through the tunnel, but we never did find much of value. Nothing that wouldn't be missed, anyway."

"That explains the noises I heard," Belle noted.

"Cerise found that one pearl in a compartment in Thomas's desk and was convinced that there was a fortune hidden somewhere, and she wasn't going to stop looking until she found it. Cerise was right, you know. That birthday party was a turning point in my life. I'd never felt like I belonged anywhere, never had anyone care about me. After that, I told Cerise that I knew for a fact that there was nothing in the house and she should just drop the whole idea."

"That's who I saw you arguing with at the town fair," Abby said.

"Unfortunately, Cerise was unwilling to let it go. I wasn't able to convince her that there was nothing to be stolen. At that point, I was so ashamed at having any part in trying to rob you that I couldn't face you, Abby."

"You lied to us," Abby said stonily. "You said you were going to Williamsburg to a sales conference. You don't work for a sporting goods company, and you don't do business with any North Carolina college."

"Well, you're half right. I didn't have a sales meeting, but I was in Williamsburg." Drew's face flushed, and his eyes settled on the tips of his shoes. "There were some very old charges pending against me there. I went back to try to clear things up. I am tired of running from things. I wanted to start over. I could not do that until I wiped the slate clean."

"What were the charges?" Colin asked.

"A check I wrote a few years back bounced. I never made good on the check. The person I had written the check to pressed charges. It isn't something I made a habit of doing. I simply didn't have the money to make good on the check. I left the state, never expecting to be back in this area."

"You lied about everything. You lied about your job, you lied about who you are . . ." Abby's face grew darker with each accusation. "Why should we believe one word of what you are saying now?"

"I didn't lie about my job. I do work for G.K. Sports."

"Then why did they say they never heard of you?" Abby's chin jutted up slightly.

"Probably because you asked for Drew Cassidy, and they know me as Andrew Brannigan." His downward gaze intensified, as if memorizing the pattern of the worn Oriental carpet. "There was a warrant because of the bad check. If I used my real name, I wouldn't have gotten the job."

"Is Drew Cassidy your real name? Are you Thomas's grandson, or was that a lie, too?" Abby's eyes began to burn.

As he opened his mouth to reply, Belle spoke up. "No, he is not Thomas Cassidy's grandson," Belle said softly, and, for the second time, all eyes turned to her.

"Then who is he?" Alex asked.

"Unless I am mistaken, Alexander," she said as tears began to well in her eyes, "Andrew is your brother."

✦ 42 ✦

The silence in the morning room following Belle's pronouncement was total.

"Gran, I don't have a brother," Alex reminded her as gently as he could.

"Yes, son, I'm afraid you do." Belle sighed and lowered herself onto her rocking chair.

"How can he be my brother?" both Alex and Drew asked at precisely the same moment.

"Oh, my, it's all so complicated." Belle shook her head slowly. "What a tangled web we do weave . . ."

"Gran, let's start at the beginning." Alex sat down on the footstool near Belle's chair.

"Oh, dear, the beginning . . ." Belle shook her head again and sighed heavily. "Suppose we start by asking Drew why he believed that Thomas Cassidy was his grandfather."

"My mother always told me that my grandfather was a wealthy man who lived in Primrose, North Carolina. My father's name was Edward Cassidy. When I read that magazine article a year or so ago about Thomas Cassidy, the adventurer from Primrose, North Carolina, I just naturally put two and two together." Drew held his hands before him as if they held his words for their inspection.

"And, unfortunately, came up with three," Belle told him. "The house you visited as a small boy stands on the opposite side of the street, Andrew. The man who lived in that house was not Thomas Cassidy but Granger Matthews."

"You've lost me, Gran." Alex looked up at Belle somewhat blankly.

"Granger's son—the one he had with his first wife—was their father." Abby spoke up. "Mr. Tillman told me about Granger's first wife and how she disappeared with their son . . ."

"Exactly so." Belle nodded. "I wasn't aware that you knew about that, Abigail."

"Grampa was married to someone else before he married you?" Alex frowned.

"For a very brief time," Belle told him. "Oh, but she was a wild one, that Annie Fields. Wanton and loose, she was. No one in Primrose was surprised when she took off. Everyone knew it was just a matter of time before she would take what she could get from Granger and leave him."

"Why would Grampa marry someone like that?" Alex asked.

"I'm afraid that Granger, like so many other young men in Primrose at that time, had a fling with Annie. When she told him she was carrying his child, he felt it was his duty to marry her." Belle swallowed hard. "He was a Matthews. He had to do what was right."

"Gran, that's the oldest trap . . ."

"Well, there was no doubt that Annie was carrying a child. For years, there was speculation that perhaps it was not Granger's. But the child was his. All one had to do was to look at the boy—Carl, they'd named him, after Granger's brother, who was killed in the early days of World War I. One look at the boy, and there was no doubt who the father was." Belle's fingers twisted a tissue into a long, thin cord.

"You were in love with Granger even then," Abby said softly.

"I cannot remember a time in my life when I was not in love with Granger Matthews." Belle's face, wet with slow tears, met Abby's from across the room. "And to know he was lost to me—and for the likes of her!" Belle shook her head at the memory. "Well, Carl wasn't but a few months old when Annie took up with a tractor-trailer driver. Used to stand right up there at the bus stop on Harper Avenue, waiting for the bus to take her to the diner out there by the interstate where she'd meet him. Everybody in town knew what she was up to. Granger pretended not to know, at first—once he knew, of course, he'd have to do something about it, you see, and divorce was unheard of in Primrose. Especially for someone in Granger's position."

Belle dabbed at her eyes and sighed deeply. "In any event, one day, Annie just packed up the boy and as much as she could carry and headed north, they said, with a salesman. Closed that door behind her and left Primrose. Of course, Granger hired a detective to bring Carl back, but they never did find them. The next year, Granger quietly divorced Annie. And two years later, he married me."

"You burned the house down," Abby said softly. "The house where Granger lived with Annie . . ."

"People said Granger did it, but anyone who knew him at all would have known that he'd never have destroyed so valuable a piece of real estate." Belle nodded, a wry smile playing on her lips. "But I didn't care a whit about that. All I knew was that as long as that house stood, it would taunt Granger. So I put a match to it. Several matches, if the truth were to be told. And I have never for a minute regretted it. Annie was gone and had taken that boy with her. I prayed every night that we'd seen the last of them. Even though he was the spitting image of Granger, that boy was all Fields."

"How would you know that, Gran?" Alex sat, still as a stone.

"Because every time he needed money, he showed up on my doorstep. Oh, never when Granger would be expected to be home. Always in the middle of the day, when Granger would be at the bank. The only thing he ever wanted from his father was his money. Which I was happy to give him, if it meant he would leave Granger alone."

"And Grampa never knew that his son had come back?"

"No." Belle set her chin firmly.

"Gran, do you really think you had a right to do that?"

"A right? I had a *duty* to protect Granger. Carl would only have hurt him. He was a con man, a petty criminal. More than once, I sent money—my own money, I might add—to bail him out of jail."

"Why would you have done that?"

"Because if I had not, he would have gone to Granger."

"You mean Carl blackmailed you?" Abby asked.

"I really didn't care about the money. Carl never understood that. Back in those days, money was not an issue. And as long as I could protect Granger, the money was unimportant." Belle began to rock slowly in the chair, her eyes glazing over, as if she were transporting herself back in time. "But then, *she* showed up."

"Who" Alex frowned. "Annie?"

"No. Annie was long gone by then. Died of pneumonia when she wasn't but forty or so. No, we never saw Annie around here again, once she'd left town," Belle told them. "No, it was Carl's wife. Hard-looking little thing, she was. Thin and angry . . . and barely half Carl's age. He must have been in his forties, maybe his fifties by then. She couldn't have been much more than twenty, twenty-two.

Stood right there on my front porch and rang my doorbell, bold as brass. One baby by the hand, one baby on her hip." Belle's eyes narrowed as if squinting to bring the memory into sharper focus.

"Alex and Drew," Abby whispered.

Belle nodded, her head down, unable to meet the eyes of anyone in the room.

"Carl had gone to prison again, she said. Managed somehow to get himself killed during some sort of brawl. Well, Carl had told her about the goose who was laying golden eggs in Primrose. She figured that Granger was responsible for the boys, now that their father was gone. Well, of course, I tossed her out on her ear." Belle rocked rhythmically. "Granger had just had his first heart attack, and I was not going to permit that little piece of business to help him along to his second. I gave her every cent I had in the house and sent her packing." Belle accepted the tissue Abby passed to her and wiped the tears from her face. "Soon after she left, I heard something out on the front porch—a cat crying, I remember thinking it was, at first. And there he was, wrapped in a blanket and crying to beat the band."

"Alex," Abby whispered.

"Yes, Alexander." Belle nodded. "I lifted him up and looked into those brown eyes—Granger's eyes—and I knew what I had to do."

"Which was?" Alex asked.

"I knew we had to keep you. I called Josie out in California and told her there was a child—the son of a local girl who'd gotten herself into trouble. I said that I'd told the girl's mother that I'd help to—discreetly—find a home for the boy. Josie never hesitated for a second. She fell in love with you the second she set eyes on you. We all did."

"Did Mom know?"

"That you were the son of her half-brother? No. She never did."

The silence began to crowd them, filling the room to its capacity and threatening to stifle all of them.

"But you must know, you must believe," Belle spoke firmly, addressing Drew directly, "that even as I have blessed that woman every day for leaving that baby on my porch, I have cursed myself for having turned the other boy away. There is no consolation for you, Andrew, in knowing that I would have given anything—*anything*—to have had a chance to bring you back. I did try to track you, but there was not a trace."

"I was probably well into the foster care system by then." Drew's eyes seemed to become hollow with the memory.

"Oh, how you must hate me." Belle buried her face in her hands and sobbed. "All you went through. All you suffered because of my spitefulness . . ."

Drew reached over and wordlessly took the old woman's hands, stroking and patting them with his own, while he struggled with the implications of Belle's story.

Finally, he asked, "Why is my name Cassidy? I saw my birth certificate. My name is Cassidy."

"Annie remarried when Carl was about five years old. Her new husband adopted Carl. The irony that Annie's new husband was named Cassidy was not, I feel certain, lost on Annie." Belle blew her nose as daintily as she could.

"So when Drew saw the article about Thomas, knowing that his father was born in Primrose, he naturally assumed that Thomas was his grandfather," Abby noted.

"Funny, isn't it?" Drew looked down at Alex, who still sat at Belle's feet. "Neither of us is who we thought we were."

"I guess we both need to decide which is more important"—Alex raised his head solemnly—"who we were or who we are. And if the past means more than the future."

"Well, there's not much in my past worth holding on to," Drew told him, "and there's never been much for me to look forward to. Maybe that will change now."

"Colin." Belle addressed the policeman, who had sat silently on the sofa at the opposite side of the room as the long-hidden truths sought their disclosure." Are you going to arrest Andrew?"

"Can't think of anything to charge him with," Colin said after a time. "He wasn't really impersonating Thomas's grandson. He truly believed he *was* Thomas's grandson. He wasn't involved with the theft of Susannah's things. Only thing he's really guilty of, far as I can see, is bad judgment in hooking up with Cerise. Unless you want to press charges against him for unlawful entry—those times he came into the house through the tunnel—I don't see where he's committed a crime. He's free to go, far as I'm concerned." Colin stood and folded up the notebook that had been resting on his knee. "So, unless there's something else, I guess I'll just check in at the station and call it a night."

"Thank you," Belle said, and Colin responded with a nod of his head as he headed out of the room.

The sound of the front door closing as Colin let himself out echoed through the first floor.

"Oh, my boys," a clearly distressed Belle cried, "how can either of you ever forgive me?"

"You've given us both a lot to think about, that's for certain," Alex told her as he stood up and stretched his legs to unkink his knees.

"Miz Matthews . . ." Drew began.

"Will you ever be able to call me 'Gran'?" Belle asked, then smiled ruefully, looking directly at Alex. "Though that, too, was part of the deception, since, of course, I'm not really your grandmother, you know."

"Gran, don't ever say that. Don't ever even think that," Alex said softly.

"I think you all have a lot of things to say to one another. So, Drew," Abby told him as she stood, "I will make up the back room at the end of the hall for you."

He nodded, and, as he looked up, Abby saw the first trace of tears on his face. She patted him on the back, then kissed Belle on the cheek before standing on tiptoe to kiss Alex's lips, which were trembling and dry.

Abby locked the front door and checked to make certain the dining-room lights were all off before heading quietly up the steps. She would have guests to tend to in the morning. They would want breakfast and conversation, and, besides, she knew, Alex and Drew and Belle needed time to redefine themselves. As much as they all loved Abby, and she them, she could be neither party nor witness to their first tentative steps toward accepting their new roles in one another's lives.

It was near dawn when Alex slid into bed beside Abby. He said very little, other than, "I think Gran and Drew will be okay."

And you, Abby wanted to ask, *will you be okay?*

Instead, she merely permitted him to entwine himself around her. When he was as close to her as he could get, he closed his eyes, though Abby suspected he did not sleep. When the sun shed the first hint of morning, she moved her legs over the side of the bed, attempting to rise quietly and begin the preparations for breakfast.

"Not yet," he whispered. "Don't go just yet."

"Alex?"

"Hmmmm?"

"Are you all right?"

"I think so. It's been a big shock, though, finding out that the woman I believed was my mother was really my aunt."

"Would you have loved her less, had you known?"

"Of course not," he replied without a second's hesitation. "She was my *mom.* Nothing can change the way I feel about her."

"And your father?"

"I never really felt that I knew my father. There was never really much of a bond between us. It's been some years since I've seen him, and I don't feel that my life is diminished in any way because of it. He never really treated me the way you would expect a father to treat his son, and he treated my mother very poorly when she needed him the most. It doesn't bother me in the least to learn that he was not my real father. Though I can't say it was a pleasure finding out what a bastard my *real* father was. And that my birth mother is out there somewhere . . ."

"Drew doesn't know where?"

"He tried to track her down a few years ago."

"Do you think you will look for her?" Abby sat up and

massaged the muscles that were tightening around his neck and shoulders.

"I don't know, Abby. I need some time to sort this all out," he said softly. "Nothing could ever make my mother less than my *mother*. And nothing could ever change the fact that Gran was—is—my grandmother. She's always been there for me, Abby. She gave me so much over the years—the fact that she and I do not share the same blood does not change what she is in my life. I'll never love her any less." Alex's voice cracked slightly.

Abby leaned over his shoulder, her arms around his neck, and felt the warm tears that flowed freely down his face.

"The hardest thing is not finding out that I have a brother, it's knowing that we didn't have each other all these years. It's knowing that if Gran had not turned him away, things could have been so different for him. All those years, Abby, he thought he had no one . . ."

"I suspect that's preying heavily on Belle's conscience."

"Gran reacted to a situation that nothing in her experience had prepared her for. She is a very good woman who made one very wrong decision. How can I hold it against her, that one mistake?" He shook his head, trying to reconcile the bits and pieces of the truth and the aftermath of their revelation.

"How does Drew feel?"

"I don't know, but I expect I'll find out in a few hours." His hands sought her arms and stroked them slowly, and he seemed to drift into deep thought. "Drew and I are going fishing."

"Now, you will remember to thank Alex for us, won't you, Abby?" Sue Turner said as she tucked the sprig of lavender Abby had offered into her purse.

"I certainly will," Abby assured her as she accepted the checks offered by Jeff and Bob, who turned to gather up the overnight bags. "And we'll look for you on Thursday, on your way back."

"Now, will you be planning something this weekend, a treasure hunt, another whodunit?" Jeff asked expectantly.

"Ah, no." Abby, whose nerves were still raw from the sight of Cerise waving a gun around the night before, shuddered at the very thought of reliving a minute of what could have been a tragedy. "As a matter of fact, Alex and I have decided that we're not really interested in repeating that type of performance."

"Well, do you think maybe you could arrange for something when I have my managers' meeting in the fall? It might add a light note to what could turn out to be some pretty intense workshops," Bob Conroy prodded.

"I doubt it." Abby shook her head. She'd had about all the intensity she could take. "I think we'd rather direct our energies toward the food and the ambience of the inn."

And away from gun-wielding intruders, real or make-believe.

Abby waved at her departing guests from the front steps. Once the car had driven off, she started back toward the house. Crossing the front porch, she noticed the wicker chairs sat somewhat askew around the table in the far corner of the porch where the guests had had their hors d'oeuvres the night before, and so she proceeded to straighten them, placing the slender white legs under the table at just the right angle. The pitcher of tulips Naomi had placed there the afternoon before still graced the center of the table, lending a casual elegance to the setting. One of the guests had left a cocktail napkin on the table, and she shook its few crumbs over the porch railing for the birds.

Come and sit for a moment, the comfortable corner seemed to insist. Unable to resist the invitation, she did.

I wonder how Alex and Drew are doing. They have so much to talk about, so many years to catch up on. How long, if ever, would it be before they will be able to accept each other, think of each other, as brothers? I wonder if Drew will ever be able to forgive Belle—and how Alex will handle the news, once it sinks in, that Josie was not in fact his mother, that Krista is not really his sister, and that everything he thought was true about his family was in fact fantasy. Is he strong enough to understand that he is who he is regardless of who his "real" parents may have been—or will the truth somehow change him, change how he sees himself, how he sees his world, how he sees even me?

Abby leaned over the railing and deadheaded some dried and spent azalea blossoms. She wanted it all to work out for all of them—wanted Drew and Alex to learn to care about each other, wanted them both to make their peace with Belle and with each other and with the past, so that they could all go forward and their lives could mesh the way families need to do. She prayed they would have the chance to do that.

All I ever wanted was Alex. Alex and a life here with him in Primrose.

An errant breeze seemed to waft a drift of lavender across the open end of the porch, surrounding Abby in the beloved fragrance. The scent never failed to comfort her, and for a moment it almost seemed as if Leila herself was there to assure her that all would indeed be well, if only she could be patient for just a little longer.

Smiling at the very thought of it—of Leila leaning over her like an elderly but loving guardian angel—Abby knew it would, in fact, all be well.

She stood and pushed the chair back in. Feeling the small wad of paper she had earlier tucked into her pocket, she withdrew the checks, unfolding them curiously. Just how much had Alex told their guests their night's lodging and dinner would cost?

Each check had been made payable to the Primrose Inn in the amount of $185, the memo portion of the Conroys' check noting "$125 room, $60 dinner."

Hmmm, she thought. Not bad: $370 for two rooms and four meals. Not a fortune, but it was the first money she had made in months.

Smiling, Abby went into the house and up to the second floor. Wandering down the hall, she threw open the doors of the rooms she had spent the last five months renovating, admiring her work as if seeing it for the first time, measuring the qualifications for guest accommodations of first one room, then the next, as if through the eyes of a stranger.

By the time she found herself in the room that was next

on her "to do" list, she knew that Sunny had been exactly right.

The house at Thirty-five Cove Road *was* screaming B&B. Up until now, Abby had not been listening.

◆ 43 ◆

The late-afternoon sun—still casting a fierce blaze, although it was only June—had shifted just enough behind the trees to allow a bit of shade to fall across the neatly groomed flower beds. Abby bent down to inspect the nasturtium transplants that Naomi had raised from seed and handed over to Abby the day after the wedding plans were announced.

"I can see the whole thing already." Naomi had beamed. "We'll do a garden party to make Leila proud. Now, let's see, we'll want to serve lots of colorful, if not slightly exotic edibles. I'll do the hors d'oeuvres, of course. I think nasturtium blossoms stuffed with an herbed cheese and some cherry tomatoes stuffed with pesto . . . Abby, are you writing this down?"

And off Naomi had gone, putting her own spin on Leila's garden tea menus and insisting upon planting certain flowers, herbs, and vegetables in Abby's garden as well as in her own. Every day for the past week, she had had Abby checking the nasturtiums, hoping for just the right amount of bloom come Saturday, just three days away. Abby lifted one large orangey blossom to inspect it. She thought they'd be right on the money for the wedding.

Abby plucked a few dried blooms from the early-blooming perennials and crushed the spent petals in the palm of her hand. She enjoyed these few moments alone in her garden, especially since the past few days had been so hectic, and the rest of the week—starting tomorrow morning, when Susannah was to arrive with her mother and three sisters—could only be bedlam. Aunt Catherine would be of enormous help, Abby knew, and, as Abby's mother's sister, Catherine would perform all those tasks normally left to the mother of the bride. Abby's cousins had already committed themselves to Naomi's work crew. The Hollisters were all hard workers, had been hard workers all their lives, but they never had the likes of Naomi to contend with. Vowing that this would be a wedding Primrose would never forget, Naomi had lists of things to do prepared for each member of Abby's extended family. God have mercy on the soul who failed to pull his or her weight—Naomi would be merciless if all was not completed properly and on time.

Abby looked to the river, shading her eyes to catch a glimpse of Alex as he worked on the boat that had been delivered just days earlier. It was everything he had ever dreamed of in a craft, and Abby had been delighted to buy it. After all, it was Alex who had found the pearl dealer in New York who had offered them such a phenomenal amount of money for the lustrous beads that had rolled out of the side of the picture frame, rendering Abby totally speechless for the first time in her adult life.

In the wake of the unfolding family drama, the pearls had been pretty much forgotten until the following day. Drew and Alex had returned to the house late that afternoon, sunburned and subdued, though clearly having scratched the first tentative surface of kinship. After dinner, they had traded childhood memories. As the intensity of the conversation had begun to wane and a more relaxed air settled over the dinner table, Belle had fetched the picture frame from the morning room and opened it on the dining-room table.

"Did you ever see such a sight?" Abby had whispered in awe as the creamy rounds rolled across the linen tablecloth.

"Wow!" both men had exclaimed simultaneously.

"What do you propose to do with them?" Alex had asked, rolling one of the cool pearls in the palm of his hand.

"I haven't the faintest idea." She had shaken her head in wonderment. "What *does* one do with such things?"

"The stuff fantasies are made of," Drew had mused.

"Pearls this big would have to be worth a king's ransom. There can't be too many more like these, anywhere in the world."

"Well, Ab, what will you spend the money on?" Alex's chin had rested in the palm of his right hand.

"Are they mine?" She'd frowned. "Do they belong to me?"

"What did Leila's will say about Thomas's possessions?"

"They belong to me." Abby's smile had spread slowly, then blossomed and lit up her face. "They belong to me. I can get a new furnace. And I can call in a mason and get the chimney fixed. And I can . . ."

". . . buy your fiancé a boat." Alex had slipped in his request.

"I could buy my fiancé a boat. Maybe. If he promised not to surprise me with unexpected guests again," she'd teased.

"Well, now, you know, a small-town law practice may not generate much income the first year or so. The time may come when you might be sending me out to scour the Outer Banks for some paying guests."

"Then again," Drew had interjected, "you never know what else Thomas may have hidden around the house."

Abby had gone to Alex, and he'd pushed his chair back from the table so that she could sit on his lap. "Just think," she'd said, "of all the fun we'll have over the years looking for little trinkets here and there around the house."

"I would hardly call these little trinkets." Belle had held a pearl up to the light and sighed. "And to think, Abigail, if you had sold everything right off as you had wanted to, some other deliriously happy soul would be facing the enviable dilemma that now faces you. What to do with the pearls, and whatever else might be hidden under your nose, just waiting to be uncovered."

"Well, Gran, we'll have a lifetime to find out," Alex had told her.

"What do you mean?" Belle's eyes had narrowed expectantly.

"I mean that Abby and I are going to get married." Alex had folded his arms around Abby and waited for Belle to react. "We are, actually, planning on living quite happily ever after, right here under this very roof."

"No! You don't say!" she'd exclaimed, bracing herself against the back of her chair.

"I do indeed say," he'd assured her.

"Why, Alexander, that is wonderful. Just wonderful. Abigail, I can't tell you how thrilled I am. Why, it's all we've ever wanted, Leila and I."

"I'm only sorry Aunt Leila couldn't be here for the wedding," Abby had said sadly.

"Oh, but, of course, she will!" Belle had declared, then paused before adding, "That is, I feel certain that she'll be here in all our thoughts. Now, do tell me all the plans . . ."

"We haven't actually made any yet," Abby had told her. "But we will. Tomorrow we will spend making plans. We will plan a wedding to set Primrose on its very ear."

Those plans had included a honeymoon they would never forget.

Once she had assured herself that the proceeds from the pearl sale had covered the cost of the needs of the house, Abby had surprised Alex by suggesting a trip to Maryland to check out the boat sales at several marinas along the Chesapeake Bay. It would be a window-shopping expedition only, they had agreed. They had barely arrived at the first boatyard when they saw her. Thirty-six feet long and newly painted white, she'd stood slightly apart from the others. It was love at first sight as far as Alex was concerned, but when Abby had rounded the back of the boat and read the name painted in black, she knew it was meant to be. Thirty minutes and one big check later, the *Layla* was theirs.

Alex had spent the best part of the past week customizing the craft and preparing for their floating honeymoon. He had scrubbed the deck, cleaned the cabin, spiffed up the small galley kitchen, and added a new refrigerator and microwave oven. He'd made up the state room's queen-sized bed with cream-colored satin sheets he had secretly purchased in Hampton the last week he spent in the employ of Pendleton and Vickers. Having declared the *Layla* off-limits to Abby until after the wedding, the groom had begun to stock up on all the necessities for a honeymoon cruise. The champagne was already chilling in the refrigerator, and by the time they were ready to set off into the sunset, Naomi would, she promised, have a picnic hamper filled with all manner of incredible goodies prepared especially for the wedding couple.

Immediately following the reception, they would cast off and follow the intercoastal waterway through North Carolina to Virginia and up into Maryland, where they would cruise the bay and dock each night at one of the marinas where they could find safe harbor as well as restaurants within walking distance to eat their fill of soft-shell crabs and ocean-fresh fish. During the day, Alex could fish from the deck while Abby lounged on the deck, slathered in sunscreen, and sipping cool drinks. It would be lazy, relaxing, and totally indulgent for ten days.

Abby's heart skipped a beat as Alex leaped the short distance from the boat to the dock to gather something before springing back to the boat. Seeing him in motion always brought a smile to her lips. He had all the grace of a big, somewhat lazy cat, whose movements were never forced or strained but always easy, always natural. Watching him stirred a warmth within her, and she smiled to herself, wondering if she'd have enough time to drag him off to the carriage house before dinner.

Of course, the carriage house was a bit of a wreck these days, she reminded herself, what with Drew and Alex having stripped a portion of the interior to frame out Alex's new law office, which would consist of two rooms—a small reception area and a larger, more open space that would serve as both library and office. Once their efforts began, Abby suggested that perhaps Drew might like to claim a section on the second floor, so that he would have an apartment there for his own use, a home base for the first time in his life. He and Alex had been working diligently and were awaiting the arrival of the electrician and the plumber at some point over the next week.

Abby slowed her pace and looked to the sky. The weather

outlook for the weekend was uncertain, and Naomi was pressing her to decide if they should abandon their plans for a garden wedding and go directly to Plan B, which would necessitate moving furniture around in the house and the construction of the garlands of ivy and multicolored roses that Naomi, who had an unrivaled eye when it came to such things, insisted should drape the stairwell and the mantels. It was a decision Abby could not put off beyond Thursday evening. The weatherman had twenty-four hours left to make up his mind and, once having done so, had better stick with it, unless he wanted to deal with Naomi's wrath. Maybe, Abby thought, they should just go with the wedding in the front parlor. If the storm remained at sea, as some predicted it would, they could still have the reception in the garden. Besides, she had loved the vision of white roses Naomi had conjured up as much as she loved the idea of exchanging vows in the same spot her parents had stood. She would discuss it once and for all with Alex later this evening.

He turned toward her as if he had sensed her presence, raising his fingers to his mouth to send a sharp whistle, quick and clean as an arrow, winging from the dock to where she stood in the midst of the geraniums. Laughing, she all but skipped down the slight incline to join him.

"Permission to come aboard, sir?" Abby batted her eyelashes with feigned innocence.

"Permission denied, as you knew it would be." He grinned. "Nice try, though."

"What are you doing there that I can't see?" she demanded with all the impatience of a child who had been put off one time too many.

"You'll have to wait until Saturday to see," he told her, "but I promise it will be worth the wait. We agreed, Abby. You take care of the wedding, I will take care of the honeymoon."

"But I told you what we were doing for the wedding . . ."

"All the more reason why the honeymoon should hold an element of surprise." With one foot on the dock and one foot on the *Layla*'s side, Alex's body spanned the space like a living bridge. "Besides, you won't let me see your wedding dress."

"That's entirely different." She appeared horrified.

"Why?"

"Because . . . because it is. It's supposed to be bad luck for the groom to see the bride in her wedding dress before the ceremony."

And, besides, she wanted to make an entrance in Leila's incredible wedding dress. Made of the finest Belgian lace over layers of tulle, the heirloom gown had been expertly fitted to Abby's small frame by Sharon, Naomi's sister, who had also helped to make the dresses for Meredy and Lilly, who would serve as flower girls. For Naomi, who would be matron of honor, they had selected a dress of pale lavender organdy from the gowns that hung, so perfectly preserved, in the attic. Abby would wear her hair up on top of her head, upon which would sit Leila's prized white garden hat, to which Sharon had added some small amount of veiling to gently frame Abby's face. Around the bride's neck would wind "something blue"—Serena's sapphires, which would also serve as "something borrowed," since they belonged to Sunny. For flowers, Abby would carry a bouquet of soft-colored roses—cream, white, palest yellow, barely pink—with trails of ivy and honeysuckle.

No, Alex would not be getting so much as a glimpse before the ceremony, nor would anyone, other than Sharon and, of course, Naomi.

"Were you coming to fetch me for dinner?" he asked hopefully.

"No. I was coming to fetch you for a fun-filled hour in the carriage house. That was before it occurred to me that, with all the lumber you and Drew have piled up in there, there is barely room to stand up, let alone to do anything else."

"Hmmm. Sad but true." Alex nodded.

"Of course, if you'd let me on the boat, then maybe we could try out that handsome stateroom . . ."

"This is one time, I fear, when your persistence will not be rewarded." He laughed, squinting into the sunlight. "At least, not today."

"Okay." She tried to appear downcast but found she could not sustain a long face in the midst of the joy she was feeling. "Anyway, if you want to take a break now, we can have an early dinner. We can sample some of the neat things Naomi and I have been making for the wedding. She is so clever, Alex. She just never fails to amaze me. I can't wait to use some of her ideas when we have teas for our guests at the inn this summer."

"Like what?" He turned off the radio, which had been tuned to a jazz and blues station and from which Howlin' Wolf was doing just exactly that.

"Like a mixed green salad with chicory flowers . . ."

"Chicory flowers?" He raised an eyebrow as he pulled on the ropes that secured the boat to the dock and eased the boat in another foot or two.

"They're perfectly edible. And the salad *looks* so gorgeous, all different shades of green leaves with these sky-blue flowers. And a potato salad made with primroses, a marigold mustard to serve with the baked ham, and, for the dessert table, a rose-petal sorbet, a marigold cake, and, of course, the wedding cake will be festooned with violets, which are an excellent source of vitamin C."

"You don't suppose Naomi made up that part, do you?" He stepped from the boat to the dock.

"Of course not. And I think it's neat. We'll have a really unique wedding."

"That's for sure." He gathered her into his arms and kissed the tip of her nose.

"Oh, and wait till you see the ice cubes," she added, wide-eyed.

"What would you possibly do to ice cubes?" He leaned toward her, forehead to forehead.

"We froze tiny flowers in the trays, lavender and violets and rose petals, which we'll use in the punch." Abby wrapped her arms around his neck as she chatted.

"Dare I ask what will be in the punch?" He feigned a look of apprehension.

"Wine and strawberries—and geranium blooms." She laughed.

"Can't wait to try it," he said dryly.

"You won't have to. There's some in the house. Unless, of course, Belle has polished it off. She absolutely loved it."

"You know, Ab, I can't remember when, if ever, I've seen Gran this happy."

"Belle is having a great time. She has been right in the midst of all the planning—even suggested that, as favors for the female guests, we make some little sachets filled with lavender. A little bit of Leila, she said." Abby stepped back from him slightly and, wrapping an arm around his waist, tugged him to begin the stroll from the dock toward the path leading back through the garden to the house.

"Well, I notice she's been busy making up those little lacy sacks herself. And it's good for her, to be involved, to feel needed. I appreciate the fact that you have allowed her to be an integral part of the preparations."

"She is an integral part of it. And I was delighted that she thought of making the favors, and even more delighted when she volunteered to actually do it. There are only so many hours in each day, and there are a million things left to do. I don't think I could have handled one more thing."

"Well, we're almost there, you know. It won't be long until the wedding will be behind us and will join the countless happy memories we'll spend the rest of our lives making."

"We will be happy, won't we?" She smiled up into his eyes, warm as brown velvet.

"Absolutely." He kissed the tip of her nose. "We can't miss, Ab. And we will live happily ever after. I promise you that."

Happily ever after. I like the sound of that.

I like it a lot.

As they passed the ancient pine, she looked up at the initials, carved into the rough bark so long ago by a lovestruck boy for his first—and only—sweetheart.

As they stepped onto the path that led through the herb garden, a cloud of lavender rose to engulf them, like an embrace.

They had, Abby knew, come full circle at last.

✦ Epilogue ✦

The gentlest of early-autumn breezes billowed through the lace curtains, sending balloons of white lace to drift over the wide window ledge. The aged fingers, impatient and curious, parted the curtains to peek out onto the front porch of the house at Thirty-five Cove Road, where every living soul Belle Matthews cared about was gathering.

Dressed in one of Leila's favorite blue-and-white dimity gowns, its high-collared neck held with a cameo, Abby paused to set a tray of tea sandwiches upon the edge of the wicker table while her fingers searched the back of her head for the hairpins she could feel were slipping, allowing the auburn tendrils to escape down her back. As her guests began to arrive, she crossed the porch to greet them.

Chuckling with amusement, Belle watched with the greatest satisfaction as a young boy of perhaps four peered around the corner of the table upon which rested a mound of presents and a mountain of a birthday cake. His small fingers traced the edge of the table until they were in striking distance of the confection that was the object of his furtive mission. Just as he slid his right hand forward to swipe at the frosting across the back of the cake, a shadow fell across the table. With guilty eyes, the boy looked up.

"Gray, you know what your momma said about keeping your fingers out of the cake," Meredy whispered. "Now, come along out of there. It won't be long before the cake is cut. You can wait a little longer."

Despite his obvious disappointment, the boy came out from behind the table. Meredy, so grown-up now at ten, beckoned to him with a crooked finger.

"Let's see if we can find your sister before she gets into trouble," Meredy told the boy.

The old woman chuckled. It was too late. The boy's sister,

Miss Charlotte Cassidy Kane, sat on the porch decking under the table, barely visible to all except the woman who watched from behind the curtain. With pudgy fingers, Charlotte smeared pudding from a fruit tart across her chubby cheeks. Blissfully sucking her fingers along with a slice of kiwi, she went unnoticed to all but her great-grandmother, who laughed softly as the youngster scratched at her ear with messy fingers, spreading the pudding into her strawberry-blond curls.

I really should tell Abby, Belle mused. *But she is so adorable . . .*

A wave of scent, faint at first, then gradually becoming more pronounced, seemed to fill the front parlor.

"Ah, but they are perfect, are they not?" Belle whispered. "Look at young Gray—isn't he the picture of Granger? And little Charlotte, bless her, looks *so* like you, dear . . . what? Oh, yes, I'd say things have gone *quite* well, all things considered. No, indeed, not *one bit* more perfect . . ."

Belle watched with pleasure as Naomi and Colin approached the front steps, Naomi the height of Victorian style in a dress of the palest lavender, a white straw hat with a netted brim, and a parasol trimmed with masses of creamy lace which she used as a cane. She slipped one arm through that of her husband, who made a dashing figure in a jacket of deep burgundy velvet and a black bowler. They chatted quietly, their faces close together, obviously lost for a brief moment in the romance of the era into which they were about to step. Naomi stopped on the third step and turned to hold her hand out to the toddler who staunchly insisted on walking up the steps unaided. It had seemed so right to Belle that Naomi had named her young daughter Faith. Belle doubted she had ever known anyone who had possessed more of that virtue than Naomi.

Belle sighed heavily. "I do hope I live to see Andrew settle down as happily as his brother has, but, ah, well, all things in good time."

Belle's nose twitched slightly as she frowned and shook her head. "Well, of course, dear, I *know* that no one lives forever, and I'm happy—grateful—to have made it to ninety-five. But if the truth were to be told, it doesn't seem like quite the right time for me . . . well, I realize it's not necessarily my choice."

The sound of the car door drew her attention back to the window. She watched as Abby ran down the steps to greet Sunny and her new husband—now, *there* was an interesting young man, Belle mused.

"Well, you're perfectly right, dear. Susannah had said she wanted a man who was the adventurous sort. She certainly got what she asked for on that score. And I must say that *he* should come as no surprise to you. After all, she *is* your blood . . ."

The back door of Sunny's car opened, and, to Belle's surprise, Drew stepped out, then leaned back toward the car with an outstretched hand to assist a woman from the car.

"Oh, dear, no, I can't see her face, just a lot of long, curly hair. Why, yes, I do believe she is one of Susannah's sisters . . . which one? Why, yes, I do believe you are right . . ."

"Gran, who on earth are you talking to?" Belle turned from the window as Alex entered the room.

"What? Oh, just thinking out loud, dear. And admiring those beautiful young ones. My, but they are a joy to me. As you are, Alexander."

"Why, thank you, Gran." He kissed her forehead.

"I must say that you are very handsome in that morning coat. Very handsome, indeed."

"Thank you, Gran. Abby thought it would be fun if we all sort of dressed in turn-of-the-century clothing in honor of your birthday."

"Well, it's a lovely sentiment, and you all look wonderful. But, as I told Abby, I've already *done* that style once and am more comfortable these days in more modern clothing."

"Well, you look beautiful to us, no matter what you are wearing." He smiled and took her arm. "Now, come on outside. Everyone is waiting to see the birthday girl."

"I'll be along in a minute, dear," she assured him. "Go along out. I'm right behind you."

"Okay, but be sure that you are. I don't know how much longer Abby can keep the children out of the cake."

The screen door slammed behind him, and he crossed the porch to where Abby was trying in vain to coax Charlotte out from under the table. Belle chuckled as Abby dangled a beautifully frosted cookie under the tablecloth to no avail. Abby shrugged good-naturedly and threw up her hands, which Alex took in his own, planting a kiss in each of her palms. A look of such love passed between them that Belle beamed with pleasure.

With a deep and happy sigh, Belle started toward the door. "Isn't it all just too perfect? Just as we'd hoped . . ."

Her nose wiggled, and she smiled as the smell of apple cider and cinnamon drifted toward her when she opened the screen door. She wondered if it would be her last autumn. She hoped it would not be.

"My, but it's a lovely day," she whispered. "Isn't it perfectly glorious to be alive on such a day? Oh, of course . . . *so* thoughtless of me. I do apologize. Do come along, Leila, dear. Our family is waiting."

Fall in love

with bestselling romances from Pocket Books!

Impulse • JoAnn Ross
A haunted man…A hunted woman…
Together they must stop a madman before he kills again.

BAD Attitude • Sherrilyn Kenyon
Sometimes even the good guys need to have a BAD attitude…

The Seduction of His Wife • Janet Chapman
He set out to seduce her for all the wrong reasons—
but fell in love with her for all the right ones.

Thrill Me to Death • Roxanne St. Claire
When a Bullet Catcher is on the job, he'll always watch
your back. But you better watch your heart.

Dirty Little Lies • Julie Leto
She's a sultry Latino bounty hunter armed with
sex, lies, and other deadly weapons.